HOT SPRINGS

an iNovel
www.HotSpringsNovel.com

HOT SPRINGS

an iNovel
www.HotSpringsNovel.com

STEVE ZIO

McArthur & Company

Toronto

First published in Canada in 2006 by
McArthur & Company
322 King St. West, Suite 402
Toronto, ON
M5V 1J2
www.mcarthur-co.com

This paperback edition published in Canada in 2007 by
McArthur & Company

Library and Archives Canada Cataloguing in Publication

Zio, Steve   Hot springs : an iNovel / Steve Zio.
ISBN 1-55278-564-5 (bound).--ISBN 1-55278-626-9 (pbk.)
    I. Title.
PS8649.I6H68 2006   C813'.6   C2006-901421-3

Design and composition by Tania Craan

The publisher would like to acknowledge the financial support of the
Government of Canada through the Book Publishing Industry Development
Program (BPIDP) and the Canada Council for our publishing activities. The
publisher further wishes to acknowledge the financial support of the
Ontario Arts Council for our publishing program.

10 9 8 7 6 5 4 3 2 1

HOT SPRINGS

PART I

HOT SPRINGS ISLAND,
BRITISH COLUMBIA, CANADA

Chapter 1

"It's all beneath the surface."

Once a voyage, regardless of the weather, he came here to the bow to feel the wind on his face and in his thatch of thick brown hair. The cleansing wind and the crisp blue and white of the ferry conjured images of strength and purity. He took a deep breath of the clean air. The muscles in his long neck unknotted for the first time in weeks.

Jason rode high above the ocean on the foredeck. Engines pulsing away in the dark chambers below, the thousands of tons of steel that was the *Spirit of Hot Springs Island* drew them closer to Active Pass. They approached a blind turn; the engineer sounded a warning. The weather was already clearing and before long the Olympic Mountains to the south would arrive into view. It had been raining on the Vancouver side since last night and only now were they leaving the drizzle and mist and heading towards a brighter sky.

Although coming home, Jason felt more like he was embarking on a new beginning. The ninety-minute ride was like a baptism or rebirth. He couldn't wait to dock.

Packing had been brutal. Every single thing he picked up or touched reminded him of something: of the career he was abandoning or the woman left behind. Saucepans, wineglasses, the stereo, CDs, the stained-glass mobile Dee Dee had given him last birthday. Even his old Rubik's Cube. Not to mention the sheets and pillows and duvet...he didn't even want to think about those. He stuffed everything into cardboard boxes, wrapped them away in newspaper.

The ferry's PA system announced that a musical performance would take place shortly in the main deck lounge. A musician himself, Jason decided to check it out.

Seats had been moved to clear a space in the center of the main lounge area and the floor was dotted with canvas bags full of musical instruments with a heavy emphasis on percussion. There were djembes, bongos and congas, tambourines, maracas, rhythm eggs, wooden fish, small triangles, jingle sticks, clavels, finger cymbals and castanets. The instruments were from Africa, South America, Asia, Hawaii — there was even a Japanese *taiko* drum set up beside an electric keyboard, which was in turn ringed by stands of mandolins, banjoes, a guitar, a ukulele, a Dobro, a couple of fiddles and more. The collection was impressive.

Removing his eyes from the instruments, Jason scanned the area, looking for the one person who could be behind such a scene. The one with his back to Jason. Glad-handing like a politician, but dressed like a Latino cowboy in a wide-brimmed hat with a colorful band and an exotic feather crowning his head. Below was a white wool serape replete with three bright stripes above the bottom hem; jeans and sandals. His long, blond ponytail flowed onto the serape back. It was Cassidy.

He embraced someone, flashed a huge white smile at another, winked and patted and shook hands. He had mastered every gesture of camaraderie. Jason saw him literally lift one girl off the ground and twirl her round, both of them laughing. This was Cassidy. Unleashing his great white smile, he had a good word for everyone. He sucked his audience into the vortex of his overflowing will and energy like dust specs into an Electrolux. Jason thought about saying hello, but decided to wait. It would be hard to break through Cassidy's circle of admirers.

Returning to the circle's center, still grinning, Cassidy bent his 6'3" frame and gave a low elaborate bow.

"Gentle ladies and gentle men, thank you for coming today. Not that you had much in the way of choice," he gained an appreciative chuckle. "My name is Cassidy Maher and I've been living on beautiful Hot Springs Island for about five years now. I make my living by playing music and helping run the unequaled Garden Center…and I've left some business cards on the table for all you green-thumbed organic-coffee-drinking tree-hugging Hot Springs Island types.

"What you're about to hear is not just music or song. Today this isn't a regular ferry. It's a time machine — and I'm not just talking about how old this boat is." Everyone laughed.

"We're going back to the very origins of music. The pulse of what drove humans to discover music in the first place. To what do I refer? Yes. Yes! As some of you have guessed, rhythm. The core, the middle of everything we do. Our breathing is rhythm. Our hearts are rhythms just as are the cycles of days, months, years, and seasons. Rhythm is life.

"But, when I say rhythm, I don't just mean listening to some drumming by a gadabout like me. Ohhh, no. This will be far beyond the realm of a mere drumming exhibition." Another laugh, but this time more cautious. "Gentle ladies and gentle men, the rhythm performance you are about to *experience* is going to be performed by none other than YOU!" In a frenzied burst of movement Cassidy handed out bags of rhythm instruments to three or four people who'd been instructed to pass them out. Whippet-quick, Cassidy delivered gourds and rhythm sticks and sandpaper blocks. Some he tossed. Jason was reminded of the invisibly quick movements of hummingbirds and sparrows, squirrels and dragonflies.

"Now! Now!" said Cassidy, gaining momentum. He maneuvered himself behind what looked like a hollow log set on the carpet in front of him. Two much smaller sticks lay nearby. He sat down behind the log, cross-legged, and seemed to enter an almost trancelike state. People strained to see him. In a commanding yet still serene voice, Cassidy spoke to the crowd: "First, just listen." Eyes closed, back straight, Cassidy began drumming.

Jason searched the faces in the crowd. Cheeks were pink where before they'd been pale. Pot-bellied men and well-coiffed matrons were starting to move in accordance with Cassidy's rhythm. Although he couldn't completely follow what they were saying,

Jason's college Japanese could at least understand the superlatives of the tourist group beside him, half of whom held Cassidy's instruments like trophies.

His left hand continuing the rhythm, Cassidy pointed to the group on his right. "YOU!" He shouted. "ALL OF YOU! NOW JOIN ME." And they did. Some latched onto his simple rhythm quickly. Some were slightly off. It didn't matter.

"Now," Cassidy said, "Keep it going. Great! That's *IT*!" Now that a third of the group was carrying the rhythm, Cassidy could quit drumming himself. He pointed to the middle of the large semicircle gathered loosely round him. "NOW YOU ALL! I want you to do *this*!" And he started a contrapuntal rhythm which the middle group picked up and started playing with a solemn but enthusiastic panache. He had them.

Cassidy started a third rhythm with the crowd to his left. Once they were set, he returned to his log. Closing his eyes again, he began pounding. *"Now! Faster!"* he cried. Then he slowed them down. He sped them up again and slowed them down. All eyes were on him. Beginning with the first group he stopped them in the same order he started them. Solo, he went faster and faster and faster until his arms were a blur. Then — without warning — he stopped. He raised his arms high. Silence reigned.

Applause replaced the drumming and was just as thunderous. Cassidy remained frozen in front of his log, arms still raised, eyes still closed. Then — again without warning — he suddenly bounded straight up high — high! — into the air. His smile dazzled.

His eyes shone. Returned from whatever spiritual outpost he'd been visiting, he leapt from group to group, person to person, praising and patting and hugging and sometimes kissing. It was a virtuoso performance of human psychology. In every face around him, couples, families — even strangers — exchanged looks that said, "See what we did!"

As the buzz subsided, Cassidy moved to the electric piano and played half a dozen songs to his admiring crowd. When he was done Jason used the break to say hello. They'd met a number of times on Hot Springs, as Cassidy had taken over the leadership of the Hot Springs Island Music Club, to which Jason was an occasional visitor whenever he returned to the island.

• • •

Cassidy recognized Jason at once. "Jason! Jason! How are you?" His enthusiasm was sincere and infectious. Despite himself, Jason was embraced like a long-lost sibling by the wiry but muscular Cassidy.

"Good to see you," Jason said, still gripped in Cassidy's bear hug. "That was quite a performance…"

Without acknowledging the compliment, Cassidy immediately zeroed in on the essential. A serious expression doused the smile. "How's Dada?"

"Well, he had another episode a few nights ago, you know, the racing heart and…"

"…the sweats and difficulty breathing," continued Cassidy. "Alexandra called me from the hospital. I meant how is he *today*?"

Jason was taken aback.

"He's good. I talked to him this morning. Al, too. She's a little tired but she's okay."

"I'm glad, my brother, I'm glad," said Cassidy. "And how about you, Jason, how are you doing? Al told me you've got a lot going on." Cassidy's intense gaze focused on Jason.

"Well, I'm moving back to Hot Springs for good."

"Will you still do that web development thing?"

"I might but—" before Jason could elaborate, a group of Cassidy's friends pounced on him, leaving Jason alone to recall the bust up with his boss and his resignation from Human Designs. From there, it wasn't far to replaying his other recent heavyweight bout, the fight with Dee Dee.

Jason went out on deck. Through the thick windows, he could see Cassidy packing up his gear and chatting with people. He wondered if Cassidy was aware of his effect on others. He moved like a satellite — or perhaps even a planet — within his own orbit.

Waves pounded the hull of the *Spirit of Hot Springs Island*. The dark indigo of the ocean was beautiful and opaque. Jason knew from sailing the area that it was hundreds of feet deep at this spot. So much down there, he thought, and it's all beneath the surface. So much we can't see. And that's how the idea for the song hit him, literally up from the blue. Hoisting himself onto the gleaming, hip-high, metal life jacket container, Jason tugged his Cambridge notebook from his backpack and scrawled down the lyrics, the song finishing itself in a remarkably short time. Maybe he was right about a new start. Maybe moving back to Hot Springs was the absolute best thing he could have done. He scanned his lyrics again and wished he had a guitar with him. He contemplated borrowing one from Cassidy but instead stayed to enjoy the clearing weather. All the way to the main ferry terminal on Hot Springs Island the melody played in his head, a soundtrack.

> *Under the Surface*
> It's all beneath the surface
> In the places we can't see
> In the darkness and the shadows
> Underneath, underneath
>
> Dreams, they are the ripples
> On the surface of our sleep
> Fathoms and fouled anchors
> That's the deep, oh that's the deep
>
> CHORUS
> Everything's under the surface
> The places that we've never been
> Everything's under the depths and the dark
> Everything we've ever dreamed
>
> You'll never — know what's down there
> It's the unknown that we fear
> Engulfing, all surrounding
> Far and near, oh far and near

Everything's under the surface
The places that we've never been
Everything's under the depths and the dark
Everything we've ever dreamed

Rivers, lakes, the same thing
Weeds tugging at our feet
As eerie, the subconscious
Oh so deep, it's oh so deep

Everything's under the surface
The places that we've never been
Everything's under the depths and the dark
Everything we've ever dreamed

Chapter 1 iNovel Link
Interested in actually hearing this song,
"Under the Surface," as recorded by Jason?
Visit **www.HotSpringsNovel.com/chapter1/**
where you can also download the lyrics and
guitar tabs.

Chapter 2

"It's time for us to return to our natural state,
to wash the dirt from outside and in."

Cassidy's beater of a pickup truck and camper combo, plastered with flags, bumper stickers, decals, and old album covers tacked on with duct tape, drove off first. It was a rare day when Cassidy wasn't at the front of the line. How he managed it, Jason never knew.

Jason's cell phone played its original Jason melody.

"Jason."

"Dada!"

"Hello, son. You on the ferry?"

"Just arriving this second. What's up?"

"Listen…I'm in the ferry parking lot. I thought I'd come and surprise you. I'm with Harvey but now I know you're here, I'll send him off."

"Great! See you in a sec." Jason smiled. Being met at the ferry docks, welcomed into warm familiar arms, is the ultimate luxury.

Jason spotted his father, but immediately his pleasure waned. He couldn't believe the change. His frame was shrunken and his skull had grown pronounced in even the few weeks since Jason's last visit. For a moment, Jason even thought he detected something in his walk. But at least the sparkling eyes and voice remained unchanged as Dada uttered his usual *Richard III* greeting: "'Small cheer and great welcome makes a merry feast!'" Then, softer: "Welcome home, son." Jason wrapped his arms tightly around his father. Despite Dada's coat and usual checked shirt and cardigan, Jason could feel how thin he was.

To reach the hotel on the southeast side of the island, Jason and Dada had to drive through Troy, Hot Springs Island's biggest and only real town. They cruised past the famous bakery and sauntered by the three espresso shops and Thrifty's grocery store. The art gallery appeared to be doing a booming trade. Jason reveled in the collection of sheep farmers and retired folk, tourists and families and kids; the glorious phalanx of West Coast humankind that made up Hot Springs. The new high school gleamed in the distance. They whizzed along the undulating North-South Road, the carotid artery of the Island. Deer grazed in a meadow between road and ocean and the bucolic backdrop eased their conversation.

"So how are you feeling, Dada?"

"I'm fine, I'm fine. Except for these…episodes, if that's what you can call them. I really don't know what's behind them. It's vexing. My ECG checks out fine, so do the other tests, there's no history of heart trouble in the family — I haven't a clue what's going on and neither do the doctors. What I do know, though, is I'm being a major pain in the behind to you and Al and everyone else."

"Maybe you're under too much stress."

"No more than usual — with the possible exception of you."

"Me? What do you mean?"

"Quitting your job, for one. Moving back here, for two."

"Don't worry about me, Dada. Human Designs was hardly first prize in the job lottery. Like Kevin says, it was Dilbert meets The Scream. Besides, your night episodes were happening a long time before I quit."

"So what happened again, exactly?"

"It's a long story."

"We've got time."

"Well...I've told you how Kevin always hangs around the water cooler? How he's over there at least twenty times a day?" Jason and the rather quirky but always interesting Kevin had been friends since their UBC computer science days, and Jason had helped land him a job at HD. "Well, as usual, he'd gone to the cooler for the tenth time that hour, and then he comes over to my desk to tell me he's drunk so much water he's starting to identify with camels, or something ridiculous. That's when Walter shows up."

"Your boss?"

"Exactly. Walter of the tight black outfits, platform heels, and Tom Petty hairdo."

"I remember."

"As usual, Walter starts getting on Kevin's case. I mean, on the one hand, I can understand but, you know what? Despite the empty pizza boxes and headless dolls, Kevin's actually a good guy and very good at his job. Anyway, you should have heard Walter light into him. Totally unnecessary, personal, demeaning stuff. It got to the point where I was thinking, employer or not, this has got to stop. He was totally out of line. I had to say something."

"In no uncertain terms, you're suggesting?"

"I guess so."

"So are you saying you were fired, essentially, for sticking up for one of your co-workers? If that's the case, you could fight it, you know." Dada was a scrapper by nature, especially where underdogs were concerned.

"I wasn't fired, Dada, I quit. I was so pissed that I didn't stop there. I think I actually took it too far." He paused. "I pointed out as loudly as possible, so that the whole office could hear, that Walter's fly was open. At first you could hear a pin drop and then everyone — and I mean everyone — burst out laughing. You should have seen Walter's face. He looked like a rockfish. I don't think he's ever been so humiliated before. Especially in front of his staff."

"Well, Jason, if you ask me—"

"I know, Dada, I know. Two wrongs don't make a right. Revenge is self-defeating. You don't need to—"

"I was going to say I'm proud of you."

"Proud of me? For what?"

"For doing the right thing. For being loyal. For standing up to a bully."

Jason took his eyes off the road momentarily. "Thanks, Dada."

"You're welcome."

They drove a few hundred yards in silence.

"And, you know, Dada, to be honest, I was really

starting to question the whole job and supposed importance of it all. The crazy deadlines and the inane jobs I was given by inane bosses for an inane client. Some of the things they were asking me to do were just plain offensive. Pop-up ads. Junk mail. I was lining up zeros and ones for no other reason than to line them up. It was starting to get to me, Dada. It really was."

• • •

The hotel's massive oak doors had six thunderbirds carved on either side. Walking through them shifted Jason's senses into overdrive; it happened without fail. As if the smells of the yard and garden and the wood in the shed weren't enough, the hotel's hall-way took him to the next olfactory level. Whiffs of freshly baked bread, hints of rich soups, and the suggestion of recently cut flowers — these smells defined nostalgia for Jason. They transported him back to a time when Mum was alive and life had been warmer, simpler. The walls cluttered with paintings, the old framed movie and concert posters (*Harold and Maude, Neil Young*), guest photos, event T-shirts, lacquered fishing trophies, framed testimonial letters, and battered sports equip-ment...Yes, this was home. Jason walked around touching this, remembering that. His father watched from the open door.

"Dada, where's Mum's tapestry?"

"Al said it needed cleaning. She was right, as usual.

Also, on your left, there, I reframed that camping shot of the three of us."

Jason picked up the photograph of father, mother, son, now in a burnished wood frame. He remembered the trip well. They'd traveled by floatplane, Mum piloting, to Hot Springs Cove on Vancouver Island's west coast. Seven glorious days of exploring the rainforests and beachcombing the rocky coast. "It looks great."

"Remember the whales in Pachena Bay?" Jason asked.

"Yes," said Dada. "Five of them and three of us. We were outnumbered." They fell silent.

"It's good to be back," Jason said, and meant it. "And, speaking of Al, where is she? And where's Golly?" Al was Alexandra, longtime family friend, cook, assistant manager, and the main reason the hotel ran efficiently. Goliath was Jason's ancient black Labrador retriever, now an astonishing seventeen years old.

"Golly was outside earlier, 'Sitting as one new-risen from a dream,' and Al's in the kitchen — at least she was. She's expecting you." With a smile and a pat on the shoulder, Dada slipped his unlit pipe into his mouth and vanished into the office.

The kitchen was full of gleaming counters, polished dishes, and intimations of dinners past and to come — but no Al. Golly couldn't be found in either of her two customary spots: the doghouse beside the hotel or the old green bath mat near the bathhouse. Jason finally found her at the beach.

The Russell Point hot springs had two close but separate locations. One spring filled the wooden bathhouse near the hotel while the other rose up in three or four warm vents through layers of rock and muck and sand into the ocean. When the tide was right, the seaside hot springs heated the frigid Pacific water nicely, although passing ferries could float in an icy wash and send bathers scampering up the white shell beach and grassy slope breathless from laughter, the sudden exercise, and the unexpected exquisite chill.

Dada had visited Japan during and after the Korean War and had fallen for the Japanese hot springs esthetic. When the hotel started turning a modest profit, Dada reinvested the money and initiated his long cherished plan to lay in and mortar extra rocks around the beachside hot springs. He'd done a beautiful job; it looked like a natural pool more than a man-made bath.

"You should see these places in Japan," Dada said to a young Jason. "Not only are they beautifully planned with every rock and tree exquisitely placed, but there are so many, each with its own distinctive elegance." Jason hoped to go. It was the reason he'd taken a Japanese elective in college.

Huge clumps of bull kelp floated around the pool. From afar, they evoked beaded cornrows — the ocean's hairstyle. This place was exceptional and a prime reason for the hotel's popularity. Waters warmer than Mexico's with access to BC scenery; verdant evergreens on the slopes across the bay and white-shell sand beaches outlining the hotel. As Dada always said, "It's hard to top warmth in unexpected places." Golly epitomized this Dada aphorism, lolling in the hot bath like some oversized black loofah.

Despite her fading hearing, Golly heeded Jason's call and lumbered from the bath, more bear than dog. For the second time in less than half an hour, the issue of mortality smacked Jason hard across the face. Even Golly's normally high-velocity shake to rid herself of water seemed in slow motion. At least her mind remained sharp; if Jason were old and arthritic, he'd hang out in hot springs too.

Golly licked Jason's hand while he patted her affectionately. He had hardly known life without her. With no brothers and sisters, and his mother gone so many years, Golly occupied an important position. She'd grown even fatter, as Labs do. In the water she'd seemed lighter and slimmer, her movements easier. The penetrating heat worked its magic, even on dogs.

"Jason!" A mop of steel-wool hair topped Al's tiny frame. Her face, leathery and tanned, evoked the kindness and strong values that defined her character. She was smiling and, despite her age, came bounding across the rocky landscape.

Taking a cue from Cassidy, Jason picked her up and spun her round easily, skirt and apron swirling like a merry-go-round.

"Oh put me down, you big lump," she said in a mock angry voice but held on even after Jason lowered her onto the lichen-covered ground. "Come on into the kitchen and I'll fix you a cup of something. What's your fancy?" They meandered back towards the hotel, through the lobby and lounge and into the kitchen where Al poured them cups of coffee. For Al, kitchens were the only suitable place for conversation.

"So tell me about Dada, Al. What's going on?"

"Well, you've seen for yourself. Tell me what *you* think." She scrunched up her nose anticipating his answer.

"I thought he looked pretty frail. Actually, I was shocked. This heart thing has knocked him for a loop."

"Jason, if you want my honest opinion, I don't think it *is* his heart."

Although Jason suspected what was coming, he asked anyway: "What do you mean?" A small vein throbbed in his forehead.

"I think you know what I'm going to say, Jason, so I'll be direct." Al was rarely anything but. "I think it's the booze. He's getting older, I know we all are, but I just don't think he can handle it like he used to. Have you seen how his shirts hang on him? He's like a scarecrow. I tried to buy him some new ones, smaller ones, but he says he won't have any of that, the old ones fit fine. Stubborn old mule…"

Despite the gravity of the topic, Jason smiled at Al's description. He also wondered if she was right. Of course Dada drank. He'd been a drinker for years. But he never missed work, never appeared hung over. Dada enjoyed tippling with guests while regaling them with stories. It was part of the hospitality business and guests loved the eccentric old hotelier. "'I drink to the general joy of the whole table,'" Dada would say, quoting from *Macbeth*.

"I worry about him driving, Jason. I worry about him with his tools. I worry about him putting too much strain on his heart. Also, when he's had too much lately, I've noticed a personality change."

"A personality change?"

"He's become, oh, I don't know how to put it. A trifle maudlin. Or sad — or *something*. I can't describe it properly. You'll have to see for yourself. Whatever it is, he's not your usual father. The only time I remember him even being close to this is, well, that period after your mother died, when I first arrived."

"Have you brought it up with the doctor?"

"Well, although I disagree, he doesn't think this has anything to do with the drink. Or his heart, really. But when you ask him what it is, he doesn't have an answer. And, by your question, I take that to mean you haven't talked to Doc Curry, I mean— lately." Jason indicated "no" with a guilty shake of head. "Will you talk to him, Jason? Dada, I mean. Please? I've tried and tried and he just puts me off. And I wonder about my place, sometimes…"

"Oh come on, Al — you're family. How could you even worry about that?" Jason suspected she knew this but liked hearing it anyway.

"That's not the way it's been sometimes lately, Jason, especially when's he had a bit too much. You'd be surprised. I just hope he'll listen to you."

"Okay, Al. I'll see what I can find out tonight in the bath." Al squeezed Jason's hand in her two smaller ones.

● ● ●

With the hotel almost full, Jason helped wait tables like he'd been doing since he was ten. Once, he'd tripped carrying a tray of cutlery and sent a cold spoon spinning down the open back of a guest's cocktail dress. While Dada desperately maintained a serious face, the diner's rather pompous husband fished and groped for the offending utensil. His wife made faces either titillated or horrific — at first it was hard to tell which. After retrieval of said spoon, Jason was sent to wash it. On the verge of tears and expecting a scolding, he found Dada and Mum laughing at the sink. They called it "Jason's spectacular spoonerism."

The last table polished and ready for breakfast, Jason joined Al, Dada and Ellery, the new guy, in the kitchen. Call it custom or tradition, when dinner was done and the guests packed off, they gathered in The Pit for a coffee and some leftover dessert. Here they rehashed the day.

"Why 'The Pit'?" Ellery asked. Jason was perched on the central island, Al and Dada on stools. Vivaldi played in the background.

"Mum started it," Jason said.

"Two reasons," Dada elaborated. "First, it's like an orchestra pit, because of the music. My wife thought that baroque music and cooking shared the same rhythms — that it somehow made the food turn out better."

"Seems to work," said Ellery.

"And the second," added Jason, "is because sometimes it gets too crazy out there and The Pit's where we take shelter."

"Like the trenches," Ellery suggested. "For regrouping."

"Exactly," said Dada.

"So there must be some good stories," Ellery said.

"Oh, there are," laughed Dada. "Like the *War of the Roses* couple who'd come here for a romantic weekend. They were ostensibly trying to get their marriage on track but it wasn't working. I was waiting their table, and as I took their order, I could hear the little cutting remarks. Then, the wine started flowing and things started to escalate—"

"—including kicking each other under the table—" continued Jason.

"—and then a full-fledged food fight," finished Al.

"Or that granddad who got so sozzled he kept forgetting the names of the bride and groom during his speech," Dada said, laughing. Jason caught Al's quick look his way.

Al said, "And how about when the mixer broke and Dada had to rig up his electric drill. We did half a dozen cakes that way."

"Don't forget the story about the missing ring in the cake, when — god forbid — we were hoping someone wouldn't break a tooth." Everyone except Ellery chuckled.

"I don't get it…"

"Jason found it. He swallowed the damned thing and his mother and I had to, um, stand sentry duty for two days after, if you know what I mean."

Jason heard someone calling from the dining room. "Excuse me! Excuse me!" He went through the swinging door to see.

The Carsons' son Stevie was in the hallway looking lost. Probably not far from Jason's age, Stevie had straight reddish hair, wore glasses, and was about five foot four. He was a Downs child.

"Excuse me, Jason."

"Hi Stevie, what can I do for you?"

"Can I have a hot chocolate, please?"

"Of course." Jason looked around for Stevie's parents but saw no one. "Why don't you come in the kitchen with us while I get it ready for you?"

"Okay," he followed Jason through the swinging door.

Everyone said hello while Al gave their visitor her stool and started heating milk.

"Did you have a good day?" Dada asked.

"Yes, thank you," Stevie said. "I like boats. I saw lots of boats and I even rode on one. And I like the ocean and I like the hot springs, too. I like it here."

"Where are your folks?" Jason asked.

"They fell asleep watching TV."

"Well, we'll go with you after you've had your hot chocolate."

"Thank you," Stevie said. Before long, Al's hot chocolate, sprinkled with cinnamon, mint, and flakes of white chocolate was ready. Once it had cooled, he finished it in one long gulp.

"That was good. Can I have one more please?"

"Of course." Al filled his cup, again he downed it.

"I like it here."

"I'm glad, Stevie," Al said. Her hand rested comfortably on his shoulder.

"Can I stay here?"

"Of course you can. In fact, you're going to be staying here two more nights," Dada said.

"No, no. I mean forever. I'd like to live here."

"I don't think your parents would want that, Stevie. They live in Seattle. You'd be too far away. They'd miss you."

"No, no, I mean after they die. I worry about that, sometimes. About what's going to happen after they die. So I thought maybe I could live here."

"Would you like some more hot chocolate?" Al asked.

"No, thank you. I had enough. But it was very good. I think I'd like to go upstairs now."

"I'll go with you," Jason said, and he escorted Stevie up to his family's room.

• • •

At midnight, Jason waited for his father in the lobby like he'd done hundreds of times. Several minutes passed. Such tardiness was rare. Imagining another heart episode, Jason rang Dada's room but was told, somewhat impatiently, that everything was fine. He'd be out in a minute.

The bath habit had begun at Mum's instigation and had become a Chiron tradition. In fact, Mum had continued it until the day before she died, taken by an aneurysm only a week after Jason's twelfth birthday. The year she'd given him Golly.

"Come, my boys," she would say in a mock regal manner, "it's time for us to return to our natural state, to wash the dirt from outside and in." First they'd scrub and then shower and soak. "The family that bathes together, stays together," was another of her axioms. Mum had always balanced practicality with affection. Jason remembered her upright posture and dexterous hands as she sat doing the books or arranging the dining room. At such times Dada would call her, "Your Grace."

She had been an only child, like Jason, and her parents had died years ago. Dada still had relatives on Cape Breton Island but, with passing years, contact faded. Distance doing what it did.

Even at a young age Jason suspected that his parents wished him to be a family man with hordes of children. It spoke of their desire to again experience the vibrant energy of babies and young parents and to hear the cries and laughter of children. Being close to youth seemed to be a touchstone hardwired into people as they got older, as if children were a tonic that worked when others wouldn't. The presence of children and their children's children would confirm they'd fulfilled life's most primal function.

When young, Jason loved looking at photo albums with his mother. Seeing the exotic places she'd lived — the house on stilts in Georgetown, the one with a huge expanse of lawn facing Sydney Harbor — and the cracked black and white photos of her father, a sturdy bald man with tanned skinned and a wide grin. "I look like Mummy more," Mum said. "I'm more the thin wiry type than the sturdy type like Daddy."

"Who do I look like?"

"Like the sun and the moon and the stars put together!" Mum grabbed him and tickled until he was laughing so hard he thought he'd pee. Despite the golden nature of his early years, Jason envied friends with nearby cousins, aunts and uncles.

Yet, the mineral baths were a blessing to the Chiron family, and hotel staff and patrons had become extended family.

The hot springs seeped up through faults and fractures into four locations around the island, including the two here on Russell Point. All were gravity fed, also known as artesian wells. The hot water that reached the surface had once fallen as rain or, rarely, snow.

"Imagine it," said Mum more than once. "This water you're sitting in is thousands of years old. Older than us. Older than countries. Older than the trees and just about anything else you can think of." These images fascinated Jason. This water linked them to the past. He was immersed in something that conjured up times and events beyond his ken.

"Sometimes I think of the earth as a person," Mum told him. "If you imagine the earth has a body, then these hot springs are its blood, the warm river within that links everything. Like with people, the deeper you go, the warmer the earth and the water." She was right. The geologically active sections of Western Canada that included Hot Springs Island were part of the so-called Ring of Fire that circled most of the Pacific Rim. The temperature of rock three or four kilometers below the island was above boiling point.

The springs, as they were known locally, had given the island an identity, and a name. Over the years they'd also delivered prosperity to people like Dada.

Who, shuffling along in slippers, towel in hand, had finally arrived.

• • •

Years ago, Dada built a boardwalk leading from the back of the hotel veranda to the first flagstone of the bathhouse. The boardwalk consisted of exactly 299 wooden planks that Dada invited guests to carve or burn their names into. Some of the signatures were quite elaborate. Some had dates and logos and cleverly phrased mottos. When they rotted and aged they were retired and replaced with new ones — blank spaces continuing the tradition. Without fail, returning guests searched for their planks. "Memory Lane" was always mentioned in the hotel's guest book.

By nature, Jason was a counter and list maker. From an early age, he developed the habit of counting the boardwalk's planks. He took solace in this constant — while at the same time worrying that he was becoming staid and boring. Sometimes he missed the relish of childhood. The freshness of everything. He fretted he'd lost the capacity to take pleasure in the minutiae of existence. He wondered if it was his job, technology, or just society in general that was wearing him down. The doubts seemed to ebb, however, whenever he returned to the outdoor life of the island. Here, with the ocean and trees and hot springs, he felt rejuvenated and more human.

In silence, Jason and Dada traversed the boardwalk to the bathhouse. Still without speaking, they undressed, showered, and slipped into the bath. The heat and the darkness soothed them within seconds. Steam rose into the night. The mood was of profound intimacy — not just between them, but with nature and the past, as well. The ritual of the bath spoke to some inner sanctum that seemed as deep as the well from which the hot springs water flowed.

Over the years, this bath had been the scene of many incidents: a couple making love so loudly that they'd woken guests through closed windows 299 planks away; teenagers on graduation night who'd filled the hot springs with bubble bath; one time Canadian geese had landed and defended the pool like knights in a castle siege until Golly finally evicted them with quick lunges and fierce barks.

Perhaps the most legendary incident was the night

two guests encountered a different kind of creature in the springs. Jason was on duty that eventful evening when his reading was interrupted by the arrival of two excited men in robes.

"There's an animal in the bath," said one, "and you'd better get something or someone over there *right away*." Arriving at the bath, Jason hadn't a clue what it was. Golly barked and lunged, barked and lunged. Jason's best guess was a baby river otter. But, with the burned-out overhead light, he couldn't tell for sure.

Jason said, "Best be prepared." From the nearby tool shed, they collected a prawn trap and some wire. A crowbar and axe were also selected — albeit with no clear strategy.

On their return, Golly's barking became frenzied.

"Have you got a gun in the hotel?" asked the older man. He had pulled on sweatpants under his robe, and for some reason, well-polished business shoes. Seeing Jason's surprised look, he added: "Not that we'll need it, of course."

"We'll use the pool net. It's got a long handle. Back me up."

"Roger," said the first man.

"Wilco," said the second.

Even Golly, sensing the tension, grew quiet.

He moved the net below the water and then, with a well-practiced upwards flick, snagged the floating animal on his first go. It didn't move. Neither did anyone else. The air was as static with tension as before a thunderstorm.

"Perhaps it's dead," suggested the first man. He

pulled his dressing gown sash tighter around his substantial midriff.

Jason couldn't understand why the creature remained motionless — and so light. It weighed next to nothing. As Jason brought the pole closer, realization dawned.

"Oh," he said. "Um, listen gentlemen, I've got to tell you something. It's, um, well, it's not an animal …" Jason moved the net closer.

"Be careful!" said the first man in a higher-than-intended voice. "If it's not an animal, then what is it?"

"Well, it's— well…it's my father's toupee," said Jason, becoming more emphatic as he neared the end of this painful sentence. He brought the object closer. Indeed, it was Dada's hairpiece.

Golly came up and disdainfully sniffed it.

"Your father's toupee?"

"Yes. I don't know what else to say. Except, well, *sorry*. This has never happened before. Really."

"Your father's *toupee*…"

Timing impeccable, a less-than-sober Dada chose this moment to enter. His bald pate underscored Jason's explanation. His son wasn't sure whether this was positive or negative.

"There it is," Dada said as if nothing was out of the ordinary. "There's my piece." He lurched towards Jason who was now holding the dripping clump of hair between two fingers.

"Okay," said Jason. "Thanks for your assistance, gentlemen. You were wonderfully helpful. Thank you. Really." He ushered them out.

The two men turned their backs and left. Jason could hear the younger man explaining, and then, thankfully, the door closed.

"I knew I'd lost it somewhere," said Dada. He then attempted to place the sopping hairpiece on his head. Jason put his arm round his father and led him off to bed. When approaching the kitchen, Golly saw the sodden mess in Jason's hand and gave one desultory half-yip then went back to sleep.

As Jason tucked Dada into bed, Dada said: "'I have very poor and unhappy brains for drinking' — *Othello*."

"You can say that again."

• • •

"You're sure about this, right?" Jason asked Dada.

"Sure about what?"

"The bath. Don't you have to be careful about getting overheated?"

"I do if it's really my heart," Dada said. "Anyway, the doctor gave me the okay as long as I don't stay in too long."

"And you really don't think your heart's the problem?"

"All I'm saying is I don't know what it is."

Jason recalled his conversation with Al. Maybe Dada's drinking was worrying him, too.

"Maybe you should lay off the wine and stuff for a while, Dada...you know, to see if that makes a difference."

"No, I don't think it's that." Dada dismissed Jason's overture without missing a beat.

Jason eyed his father through the steam. "If there's something on your mind, Dada, you can tell me, you know. Just go with it."

Dada looked back. He seemed to be mulling something in the way a tongue flicks a painful tooth.

"What is it, Dada? I can tell something's bothering you."

There was another long pause before he spoke. "Well, like you said, I probably shouldn't stay in too long. Just in case. I'm about done here, I think. Good night, Jason."

As Dada dressed, Jason watched him closely, searching for clues.

Dripping wet, Dada couldn't have weighed more than 130 pounds. As always, he sported a beard, a scraggly mixture of sandy red and salt and pepper — "a bit of the old spice rack." Set into a kindly, expressive, face, Dada's bright curious eyes spoke of the musician, builder, actor, artist, and bon vivant he was. Recently those eyes had lost some of their luster. Although he was older than Jason's friends' fathers, until his recent health issues, Dada possessed an ageless quality that made his present appearance all the more troubling. But, regardless of what he struggled with, Dada was uniquely Dada, a certified character on an island redolent with them.

• • •

Jason soaked for another twenty minutes. Readying to emerge from the steaming water, he realized he was towel-less; it was drooped over the back veranda railing. Jason gambled that no one would see him scurry nude from the bath to the rear deck and back. Halfway there, luck deserted him. Coming around the side of the hotel were a man and woman, probably guests out for a romantic moonlit stroll.

Since romantic moonlit strolls are rarely meant to include buck-naked hotel staff, Jason scanned the area for cover. A dash back to the bath seemed his best bet, but doing so would require crossing their line of vision and Jason feared his pale white butt becoming an alternative source of moonlight. A better option was the woodshed to his left. The wood chips and rough ground hurt his feet as he did a shoeless dance across them.

The couple paused on the path, watching the mist rolling in off the ocean and remarking on the quality of the moon through the fog. They sat down. He was wet, the evening was far from warm, and the fog meant damper, colder air. But the fog was also an ally, Jason's best chance for cover. Finally a cloudbank obscured the moon, and the couple rose. The increasing clouds and fog provided just the camouflage Jason needed. Dying to dive in and be re-embraced by the bathwater, he darted from his hiding spot. He hadn't taken three steps, however, when a phone rang in the still night. Jason froze. The couple stopped too. They were only meters away.

"Is that our phone, dear?"

Damn! Jason recognized the distinctive ring tone. His phone was lodged in his pants pocket, back in the bathhouse.

He prepared to sprint away at their slightest movement. Either that or cover the most embarrassing part of his body — his face. The phone went silent and he heard the man say, "No, dear, that's not ours."

Despite his temporary adrenalin rush, Jason continued shivering. Thank god for the hot springs. He returned to the bathhouse, pausing there for a moment to make sure the couple was gone, and entered. It was darker inside the bathhouse. He plunged in, submersing his head to get the full benefit of the heat. He wanted to warm himself as quickly as possible; the phone could wait.

The heat enveloped him like gloves warmed on a radiator. He stayed under until he had to breathe. Coming up for air, the last thing he expected to see was someone stepping out of the bath.

"Dada?" Jason rubbed the water from his eyes, which widened as he saw the other person wasn't his father at all, but a woman. She was maybe Asian, slight but shapely with a thick rope of black hair which she'd tied up behind her head. She held a rectangular white towel in front of her.

Acknowledging Jason's startled reaction, the woman stopped and spoke for the first time.

"I'm sorry," she said. Then, without rushing, she walked gracefully through the changing room door. From behind, her skin was a pale glow in the darkness. Jason registered an elegant torso as she disappeared.

Who was she? A hotel guest? Should he say something about guests requiring bathing suits — but, then, who was he to talk? He hadn't even bothered with the changing room. He slid deeper into the water. He didn't want to risk offending her. And, to be honest, he was more than intrigued.

Quicker than expected, the woman stepped out in jeans and a wool sweater. She said, "I'm sorry" again and then, with a minimum of movement, stepped into a pair of sandals Jason hadn't noticed earlier, and moved to the bathhouse door. She was far enough away that Jason could barely discern her. The darkness and the steam and the mist were veils separating them. He heard the door crack open and then she said, "Good night."

Then she was gone.

• • •

What was *that*? Despite an urge to leap from the bath and follow her, Jason stayed put. He should have peppered her with questions. Who was she? Didn't she know that the bath was closed to the public? She'd been so composed, so unconsciously seductive.

Warmed and brimming with speculation, Jason left the bath. Still towel-less, he dried himself with his T-shirt and dressed. Back in the hotel, his immediate objective was the guest log. As he remembered, there were no single women booked. Later, in bed, sleep was the last thing on his mind. He asked himself questions but no answers seemed right. He thought about the girl until finally sleep closed in and captured him.

But that wasn't the last of her. He dreamed. He was at the beachside hot springs and it was early in the evening, just past dusk, before the light had fully escaped and the sky was not yet black. He passed through the gate and saw her, back to him, facing out to sea, immersed in the hot water just below her shoulders. Tendrils of steam escaped upwards like tiny gossamer nymphs. A hint of wind ruffled the tops of the arbutus trees behind him. As in real life, the girl's hair was thick and up. Her shoulders completely visible, lithe and of perfect contour. Slowly, without effort, she waded through the pool to the outermost rocks that formed the border between ocean and hot springs. Like a mermaid or Venus on the half-shell, she stepped onto the largest rock on the outer perimeter of the pool without using her hands. As she'd done since Jason arrived, she continued her watch over the body of water. He willed her to turn, to see her more fully, but she remained motionless despite the occasional influx of seawater that ran across her feet in a surge of froth and foam like something alive fleeing the cold. Still she kept looking. Jason could not see the focus of her gaze. And then, like steam from the hot springs vanishing into the darkening night, she faded, pixel by illusionary pixel, and Jason slipped into a deeper sleep.

• • •

Part-timers bolster the staff of any busy hotel. Ellery was hard-working, personable, and popular with guests. Although twenty-seven, his pierced ears and tattoos made him look younger. Dada wanted Ellery to take on more hours but he couldn't because of frequent trips into Vancouver.

After the usual small talk, Jason asked Ellery about Asian guests.

"None as far as I know," Ellery replied. "Why?"

Next, Jason went looking for Al but instead found Dada in the office studying a supply list.

"Morning. Dada," Jason said.

"Ah— 'the cock, that is the trumpet to the morn.'" Before Jason could retort or ask about guests, Dada looked at Jason and asked: "Did you stay long last night?" He swiveled his ever-present unlit brown and black briar pipe from one side of his mouth to the other.

"A while..." Jason paused. "And we're going again tonight, right?"

The moment the question was out, Jason regretted it. What if the mystery woman returned — and what would Dada say at such an encounter? Jason changed the subject. "Is Music Club happening tomorrow night?"

"Indeed it is. Shall we go?"

"Where's it at?"

"Bobbi Lee Hunter's. She's a friend of Cassidy's. I'm not sure you know her. She's got a big place on the harbor."

"Sure. It'll be fun."

He swiveled his pipe again. Jason readied to leave.

"Oh, Jason..." Dada called him back.

"What is it?"

"I forgot to mention. Don't be surprised if you run into a Japanese girl, name of Kiriko, in the bath if you go late, after closing hours."

"What...what's her name?"

As in hockey, a deflection is always a good play.

"Her name's Kiriko. She's the daughter of a family I met while I was in Japan years ago, you know, doing my hot springs tour. She's living on the island now and I gave her a key and told her to use the bath whenever she wants. The family owns a small hot springs inn in Kyushu."

"What's she doing here?"

"She's an artist, a painter. She's got some stuff in the Troy Gallery; you should go take a look. She's very good. Very talented. Her work is amazingly detailed and delicate. Subtle. I was hoping you'd get to know her. Maybe you could practice your Japanese."

"I'll check out her work next time I'm in town. And I'll watch out for her in the bath." This was all the composure he could muster.

"I think Al's got some shopping for you."

"I'll see if I can find her."

Dada smiled and said, "Perhaps you best do that."

Chapter 2 iNovel Links

There are two iNovel Links for Chapter 2. The first is an artistic one. Three artists have been asked to draw, sketch, paint – whatever – their impressions of the Hot Springs Island Hotel. Why three? To illustrate how we all see the same thing in different ways and how perspective is everything – to make the hotel seem more real but more elusive at the same time. The second link is an interactive map (including photographs and a QuickTime movie) of Hot Springs Island and the town of Troy. Please **visitwww.HotSpringsNovel.com/chapter2/** for both links.

Chapter 3

"How's that for a coincidence?"

Al wasn't in the kitchen or upstairs. Jason couldn't find her in the garden or in the basement. He finally came across her sitting on a chair atop the outcrop overlooking the beachside hot springs. She was staring out at the ocean. At this time of day it was rare to find Al unengaged in some energetic task.

"Al?" She started slightly at Jason's voice. Then she moved her hand to her face as Jason came closer.

"Al— you okay?"

She laughed. Jason could tell it was a feint.

"Oh, you know me, I'll cry at anything."

Jason sat next to her.

"Not out here, you usually don't." The view looked out over Ford Harbor and across to the southwest. Guests liked to come here and watch the sun descend behind Mt. Sansum.

"It's Frankie." Frankie was Al's only son, from her third marriage. Frankie's father, Al's love, had shot himself in the back room of their bungalow in Esquimalt.

"You know, when I moved here to Hot Springs," Al said, "I thought I was going to be able to put all of it behind me."

Jason nodded.

"I know it's naïve, but when I moved here I thought I'd finally found my own little oasis, a place where I could leave my nightmares back on the other shores...for a little while, anyway. I remember when I was growing up on the prairies; there was land everywhere you looked, as far as you could see. How could you ever defend yourself or protect yourself in a place like this, I remember thinking. But, here, with this water. I thought the island was a castle and the ocean a giant moat."

"Al...don't start getting all melodramatic on me, now." She smiled. "And, okay, if you want to be serious for a minute, just think how much you helped us by coming here. Think how much *I* needed you, for one. And how much Dada needed your help after Mum died."

"I remember how he was. How badly your mother's passing affected him. We didn't even have to say anything to each other. We spoke the same language of loss. We'd developed our own dialect that only the two of us understood."

More than once Jason had wondered if Al and Dada had been lovers. Part of him hoped so. Two lonely people in need of such profound solace. How could they not have been?

"So what's the story with Frankie?"

"Money. As usual."

"What for, this time?"

"He's been evicted again. He has to find somewhere else to live. It's not the money. It's just that it's the only time he calls."

"What are you going to do?"

"What is there to do?"

He looked out at the calm water and watched the otherwise invisible wind kick up the occasional cat paw before again disappearing. A chainsaw fired up in the distance and a seagull floated above them.

Al faced Jason.

"What about last night? Did you talk to Dada in the bath?"

"About?"

"You know."

"Sort of."

"Sort of?" Her tone indicated that the old, less melancholy, Al was back.

"Well, I only bridged the topic. I didn't want to sound too accusatory, especially so soon after coming back."

"But you talked about it?"

"We did."

"And?"

"He doesn't think his drinking is connected to the heart problem. Or a problem at all, for that matter."

"He wouldn't. But if it isn't, then what, pray tell, is?"

• • •

The regular Thursday routine was shopping then banking. The hotel always needed extra food and liquor on busy weekends so Jason volunteered.

Before setting out with Al's shopping list, Jason inventoried the hotel's beer, wine, and spirits supply with the intention of gauging Dada's drinking.

Although he'd been watching closely, Dada was either imbibing in skilled solitude or hardly drinking at all. The only thing Jason got from sniffing Dada's morning coffee cup was the sense of feeling ridiculous.

A few yards from the liquor store, Jason had his head down checking his list.

"Hey, stranger." That voice — husky and female — could belong to only one person: the inimitable Tina Magdalene Love. Tina. *Tina Love*. Tina was Jason's first. His first love, his first lover. They had dated since their third year of high school and, in many ways, they'd become adults together. The relationship was tempestuous, he hadn't known such heights of passion or depths of despair before or since — Dee Dee included. Maybe it was the first-love thing. Possibly it was something more. Her, perhaps, or chemistry, or all of the above.

"Tina…" said Jason. He remembered the last time he'd seen her: at a party three Christmases ago. The next week he'd changed jobs and moved to Human Designs. The time before that, Jason's place in Vancouver had been robbed while they shared a bottle of wine.

He was surprised to run into her. She was supposed to be married and living out east. But Tina never disappeared for long. They were connected by family and history and by this small island. Like it or not, their bonds of time and circumstances were stout.

Tina and Jason had parted and made up too many times to count, and even during the off periods, her appearances were always harbingers. Major events in

Jason's life always followed a Tina-Jason reunion, regardless of the form that reunion took.

Tina's long auburn hair was pulled back with a shell barrette he remembered her making. As usual, her smile made him think of summer. Visceral memories flooded back. "Marriage seems to agree with you," Jason said. They hugged. There's nothing like embracing an old flame. Bodies merge easily and memories are instantly rebooted.

"How long you back for this time? It's so good to see you!" A licensed veterinarian and, like Jason, twenty-nine, Tina still hadn't lost her habit of finishing most sentences with a rising intonation— question or not — a Valley Girl thing that had always bewildered Jason in someone so smart.

"I'm back for good," Jason said. "Gave up my apartment in Vancouver and quit my job. Back to my old life."

"You're kidding! That's amazing! Me too. I'm back for good, too."

Tina's brains and unrelenting work ethic had taken her off Hot Springs Island and into the University of Alberta's veterinary program before she'd transferred to Guelph in Ontario her second year. This separation ended their initial romance, but it was followed by enough returns and breaks for a five-set tennis match. The final split occurred more than three years ago.

"Permanently?" Jason asked. "You're back permanently? With..." Jason scrambled to remember his name.

"Well, yes to the first and no to the second."

Tina looked nonplussed. "I'm recently...no longer married..."

"You're divorced?" Tina nodded. Jason could only stare in disbelief. "This was the guy back east? The psychologist?" She nodded. Trying to recover, he attempted a joke. "Well, you always were a quick worker."

"You bastard," she said, thumping him on the shoulder. He couldn't tell if she was kidding or if he'd crossed the line. "And what about you? You still with that Newfie girl? What was her name — Doo Doo, Pee Pee?"

"You're the one who's a bastard," Jason said, thumping her in return. Her sense of the absurd remained intact. "It's Dee Dee, and, to be perfectly honest, I don't really know..."

"You don't really know?"

"Short version. I don't know if you know, but Dee Dee and I worked together at Human Designs. She'd been laid off a couple of months before, you know, during a 'restructuring,' and when I quit, she thought I'd done it purely out of solidarity. That I was doing it for her."

"So what's wrong with that?"

"My quitting had nothing to do with committing or us whatsoever. ...If it was about anything, if was about me getting fed up with so-called technological advances and what I was being asked to do with them."

"But there's got to be more, right? Sounds like there's history, here."

"Isn't there always?"

Tina continued. "But, if I hear you right, you haven't officially broken up, is that it?"

"Essentially, yes."

"Well, well, young man, how about that? We should get together and talk. Trade some stories."

"We should." Memories of lying in the back of Dada's old station wagon came rushing back. Then her room with her parents away, and the tent on Sansum Point. He shut them off quickly.

Jason looked at his watch. "Listen, I should go. I've got something."

"Yeah, me too," said Tina. "Call me."

"I will."

• • •

Jason carried the cases of booze to the pickup. He had brought Golly along for company and today she was relatively spry, needing only a slight boost into the truck's cab. Seeing Jason return, her thick tail went *bam bam bam* against the seatback.

Groceries were next. He found a parking space and left Golly in the truck. Inside the store he grabbed a buggy and set to work. In the soft drinks aisle, he came across an old school buddy. They exchanged island news and talked about their latest gadgets and machinery. The inexorable shift to a sports-related topic was imminent.

Suddenly, Jason saw someone crossing the aisle at the far end. If he wasn't mistaken it was the beautiful

Asian woman with long black hair. What was her name — Kiriko? She disappeared before he could confirm his guess. He'd only managed a quick glimpse and was anxious to investigate.

Jason cut off his friend. "Mark...Buddy. Something's come up. Gotta run."

Mark didn't flinch. "Sure, Jase. See you around. We should go for a beer."

He was already halfway down the aisle. He scanned the cash registers, he checked the doors. Then he dashed to the bakery section on one side of the store and all the way back to fruits and veggies. Nothing.

Then he had a thought: maybe she'd gone to the Troy Gallery. He'd check it out after shopping. Even if she wasn't there he could at least see her paintings.

The Troy Gallery was more than thirty years old but had made money only in the past five as the island grew in popularity as a tourist destination. Hot Springs Island was artist dense and the collection reflected it, often displaying fifteen to twenty artists at a time, almost all local. Jason's Music Club friend, Cristine, showed regularly. Now, apparently, so did Kiriko.

Three of Kiriko's paintings were on display. Jason agreed with Dada's assessment: she was very good. Three themes seemed to dominate her work: mountains, the ocean, and floral motifs. But it was her bio card that interested him the most.

Japanese Artist: Kiriko

Kiriko was born in the Japanese hot springs resort of Kurokawa Onsen (Hot Springs) on the southern island of Kyushu. She graduated from the Musashino Institute of Art in Tokyo and has studied with Hiroshi Inoue and Akiyo Ueda since. She specializes in the medium of *Nihonga*, translated as "traditional Japanese painting." One of the main features of *Nihonga* is the use of powdered, organic mineral pigments, which Kiriko grinds herself. Kiriko is now a resident of Hot Springs Island.

Trying to absorb as much as possible, Jason examined the painting titled *Silent Solitude*, an incredibly intricate rendering of rocky hills dotted with lichen and a sharp, soaring peak in the background. Next to the painting was another card.

Silent Solitude (not for sale)
The title of this painting is *Jakujo*, a Buddhist term relating to a particular state of the heart after a time of sadness. I painted this as one of a series after an event of sadness had visited my own life, the passing of a loved one — my beloved mother. This painting represents the ability of humans to transcend pain. Mountains stand firm and unyielding despite the harsh conditions nature sometimes chooses to bring. At the foot of the mountain, lovely spring flowers bloom, telling us that life is a cycle that repeats and repeats itself, regardless of what has come before.

"They're beautiful, aren't they?"

The gallery assistant startled him.

"Yes...yes, they are."

"I look at them and feel this calmness, this serenity, come over me. It's a state, almost meditative, I'd say. And you're in luck. If you'd like to meet the artist, she's right over there...Kiriko! Kiriko, would you mind coming over here for a moment?"

Kiriko emerged from the half shadows of the framing area into the brightly lit gallery. It was her.

"Kiriko, I'd like you to meet..."

"Jason, Jason Chiron."

"Nice to meet you, Jason." Their eyes met briefly before Kiriko looked away at one of her paintings. In his panic to know if she recognized him from last night, Jason hardly saw her face.

"Your paintings are extremely beautiful," Jason said.

"Thank you."

"But this one's not for sale. Isn't that unusual in a gallery?"

"It is," answered the assistant. "But Kiriko always displays this particular piece whenever she shows, as a way of remembering her family. And it's so beautiful...how could we resist?" The assistant smiled before darting away to answer a ringing phone.

"I'm Joseph Chiron's son. Dada's son."

"Your father's been very kind to me." Kiriko's English was clear, if somewhat measured.

"And I think we already met, last night, in the bath. I'm sorry, I didn't..." Jason fumbled for words.

"I should say sorry instead. It was a little...embarrassing...I think. For both of us."

"Yes," Jason said.

Then Kiriko looked up and Jason saw for the first time her remarkable amber eyes.

Chapter 3 iNovel Link

By going to the iNovel link at **www.HotSpringsNovel.com/chapter3/** you'll see a large, full-color rendition (and a description in the artist's own words about *Nihonga* – traditional Japanese painting) of Kiriko's *Silent Solitude*. And, if you choose, you can actually buy prints of *Silent Solitude* as well as originals and prints of other *Nihonga* painting by this talented Japanese artist.

Chapter 4

"You must have come a long way."

The hotel was full and dinner busy. It reminded Jason of the first time he'd helped out in the kitchen. It was organized chaos with Mum as traffic cop and staff the rapidly moving delivery vehicles. The sound, the smells, the bustle and the post-dinner gatherings in The Pit returned Jason to the rhythms of hotel and Hot Springs life. He was glad to be back.

Speeding about with full, then dirty, plates, Jason cornered Dada long enough to confirm they'd meet in the lobby at midnight. Dada's agreement was punctuated with a quote from the end of *A Midsummer Night's Dream*, one of his favorite plays. Jason hoped this was a good sign. "'If we shadows have offended / Think but this, and all is mended, / That you have but slumber'd here / While these visions did appear.'" Jason interpreted this as an apology for Dada's tardiness the last couple of nights.

Jason watched Dada for signs of inebriation. To the good, he seemed in control at all times, a model of moderation. On the minus side, he'd taken up chewing gum. The verdict was still out.

Post-dinner and Pit session, Jason headed for the office. He wanted to check his e-mail and begin a much-needed upgrade of the hotel's website.

Despite his problems with Human Designs, one of

Vancouver's largest graphic shops, Jason excelled as a web developer and web and graphic designer. He instinctively saw shortcuts where others saw obstacles and he could picture a large, complex website in its entirety with unnerving ease. He could talk to and understand either developers or artists and, at heart, he identified with both groups — a rare gift.

He also instinctively understood what clients needed, even when they didn't. Websites were still a relatively new medium and many people, Jason realized, had trouble picturing them. Just as importantly, they lacked the vocabulary to describe them and what they could and couldn't do. Jason did the on-screen equivalent of reading between the lines. He visualized the end result people wanted and explained it in terms they understood. Although this sounded simple, it wasn't. Like all good teachers, he moved from intention, to process, to result. Using a website skillfully required a new visual syntax that few people knew about yet, one still not taught in mainstream schools.

Jason was hunkered down in front of his screen when he heard the distinctive "ping" of arriving e-mail. Two he opened right away.

Kevin's was first. In Jason's apartment the night he resigned, Kevin had toasted his friend's loyalty and pledged eternal friendship. The tone of this particular message, however, was anything but.

What the—? The gist of Kevin's e-mail centered on the Dee Dee breakup. Bluntly, Kevin asked why Jason had dumped her and who'd initiated it. He wanted "the real lowdown." Kevin called Jason "a major dumbass" and wrote that "bad things happen when bad things get done."

Jason clicked the next message. Ironically, it was from Dee Dee herself. He read the note three times in succession.

Jason, sweetie (I hope it's still okay to call you that :)

I hope you're well. I really truly do. I haven't heard from you since you left. I was hoping you'd at least write and tell me that you and Dada were okay but I suppose I can understand, even if I don't agree with your reasons.

Of course I've been thinking. All the time. Thinking at night. Thinking in bed. Thinking as I take a walk — and I've been taking plenty of walks lately. Thinking about you and me and us and, every time, reaching the conclusion that there are just too many loose ends, that there's too much unresolved. You know I didn't want events to play out as they did and I hate this place we're in. We've meant — and mean — so much to each other so you shouldn't be surprised to hear from me, to know that I have to see things through and do my best to salvage what I think we can. I hate giving up. That's what love and commitment are all about. Aren't they?

I tried calling you late one night but you

didn't answer. Maybe you were in the bath with Dada — or maybe you just didn't want to hear from me. I hope it's the first reason.

What I'm proposing is this. I want to come and visit you tomorrow. And just so you don't think too much of yourself, I'm not just coming to see you but Dada and Al, also :) And don't say no, Jason. We HAVE to talk. You know that as well as I do. So, I'll be there, hopefully sometime after two. I decided to drive so you don't have to pick me up. I'll call if there's any change of plans.

All my love, (I hope it's okay to write that, too...)
Dee Dee

Jason clicked the reply button but his hands were motionless on the keys, his face lit by the glow from his screen. Every second, hundreds of cathode rays, undetectable to the eye, shot down the monitor and disappeared into the electronic vacuum. Jason continued working on the website. Tomorrow would bring what tomorrow would bring.

• • •

When he finally checked his watch, it was nearing midnight and time to meet Dada. Would Kiriko show, too? How would the dynamic work then?

Jason decided to pick Dada up in his room.

After Jason's birth, the family ran short of room. In typical energetic fashion, Dada used his considerable carpentry skills to make an extension for use as a family residence. He built a living room, kitchenette, two bedrooms and an en suite, all reached by a hall off the main dining area. A "No Entry" sign was bolted to the suite's door.

Jason knocked once, listened, and then tried the door. It was five minutes to midnight.

The lights were off. Jason could hear a clock ticking. "Dada? You there?" Silence. He turned on a table lamp and crept to the bedroom door. It was ajar. Peeking in, Jason saw Dada in bed, lights out. He was breathing peacefully. Like it or not, Dada was getting old. Jason had to accept it. How small he looked in the big bed, one thin arm lying out in the open. Feeling a mixture of affection and regret, Jason came close to pull up the covers. The unmistakable smell of alcohol hovered by Dada's bedside.

• • •

Dada had never missed a bath before. Not once. He contemplated waking him. But he couldn't. He didn't have the heart. Dada was seventy. Surely his rest and health took precedent over anything else — including his and Al's suspicions. It had been a busy day and maybe he wasn't feeling well.

He'd just have to bathe by himself. This time, Jason fetched his robe and bathing suit. He also made sure to leave his cell phone behind and off. Walking down the boardwalk (he counted) from the back deck, he looked for moonlight strollers. Even when he stopped and listened he heard nothing. His thoughts gravitated to Kiriko.

Holding his breath in anticipation, Jason tried the door. It was locked and the bathhouse empty.

The total immersion produced a blanketing effect and the sensation that his entire body was being massaged with no place untouched, no part of his body neglected. Mum thought that people loved hot springs because of the unconscious association with the womb, to that period of ultimate security, protection and love. We need touch, Mum said. It's our first and most fundamental sense, our primary desire. "Babies and children know," she said. "It's just that somewhere along the line we lose the connection to intimacy, although we never lose the need. Hot springs draw us back to that. They comfort us in ways other things can't."

Fifteen minutes in and Jason felt baked. Beads of sweat spotted his brow. He heaved himself onto the edge of the bath, leaving only his feet dangling. When cooled, he re-immersed himself and repeated this cycle. Then he went to wash his hair.

While rinsing he thought he heard a knock. He turned off the water and he heard it again. A soft but distinct knocking. Still lathered, Jason said, "One sec," and rinsed off the last traces of shampoo. His heart pounded. But before he could reach the door, the key turned and Kiriko stood at the open door.

After a moment, Jason spoke: "Please come in," he said.

Kiriko paused, too. "Are you sure...you don't

mind? I could wait…" She wore the same jeans and sweater.

"No, not at all. Please go ahead. If you want, I can leave."

"No, no. I'm sorry…"

A brief awkward silence ensued.

"Please, Kiriko. You must have come a long way." She hesitated. "Please," Jason repeated, this time in Japanese.

"You speak Japanese?"

"Only a little," he replied in her language. Then, in English: "I had two years at university. But, please, come in."

Slowly, Kiriko entered the bathhouse. She disappeared into the changing room. After showering, she emerged several minutes later wrapped in a white towel much larger than the long rectangular one of the other night. He remembered how she'd looked that evening, walking away, her back exposed to the air. He'd dreamt of her that night; but images from that and other dreams were stored and retrieved differently within his memory. His subconscious remembered things he did not.

Still in her towel, Kiriko slid into the opposite end of the bath.

Whether from mutual shyness or pure serendipity, both man and woman looked skyward at exactly the same moment. The night was perfect for outdoor bathing. A frosty hint in the air made the water temperature even more welcoming and gave the air a crisp, high-definition clarity. Thus, when a shooting star burst into a trail of white and silver across the glossy blackness of sky before instantly disappearing, Jason and Kiriko let out tiny but audible gasps of delight and surprise.

"Did you see that?" asked Jason.

"Yes," said Kiriko. "It was amazing."

"Was it ever," said Jason. "What timing...Is it the same in Japan — we have the idea here that if you see a shooting star and make a wish, then you have a better chance of it coming true," said Jason.

"It's the same for us," said Kiriko.

"We also call them falling stars. What about in Japanese?"

"We say *nagare boshi*," said Kiriko. She pronounced the words very slowly and Jason repeated them, with good pronunciation, until he memorized them. "*Nagare,*" continued Kiriko, "means flowing, or pouring. *Boshi*, or *hoshi*, is star."

"*Nagare boshi* — a flowing star," said Jason. "I can remember the first time I saw one — actually it was more than one. It was summer and I was in the other bath, the one down by the beach. I was with my mother and father and there were showers of them, literally showers. We kept looking up and there they were, one after another, all over the place. Mum said, 'We were showering under the stars.' The funny thing was, I had no idea. I thought that was normal." He laughed lightly. "And then I didn't see another one until I was in high school, even though I can remember going to Cape Sansum for the specific purpose of watching them and not seeing even one all summer. What about you, Kiriko-san, when did you first see one for the first time?"

Kiriko smiled at Jason's use of "*san*," the honorific meaning Ms. or Miss or Mrs. or even Mister. It made him sound formal but familiar at the same time. She liked that he showed equal respect for her and her culture.

"For me it was also the summer. I was a little girl and there was a summer festival, I can remember. We wore *yukata*, which are cotton kimono, and ate lots of delicious foods. The night before we were catching — I don't know the English word — *hotaru*, the kind of insect that glows in the dark—"

"Fireflies," said Jason. The concept of catching fireflies struck him as novel.

"Fireflies," continued Kiriko, "and, then, the next night, I saw a 'flowing star' and remember how I thought the stars and the fireflies were almost the same."

"Remember how I told you that I took two years of Japanese?" Jason asked.

"Yes."

"Well, in one of my classes, my professor told us about the Star Festival in Japan. I know it's on July 7th but that's about all I can remember."

"Oh yes, it's celebrated on July 7th — I love the story of the Star Festival because my birthday is July 8th. When I was a child it seemed like this festival was especially for me. There is a big one in Oita, not far from where I grew up. Sometimes I'd go with my uncle and aunt and cousins. People write their wishes for the future on small pieces of paper and tie them to little trees. There are parades and fireworks and very colorful decorations."

"What's the story?" Jason asked.

"The festival is about two stars, Hikoboshi and Orihime, who became lovers. Orihime was a princess and a weaver and she fell in love with Hikoboshi, a herdsman who was very brave and handsome. They were so much in love that all they could think of was each other and they began neglecting their work, which made her father very angry. As a result, he separated Hikoboshi and Orihime across a river of stars and, after that, they were only allowed to meet once a year, on July 7th. The story also says that if it is rainy on this day, the two lovers are unable to meet and it is very sad. But if the sky is clear, like tonight, they can meet and it's very happy and romantic."

Again, in unrehearsed unison, the two of them looked up at the sky.

"I wrote a song about the stars once," said Jason. "It's called 'Stars Tonight.'"

"That sounds like a perfect title, especially for tonight. Would you sing it?"

"Oh, no, I couldn't, not without my guitar or piano."

"Please, I'd love to hear it. Especially after we've just seen the *nagare boshi* together and talked about *Tanabata*," said Kiriko. "It seems the evening won't be perfect to me unless you sing it. Please."

He knew from experience that sound echoed well off the rock and stone and wood of the bath. In his soft tenor voice and without instrumentation except for the mood evoked by the hot springs and what they'd seen above them, Jason began to sing, his words and voice carrying into the night.

Look up at the sky, look up in the night
Look at just what could have been and look
    at just what might

See the stars and wonder just how do they
glow
See into the heavens from far down here
below

Watch the change of seasons, feel it in the air
Watch the planets passing in the night sky as
you stare

Look up at the moon and think just how
    small we are
The galaxies beyond us have a billion burning
    stars

Stars tonight, sky tonight, they shine and they
    glow
Stars tonight, sky tonight, so much we don't
    know
Stars tonight, sky tonight, we feel so alone
We feel so alone in the night

Look there goes a shooting star, it's time to
    make a wish

As it fades into the darkness, as fleeting as
   a kiss
I'll fall asleep in two hours' time, it's there
   my dreams
      come true
A different kind of blackness but I hope the
   stars shine through

Stars tonight, sky tonight, they shine and they
   glow
Stars tonight, sky tonight, so much we don't
   know
Stars tonight, sky tonight, we feel so alone
We feel so alone in the night

Kiriko listened carefully. She tried to capture the
words as she had the fireflies that summer night as a
child. Stars and fireflies. Fireflies and stars. Suddenly
she recalled that in ancient Japan, *nagare boshi* were
not the upbeat purveyors of hopes and wishes they
were now. Instead they had a more ominous cast —
harbingers of doom and natural disaster and scourge.
She'd even heard it told that to see a falling star was
to see the last flash of a soul as it left life forever in
death. She chose not to tell this to Jason, however.
On a night like this she preferred not to talk of dying
or doom. All she wanted to feel was the melody and
power of his voice coming to her across the water.
That was enough.

• • •

The next morning, Al found Jason the second he was down the stairs. "So?" she asked, almost bouncing in anticipation. "What did you find out?"

Her question took Jason aback but, of course, she was referring to Dada. "He didn't show," he stammered. "I went to find him, just before midnight, but he was dead to the world. I didn't have the heart to wake him."

Al made a wry face. "He'd probably had a snoutful. Wouldn't be surprised if he was uttering some nonsense in his sleep about 'poor brains for drinking.'"

"Al...don't you think you might be a little...harsh here? I'm not really convinced things are as bad as you think."

"That's easy for you to say, isn't it?" Al rarely used this clipped voice. "You haven't been back long, you know...Have you any idea what he's been like this past little while? And what about missing your bath? Doesn't that strike you as odd?"

"Odd's one thing, but c'mon, Al..." She looked unappeased. "You know," Jason continued, "I'm just wondering if it's not something else. Like there's something we don't know about, something under the surface. I don't know what he's been like the past while. And you're right, it *is* unusual about missing the bath and being late." Al relaxed, concession silently accepted. "But, I'm wondering if his odd behavior lately and his drinking, I'm wondering if they aren't symptoms of something else. Something we can't put our fingers on. How long's this been going on, anyway? When did you notice a change in him?"

"Don't you remember? His first heart episode was after your last birthday. And not long after that, if I recall, is when he starting drinking more and acting, in my opinion, peculiar." Al removed her glasses and rubbed her eyes.

"My birthday?" Jason tried to remember something unusual. "Where is he, Al? Now, I mean."

"Fishing. He left early."

"Fishing? He didn't even tell me he was going—"

"There you go. See, I *told* you he's been acting peculiar. He had his big tackle box — the black one — with him," Al added, implying that fishing gear wasn't the only thing inside. "We've got to get to the bottom of this, Jason, or you've got to. And soon."

"I know," replied Jason, puzzled. "And, by the way, I didn't have the chance to tell you. Dee Dee's coming."

• • •

Dada's aluminum skiff returned to the dock mid-morning. He was with Harvey, one of his oldest buddies. The expedition had to have been planned, so why hadn't Dada asked him along? Fishing had been a father and son fixture for as long as Jason could remember. Next to the nightly bath, it was their most sacred ritual. They sat. They talked. They had an early morning together. For the moment, however, Jason was limited to making small talk and tying the boat to the toe rail.

Carrying rods and the tackle (but no fish) to the

shed, Jason kept the tone light: "You going to music club tonight, Dada?"

"Of course. I thought we'd decided."

"Just checking."

Harvey, tall and slightly stooped, a beat-up BC ferries cap reining in his wild thatch of long white hair, glanced over.

Dada stopped.

"Son, I'm sorry. I fell asleep and just didn't make it. I'm getting a bit old and, believe you me, I'm sorrier about that unfortunate fact than you are. Like Lear said, I'm 'A poor, infirm, weak, and despis'd old man.'"

"Dada..." Jason felt a cold guilt come over him like an influx of icy ocean water swamping the beachside hot springs. Minutes ago he'd been full of self-righteousness. Now he only felt chastened and insensitive.

• • •

For the rest of the morning Jason buried himself in hotel work. He served meals, continued renovating the website and even started some much-needed painting on the back veranda.

Keeping tabs on the time, he jumped in the shower to ready for Dee Dee's two o'clock arrival. He kept listening for her car, but hurry as he might, Al beat him to it. By the time Jason emerged through the front door, Dee Dee was already embracing Al. Jason let their moment unfold.

She was wearing the white, wool garment that Jason referred to as her 'ice cream coat.' She always wore light colors and today was no exception. Under her jacket she wore a thick cream turtleneck and off-white jeans. Her blonde hair tumbled to her shoulders but was kept from her face by a pair of sunglasses pushed up high on her aristocrat's forehead.

Dee Dee was handing a beautifully wrapped present to Al when Dada materialized behind Jason.

"What're you waiting for?"

"I wish I knew," Jason answered under his breath.

He was the last to embrace her. In close, he wondered what exactly they were holding on to as he felt her arms clasp him with a strength born of — what? Hope? Desperation? A nervousness about what the afternoon would bring? If so, they shared the same uncertainty.

After the requisite hot beverage in the kitchen and reports on Dee Dee's family, Al and Dada each took their leave with a subtle glance backwards.

"What if we head to the beach?" Jason suggested. "We can sit on the point and talk. There's usually no one there at this time of day."

"I was thinking the same thing."

On the way, they kept their thoughts private. He remembered Dee Dee sitting in her kitchen as she told him about Newfoundland and what it — and her large family — meant to her. He imagined her outside one of her vegetarian restaurants stooping to talk to a homeless person sitting against a brick wall. Or battling with Walter in the office about some ethical issue. And, most recently, in his apartment arguing that commitment was the source of, and the solution to, their problems. Just who was this girl, this woman, he found himself asking. ...Despite the months they'd spent together, the intimacies shared, he couldn't escape the fact that he didn't know her, not in the deepest places or in the sense that mattered. He thought about her idealism, her sense of self, her intelligence, her kindness. Perhaps Dee Dee had it right after all, maybe commitment was the only road out of the twin cities of doubt and uncertainty.

"I love this place," Dee Dee said, standing on the rocky point with her back to Jason who, instead of watching the landscape, watched her. "The rocks remind me of home." Dee Dee had been born in Heart's Content, Newfoundland. She spoke of it often. But despite her best intentions, whenever she spoke of her hometown and of her mother and sisters as her best friends, Jason felt somehow left out, like he was missing an important connection. Whether it was his sibling-less status, or because his mother had died young and left an unfillable void, he didn't know. But whenever Dee Dee mentioned Heart's Content, he felt an emptiness and envy that he couldn't express. Perhaps someone who had these things couldn't comprehend life without them, and vice-versa.

"I love it, too," Jason said.

Dee Dee turned. "But do you love *me*, Jason, that's the million-dollar question." He said nothing. "Because, you know, if you want the honest truth,

I've never really truly been sure," she pulled her hair behind her ear. "Oh, I know you've told me you loved me and I think you thought so at the time, I really think you did. And I probably did too, I wanted to believe it. But, later, when I thought about it, I wondered. And the reason I wasn't sure, I think, is that deep down, I'm not sure you were ever really sure yourself. Which is why I probably kept — keep — harping on about commitment. I think I wanted proof, needed proof. Oh, I'm not just talking about our differences about wanting kids, although I suppose that's part of it. I thought with you being an only child and the way you got along with your parents so well...I could never figure out why you were so hesitant."

"Dee Dee," Jason looked at the expanse of the ocean "It's one thing to commit and another thing entirely to commit when you're not one hundred percent certain. You can't fake certainty. It has to come from some deep inner conviction — it's like faith. You can't talk someone into it."

"So what you're saying is...that you're probably capable of commitment — but just not with me."

"Uncertainty isn't just a function of who your partner is — timing plays a role, too, wouldn't you agree?"

She turned to face the ocean and hills with the higher mountains in the distance. "But it could be. Who your partner is..."

"What do you mean?"

"Jason, when you said you were coming back to

Hot Springs Island, alone, do you know how I felt? Can you imagine what that did to me? Oh, I'm not stupid, I know things hadn't been going that well, but I put a lot of that down to me being out of work, and you having to slave away in the techno sweatshop. But what I couldn't take was that you unilaterally decided, you denied me my stake in this relationship. I felt like you'd tried to steal my voice. But at the same time, you never really came out and said it, that we were over. It was like you were hedging your bets, trying to give yourself time to make up your mind."

He tried to order his thoughts and at least put a façade of reason on what was actually anything but.

"If I'm being honest to you, and to me, which I'm struggling to do...well, then, I can't say you're wrong. Yes, I needed time to think. Yes, I did have doubts about us, our future, and commitment, all of those things. All I can say is, if you think I left because I was emotional fence-sitting, well, I'm probably guilty as charged."

Dee Dee began pacing the outcrop. She bowed her head for a moment and then came and sat next to him.

"The thing is, Jason, we were a couple. We were together. And the central element of being a couple, it seems to me, is that it takes two. Both of them have to agree that, yes, we're a pair, a team, and we're going to back each other up, no matter what happens. But when a couple breaks up, it only takes one. Suddenly it's no longer a couple but two individuals and one of those individuals can destroy the pair even if the other doesn't want that to happen. And that's no good, is it? In fact, it's even kind of pathetic in a way, don't you think? What I mean is, how could you like, or even still love, a person and want to stay with them if they don't want you in return? It's a bit like a kicked dog that keeps coming back for more. Don't you think what I'm saying is true, that it takes two to be together and only one to end it?"

"I suppose I do."

There was another long pause and then Dee Dee's blue eyes looked into Jason's brown ones. "Well, in that case, I'm the one, then. I'm ending it, Jason. I'm ending us. If you're not certain, then I am."

• • •

For the rest of the day, Dada and Al did their best to lighten the mood, but Jason's mind couldn't clear Dee Dee's visit. Dada was keen to get Jason off to music night, to distract him in a more positive way. Yet the funny thing was, as empty as Jason felt about the finality of he and Dee Dee, he also saw much truth in what she'd said. It was almost freeing.

As Jason walked Kiriko to her car the other night, Kiriko had told him about the death of her mother from cancer, how she'd been devastated while at the same time recognizing that any prolonging was actually a diminishment. "There is a time to end, and the silence of ending is more valuable when the moment has come. It is like after a song has finished, but you can still hear the music inside your mind. It is like the empty space in a painting. Because of what is next, what is left behind becomes more beautiful."

• • •

Dada removed his Gibson mandolin and Washburn banjo from their stands and placed them in hard-shell velour-lined cases. Seeing the square mandolin case, Jason smiled, reminded of an incident when he'd been about eight years old. He and Duncan from up the road had been playing outside in the woods after a big rain. They'd been trying to scramble up a slippery, grassy slope off the road not far from the hotel when a brilliant idea struck him: sliding! Why not sliding? The place was perfect. The conditions were ideal. There was only one problem: no slide. After one unsatisfactory makeshift slide after another, Jason had another brainstorm. He snuck back into the hotel and, there it was, the perfect vehicle: Dada's fiddle case. Luckily the fiddle wasn't inside, but the square case served the two boys well as they slid and tumbled in the slick, muddy grass for a good part of the afternoon. When Dada found out, he was livid. He preached that musical instruments, like animals, were invaluable and should never be abused. Jason's cheeky retort that cases weren't instruments didn't help *his* case at all.

Jason was glad that Dada was revving up for music night. Except for the rare evenings when group dynamics intervened, these musical interludes pumped up the soul. Everyone needs unwinding and what better way than music? Jason invited Al but she had declined with a grateful smile.

Dada caught up with Jason just before eight.

"Jason, I forgot to tell you. Harvey's picking me up. We're going to look at some property he's thinking of buying, then he'll drop me off at Bobbi Lee's. I'll meet you there. Do you mind going alone?"

"No, I just—"

"Sorry, Jason. My memory must be going. I meant to tell you this morning but it slipped my addled old mind. We'll ride home together, right?" Then a horn honked. Jason helped his father carry his instruments.

As the car pulled away, Jason realized he didn't even know where Bobbi Lee Hunter lived. Ellery had seen and heard the exchange and was quietly observing Jason's somewhat defensive reaction. Jason found Bobbi Lee in the phonebook. She sounded very nice — all bubbly good spirits. After his exchange with Dada, he thought of staying home; but the combination of Bobbi Lee's engaging voice and his need for something uplifting decided him. Music would soothe his brooding over Dee Dee, and Jason knew no better way of breaking the tight invisible bands constricting his chest than notes and voices floating up into the evening. With that in mind, he packed his old Yamaha acoustic with the rosewood fret board and new tuning pegs and prepared to go. As he closed the door behind him, Jason heard Al call out, "Have a great time!"

• • •

Jason's headlights stabbed into the dark night. He approached the end of the hotel's long private drive and lit up the carved wooden sign proclaiming Hot Springs Island Hotel. Trees formed a cover across the middle section of the perpetually dark driveway; coming home at night as a kid, Jason had always run or cycled as fast as he could through the natural tunnel.

Jason sped up one hill and down the next. So much was happening. His encounters with Kiriko, the breakup with Dee Dee, his ongoing questions about Dada...

He found Bobbi's house easily; the bright lights and numerous parked cars confirmed Music Club was on. A quick search for Harvey's old Rabbit drew a blank. Either Dada hadn't arrived or Harvey had dropped him and left. In line with Music Club custom, Jason rang the bell once and went in.

"How do you do?" Coming into the entrance hall was a smiling face with rosy cheeks and round glasses framed by the white curls of a recently coiffed poodle.

"I'm Jason Chiron. I think we just talked on the phone. You must be Bobbi Lee."

"That's me, honey!" Raised in Savannah, Bobbie Lee had a voice that still carried the warm breeze of the South and a hint of magnolias. Jason put her age at somewhere near Dada's.

"Thanks very much for having us," Jason said.

"Well, the night's still young and *I'm* willing!" She

gave a hearty laugh. "Come on in!" She looked Jason up and down. "My! You're a cute one, aren't you?"

"Do you know if my father's here yet?"

"You didn't come together?"

"No, he had something to do. He said he'd meet me here."

"Sorry, honey. I haven't seen him. But why don't you just come on in and say hi to everyone and let's play us some music." Her enthusiasm and laugh were infectious.

"Hiya, Jason," Tony the harp player called. "Jason!" Greetings pinged like sonar echoes around the room. Good cheer was ubiquitous, the mood festive. Pats on backs, vigorous handshaking and hugs — most of all hugs — were everywhere.

Jason found you could learn much about a person by how they hugged, not to mention the relationship between huggers. How desperately they cling. How reserved and how shy. Like driving, hugging reveals the inner person.

Hearing music in the background, Jason remembered "Under the Surface" and wondered if he should play it tonight. The lines came back to him ("The places that we've never been") and the melody lodged itself there for the next little while.

The air of expectation in the house meant Cassidy wasn't there yet. Although people usually started showing up around eight, nothing really began until Cassidy made his grand entrance. His rusty pickup arrival, filled with percussion instruments, electric piano, camera, fiddles and guitars was like a party in itself.

Probably twenty-five to thirty people lounged in Bobbi's living room and luxurious kitchen.

"Jason." Cristine, painter and friend, took Jason by the arm. He put down his guitar case and they hugged, a good long one. Cristine was an intriguing soul. She had an inquisitive mind, she knew lots about lots, but there were gaps in her learning that she was wary of showing; this gave her both an edge and an attractive vulnerability.

Cristine and Jason had met at the Music Club four years earlier, when he'd been visiting from Vancouver. Both of them loved the Indigo Girls and they'd done a duet of "Closer to Fine." In doing so, they'd achieved that state that Jason had found only when making love or playing music, that moment when words become irrelevant and telepathy takes over. You knew, actually *knew*, what the other person was feeling and what they'd do next. It was fleeting. But it was that very fleetingness that kept you coming back. Once you'd achieved a state of grace you needed it again. Perhaps this profound neediness was the definition of addiction — or just pleasure — Jason didn't know. He did know, however, that he and Cristine had found it musically a number of times; it forged something between them that both understood but had never verbally acknowledged.

Hug ended, they exchanged smiles — Cristine's distinguished by a crooked tooth. She cut her sandy hair herself and it was different every week. Today it was pulled back and up.

Cristine had headline news. Her unmarried, unattached, unemployed, eighteen-year-old daughter was five months pregnant. She'd bolted from home and come back a month ago, "knocked-up," to use Cristine's delicate phrase. Angel refused to divulge the father's identity and was equally insistent on keeping the baby. Cristine wasn't prepared to play grandma or, worse, mother. "A grandmother at thirty-seven? Lovely. Great. Just what I need." She'd become Angel's mother herself at nineteen and knew the hardships firsthand. Jason listened intently, not only out of friendship to Cristine.

"The difference between us is that at least I had a husband," Cristine laughed self-deprecatingly. Cristine and Abner had been married a year when Angel was born but split up four years later. "All she has is me, and that's not all that much, believe me. What does she think I am, a magician who's going to pull a rabbit out of my hat and make everything okay?" At least her paintings were selling. But she never knew when the money would be coming in.

Cristine was staging an exhibition of new work at the Hot Springs Hotel next week. She and Dada were pals and Dada had offered the hotel as an exhibit space — something he'd done for other local artists in the past. That guests enjoyed the shows didn't hurt either; they often bought the works on display. Dada liked to say that hotels should give visitors something to talk about when they went home — as long as it wasn't dirty bathrooms. Also, Dada has once been a painter himself, a surrealist, which is how he'd earned his nickname.

Lacking better plans, Angel and the baby would live with her and Layla in Cristine's small house on the road up to Mt. Trincomali. "It's going to be tough," Cristine said. "And I'm not even talking about money."

Layla was Cristine's other daughter, half-sister to Angel. She was ten years old and acting, according to Cristine, "probably the most mature of us all."

Jason was about to ask what she meant when someone interrupted to say hello to Cristine. Jason checked his watch. It was almost nine and no sign of Dada. I'll wait until 9:30, he decided.

By 9:40 Dada still hadn't arrived. Normally, Jason wouldn't have given his absence a second thought. But lately...First Jason called around. Harvey told him that, yes, they'd looked at the property but had left Dada outside Salty's Pub afterwards.

Jason stashed his guitar and headed for town. On the way, he scrutinized pedestrians. With his instruments slung across his shoulders, Dada shouldn't be hard to spot; he was nowhere to be found. A tour of the tables at Salty's turned up nothing. Dada wasn't in the washroom or out back, either.

"Moses, you seen my dad?" Jason shouted, when he finally caught the proprietor's eye.

"Sure. He was in here till, I dunno, maybe a half-hour ago. Forty minutes."

"Did he say where he was going?"

"Nope."

"Did he have his instruments with him?"

"I'm not sure Jason...it's kind of busy in here, you know," he gestured at the large crowd with his big head and small eyes. Moses bustled off, crusty to the core; everyone said that Salty's had been named for his personality.

Jason searched the coffee shop across the street and then two nearby restaurants. Returning to his car, he zoomed down the ramp to the parking area fronting the government dock. Leaving the car unlocked, he loped down the path along the harbor, which, on sunny days, made a lovely walk. He started to sweat. There were some kids smoking dope on the hill and he asked them if they'd seen an old man walking by. They hadn't, they replied politely, and went back to their joint.

He could try searching Troy's two other bars but what was the point? Dada could be at one of the hotels, at a friend's, anywhere. ...I'll check out the the Smuggler and the Troy Pub and that's it, Jason decided.

As expected, the final two locations provided no clues. Jason returned to Bobbi Lee's. The glowing car clock told him he'd been gone almost two hours. If Dada was home, at least they could grab a bath together and talk. Jason knocked on Bobbi Lee's front door and walked in. Jason said hi to a few people and went for his guitar. As he was bending down, flicking the clips on his guitar case, Bobbi Lee approached him from behind and placed a hand on his shoulder.

"Jason."

"Hi Bobbi Lee."

"Your dad's here."

Jason's first reaction was relief. "Thanks, Bobbi

Lee." Then he felt like a jerk. Typical, Jason thought. Here I am, worrying for no reason when Dada had done exactly as promised. I missed him somewhere along the way, simple as that. "Where is he? When did he get here?"

"Oh, not that long ago...and, well, I don't really know how to say this, Jason, but he's really, well, quite sozzled. He's in the living room and he won't be hard to find, believe me." She gave a nervous little laugh, and her white poodley hair bobbed up and down.

"How sozzled?"

Bobbi Lee put her hand on Jason's forearm.

"Somewhere between very and extremely. Or, as we say from where I'm from, 'pissed as a possum.' I think it might be best if you got him home soon, honey. In fact, I'd appreciate it if you did."

Jason entered the living room to find Dada dancing with Cassidy; to describe their dance as wild would be blatant understatement. Accompanied by fiddle, guitars, electric bass, and hand drums, their Celtic jig was more like a tantrum. Dada's eyes were shut and he made Jason think of a combination rag doll and a child's top as he was literally spun around by the much bigger, taller Cassidy. The jig ended to wild cheers and applause.

Reaching for his semi-collapsed father, Jason saw Dada begin to heave. Everyone heard dangerous noises emitting from Dada's throat and immediately eyed Bobbi's brand-new, Virgin Wool, ivory wall-to-wall carpet. Like a slow motion intro on a sports network,

Jason leapt for a wastepaper basket, a bowl — anything — to prevent the ignominy of his father barfing on Bobbi's expensive rug. Luckily, however, disaster was averted. Dada gained control. The tense silence was broken and Jason and Cassidy scooped Dada up and whisked him outside before even a thimbleful of spittle passed his lips. He caught the looks on everyone's faces. Concern, worry, relief.

Dada slept most of the way home.

• • •

Ellery maintained a tactful silence as they helped Dada from the car. Thankfully, no guests appeared. Silently exasperated — as he was most of the whole way home — Jason undressed his father. But seeing Dada minus checked shirt and other clothes changed everything. The sparse white chest hair, visible ribs, and sticklike arms contrasted sadly with the robust muscles of Jason's memory. Dada's toupee was also askew. He hated seeing him like this. He put the old man to bed and started back towards the stairs and his room. "Thank you, Jason," Dada managed to call as Jason left the suite.

Returning to the lobby area, Jason surprised Ellery playing Tetris on the front desk's computer. Ellery minimized the window and grew busy, shifting forms and grabbing at a pen. In truth, Jason didn't care. Especially not tonight.

Years ago he'd had his own short-lived Tetris obsession. Boxes dropped from heaven by a geometry-armed God trying to smite you according to some random celestial color scheme. Your reward for higher achievement, more blocks — sort of how things ran at Human Designs. If you wanted, you could choose the preview option. Or, if you preferred, you could play blind and earn more points. In a way you were patted on the back for taking destiny as it comes. But the last few days the blocks of his life were falling way too fast and he didn't know where to put them. He was leaving spaces where he shouldn't and piling things in the wrong places.

Jason was exhausted. He was of two minds about visiting the hot springs. The tobacco smoke on his clothes decided him. The bath would relax him. Soaking alone would only remind him of Dada's absence but then, maybe he *wouldn't* be alone. Perhaps Kiriko would put in another appearance. He hoped she would.

By the time he reached the bath, he was chilled. On colder nights, the steam rising from the bath became more pronounced, adding another layer of atmosphere to a place already steeped in it. Jason followed Kiriko's lead and kept a towel nearby. Five minutes later he heard some footsteps on the path. He wrapped himself in his towel and waited for her to enter.

The door swung open. It wasn't Kiriko at all.

"Dada! What are you doing here? You should be in bed."

"I'm fine," Dada said, his speech almost normal. "We have to talk." Surprisingly adept for someone in his state, Dada — waving off Jason's assistance — stripped, showered, and entered the bath.

"You shouldn't stay in too long, remember," cautioned Jason.

"I know. But we have to talk."

"My feelings exactly."

"You want to talk about my so-called drinking problem — you and Al, I know what she thinks. What you two are saying behind my back. But that's not it. That's not what I want to talk about."

Jason waited for Dada to speak of his own accord. He wouldn't have gotten out of bed to come here in his present state unless he had something important to say.

"You know that *Lear*'s my favorite tragedy?" Dada asked. "And that I think Shakespeare was a very wise man, indeed, perhaps the most insightful that the world...and that we can't learn enough from him and that we should put great store in what he says."

Jason smiled. "How could I not?"

Dada wasn't listening. "'I have full cause of weeping, but this heart / Shall break into a hundred thousand flaws / Or e'er I'll weep. O fool! I shall go mad.'"

Dada paused. Jason realized what a good Lear his father would make.

Dada spoke again: "Jason. The first thing you have to know is that I love you. I've always loved you — as did your mother. I want to make sure you know that."

"Of course I do," Jason said, pulling himself upright.

"Well...this is the hardest thing I've ever had to do in my entire life. That's why I'm telling you now, when I've had a little too much to drink." Jason could hear his father gulp, gasp, fight for words. "Well...the truth is...the fact is...that, well, for twenty-nine years we've been hiding something. We— I— have kept the truth from you, Jason." The longest pause yet. "I must tell you something that I never wanted to have to tell you, something that I hoped I'd never have to say...and that is...Mum and I aren't your biological parents — we weren't your birth parents. You're...adopted."

Jason no longer felt the heat of the water. Before Dada could say anything more, he plunged his head under. He could feel his lungs bursting and his eyes stinging. He relished the sweet pain. When he finally broke the surface gasping he wiped from his eyes and mouth the hot water that smelled of sulfur and rotten eggs.

Dada turned to face him, his expression humble and pained.

"I'm sorry, Jason. I know we should have told you when you were younger. I know that. Now, of course, I wish I had. Mum and I planned to tell you...before she died, when we thought you were old enough. But, then with her death it was...well, just too much for me to do alone. It was just too much." Dada's head was down. He stared without seeing.

"And then with each month, with each passing year, it kept getting harder. The longer I put it off, the easier it was to say nothing and maintain the status quo. I kept waiting for the right time, the right moment, but it never came. And then, foolishly, I thought maybe I'd never have to tell you. That perhaps I'd die and the secret would die with me."

Jason remained silent not only from the profound shock but also because he had a hundred — no, a thousand — questions and every question collided with was another in an endless bunched-up traffic snarl.

"Your mother and I couldn't have children. As you know, she miscarried twice. They were both hard, of course, but the second time almost killed her. I...I mean physically as well as emotionally. The doctor said that if we wanted kids the only thing to do was adopt and—"

"Where from? Where was I adopted from?" His voice shook. It didn't seem his.

"I'll explain everything. Please be patient."

"Patient?" Jason asked. "After thirty years and you're asking me to be patient?"

"Can't you understand?" He pulled a wet hand across his scarred skull. "We didn't know what to do. We wanted a child badly and Mum was so devastated after the miscarriages. Then, around that time, we had a visitor. A young woman. In her mid-twenties. From England."

"My mother."

"No!" said Dada with a surprising force. "Mum is — and was, and always will be — your mother. Don't ever forget that." Dada stopped for a moment. "Please don't ever forget that. The person I'm going to tell you about is the person who carried you. She conceived you and gave birth to you, yes, but that's all — nothing more. She was single and left England because she didn't want anyone, her family in particular, to know she was going to have the baby. Providence brought her here; she stayed at the hotel as a guest. She was such a nice young woman...wonderful, in fact...and as we grew close, she confided in us. She was going to have a baby she couldn't care for, and we wanted a child more than anything in the world.

Jason's mind raced. Who was she? Why couldn't she keep me? Or was it just that she didn't want to? Was it something to do with my father? Who was he?

How could Dad have kept this buried so long?

"We agreed that you'd be ours — totally ours — and that she'd fade from the picture and our lives forever. She was thrilled to find a loving, caring home for you — it was more than she deserved, she said, more than she could have asked for. So we embarked on our great deception. We told everyone that Mum was pregnant. We even went so far as to pad Mum's stomach. And, as the time approached, both of them went east to Ontario. We said it was to be with family. No one else knows, Jason, not even Al. But the most important thing is that *you* know. At last." Dada paused for a moment. "'And oftentimes, to win us to our harm, / The instruments of darkness tell us truths, / Win us with honest trifles, to betray's / In deepest consequence.'"

• • •

Jason's biological father was married but Dada knew nothing more about him. No, as far as Dada knew, Jason had no siblings, although there was the possibility of half-brothers and sisters.

"And, have you heard from her? What's her name? Is she still alive? Where does she live?"

Dada looked pained. "Jason, both of us have to acknowledge that this is a lot to take in. Once you know something, you can never unknow it."

"But I have to know something. ...Her first name, what was her first name?"

Dada paused. "Elizabeth."

"Elizabeth?"

"Like the queen."

"Elizabeth," he said, sounding the name of his natural mother for the first time. Dada said nothing. "Has she ever tried to contact you or me, to find out about me?"

"You're sure about this?"

"I'm positive."

"The answer's yes. She calls periodically. But rarely."

"When was the last time?"

"Actually, not that long ago."

"So that's it," Jason said.

"What's it?"

"Your heart episodes. They started just this year."

"Don't be silly, Jason," said Dada.

"What did you talk about?"

"What we're talking about now."

"Dada."

"She asked if you knew about her. She thought it was well past the time to tell you. And she said, well, implied, really, that if I didn't say something, she would."

"So what did you tell her?"

"I told her I would. It's partially the reason I'm telling you now."

"Does that mean she wanted to see me or meet me?"

"She agreed to stay out of our lives, Jason. Right from the beginning, she said so. It was her idea. To respect that we were your parents, us alone. She even asked for permission to call. That was our arrangement."

"So I still don't see why you didn't tell me? You promised her."

"Well, I've told you now, haven't I? 'I pray you now forgive and forget.' You have to understand, son, that I *was* going to tell you. It's just that—"

"So this last call," Jason said, interrupting. "It was around my birthday?"

"Actually, it was *on* your birthday." Al's timing had been spot on. "Jason, I know this is a shock, but it's important — terribly important to me, as I know it was to your mother — that you understand why we didn't tell you. It was to protect you and keep you from the pain and to make you feel totally ours. You understand that, don't you?"

"All I can say is I'll try, Dada. But this is a lot to take in."

"Of course it is. And I can't tell you how sorry I am. I only wish that Mum was here to tell her side of things. That way I'm sure you'd understand better. She was always better at explaining things, especially important ones like this. You know how much she loved you, Jason, don't you?"

"Of course I do."

"Please keep that foremost in your mind. If you remember that, it should help guide you through the difficult times, I hope. Mum and I are your true parents. Nothing can ever change that. Nothing."

Jason kept his eyes on the water. "Dada, let's go. You shouldn't stay in too long."

• • •

Jason's predominant sense was one of solitariness. It was one thing for Dada to proclaim that he and Mum were his parents in all senses except the biological, but it wasn't that simple. There were incontrovertible truths. He might have siblings. He might have relatives. An entire family from another continent.

Identity is linked to the immediacy of the here and now, Dada said. Our nearby families. Our homes. But what about our collective pasts? Pasts that once taken from you or called into doubt, caused everything else to come tumbling down like one of those fragile human pyramids you build out of bodies in gym glass.

Of course he couldn't sleep. He lay on his back staring up into the night's void. Darkness. The sheets cloyed. Part of the burden was bearing this alone. Dada wanted Jason to keep this between them.

Why did Dada seek to keep the situation under wrap? It wasn't like he had anyone to protect, particularly Mum, not now. It was shame. Shame at their inability to conceive on their own, that the most basic human function was beyond them. The word "bastard" also floated in. Things had been different then, closed. Talking about it would also expose his parents' decades-old cover-up. Yet, Jason knew he *wanted* to protect Dada and Mum.

Unable to even flirt with sleep, he rose before five and crept through the still hotel. Golly woke when she sensed his presence, and joined him outside in the pre-dawn. The faintest of glows hinted in the east. A twig cracked and the dog turned her head. Straining his eyes, Jason saw a solitary fawn, probably a yearling. It stood perfectly still, only its ears twitching, and then it moved out of sight. Jason and Golly continued towards the beach. Perhaps the ocean would calm him.

Sitting on the retaining wall between lawn and beach, Jason tossed pebbles half-heartedly into the ocean. The morning was calm and the sea flat. In the burgeoning light, he could see the ripples expand exponentially, the last hurrah of the disappearing pebbles as they wobbled down to their resting place.

He descended to the beach. On sunny mornings, the white crushed shells gleamed almost too bright to look at. He picked up a broken branch and used it to write Mum's name, Mary, in the sand. Before long, the water lapped onto the beach, obscuring his writing and erasing the name. It isn't ashes to ashes, dust to dust, Jason thought. It's water to water. He remembered playing a game on the beach with Mum. Waves would arrive from a passing boat and he'd dash away at the last instant. "Don't let them get you, Mum, don't let them get you!" Jason would shriek. Toweling him off later, Mum had hugged him and said, "See how good this feels. It's more valuable than money, Jason. It's more valuable than anything. Always remember that, okay?"

Looking down at the sand and the last traces of his mother's name, Jason vowed to visit her grave. It had been too long.

"Good morning, son." The "son" was intentional. "I couldn't sleep either."

Jason looked into Dada's eyes. "I've got questions for you. I've been thinking about them all night."

"Well, I can't say that surprises me. Or pleases me, to tell you the truth. But anyway, fire away."

"First, I noticed a change in you — Al did too — around the time of my birthday. The drinking and your health problems...they're connected to Elizabeth's call, aren't they?"

Dada put his hand to his toupee and considered. "Not consciously, no. But, I suppose it could have been." He tried for a smile. "What else?"

"Do you know how to get hold of her? How to reach her?"

"All I can say is...are you sure, absolutely sure

that you want to know this?" Jason nodded. "I don't really know very much. All I know is which city she's living in in England," said Dada. "Or was, at least."

"Which is…?"

"Please don't ask me, Jason."

"Why not?"

"If not for me, then for your mother, at least. We talked about it and I know this is what she would want. Please, Jason, please." Jason had never heard this tone in Dada's voice. How could Dada make such an impossible request? And, Jason realized, how could he deny it?

Chapter 4 iNovel Link
The iNovel Link for Chapter 4 is another musical one.
Please go to **www.HotSpringsNovel.com/chapter4/**
to listen to Jason's song, "Stars Tonight."

Chapter 5

"Maybe all people are all alike in this,
at least in some ways."

Dada was already doing chores by the time Jason made it down to the kitchen after showering. Impressive, given the probable size of his hangover. With an inquiring look from Al, he grabbed two mugs of coffee and went searching for his dad.

Jason didn't have to look long. He found both Golly and Dada out back near the bathhouse: the dog on her green bath mat, his father brushing her. Seeing such domesticity, Jason felt more protective than upset.

"Dada? How are you feeling this morning? I brought you a coffee."

Dada took the coffee with red-eyed gratitude.

"Thank you, son. I'm sorry again about last night. You must still be in shock..." Dada gazed into the distance. "'My conscience hath a thousand several tongues / And every tongue brings in a several tale / And every tale condemns me for a villain.'"

"Speaking of apologies, you might want to phone Bobbi Lee later."

"I'd planned to. Was I that bad?"

"Did you know that I'd gone looking for you earlier in the evening? At Salty's, at the Troy — all over." Suddenly, it struck Jason that if he'd found Dada when sober, he might not have found out.

"Sounds like I have a lot to apologize for." Golly's tail thumped as if, as far as she was concerned, all was forgiven.

Dada took Jason's silence as acceptance. "Come and give your old dad a hug so we can put this behind us, at least for the time being. There'll be more to talk about but, for the moment, at least, why don't we go and get some breakfast." When they hugged, Jason was reminded yet again just how fragile he was, how fragile everything was.

"And, you know what, Jason?" Dada said. "I think I probably will cut back a bit on what's good for me. Maybe even give it up. How's that sound?"

"Fine, Dada, just fine."

Walking back to the hotel arm in arm with Dada, Jason saw Al move away from the window, a broad smile gracing her face.

• • •

Al wanted the lowdown on the father-and-son tête-à-tête immediately, of course, which forced Jason to be inventive. At least, however, he could report on Dada's volunteer abstinence program.

"He's agreed to cut back, Al," Jason said. "He more or less admitted that things started getting bad after my last birthday."

"I already had a call about his behavior at Music Night. Maybe public embarrassment isn't a bad thing, after all. I would have given anything to see him dancing like that," Al giggled. "Anyway, our mission is to make sure he sticks to it. We've got to help him any way we can."

For Al and Dada, at least, the Big Talk of the night before reaped immediate benefits. Dada seemed more lively and eager to spend time with both of them. Jason wished he felt the same way.

• • •

He was reading another peculiar e-mail from Kevin when his cell phone rang. Phillip Hung was on the line.

"Jason — Phillip here."

"Well — Hung!" Jason said, using his standard greeting.

"Very funny," said Phillip, using his standard reply.

"You aren't calling me about Kevin, are you?"

"No, why?"

"I keep getting these weird e-mails from him. About Dee Dee and me."

"What do you mean? What's in them?"

"They're just weird. Typical Kevin stuff, I suppose."

Phillip Hung was both solicitous and brilliant; he was as concerned as he was grounded, and as trustworthy as he was well groomed. Even his work, managing databases for a major bank seemed solid and stable. Hung and his girlfriend, Irene, had been dating for seven years and they were the source of envy among every couple they knew. His life was solid, well planned, stable and crisis-free — everything Jason's was not.

"What about your career?" Phillip had said as Jason packed for the island. "Isn't working at the hotel a major step backward? C'mon, you're not eighteen anymore and this isn't a summer job." He wasn't being judgmental, he was genuinely concerned.

"So what do you mean by 'weird stuff'?" Phillip asked again. "Tell me more about these e-mails — there's more than one?"

"He keeps bugging me about Dee Dee. About why I left. While we're on the topic, she came to visit…we're officially over."

Phillip paused, "How did it go?"

"Civil. Reasonable. Painful. Typical Dee Dee, I suppose."

Phillip kept talking. "But — that's not why I'm calling. I've got some work for you, web stuff — if you want it, that is."

"What is it?"

"It's kinda cool, actually. Our employees are organizing a charity run and we're setting up an independent website for it linked to the bank's main corporate site. The bank's agreed to sponsor the event and fund the website so I thought of you."

"Sure, sounds great."

"You might need to come to Vancouver for a couple of days. You can stay with me, if you want."

"Thanks. When?" Jason wondered if Phillip was just being kind by throwing work his way.

"ASAP, really. Sorry for the short notice. When could you make it?"

"Let me check, but how does the day after tomorrow sound?"

"Good. Just get back to me. And don't worry too much about Kevin and his e-mails. You know what he's like."

"I do, I do," said Jason. "And thanks, man."

• • •

This time the ferry ride across the Georgia Strait wasn't quite so pleasant. Rainy weather forced Jason inside after he'd spent only a minute or so at his usual spot at the bow.

He came through the reluctant metal door and immediately spotted Kiriko on an aisle seat. He felt a flush of real pleasure. She was alone. Next to her was a large artist's portfolio.

"*Konnichawa*," Jason said.

"Jason," Kiriko looked up from her book. Jason thought she looked pleased.

"It looks like you're going somewhere on business," Jason said.

"Yes, I'm showing my work to a gallery in downtown Vancouver."

"How are you getting downtown?"

"By bus. I just bought a ticket," said Kiriko.

"Let's return it. I'll drive you."

• • •

Rain always worsened the traffic into Vancouver and today was no exception. They were at a standstill on the long man-made causeway leading from the ferry terminal into the flat expanse of Tsawwassen.

"Tell me more about your painting," Jason said.

"What would you like to know?"

"How about why you paint?"

"That's a very a difficult question."

"I was trying to ask an easy one." Jason smiled.

Kiriko thought about her answer. That was one of the things about her. Everything she said was considered. "I suppose I paint for many reasons. Because I want to show beauty. Because, sometimes, there are so many things in my mind that...that I have to find a way to let them out and express them. I can't do so any other way. I suppose I also paint to...what's the word...to let my thoughts escape. And, by doing so, I can escape them, too."

"Now there's something I know about," Jason laughed. "So what are you escaping from?"

Kiriko had been looking at Jason. At his question, however, she turned towards the rain-streaked window.

"I think most people — perhaps all people — are escaping. Either that or they are searching for something or someone, even if they don't know what it is," she said. She looked up again.

"I think you're right. Secrets and searching. Two of life's S-words," Jason said. The car inched forward. The rain splattered rhythmically against the glass. The wipers squeaked in counterpoint. He squeezed the wheel. Then Jason took a deep breath. "Secrets and searching," he repeated. "That describes me perfectly."

"I'm sorry, I don't think I understand," said Kiriko.

"I remember you telling me about your mother passing away from cancer."

"Yes?"

"And you know how my mother died when I was twelve?"

"Yes?"

"Well, I just found out that she wasn't really my mother."

"What?"

"I found out from my father a few days ago. I'm adopted. It turns out my real mother was an Englishwoman who came to Canada, to Hot Springs Island, because she couldn't keep her baby in England. It's a long, complicated story and I don't know the half of it. I'm still in shock."

"Do you know your real mother and father? Do you know anything about them?"

"All I know is that they abandoned me and they've never bothered trying to contact me since, although apparently my mother — her name's Elizabeth — calls every now and then to find out how I'm doing but that's about it. My biological father was married and he's completely out of the picture. I feel like the carpet of my identity was yanked from under me, and the floor underneath is hard and bare. I feel like everyone in this story was putting themselves ahead of me, that all these selfish decisions were being made and people weren't think-ing about me at all when they did the things they did. All they thought about was what they wanted and what they needed. It seems to me that all of these people — Dada, Mum, Elizabeth, my other father — had a responsibility to me that they ignored for years and years and years. I can't tell you how hard that is to come to grips with, these feelings of abandonment, these feelings that everything you took for granted and counted on no longer applies. That the people whom I trusted and loved and respected pulled one over on me for my whole life. What kind of people give up their child? What kind of people lie to their child for thirty years?"

Throughout Jason's monologue, Kiriko remained silent. Her movements were restricted to an unconscious tightening of her hands and lips.

"I'm sorry, Kiriko. I just unloaded on you out of nowhere. Half of what I said I don't even know if I meant. I don't know...All I can say is thank you for listening. Thank you for listening to me."

The traffic jam unclogged. As they were about to pass under the Fraser River on their way into the sprawling city, their eyes met in the rearview mirror. In the darkness of the tunnel, Kiriko wept. And she finally spoke. "*Wakarimashita*," she said. "*Yoku wakarimashita.*" Jason knew these words. They meant that she knew. That she understood. That she understood deeply. Everything she did, Jason thought, she did deeply.

● ● ●

Jason let Kiriko off near her gallery and watched her

disappear into the late-morning crowd. Traces of her lingered inside the car.

He spoke to the receptionist behind a long maple desk fronted with the bank's logo, a red globe backed with a stylized letter. He didn't wait long. Phillip Hung soon strode out in a crisply pressed pinstriped suit. The collar of his white shirt looked like an expensive envelope more than a piece of clothing.

Phillip brought him to a leather and wood meeting room and introduced him to Tom, Cynthia and Taylor. Like Phillip, they were well dressed, intelligent and personable. After his week, Jason wondered which of them — appearances to the contrary — might be in the throes of some personal crisis. A marriage breakup perhaps, or an illness. He looked again at the four of them hunkered over some documentation. Probably exactly like me, thought Jason. Fine on the outside, filled with uncertainty within.

The charity run project was a good one, small but worthwhile. They spent the morning talking about parameters and cost options and time flew by. Soon they were ready for lunch — all except Phillip who'd been called back. Amazingly, work was hardly discussed. Maybe it was because Jason was an outsider, or perhaps he'd just lucked into a group of well-balanced people.

"Phillip was saying you've just moved back to bucolic Hot Springs Island," said Tom, the group's senior member. In his early fifties, Tom looked in great shape and his great bush of brown hair showed only a few flecks of gray.

"I was on Hot Springs Island a couple of years ago," Cynthia said later. The others were in the restroom. Cynthia had that runner's look, gaunt but loaded with energy. "I stayed at this funky little hotel."

"The Hot Springs Island Hotel, by any chance?" Jason asked, smiling, "the one with the bath in the ocean?"

"Exactly! You know it, then?"

"My family owns it. That's where I work now. In fact, that's where your website will be developed."

"I love that hotel! And are you running your web business from there, or do you work for the hotel?" Cynthia asked.

"A bit of both, actually. My father hasn't been well lately and I've gone back to help out. You must have met him when you were there. Checked sweater and, how shall I put it, an unusual hairstyle?" Jason smiled

"Of course I remember! That's your dad?" She laughed. "Wow. And does your mum work there too? I think I remember meeting her," Cynthia said.

"No, that was probably Alexandra — Al. My mother died when I was twelve." The instant he said this, he regretted it. He'd hit some nerve in Cynthia. "Are you okay, Cynthia? Did I say something wrong?"

"No, no. You just surprised me. Another coincidence. My mother died when I was twelve, too. That's amazing. ...You must miss her. I sure do."

"I know what you mean."

"I really missed mine growing up. I mean I miss her now too, of course, but there were times when I just needed her. I've got two brothers and, well, I grew up surrounded by men. All that male energy. Turned me into a tomboy. They're the ones who got me running." Then, more serious: "But you know what, there's not a day goes by when I don't think about her."

"I know what you mean."

"A lot of people don't. You really have to experience that kind of loss to understand it."

"Can I ask how she died? You okay to talk about it?"

"I'm fine. It was a car accident. She was coming to pick me up at my friend's house on a Friday night. Some guy ran a red light and plowed into her. He died as well. What about your mum? Do you mind telling me?"

Jason recalled his conversation with Kiriko in the car. "I don't mind at all," said Jason. "Actually, I think it kind of helps to talk about it. She died of an aneurysm. The amazing thing is, she'd never been sick a day in her life. One of those amazingly robust, healthy people. Never a cold, never the flu. Nothing. But, there, waiting inside her, was a little ticking time bomb waiting to go off at some appointed hour that no one knew anything about. It's just so random."

"That's what I think about all the time, too. If my mum had driven just a tiny bit faster or a tiny bit slower, if she'd missed one light or made another, then that guy would have missed her completely, she wouldn't even have been there. How lives or fate or destiny or whatever you want to call it can intersect at…at an intersection, of all places, just amazes me," Cynthia said.

"I can remember at both my high school graduation and when I finished UBC, at the ceremony my dad saved an extra seat next to him for my mother. She was big-time into education; it was the surefire route to success. Even from the time I was little she used to say how much she was looking forward to seeing me graduate."

"I know what you mean."

"And the three of us used to take these fishing and camping trips. My dad and I went on a couple after she was gone, just the two of us, but we stopped going. It was just too different without her. She's all we thought about the whole trip. How she wasn't there. What she would've said. How she would've done things."

"My mum used to come to tuck me in," said Cynthia. "And she'd always spend a half-hour or more. Oh, usually it wasn't important stuff. We'd just talk about the day and that kind of thing. But, sometimes, when I was worried about something, we'd talk about that, too, and I always felt so much better that I'd go to sleep easier and wake up refreshed the next day."

"My mum used to do that, too," said Jason.

"I've never been a good sleeper since," said Cynthia.

"Me either," said Jason.

At this point, Tom and Taylor slipped back into the booth. The conversation returned to websites and expanded to include concepts of charity. These two topics occupied the rest of the afternoon, at least in terms of the things that were said.

• • •

At quitting time, Cynthia begged off but Tom and Taylor gracefully asked Jason to join them for a beer. They had several. Phillip planned to join but called to say he was running late. He called again an hour later to inform Jason they'd best meet at home. Jason felt a little light-headed as he and his new colleagues parted. But it wasn't just the booze. In only a matter of weeks, Vancouver had become a foreign land. He and Dee Dee were finished. He'd left his job. All he had left here were memories and friends like Phillip.

• • •

Jason decided to get the car later; movement would help clear his head. He walked past the convention center along West Georgia. Normally he loved this route. The ocean and mountains to your right, hidden behind the towers of glass and steel until you came to an intersection and there it was, the true north of Vancouver.

Tonight he walked with his head down, and by the time he looked up, he had reached Stanley Park. A few more minutes and he'd be walking the famous seawall that helped give the park its identity. At Brockton Point, he saw the sails of Canada Place and the high-rises of downtown. Across Burrard Inlet yellow pinpoints of lights from streetlamps dotted North Vancouver. The Lions Gate Bridge made its presence known before you could see it. The sound of whining tires and engines on the tarmac high above carried a long way.

Jason stopped to gaze at the bridge, steel girders and cable resting on massive stone and concrete supports. The bridge symbolized the power and the capabilities of human ingenuity. Yet the focus of news reports over the past few years weren't on the bridge's strength, but its weakness. It was crumbling. There were a few other souls walking the seawall that night, looking at the lights of communities linked by a bridge that seemed so noble and strong from a distance.

By the time he returned to his car, Jason was completely sober.

The drive to Phillip and Irene's place near the university took only twenty minutes at this time of night. As Jason pulled into a parking space not far from the house, a car peeled around the corner with tires squealing. For a moment, Jason could have sworn the driver was Kevin.

• • •

"Jason, it's Tina."

"Hey, stranger." Jason was pleased to hear a comforting voice.

"Stranger is right. What've you been up to? I thought you were going to call me."

"I thought you were going to call *me*," Jason said.

"You haven't changed a bit, have you? What've you been up to?"

"Oh, I've been in Vancouver doing some work for Phillip and helping out around here. How about you?"

"Nothing so interesting, I'm afraid. That's why I'm calling. I'm going crazy 'round here. I was thinking we could get together."

"Sounds great. What'd you have in mind?"

"Something outdoorsy. Maybe we could go for a hike at Cape Sansum."

"That's an idea. I haven't been there in ages. Sure, why not? The weekend's not good, but how about after that? I've got lots to tell you," Jason said.

"Same here," said Tina.

• • •

On a crisp autumn Monday, Tina rolled up to the hotel exactly on time in her brother's four-wheel drive. The road to the cape was rough even in good weather.

Tina loved Golly and suggested they bring her along. Jason's heart swelled in gratitude. Golly was having a good day, so they arranged a bed in the back of the pickup, Jason hoisted her in, and off they went. On the way, Golly's nose never stopped; Jason hadn't seen her so alert in ages.

The turnoff for the cape wasn't far. They talked

easily on the way. Off the main road, the dirt track was potted and gully-ridden from heavy rains two weeks prior. A skilled driver, Tina navigated the hazards, and minutes later they pulled into what was once their regular spot. They'd visited often as teenagers — even lost their virginity together one summer night cuddled in a tent high above the ocean. Cape Sansum memories were as thick as the trees.

Jason lifted Golly down and they set off down the meandering trail that would bring them to the water's edge in half an hour. The path was a steep series of switchbacks and near its end was their special grassy knoll with its stunning view of the channel. They sat down to rest beside campfire remains and a few empty beer bottles.

"Looks like we're not the only ones who know about this place." Tina nodded, smiling. "Kids," she said. They admired the afternoon. Before long the winds and rains of winter would arrive. Mt. Sansum, high behind and above where they sat, would be dusted by snow and play its part in chalking up the passing of one season to the next.

Golly was in fine form. She squeezed herself between them, wriggling in headfirst. She reveled in the scratching and rubbing and attention, lolling her head back and forth, as content as a child snuggling with its parents on a lazy Sunday morning. Then, catching some irresistible scent, she was off down the trail.

Golly's departure left a gap. Jason and Tina filled it by moving their bums closer together. It felt natural and right, the ease and intimacy of old lovers, now friends, on a good day.

"So," said Tina. "Who starts?"

"You do," Jason laughed. Then, more seriously, "You want to talk about it?"

Tina took a big breath, letting the silence linger a moment longer. "I've had a rough time, Jason. The last three years were a roller coaster. The long climb up and then the big plunge down."

"Tell me about it."

"I mean, I got married, put a hold on my career, and got divorced, all in less than three years. Not bad going, eh?"

"You don't have to joke about it, Tina."

"Where do I start? Curtis was...well, he was like nobody I'd ever come across before. We met at a party in Toronto. A friend of mine had just moved there from Guelph and I was visiting for the weekend. I was just hanging around the fringes eating, pigging out — you know me — and I didn't even really notice him at first. He was talking to some people next to me and I started listening in. And the more I listened, the more it dawned on me that this guy was brilliant. He knew so much about everything, and I was drawn to him, to what he was saying. After a while, the other people moved off and we were suddenly left alone. The eavesdropper and the genius. He introduced himself, said something funny, and we started talking. I mean really talking. He told me about growing up with Catholic Storm Trooper parents. That's what he called them. Then he asked me all kinds of questions about my work, and he knew a lot about animal physiology...and he was interested in what I had to say. At the end of it all, he wanted to know if I was seeing anybody and asked for my number, which I willingly gave. Before I knew it, I was coming into Toronto as often as I could. He's a lot older than me and, although I worried about that at first, pretty soon it didn't seem to matter. He was romantic and charming and intelligent, and probably the most considerate man I'd ever been involved with — present company excluded, of course. At first, at least."

"Tina, I told you, talking good, jokes bad."

"It's something I learned from you, buster, so tough shit, okay?" She gave her little smile, and then continued.

"Anyway, I said 'at first' because he changed. This is after we got married. Once he had me, once he'd trapped me, he could strip off his camouflage. That's when I started seeing this other side. Day by day the kindnesses, the consideration, started to peel off layer by layer like some kind of cheap varnish. Onion man.

"After a while I realized that this wasn't the other side but the *real* side. He used to say the most wonderful things, things I really wanted and needed to hear. How he was getting older and how he wanted kids — with me — more than anything he'd ever wanted in his whole life. Do you know how powerful that was? Do you have any idea what that meant to me?"

Jason did. The question of children — her wanting them and wanting them soon — had been a chasm between them. Or maybe it was a wall — their own Great Wall.

"But when things started changing, they were so gradual and insidious that I can't even tell you when it began. I've tried and tried and still can't mark the day or the event when things really started to slide. He wanted me to do things for him. Little things, which I gladly did. I wasn't working very much and I loved helping him. Helping with his research, making phone calls, doing domestic stuff. It all seemed so natural. But his 'favors' kept increasing at the same time he was telling me to be free. And whenever I'd try to bring it up, he's so good with words, he'd turn things around. Then he'd treat me like a child, acting beneficent and condescending like he'd bestowed some great favor on me by even listening to my 'concerns' — that was the word he used. It was like we weren't husband and wife anymore but doting parent and slightly simple child." She paused. "But the real change came when I got pregnant."

Jason gripped her hand. He had no idea she had been pregnant. Tina gave him that smile, the one where she bit her lower lip. Her eyes were wet. She'd never looked more vulnerable.

"Yeah, surprise. At first I was overjoyed. And so was Curtis. Or so I thought. But then, almost overnight, he changed. He became so controlling. When he'd travel he'd leave me — get this — a typed list of do's and don'ts. Can you believe it? Typed, for God's sake." Tina's voice quavered. "Then, when he'd come home, he'd check up on me. He'd actually check to see if I'd followed his instructions. He'd call the doctor to make sure I'd gone; he'd measure food to see what I'd eaten. But it was 'all for my own good,' he'd say. 'For the baby's sake, our baby.'" Tina imitated him, her voice horribly pompous.

"And then…" she stopped talking for a moment, composing herself. "And then…I had a miscarriage. Oh, it was horrible, Jason. It was horr—" She was crying now and half-hugging him. "It was around eighteen weeks. One night, I went to bed, same as usual. And then, in the middle of the night, I woke up in terrible pain. I was bleeding and cramping. They rushed me to the hospital…and when we got there, there was no heartbeat…it turns out the baby had been dead for almost two weeks. Two weeks. Can you imagine?" Jason couldn't. "For two weeks I was carrying around my poor little dead Samuel — Sam. That's not the way it's supposed to be…it's just not…he was supposed to be born." She couldn't go on. He held her tight and rubbed her back. Whispered that everything was going to be all right. Tina eventually composed herself enough to go on.

"And you know what Curtis did? This so-called brilliant doctor, this so-called caring psychologist? That bastard. He blamed me. He *blamed* me. I hadn't followed instructions, I hadn't listened to him, and that's why Sam died. My poor beautiful little baby boy died inside me and he said it was *my* fault. It was the most hateful thing, the most totally hateful thing I've ever, ever experienced. After that, I couldn't stand the sight of him. I couldn't even look at his face. I hated him, Jason, I actually *hated* him. I still do. I didn't really understand what hate was before, but now I do. The only person I've ever really truly hated in my whole life is the man I married."

"You poor thing...poor you," Jason murmured, holding her, not knowing what else to say. "I had no idea..."

Tears fled down her streaky face. She waited, as if willing Jason to understand the rest.

"There were complications after the miscarriage...and I had to have a hysterectomy." She looked directly at him. "I can never have children, Jason. I can never have children. Me, Jason, me. Me, who's always wanted kids so badly. How sad is that? Turns out I might have been the right girl for you after all..." She tried to laugh, but she couldn't. Instead she cried — hopelessly, helplessly, rocking back and forth and moaning. Jason felt useless.

He had no idea how long she'd spoken, or how long he held her. Her torrent of tears slowed. They sat in silence. Both of them contemplated the meaning of pain, of children, of motherhood, of things that were and would never be.

Jason finally spoke. "There's something I've got to tell you, too." Until this moment, Jason hadn't made up his mind to tell her. But how could he not?

As he revealed everything, Jason looked straight out at the ocean. Even during this second retelling, the story seemed surreal, a disassociation from who he was — or at least from who he'd *thought* he was. Part of him remained numb so that he hardly registered Tina's shock, her disbelief, her head first on his shoulder and then on his back.

"It's beyond belief, Jason. I don't know what to say. I'm...speechless..."

"I don't either. We're quite the pair, aren't we — full of surprises."

Suddenly, from below, down by the water, Golly began barking madly. In a way it was a relief. Some outside force had intervened. It was time, literally, to move on.

They found Golly on the beach, barking towards a large rock perhaps fifteen feet from shore. When they looked closely, they saw more than rock. Atop it lay a seal pup, alone and injured, one flipper badly gouged and bloody. It stared directly at Tina and Jason and Golly as if imploring them to act.

"There's nothing we can do," the veterinarian in Tina spoke. "Who knows what happened...maybe an Orca, maybe a boat prop."

"Are you sure?" asked Jason.

"There's nothing," said Tina. "We have to leave it. His mother may come back, so we can't touch him. How would we get over there, anyway? It's too deep to wade out." Jason noticed Tina had instinctively labeled the pup a boy. "Let nature take its course, cruel as it may seem. Mother Nature's not very sentimental."

A large wave from a distant passing boat arrived and nearly swept the gray and white pup from its perch. Jason moved to Tina and hugged her long and hard. Not a Music Club hug, it was an embrace full of grief and loss for a baby called Sam and a man named Jason. It was a hug for the mothers who'd lost them. Jason thought about Cristine and her daughter's unplanned pregnancy. Then another image came unbidden to him: Kiriko sitting in his car, saying: *"Yoku wakarimashita."*

• • •

The wheels spun on the gravel, shooting rocks and pebbles in every direction. Then they were onto the tarmac, heading north again. Now the sounds of the wheels were a whir. Wind entered through the slit of the open window. Finally, someone spoke.

"Jason...can I ask you something?"

"Of course."

"Have you told anyone else? Have you told Al or Dee Dee about Dada and..." Unable to help herself, Tina started to giggle.

Jason laughed, too. "You're right. I've never thought of that before...Dee Dee and Dada. It's ridiculous, isn't it?" For the first time that afternoon, they laughed and laughed.

"Okay, enough's enough," a still smiling Tina said. "But you still haven't answered the question."

"Actually, I have told someone else."

"You have? Who?"

"Her name's Kiriko."

Tina studied Jason's profile.

"She must be very special," Tina said.

Chapter 5 iNovel Link

The World Wide Web provides untold opportunity for viewing photos, illustrations, videos and other visual offerings. It's also an amazing vehicle for audio delivery: the Chapter 5 iNovel link is an audio play – a short audio book that delivers in dramatic fashion the scene featuring Jason and Tina Love as they talk about marriage and loss on the grassy knoll of Cape Sansum (pp. 91–95). Please go to **www.HotSpringsNovel.com/chapter5/** if you wonder what they sound like.

Chapter 6

"I'm not sure anyone's really got an answer to that."

Jason started working on the charity website the night he'd returned from Vancouver. He always worked best when ideas were fresh and before the act of dragging them out of his biological hard disc became a chore in itself.

For Jason, the design of websites and buildings had much in common. Even their vocabulary overlapped; a slew of computer terms are borrowed from architecture: site, address, firewall, domain, access, portal — even the word "architecture" itself. He had flirted with a career in architecture. It combined art and science in the way jazz combined the discipline of classical music with the passion and soul of blues and gospel. Jason visualized his websites as apartments or offices, the object of the site driving his metaphors. For the bank's charity run, he thought of an athletic complex. A complete site had depth and dimensionality. Some soaring structures require high-speed elevators while more modest versions need only stairs. Jason sought to match function with design. In this he excelled.

While engrossed in these thoughts, Jason's computer announced he had mail. When he saw the sender's name — Kevin — he pictured the squealing car outside Phillip's house.

The e-mail came from a Kevin alias Jason knew well: upwithdown@rebelrebellion.com. It was a single link to an audio file. When Jason clicked, he was treated to an endless loop of two lines from one of Kevin's death-metal favorites. Spinning himself in slow circles on one of the office's swivel chairs, Jason listened: "You never know nothing about nothing until it's gone / and that's why you always got to get it before it leaves for good."

From the moment he'd met her, Kevin had been a full-fledged member of the Dee Dee fan club. As she did everybody, Dee Dee treated Kevin kindly and with respect — a rarity for Kevin. Despite his flaws — relentless hyperbolic nerd-speak, sartorial and hygiene challenges, a horrific diet and uncanny ability to never buy a round of drinks — Kevin was human, too. Dee Dee and Jason had discussed his deep but purposely well-hidden intellect.

But why Kevin continued plaguing him with these guilt-trip e-mails, Jason couldn't begin to guess. He decided to take a bath.

Immersed in his hot springs, he couldn't stop thinking about Kevin's e-mail barrage. Kevin and Dee Dee. The names tumbled together like socks in a dryer. Had Dee Dee actually ended their relationship for Kevin? Kevin of the Diet Cokes? Kevin of the ankle-deep refuse and stinkathon T-shirts. ...It was unimaginable.

He left the main bathhouse, but instead of returning to the hotel he meandered to the seaside hot springs. He was still hot. The breeze off the ocean would cool him. Access to the beachside bath was via a path and gate. Mainly because of the tides and inconvenient distance from the hotel, the beachside springs generally saw less use than the bathhouse, except during the summer. Naturally, the hardier types — like Mum — loved this spot best. The wildness of the place, the fact that you became part of nature, and not merely witness to it. Dee Dee had been right. Landscapes did tie you to them. How many key scenes in Jason's life had taken place within shouting distance of where he now stood?

● ● ●

Cristine's exhibition was scheduled for tomorrow, and preparations were well underway. Today's main event was the hanging and placing of her paintings, supervised by Dada. Food had been arranged by Al and Cristine in tandem. All had worked together on the guest list and program.

The guest of honor arrived around noon. The back of her old Ford Ranger pickup overflowed with easels and paintings wrapped in blankets and boxes and bubble wrap. Younger daughter Layla rode shotgun but the pregnant Angel stayed home so "we could keep out of each other's hair for a while," said Cristine. "But she'll be here tomorrow — she never misses a party." She rolled her eyes. Layla pitched in with all the enthusiasm and effort her skinny arms and gawky ten-year-old body could manage.

The most remarkable thing about Layla wasn't her energy — most kids her age had power to burn. It was her mesmerizing gaze. Her pale blue eyes were rimmed with extraordinarily dark lashes. Although usually a blur of motion, when she looked — really looked — at something, she became totally motionless. Once in this zone, her head would tilt and mouth open as every ounce of her being zeroed in on the object of her gaze. It was slightly unnerving for those who didn't know her, and even sometimes for those that did.

Earlier in the day, Dada and Jason and Ellery had cleared the wall of the hotel's great room. The voluminous memorabilia was stored in the attic and the wood paneling received a long overdue polish. Guests came and went all the while, and most had an encouraging word or a question to ask about Cristine's work. The electricity at the center of such events draws everyone to it like metal attracted to a charged magnet. Dada smiled so hard you could see his teeth beneath his beard. "He looks fifteen years younger, doesn't he?" Al winked.

Tina stopped by with cookies. The phone rang off the hook. Al shouted orders, Ellery ran back and forth, and Layla was asking anyone and everyone if they needed help. Jason acted as rover and general dog's body. Cristine's initial worries about sparse attendance seemed ridiculous now. Her flushed face glowed almost neon. Then, a middle-aged hardware-store owner from Yakima bought her most expensive painting only minutes after being hung — she'd achieved a major milestone before the exhibition even opened. Dada treated the hero of Yakima and everyone else to champagne. The mood grew suddenly turbo-festive.

Everyone clinked glasses, and then sat down for a break among the easels, strewn towels and wrapping paper, and the tools and empty coffee cups. The room was semi-calm for the first time in hours, with the kind of self-congratulation that hard-working groups know well.

Then the door swung open and in walked Abner van Gelderen, nicknamed L'il Abner, Cristine's ex-husband and Angel's father. Since he lived on a boat north of Prince Rupert far up the mainland coast, his appearance surprised everyone. Cristine actually gasped. Her first reaction was to wrinkle her nose as if for a bad smell. She shook her head, and closed her eyes. Golly, a good judge of character, growled, echoing the sentiments of everyone in the room.

Abner was a mean drunk and violent. Cristine left him after he'd broken her nose for denting their already battered truck. Not that he hadn't hit her before — that one was just the last straw. Layla hid behind a pillar. She searched for her mother with panicked eyes.

"Where's Cris?" Abner demanded in a voice as big as he was.

Jason stepped up. "Abner, come on, why don't you just relax for a while. We've got guests—"

"Like I give a shit, Jason. Fuck right off, you hear me?" His voice boomed off the walls. He was plainly aching for a fight. "Now, I want to know, who the hell knocked up Angel?" Abner's fists and mouth clenched. Jason sought ways to defuse the situation but was drawing blanks.

"You been drinking, Abner?" Dada strode forward

at the ready, even though he was half Abner's size. About the only thing these two men had in common were beards and fearlessness.

"Fuck off, Joe. I want Cris."

Al cautioned Dada. She knew how unpredictable men could be. Everyone else stood still, not knowing what to do. Cristine leapt up and took her turn.

"Let's go out to the truck and talk, Ab, or out back somewhere," she said in her softest, most compelling voice. She was pleading. Jason moved closer.

"We can talk here," said Abner.

"Everyone will be able to hear us."

"I don't give a fuck what anyone hears. I'm here to talk about that slut daughter of yours."

"Abner, *please...*" In less than a minute, she'd devolved from successful and popular artist to star of a public trailer-park drama. Her face was red from shame; five minutes earlier it had been flushed with pleasure. Jason noticed Al's absence and suspected the police were about to be called. The nearest detachment was in Troy; the twenty or thirty minutes it would take them to get here would be long ones indeed.

Cristine tried once more to steer her ex-husband outdoors but failed again. When she took Abner's arm, he pushed her, hard. Luckily, she landed uninjured against a chair.

Abner moved towards the sobbing Cristine. With no choice, Jason jumped between them.

"So, you wanna a piece of this, do you, Junior?" A hint of spittle left Abner's mouth.

Both Abner and Jason were breathing hard. Jason held no illusions. In a fight, Abner would be merciless.

Abner advanced.

"Hi everyone!" shouted Cassidy, a big grin on his face and a huge bunch of flowers in his arms. If he noticed the room's palpable tension, he didn't let on. He handed the flowers to Cristine, pecked her on the cheek, and then turned to Abner. Since Cassidy was the only one remotely close in height to Abner, when he spoke they were almost eye to eye.

"Abner! It's YOU!" said Cassidy. He grabbed the confused-looking Abner by both shoulders and said, "How you DOING brother, How you *DOING*?" Cassidy gave Abner a hard hug and, while doing so, whispered something into the larger man's ear. By the time they separated Abner's face was split wide by a gap-toothed grin.

"So, whaddya say, let's go then!" He turned to the gawking crowd and said, "See ya, guys! See ya at the show!" With that, he linked arms with Abner — who didn't look back once — and left. With the click of the door latch, the room erupted into excited chatter. All, except Cristine, of course. Layla ran and hugged her mother until she stopped crying. Cristine asked Layla for a glass of water. Later, after composing herself, she made a collective apology and then turned to go.

"Jason, can I leave Layla here with you for a bit? I have to go and check on Angel and make sure she's okay." Of course, Jason agreed.

Layla divided the rest of her evening between

Dada, Al, Tina, and Jason. When Jason suggested they walk Golly, the little girl immediately jumped up, ready to go. Once outside and walking, Layla suddenly stopped and gave Jason her stare. "Jason, can I ask you a question?"

"Sure."

"It's kinda a strange one"

"That's okay. Shoot."

"Why do people have babies if they don't really want them?"

He stalled. "Why do you ask, Layla? Because of what happened tonight?"

"Yeah, and all the fighting between Mum and Angel."

"I see…well, you know, sometimes we fight most with people we love."

"That sounds silly. Why?"

"I agree it does. It's because we care about them so much…but the thing to remember, Layla, is that your mum loves both you and Angel a lot. She's told me that, how great you are."

"I know," said Layla with a complacency that was oddly comforting. "But do parents love those kids just the same then?" asked Layla.

"Well, usually, yes, but you also have to under-stand there are lots of different kinds of love. Different people love in different ways."

Layla stared up at him. Perhaps even at her age, she thought his answer lame.

"So why does Abner do stuff like that?" she asked. Even as she bent to pet Golly she continued staring at him.

"Well, it could be lots of things, Layla."

"Like what?"

"Like it could be alcohol doing the talking or…"

"Or what?"

"Or he could be unhappy about something."

"You mean like Angel having a baby without getting married?"

"Well, yes. He was obviously upset about that."

"But he and Mum weren't married when Angel was born. Angel told me. And, also, Angel said that he always used to get mad about anything, even real little stuff."

"Well, I guess some people get mad more easily than others." Jason wished he had greater insight.

"But why?"

"Maybe he's just mad at the world." Jason tried.

"Why?"

"I don't know. Sometimes you don't know the reason and sometimes neither do they. If I had to guess, I'd say he had an unhappy childhood. That can affect people really badly."

"Angel told me that his dad died when he was young and that his stepfather used to beat him up."

"There you go. It sounds like you know quite a lot."

"So do you think it's better if you don't have a father at all rather than a bad one?"

"I'm not sure Layla. I'm not sure anyone's really got an answer to that."

"Because there's a kid in my class, Jamie Burr, and he's got a bad father but he's okay."

"That's what I mean…it's impossible to tell how

someone's going to turn out. I mean your dad doesn't live with you guys but you're a nice girl."

"I like *your* father," Layla said, shyness blooming forth at Jason's compliment. "He's funny," she said.

"He sure is," said Jason bending down to join Layla in patting Golly. Suddenly, Dada's recent actions and requests had found a new context. "He sure is," he repeated. "And you're a very smart little girl."

• • •

"Jason," Cristine was on the other end of the line.

"Are you okay? How's Angel?"

"She's fine. We all are. Abner did come by the house earlier but Angel pretended she wasn't here. I think he must've come to the hotel directly after. Or maybe after he got loaded. I don't know exactly."

"How did he find out you were here?"

"No idea. Maybe he saw a poster. Anyway, many thanks on the Layla front. I hope she hasn't been too much trouble."

"The exact opposite. She's a great kid."

"Listen, have you heard from Cassidy?" asked Cristine. She sounded worried.

"Not a word."

"Thank god he came along."

"He was amazing," said Jason.

"So were you. All of you. And Jason, I'm so sorry — that was unbelievably embarrassing. It could have been a total disaster."

"Don't worry about it."

Cristine paused, "Have you talked to your dad?"

"What do you mean?"

"If he wants to cancel tomorrow night, I understand."

"Don't be crazy. There's no way he'd want to do that."

"But what if Asshole Abner shows up again?"

"We'll just make sure Cassidy's here, then. ...Do you want to talk to Layla now?"

"That'd be great. And thank everyone for everything, would you, Jason?"

Jason handed the phone to the eager girl and went looking for Dada and Al to pass on Cristine's sentiments. He found them in The Pit.

"I shoulda smacked him," Dada was saying. "That would have taught the S.O.B. a lesson."

"And you one, as well," commented Al, winking at Jason across the big kitchen island.

Jason started to tell them about Cristine's call when he heard Layla calling his name.

"Yeah, Layla?"

"My mum wants to talk to you again," she said with a mischievous grin.

"Jason, Layla just asked me if she could spend the night. There's a pro-D day tomorrow so she doesn't have school. I told her no, that I'd come by and get her but she made me promise that I'd at least ask you."

"Hey, no problem — in fact, it's kind of flattering. I didn't know we were so popular with kids at the hotel. I'll make sure you get the special kid's rate."

"Pardon?"

"I'm kidding, Cristine, I'm kidding."

Cristine got it. "But seriously, are you sure it's all right? Have you got room for her?"

"We'll come up with something."

"Thanks Jason." While Jason spoke, in that inept but winning way kids have, Layla pretended disinterest while listening as hard as she could. When Jason gave her the silent okay, she danced in circles. Jason turned his back on Layla and lowered his voice.

"But can I ask you a question, Cristine? Why does she want to stay? Is she scared?"

"Well, maybe partly but that's not what she said. She mentioned two things: that Golly was there — you know how much she loves dogs — and you. She called you her big brother."

Thinking a female companion for Layla might be a good idea, Jason asked Tina to spend the night. Layla stayed in his room while he'd carve some space in his old room inside Dada's suite — the first time they'd shared it in years. In keeping with the celebratory mood, Layla stayed up till midnight and the four of them — Dada, Jason, Tina, and Layla — went to the bathhouse together. They sang songs, had a water fight and Jason was tickled to see Layla so happy. Yet, despite the hijinks, the jovial company, and the tumultuous events of the evening, all Jason could think of were two people whose absence never seemed to leave him: Elizabeth. And Kiriko.

Chapter 6 iNovel Link

The Chapter 6iNovel Link shows a selection of artwork by the painter Cristine. Please go to **www.HotSpringsNovel.com/chapter6/** to see paintings exhibited at the Hot Springs Island show.

Chapter 7

"Fire dancing is hot work."

Drinks and chatter flowed, hugs, kisses, flowers, waves and shouts and music were everywhere. Layla kept popping up with chocolate and hors d'oeuvres as fragrant as they were delicious. Al smiled and looked lovely in a new periwinkle one-piece.

Dada had foregone a checked sweater or shirt for the first time in ages and wore his tuxedo jacket and dress shirt. Jason called him Dapper Dada.

Cristine stood next to one of her paintings, a piece titled *Two Selves*, which showed a crouching woman contemplating her significantly altered reflection in water.

Her appearance proved what a difference twenty-four hours can make. Bedecked in a black silk floor-length dress with an alluring slit up one side and her head festooned with a jeweled headband and accompanying feather, Cristine was a gorgeous flapper from the twenties. One gloved hand held a long ivory cigarette holder and her cheeks were pink from more than makeup: four more paintings had already sold and there were offers on three more.

As emcee, Dada introduced the noted guests, including the mayor of Troy, the local naturalist writer J. Ames Aubrey, and Layla, whose simple, "I think my mum is great!" earned the largest ovation. Angel was there too, but she remained assiduously in the background. She'd dressed for the occasion in a sleeveless dress that Jason guessed was Cristine's. Noticeably pregnant, she rubbed her belly with both hands, but would draw them away when anyone came near. The only missing guests of note were Cassidy and Kiriko. Jason's frequent scans of the crowd couldn't find either. The party wouldn't be the same without them, although for entirely different reasons.

Cassidy's absence raised the question of Abner. "We need a 44-magnum stun-gun," Jason suggested, "or a double-barreled Cassidy."

Dada rose to speak: "Thank 'ee, thank 'ee, thank 'ee. From the bottom of my heart and the bottom of Cristine's art, I thank 'ee for attending. And for the spirit as warm as the hot springs that bubble up only yards from where we stand, and for coming together with friends and neighbors and loved ones — and even me, as well." The crowd laughed. "As host of the event, I will abscond with my tithe and say a few words of my own. For those who know me, and that's most everyone here, I suspect that you may be, well...perhaps...expecting a quotation of some sort?" There was another laugh. "Well, aren't you?" More laughter and cries of assent. "Indeed," said Dada. "And, you might well predict that said quote be from the Bard himself, might you not?"

"Hear hear!" a wag in the back yelled.

"Well," continued Dada, "I've got news for you — because for once I am *not* going to be giving you one." Collective surprise rippled through the room.

"No, indeed. I'm going to be giving you *two*!

"First, to one and all I remind you that, 'Small

cheer and great welcome makes a merry feast!' And I suspect that the opposite is true. But, without further ado, for my next quote I go to *Henry V*, Act III, Scene ii. And I suggest everyone ready for this one…" There was a jovial groan. Dada stood silent, his timing impeccable. He scanned his audience and then looked directly into the eyes of five, six, seven people. He held the room in his hand and his eyes burned. He was no longer an old man.

"The lesson learned from this quote is a fundamental one, and one I hope I've taken well to heart. So as to hold you in suspense no longer, here it is…'Men of few words are the best men.'"

With that — plus a bow and boyish grin — Dada walked off to rapturous laughter and applause. He wasn't quite done, however. As he was patted on the back for what one guest described as "the best kind of speech," Dada had one quote left: "'I would give all my fame for a pot of beer and safety.'"

• • •

With timing scrupulously rehearsed, a trumpet blared in brassy glory from behind the hotel at the very instant the clapping and laughter inside subsided. Heads turned and ears perked. In a rush, everyone stampeded to the back windows while Al pointed out the absence of the garden tables and chairs from their usual spots on the back deck. The interior and exterior lights were suddenly extinguished. A gasp shot through the group. In the dim ambient light Jason saw Kiriko at the light switch. As their eyes met,

Kiriko smiled and placed a finger to her lip in the universal conspirator's gesture of silence.

Outside, the trumpet's mournful notes devolved into silence and four figures dressed in monk's robes appeared on the back deck. All carried flaming torches. Oversized hoods hid their faces. Their footfalls kept time to a drum beating somewhere out of sight. First they marched in a clockwise circle and then, after a moment of silence, reversed their course. After four cycles of this, the beat suddenly gained intensity and the four figures began dancing as if possessed. The drumming increased again. Responding, the crowd pressed harder against the window. Then, again without apparent signal, the pace of the drumming diminished and the four figures lined up to face the crowd through the glass, their heads bowed. Two seconds passed, then five, the drum still beating softly, slowly. On cue, in a flurry of coordinated movement, they lifted their robes. Painted on four exposed male torsos were the words: "WAY TO GO CRIS!" Everyone erupted into wild cheers, shouting, whistling and god knows what else. Standing forward of the other dancers, breathing hard and with a smile as wide and white as a glacier in the sun, was Cassidy.

After such a performance, the party took a few minutes to return to more usual levels of festivity. Cassidy, of course, was feted and pawed, and Cristine appeared giddy with gratitude.

Jason and Tina tried to elbow their way to Cassidy. They were desperate to learn the whereabouts of L'il Abner and to discover exactly how

Cassidy had taken him away the previous day. Only through concerted efforts were they finally able to drag him to a place of relative quiet. Jason found himself looking for Kiriko without any luck.

"Okay," Cassidy said. "First of all, there's nothing to worry about. Abner's not even on the island." From across the room Jason gave Cristine a thumbs-up and she visibly relaxed.

"But what happened?" Tina asked. "How did you get him to leave so easily last night after we couldn't do anything with him? I thought he was going to belt someone."

"Yeah, me," said Jason.

"Well," said Cassidy, enjoying the moment. "I saw his truck when I got here. It was parked really badly, half up on the lawn, keys still in it, so I suspected there might be trouble."

"Come on," said Tina excitedly, "Get to the point! How did you get him out of here so quickly?"

"Easy," said Cassidy. "I told him I'd just gotten some dynamite hash and that we should go out and smoke some." Tina and Jason half-collapsed with laughter. Cassidy's grin said it all.

"We went out and smoked. First off, this was some pretty mellow stuff and, you know, I could see that Abner was drunk and in need of some major iceberging!" Cassidy's eyes shot sparks of excitement. "He'd been driving for days, so I told him he'd better get some shuteye in the truck 'cause we were going to a party."

"And was there actually a party?" Tina asked.

"You bet."

"What party? Where?"

"That's the thing. It was in Vancouver."

"Vancouver!" They almost collapsed a second time.

"Well, not Vancouver, exactly," Cassidy said, grinning his million-buck smile again. "White Rock. We caught the last ferry, had a little nap, partied all night, and I convinced him this morning that I'd look after everything for him over here and that all he had to do was drive back up north. I got a ride back to the ferry today and here I am. End of story."

"You, my friend," Jason said, "are amazing."

Cassidy grinned in reply. "Now, how about a drink? Fire dancing is hot work."

At this moment Kiriko appeared. The white gleam of her single strand of pearls elegantly contrasted with the black velvet of her dress and the equally velvet texture of her long dark hair, worn down. Before Jason could even greet her, however, Cassidy moved in and said, "Great job on the lights there." Then he embraced her.

Chapter 7 iNovel Link
The Chapter 7 Hot Springs iNovel Link is another musical one — although this time it's about drumming. Please visit **www.HotSpringsNovel.com/chapter7/** to listen to the drumming at Cristine's exhibition launch party.

Chapter 8

"Do you even know what it means?"

The party was the talk of the island. It was so successful Dada pledged an annual Cristine exhibition, "same time, same place, same elegant MC!" Her paintings were flying out the door. She'd earned nearly a year's income in one show. She was ecstatic.

Everyone's mood migrated two notches upward; yet, the question of Elizabeth still nagged at Jason. Since that first conversation they'd hardly broached the subject. As far as Dada was concerned, the problem had been aired and discussed and it was time to move on. He expected Jason to honor his wishes. Doing otherwise was an insult to Mum, he implied. But, with each passing day, doubts circled Jason's mental camp.

Elizabeth and Dada weren't the only people occupying Jason's mind. Speculation about Cassidy and Kiriko slipped into his thoughts, too. They were as constant and annoying as a draft under an ill-fitting door.

• • •

Jason made Dada promise to go to the next Music Club together. He wanted to sing and play with his father, and he needed something positive to stay the rumblings of his uncertainty. Music always brought them closer together. Also, since Cassidy was hosting, Jason intended to find out more about Kiriko and her relationship — if that's what you could call it — with Cassidy.

On Thursday, the night before Music Club, Jason got another e-mail from Kevin, this one with a Flash animation. A click on the icon made two words, "FRIENDSHIP" and "LOYALTY," pop up in their own window. A gray thundercloud moved in, followed by lightning bolts striking the two words and causing them to burst into flame and burn to a pile of ashes. The clouds then rained on the ashes and the screen dissolved into darkness. How much time and effort had Kevin spent creating what was essentially cyber-stalking?

In his early days with computers, Jason had believed in the limitless potential of the web and the Internet. But disappointment kidnapped his optimism. He saw kids increasingly tethered to their computers, kids ignorant of forest, ocean, nature — the landscapes that formed character and tied you to them. And adults were no better. Pornography, Internet abductions, pedophilia, Kevin-like abuse, identity theft — these manifestations seemed to indict the concept of technological progress. No wonder it was called "the web."

• • •

On Friday night Dada, Jason, and their instruments piled into Jason's car heading north for Cassidy's place. Tina, they picked up on the way.

A pack-rat extraordinaire with a small, cramped

house, Cassidy liked using the old barn on his property for music nights. Knowing Cassidy, he'd have portable heaters and mobile hot tubs.

Once there, father and son circulated. Hugs, greetings, gossip, food, drink, more hugs, a song or two, and then repeat the cycle. Everyone was present, usually the case at Cassidy's. Cristine gave both Dada and Jason sloppy kisses and warm hugs and went on for an embarrassingly long time about their kindness. Angel roamed the shadows.

The ramshackle barn had three entrances. The big main doors were closed but a regular-sized one led towards the house while another opened onto a white-fenced field and a view down the valley. Lawn chairs under the eaves were the default smoker's hangout. Before long, Jason emerged to share a joint, a minor Cassidy's Barn ritual.

Angel appeared then wandered off, separating herself from both the marijuana and tobacco crowd. She lit a hand-rolled cigarette — tobacco, as far as Jason could tell. Before long, Cristine came out for a smoke herself. At first she didn't notice Angel in the distance but she sensed the unusual hush among the other smokers and looked around. On seeing her pregnant daughter, butt in hand, Cristine erupted.

"What the hell do you think you're doing?"

"What the hell does it look like I'm doing?"

"It looks like you're trying to kill yourself and the baby as well, that's what...how could you? How could you, Angel? You keep telling me you want this baby and then you go and do something like this."

"Look who's talking..."

"What's that supposed to mean?"

"Ever heard of the word 'hypocrite,' Mom? Do you even know what it means? I don't know how you can act so holier than thou when you smoked when you were pregnant with me. Abner told me. And you drank too — hey, maybe *that's* why I'm all screwed up. Oh I get it…maybe you've finally realized it's all your fault and now you feel so guilty that the only way you can get rid of it is by yelling at me. And look at you — you *still* smoke while you're preaching at me."

"How dare you talk to me like that! I—"

"It's your fault. You started it."

"Listen to me — I don't care what you do to yourself. This isn't just about you or me. For the baby's sake, you've got to put that thing out and quit smoking until it's born. Please." Angel ignored her. Getting nowhere, Cristine lunged for the offending cigarette, but the girl was too fast. Angel stepped back quickly. Then she started yelling.

"Leave me alone! Would you just leave me alone, for god's sake! Leave me alone!" She was borderline hysterical. Her mother stood dead still, stunned. Devastated, she then turned on her heel, and half-ran around the end of the barn, sobs escaping as if from a wounded animal. Jason stood up but she raised a hand — she wanted to be left alone. Angel stood haughtily, defiantly triumphant. If anything, the only change to her demeanor was to smoke more aggressively. She finished one cigarette and then immediately lit another.

Cassidy waited a few moments and then approached quietly. He rubbed Angel's shoulders and whispered in her ear, not unlike what he'd done with her father days before. Without a word, just some nodding, Angel stubbed out her butt in the long dewy grass, and they hugged. With his arm around her shoulders and hers around his waist, Cassidy and Angel walked into the barn.

● ● ●

Later, Jason found Tina on the back porch. He related the incident behind the barn.

"What do you think Cassidy said to her? Angel, I mean," Tina said.

"Sure hope it wasn't a suggestion to go smoke some hash."

"Jason."

"I know."

Looking in through the kitchen window, Jason saw something that turned him temporarily deaf.

"Tina, look. There she is, with Cassidy. It's Kiriko. Remember? I told you about her on the way back from the cape." Jason didn't have to remind her. She remembered every moment of that afternoon like it was a film she'd seen a hundred times.

"You should go talk to her," said Tina.

"You don't mind?" Jason asked.

"Why would I?" said Tina, her mouth pulled purposefully into a kind of half-smile.

Jason searched Tina's eyes and expression. "Thanks, Tina. I'll be back."

"Go," she said.

He tracked her down in the barn.

The music throbbed. They were playing a reel and Dada was fiddling away in the center of a large irregular circle. Sasha, the long white-haired Russian, was soaring on a solo and everything and everybody was rushing along. Banjo, bass, a single snare drum and guitars of every description were strummed and picked. People clapped their hands, banging and shaking things in time to the frantic beat. While everyone pounded or stomped their feet, he saw Kiriko gracefully swaying. Once again, Jason marveled at her...serenity. Although he had no trouble recognizing her special aura, Jason still had trouble classifying it. He'd noticed this quality the moment he'd first seen her. Jason transported himself back. The way her towel had fallen in front of her. Her glistening black hair. Her walk.

He had to talk to her, to gauge if their shared bath and time in the car after the ferry ride carried for her any of the import it did for him. He moved around the room until only a few feet and several people — including Cassidy — separated them. He caught her fragrance, the one he remembered from the car trip.

Jason moved closer and touched Kiriko's shoulder. She smiled. Then the up tempo number ended and the nimble Cassidy appeared in the center of the ring.

"Now, friends," he said. "Are you ready to do some *singin'*?" He pronounced the last word with a countrified accent. Cheers and unanimous agreement answered him. "Okay, then. Let's do 'Seven Bridges Road.' You ready?" This Eagles song was a tradition with the Music Club. Tonight's crowd was fifty strong. Like a choir whose only religion was music, when the blend of voices kicked in — female, male, young, middle-aged, old, beery hoarse and mellow rich — oh! — how you felt it. He loved these moments, feeling the mass vibrations of harmonious voices and knowing you belonged to it.

The last note of the song evaporated but before Jason could move, Cassidy strode to Kiriko, grabbed her by the hand and dragged her into the circle's center.

"Friends, I would now like to introduce you to our newest member. This is Kiriko — am I pronouncing that right? — who comes to us from a small hot springs town of her own, one in Japan. What's the name of the place again, Kiriko?"

Her voice was melodic and soft. Again, Jason time-slipped.

"Thank you…I come from the town of Kurokawa Onsen — which means Black River Hot Springs. It is in Kumamoto Prefecture, in the south of Japan. I am so thankful to be here," she said. Then she stepped back to the rim of the circle. Jason thought she sounded regal, like royalty who'd given up a life of privilege but was incapable of hiding her natural bearing. When his eyes met hers again, he felt locked in.

"Anyway, Kiriko is one darn-tooting fine painter and, when you get the chance, I want every one of you to drop by the Troy Gallery and check out her work. She only arrived in Hot Springs a couple of months ago, thanks to Dada here (Dada bowed in acknowledgement) so give her a big hand and welcome her to the island and to the music group — her new Canadian family!"

Even as the applause was subsiding, someone started in on the distinctive opening guitar riff of Van Morrison's "Brown-Eyed Girl" and the room changed once more. Again it was about music. Cassidy leaned over to say something into Kiriko's ear and his hand rested low on her waist. Kiriko made no move to escape, nor did she look uncomfortable. The gesture was unmistakably intimate.

• • •

"That was a good night, wasn't it?" Dada sat on the stone flagging rimming the bath. His legs remained in the water and his torso steamed in the cold air like dry ice.

Jason didn't reply.

"That Cassidy's really something."

"Dada, I've been thinking."

"I guessed something was up. Okay. I'm ready."

"I want to know more about Elizabeth."

"I thought that might be it."

"Well, you can't be that surprised, can you?"

"I suppose not. But I thought we'd been over this, Jason. There's nothing to gain by this."

"Are you suggesting there's something to lose?"

Dada paused. "Let me tell you a story. It's about why I quit painting. There was this Frenchmen, a fellow who went by the pseudonym Max Reál, and he was the leading light of surrealism at the time. I admired Reál tremendously, I really did, so I decided to try and bring him to Canada. I organized a group and prodded and begged, and we managed to actually come up with the money and get the galleries in Toronto, Montreal, and Vancouver. Damned if it wasn't actually going to happen. The man was a hero of mine and I couldn't wait to meet him. He stood for everything I admired at the time. He was antiwar, he believed in the power of art as a catalyst to change, and in the idea that surrealism allowed us to look into the human soul. But, when he arrived, I couldn't have been more disappointed. He was a complete and utter fraud, a total phony who'd just seen a niche and jumped in, headfirst. All he was after was money, getting laid, inflating his ego. I can't tell you how disillusioned I felt. ...You should never meet your heroes, Jason, that's what I'm saying. We need ideals, sure, but not the messy and complicated reality behind them. The best way to keep things in perspective is to recognize things for what they are, realize that you can't change what can't be changed, and move on."

"And you're saying that, if I pursue this, all I'm going to find at the end is some new kind of messy reality?"

"In a word, yes."

"But Dada, this isn't some artist or hero we're talking about, here. It's my mother."

"As I've already said, Mum is, was, and always will be your mother. ...Please, Jason, I've asked you before and I'll ask you again. Please let's just move on."

"What if I told you I want to find her?"

"Well, I know how Lear would reply."

"Dada, for once—"

Dada ignored him. "How sharper than a serpent's tooth it is / To have a thankless child…"

Without another word and before Jason could register anything beyond silent but abject disbelief, Dada rose from the water and left him behind.

• • •

He wanted to speak with Kiriko. He remembered how she had listened with an intensity that matched his words. But her ties to Cassidy were a storm cloud sitting on the horizon. His other, safer refuge was — of course — Tina. She, too, was a fount of compassion, discretion, and good sense. His uncertainty about Kiriko and Cassidy decided him.

He called Tina from the office.

"Hi, Tina. Jason."

"Hi. Thanks for the ride last night."

"You're welcome. Listen, I was wondering. Can we get together and talk?"

"Doesn't sound good."

"No, no, it's fine. I need some advice from someone I trust. I need a friend."

"That's me," Tina said gamely.

Again in Tina's brother's truck, they headed for the cape. Unlike their last visit, Golly remained behind. She was having a bad day, too. They talked generalities in the car. By unspoken agreement, the big stuff could wait.

The half-hour walk warmed them. Tina had brought a blanket; like last time, they perched on the grassy knoll.

"So, there you have it," Jason said. "I don't know what to do. Or how to feel. I'm getting torn apart. Whichever way I go, someone's bound to be dissatisfied. It's a total no-win. What bothers me most is that he might be right — maybe you shouldn't meet your heroes. And the longer this goes on, the more she's taking on mythical proportions. What if I find Elizabeth's and hate her? I could go on this wild goose chase that alienates my father only to find that she's horrible. And that's *if* I find her. What if she doesn't want to meet *me*?"

"Jason...I know this is hard for you, but do you want to hear what I think?"

"Of course. That's why I called you."

"You're sure?"

"Waivers signed. Release duly given."

"First of all, didn't Dada tell you that she was a wonderful person?"

"Yes."

"Okay, so that's worry number one out of the way. You're either nice or you're not, you know what I mean?"

"Go on."

"And, she keeps calling Dada, right, even if sporadically?"

"Yes."

"So you know she's interested."

"Possibly."

"Well, if you ask me, I think your choice is obvious."

"Out with it."

"You have to go."

"Go?"

"To England. To find her. I mean, how can you *not*? If you don't find out everything you can, this is going to haunt you for the rest of your life. I know what you're like. There'll be so many unanswered questions and possible scenarios that you'll go out of your skull just trying to list them all. And, if you don't go, you'll resent Dada forever. If you ask me, you're already starting to feel that way."

"But what about a worst-case scenario and I hate her? Or I find out how terrific she is and I resent Dada even more for not telling me? The years we've lost. ...What will that do to Dada? To me? To Dada and me combined? And he's already told me that he equates any search as a personal rejection. That's what he's thinking, I know he is."

"You've got to realize, this isn't about Dada. It's about you. Dada had to know that your finding out was a possibility. I mean, he's been holding this inside for years. Didn't he even say that he meant to tell you earlier? I don't want to be too hard on him but isn't he being a trifle...manipulative?"

"What if I'd never known? I would have sailed through life quite happily, doing what I do, living as

I live, right? I mean, if I want to, I can still have that. All it requires is the will to do so. Nothing's changed if I don't change it."

"You should listen to yourself. Jason Chiron — ostrich. Do you honestly believe that?"

"I don't know *what* I believe. I'm just trying to think every scenario through."

"Well, that's good...devil's advocate is good. I thought you were just acting sorry for yourself for a minute."

"Ouch."

"Sorry," Tina said. "That was out of line."

They talked about another decision facing Jason, one he'd been mulling over since the day he'd confessed to Kiriko: telling Al. For all intents and purposes, Al has been his one and only mother and had been since Mum's death eighteen years ago. How would she react? Dada was right: things said could never be *un*said. Tina, true to her nature, urged him towards openness.

They'd been sitting in the same spot for some time and despite the blanket, it was getting cold. Needing to move, they headed for the beach. Naturally, the baby seal they'd seen last time was gone. Whether its mother had returned to reclaim it, whether it had swum off under its own power, or whether it had died and been taken by the tide, they'd never know.

• • •

"This has nothing to do with replacements, Dada. How could you think that? This is about origin and identity and being open for once." As with the last conversation, it wasn't going well. "Can I remind you that if you'd told me years ago, when I was a kid, like you said to me you should have, and then we wouldn't even be having this conversation? Listen, Dada, I'm sorry, but this is a problem created by you and Mum and Elizabeth — not me. I'm just trying to deal with it the best way I know how. I mean, come on…she called here how many times over the years, even after I was old enough to understand, and you never told me, not once…"

The older man flinched. "I'm sorry. I'm sorry…you're right. I understand that. Of course I understand that." He regained his composure a little and continued. "But, Jason, please…I wouldn't mind a little empathy or understanding too. You don't know what it was like losing Mum, what it's been like since. …I didn't want to lose you, as well."

Jason wanted to point out that Dada wasn't the only one who'd lost somebody important, but he managed to rein it in.

"Look. If you persist in trying to find Elizabeth, of course I can't stop you. But if you decide to go to England, I'm sorry, you're going to have to do it on your own. I don't want to go or have any part of it. Your decision, which I would respect, might be to go. But mine — which I would expect you to respect in return — is to stay. As far as I'm concerned, this is a chapter of my life — our lives — that I consider finished, and, to be perfectly honest, that I wish you'd consider finished as well." Dada's mouth tightened around his pipe. He turned to go.

"Dada, one more question: Where are Mum's old things?"

"What old things?"

"I remember you telling me that there were some boxes with her letters — keepsakes and stuff. We looked at them, I don't remember when, years ago. One Christmas, maybe."

"I don't know," said Dada.

"You must."

"I'm afraid I don't." Jason hated even considering the idea that...well, Dada could be lying.

With a perfunctory word to Ellery, Jason left the hotel. He was heading towards Mum's grave.

He sped north towards the hill behind St. Mary's Church where the Chiron family plot was located. Although neither of his parents were churchgoers, they'd still bought space there. "Hedging our bets," Dada winked.

Jason bought a large bouquet in Troy and then carried it up the rise overlooking Troy and its eponymous harbor behind. As a boy, Jason never understood why cemeteries had such scenic locations. Why not use these prime spots for houses or a park or school — something useful? Only recently had he realized that cemeteries were for the living. To make those left behind feel better about putting someone they loved into the ground.

The Chiron plot was for two, "a doublewide for the hereafter," Dada joked.

Engraved into the rough gray marble were his mother's name, her date of birth and death, and

Dada's name with his birthday and a blank space that always unsettled Jason. He swept the grave of leaves, and then carefully laid down the flowers. Mum had been cremated and reduced to ashes, her body stolen of the water and moisture that define life. Jason tried not to cry at her funeral. He wanted to "act like a man." But it hadn't worked. Just more life-affirming water.

He shut his eyes and came as close to praying as he ever did. Part of his ritual involved thanking Mum for his life. Now he had to edit it. He reaffirmed his love for her and, this time, asked for the wisdom to find his way through this maze of confusion.

The sun broke through and sent shafts of light onto the ocean, as beautiful as a scene from a movie. The wind blew cold on the exposed hillside, and Jason felt the chill. He imagined himself sitting in the hot springs or next to a fireplace inside the hotel. Or that he had someone to embrace and be embraced in return.

He stayed a while longer, bearing the cold, looking down at the town and the harbor behind it.

Chapter 8 iNovel Link
Music is naturally the lifeblood of the Hot Springs
Island Music Club. Go to the Chapter 8 iNovel Link at
www.HotSpringsNovel.com/chapter8/ to feel the
mood and listen.

Chapter 9

"You know, I'm not sure."

Jason spent the rest of Sunday on hotel business, and surfing the web.

A tap on the door revealed Al behind it. She seemed uncustomarily reserved.

"Can I talk to you?" Al asked.

"Of course."

She carried in an old cardboard box, and then checked the door twice before taking the other chair.

"What's in the box?"

"I'll get to that." She leaned over and placed a wrinkled hand on Jason's knee. "Jason, I have no right to be saying any of this, and perhaps I don't even have the right to be here right now. I know that. But, I've thought about it and thought about it and I decided I have to tell you. I overheard you and Dada talking in the dining room. I was in the kitchen and I heard everything."

"What exactly did you hear?" Jason asked.

"I heard everything, Jason. How you'd been adopted. And that a woman, Elizabeth— oh, Jason, you must be so upset. What a shock...you poor thing." She reached out for him. And that's when, inexplicably, uncontrollably, Jason started blubbering. Where it came from and how to stop it, he didn't know. He was twelve years old again and crying at his mother's funeral. Al comforted him, and finally, recovered but embarrassed, Jason managed to eke out a question about the box.

"Well, I heard you talking about your mother's box. The letters and keepsakes one." She folded her hands.

"And this is it?"

"This is it. I found it in the cellar. I thought you'd want it."

"Thank you, Al," Jason said.

"I'm one hundred percent with you on this, Jason. I think you should know everything and you should have been told long ago. I think you should have been told from the start. Being straight about these things is the only way to handle them. Believe me. I know."

He lowered his head with gratitude.

"I'll leave you alone with this stuff. Oh, and Jason?" He looked up from the box. "You won't tell your father I gave this to you, or that I know, will you?"

"I thought you wanted to be straight," said Jason.

"Don't be cheeky." She kissed him on the cheek.

Jason lugged the cardboard box to his room. The musty smell reminded Jason he'd opened it before — sometime after Mum died. He pulled out a handful of Christmas cards, some from friends but most of them hand-drawn by him. Dada had encouraged him to keep writing even after Mum's death. He'd done so until he was fifteen and too cool to continue.

There were letters too. Some were in envelopes, others merely folded. Jason also found old aerograms, their paper brittle and ink dulled. Since their chronology was haphazard, he skimmed for clues or connections to Elizabeth. He found a love letter from Dada to Mum after Dada's departure from Australia. But from Elizabeth there was nothing.

Jason separated everything into piles. On finding a book of old black and white photos his heart moved up-tempo until he discovered they were only old fishing trip shots. He kept one as a keepsake.

There were a dozen or so items left when he found it: a small color photo inside a plain unsealed envelope. A young woman with long straight dark hair atop a large stone on the rocky outcrop above the beachside hot springs. She had a beautiful complexion and luminous eyes that appeared clear and light brown in the fading color of the old photograph. She wore a cardigan, a white blouse beneath, and a long dark skirt which matched her hair. Her restrained smile reminded Jason of the *Mona Lisa*. He examined the photo minutely. Although impossible to say definitively, she looked pregnant. On the back, written in cursive pencil script was a single word: Elizabeth.

What did she look like now? How had time changed her? At the time of this photo, she was probably almost the same age as Jason now. He searched for a resemblance.

Jason wondered if Dada knew about this photo's existence. Maybe that was why he'd claimed not to know where the box was. He went through the last of the contents but found nothing more of real interest.

He also went through the discard pile again with the same result. As a next step, Jason would deliver the box to Al so she could return it. Al understood, Jason thought. She really got it. He wished Dada did too.

• • •

Jason faced his computer. Although abysmally ignorant of the subject or where to start, he knew that the Internet had sparked a new and widespread interest in genealogy; some said the web was the greatest tool in history for those seeking answers of their past. He started with two assumptions: that Elizabeth was alive and still in England — not much to go on.

The word "adoption" got 10.5 million results. Narrow it; he had to narrow it. He searched the phrase: "finding parents." There were 3,400 results. He tried a few hits but the first four were commercial agencies. He could always come back to those.

Next, he entered a genealogy forum. There were hundreds of messages on a vast array of bulletin boards. Desperation screamed from the headers: "My deadbeat dad doesn't want to be found"; "Desperately Seeking Sharon Wolestone"; "URGENT! Help needed in finding MISSING PERSON." Jason opened maybe twenty postings and not one — not one — had received a response. They were like unanswered screams in the night.

After an hour of fruitless searching, he grew despondent. He'd never realized how people were trying to adopt. Or that so many children lacked parents or families. The scale of the situation astonished him. It was like opening a door and behind it — instead of the small room you'd been expecting — you encountered a vast auditorium filled with lonely faces and upraised hands clamoring for attention.

Tired but determined, he tried other query strings with the same result. He needed more from Dada. At the very least he would get a last name and address.

• • •

Jason's persistent questions only upset Dada further. "Please, Jason...I told you, I'm ready to move on, and I wish you would, too. That's all I have to say about it." Jason was getting increasingly angry.

"Come over and talk," Tina said. "We'll have grilled-cheese sandwiches and tomato soup."

The food and place reminded Jason of high school. The crunch of the brown buttered toast, melted cheese and rich tomato aroma made him feel seventeen again. The walls of the smallish kitchen were still the same shade of yellow and were essentially hidden by decorative plates and plaques. The thought of an earthquake made Jason cringe. "I have nothing to do with this," Tina said. "Nothing! Nothing!"

Jason put down his spoon. "I just can't believe Dada's being so uncooperative. He's everyone's best friend except mine."

"Imagine what it's like for him, Jason," she said. "It's his worst nightmare. He's been absolutely dreading this for years and now it's finally happened.

He's probably feeling alone and alienated from the person he loves most in the whole world."

"I hate it when you're so reasonable," said Jason. "Where's the leftover self-righteousness disposal unit?"

Tina brushed some golden crumbs from her fingers. Then her eyes widened. She wanted to say something so badly she swallowed the rest of the sandwich in one go.

"Listen, I've got an idea," she said, spitting one or two crumbs.

"Got what?" Her excitement was infectious.

"The hotel records! What about the hotel records? If your dad's kept the old guest registers, then she's got to be in there somewhere. Is there any chance he still has them? Do you know?"

The idea had merit. Jason thought hard. "Al's the person to ask. Dada keeps the recent ones stored in the cellar. And he's a bit of a pat rack too so, yeah, maybe there is a chance."

"Go for it," said Tina. She was feeling quite pleased with herself. Jason was so pleased with her, too — so much so, in fact, he leaned over and gave her a cheesy kiss. For a moment she fell quiet. But then, quickly, her expression changed, like she was working out something new.

"But, wait a second. Okay, imagine you find out where she is, where she lives and stuff…"

"Uh huh."

"Have you decided what you're going to do about it?"

"I've thought about this a lot since we last talked," said Jason. "A lot."

"And?"

"I'm thinking about going after her. To England, I mean."

"Don't forget Dianna's in London. You could stay with her." Dianna was Tina's twin sister. Making use of her mother's Scottish heritage, Dianna had a British passport and was working in London. "What's stopping you?"

Before they could say anything more, the phone rang.

"Mum's expecting a call," Tina said. "Something about Saturday." Tina's mother ran the local thrift store and helped manage Troy's popular weekly outdoor market.

Jason left for the equally cluttered washroom. On the way he tried to recollect seeing any old hotel records. Again, the best strategy was to ask Al.

When he re-entered the kitchen Tina was hanging up. Minutes ago her face had shone with delight. Now it was grim.

"What is it? What happened?"

"That was Cristine. Angel's taken off again." They jumped into the car, heading for Cristine's.

• • •

"We had another fight. That's all we've been doing lately," Cristine said. On the couch, Layla made herself invisible listening to the grownup talk.

"Layla and I went shopping and when we got back we found this note." Still pacing, still smoking, she gestured towards a paper on the table.

> *I can't take it anymore. I can't take you or your bitchiness or your yelling anymore. And I know you don't want me here anyway. I've gone away before so what's one more time. And don't bother looking for me cause I don't want you to find me. What's the point?*
> *— Angel*

"She keeps saying that there's nothing I can do now that she's legal."

"Should we call the police?" asked Tina.

"No. Not yet. I'm not ready. I don't want to complicate things," replied Cristine.

"Where did she go last time?" asked Tina.

"All over the place, from what I can gather. Victoria. Up-island. Vancouver. She was gone almost three months. And came back pregnant."

"How did she go — I mean how's she traveling? Has she got transportation? Cash?"

"She's got her little scooter. I don't know about money."

"We could check the ferry terminals and see if the scooter's there," Jason suggested.

"I think she's scared and angry and doesn't know where to go," said Tina. "I don't think this is a well-thought-out plan or anything. I think she'd go to someone she'd trust. A friend's."

"But you know what worries me?" Cristine said. "It's what happens if we find her."

"I don't understand," said Tina.

"It's just going to be more of the same. We can't get along. I can't stand seeing her throwing her life away and she can't stand me saying it. I can't bear it — she reminds me too much of myself. She says she wants the baby on the one hand but then she smokes and drinks like she couldn't care one way or the other. God — I love her so much it's killing me…"

Layla said something for the first time. "I think I know where she is."

Tina used her calmest voice. "Where do you think that might be, Layla?"

"Cassidy's. I heard her talking to him yesterday on the phone."

They thought about calling but Tina and Jason volunteered to go instead.

They pulled up beside the barn with its worn wooden walls and red trim. A little Honda scooter, also red, was parked just inside the barn doors. In terms of hiding Angel's presence, the execution seemed sloppy. Perhaps Cassidy planned it this way.

"So. Now what? Call Cristine and let her deal with it? Go talk to them? Talk to Cassidy alone? I'm not sure what our role here is."

"We're going to have to decide pretty quick," Tina said. "Look." Cassidy walked out the front door.

"Hello brother! Hello sister!" He was smiling with outstretched arms. "I think a group hug might be the first order of business."

"Why don't we go for a walk?" They moved down past the barn into the field, not far from where Cristine and Angel had quarreled so bitterly. Turning the corner, he saw Angel looking out the window.

"Cris sent you, I bet," said Cassidy. "And, to answer your question, yes, she's here. And she's all right. She's fine," said Cassidy.

"That's a relief," Tina said.

"But she doesn't want to go home and I don't want you to try and persuade her. She's very upset and, if you ask me, she doesn't know what she wants. She's angry at Cristine; she thinks she's acting like a hypocrite. Parent-child baggage," said Cassidy. "And there's more."

"I'm sure there must be," Tina said.

"There's a lot I can't talk about, things that Angel's asked me not to say. I promised not to."

"Of course."

"And Angel's going to stay here?" Tina asked.

"For a while at least," said Cassidy. "I think we've got to take things one day at a time. She's very fragile now and I don't think we should force anything. Just when you got here I was trying to convince her to at least call Cris and let her know where she is. It's been tough going though…"

"What do we tell Cristine?" asked Tina.

"I'll call her if Angel won't," said Cassidy. "Just give me a bit more time."

Their mission, at least for now, seemed accomplished. Angel was safe. The immediate crisis was averted. In fact, it had been somewhat anticlimactic.

Cassidy hugged them goodbye and returned to the house.

"Give me your phone, Jason. I'm calling Cristine." As Tina punched the number, Cassidy opened the door and yelled, "Jason! Tina! Get in here! *QUICK!*"

They ran to the door. "What's happening? What's wrong?" For once, the light had departed Cassidy's eyes.

"She's tried to hang herself. Call an ambulance — omigod omigod—" She was lying on the bed, a silk tie now loose around her neck. Cassidy had managed to lift her down from a hook on the bedroom wall. She was barely breathing. Except for the angry welt on her neck, she was white. Her medical training kicking in, Tina took charge. Jason called 911 while Cassidy bent over Tina and Angel, willing her, commanding the girl to live. By the time the ambulance arrived, Angel was revived. She sobbed weakly that she wanted to die. Over and over she repeated that she didn't want to live, that she had no reason to continue living. Jason phoned Cristine. He was sure the pounding of his heart was louder than his voice.

Chapter 9 iNovel Link

Please go to **www.HotSpringsNovel.com/chapter9/** for a list of interactive links concerning adoption. Some are informative. Some are heartbreaking. Please be prepared.

Chapter 10

*"Being here, the reason we're here,
it's all been making me think."*

By now everyone in the hotel knew of yesterday's events but the news this morning was uncertain. The prognosis for Angel and child remained unclear.

It was late morning before Jason and Dada managed to leave for the hospital. Each felt a mixture of grief and tension. They sought words of comfort in preparation for seeing Cristine and Angel. They could find none that weren't hopelessly clichéd or inadequate.

Cristine's supporters filled the waiting room. Her sister was apparently arriving from Alberta. Cristine and Layla were with Angel at the moment but no other visitors were permitted. Everyone spoke quietly, and the invisible veil of sadness hung over the room. After a while, Jason felt the need to separate himself from the crowd if even for only a moment.

Jason spotted her sitting on a chair by herself at the far end of the hall. It was Kiriko. As Jason went towards her, two things happened. Dada emerged from the waiting room behind him, while Cristine and Layla exited Angel's room from a door halfway down the hall between Jason and Kiriko.

Jason, Dada, Cristine and Layla came together like cold travelers around a fire. Cristine broke down instantly. Jason could feel Layla's small arms clutching him, seeking solace, seeking anything. Cristine spoke first.

"She lost the baby, Jason, Dada. ...She lost the baby." Wracked again with tears, Cristine stopped speaking.

"Shh, shh," said Dada.

"Angel's going to be okay, she's strong and she'll pull through...but—" Layla's normally blonde complexion was red and streaked. She looked up at Jason as if for answers, but he had none to give. They moved to the waiting room where Cristine and her daughter were engulfed in the arms of their other friends. By this time, Kiriko had made her way to the waiting room. Cassidy had been back and forth all night.

Jason felt physically ill. Despite Dada's attempts to be strong, it was obvious he'd been affected badly, too. "Dada, sit down," Jason urged.

Cristine was exhausted. Finally, at gentle but insistent urging, she agreed to be taken home with Layla to rest. Jason and Dada volunteered to stay at the hospital. After more tears, another round of hugs, Jason and Dada were alone.

A large window dominated one end of the waiting room. Local scenes of sailboats at anchor decorated the room in an attempt to make it cheery. So much bad news was heard here. So much hardship endured. "Dada..."

"Yes, son?"

"Being here, the reason we're here, it's all been making me think."

"Me, too."

"I've been thinking how precious life is, how easy it is to lose it."

"You don't have to say anything...I understand."

"No, I don't think you do," said Jason. "You see, Dada, I've just realized, I mean really realized. I have to go."

"Go where?" asked Dada.

"Go after her. It's something I have to do."

"Jason, no, not here, not now. Please—"

"But don't you see, I have to go? Having your blessing would make the world of difference to me."

Dada turned so they were face-to-face, with only inches separating them. But where Jason had expected either Dada's continuing opposition or perhaps, at last, some measure of understanding, was a look of pained incomprehension.

"Jason—" Dada said, his façade of strength crumbling. "Don't go, please don't go." His voice broke. "I've already lost your mother. I'm begging you. I'm begging you..."

Only then did Jason notice Kiriko sitting quietly, not far away from them, the sun from the blinds alighting on her face and illuminating a single teardrop in one of her remarkable eyes.

Chapter 10 iNovel Link
The Chapter 10 iNovel Link is a written one, about perspective, about how one person's view differs from the rest and puts things in a different light – the Rashomon phenomenon. Please go to **www.HotSpringsNovel.com/chapter10/** if you would like to read excerpts from Angel's diary.

PART II

BATH, ENGLAND,
UNITED KINGDOM

Chapter 11

*"Regardless of how tenuous our bonds,
we seem to feel the need to congregate."*

A dark limousine bus carried them to the airport. Jason watched Tina and Kiriko's reflections in the semitransparent glass. They walked through the terminal to the check-in counter. As they did, an old man in a fluorescent orange baseball cap barged in front of them. He looked like a madcap professor, with white frizzy wings of hair protruding from the sides of his cap, as he shouted for his wife to "hurry up goddammit" because "we can't let nobody get in front of us." Jason had to admire his singularity of purpose. It's not the meek who shall inherit the earth, he thought — it's the pushy ones in orange caps.

They moved to the soundtrack of planes roaring over runways. Kiriko stood back to let Jason hug Tina, who embraced him and then kissed him on both cheeks with enough force to make him step back.

Jason wanted the hug with Kiriko to last. He tried to sear every detail of the moment into his memory so that he could draw on it later. As he held her, she whispered in his ear: "Be successful in your search." Then she handed him a white envelope the size of a large Christmas card, which Jason put in his jacket pocket. Their calls of "Bon voyage" and "Take care" followed him into the security zone, and then they were gone.

There was the usual forgettable film and a tasteless

meal. They flew east, away from the sun, into the darkening sky and the hours that had already disappeared ahead of them. Cabin lights were dimmed and the plane was silent. The constant whoosh of the brawny engines on the wings was reassuring, however, and the only sound, until Jason's seatmate spoke, her first words since a brief initial exchange when boarding.

"So...where are you headed? Oh, that's a silly question, isn't it? You're going to London." She laughed pleasantly. "I suppose I meant is that your final destination?" Jason tried to guess her age. Around Al's, he supposed. A distinctly Irish voice.

"Yes, London for me. How about you?"

"Just a brief stopover to change planes. I'll be on my way to Dublin shortly thereafter. That is, if my bags all arrive," she laughed. "They didn't on the way out, you know, although I did finally get them in the end. First time in my life without a lot of baggage." Her laugh carried over the engines.

"Were you in Vancouver on holiday?" Jason asked.

"No, I was there for a funeral, actually."

"Oh." Now he'd done it. "I'm sorry to hear that."

She was silent for a moment. "Yes. My sister."

"I'm so sorry." A single platitude was the best he could manage.

"No, no, never you mind. We haven't seen each other in years and we weren't that close, if truth be told. But still, we felt the need to congregate. Family and friends, I mean."

Anxious to change a subject that seemed too raw

for so early an acquaintance, Jason asked what she did in Dublin.

"I teach and do research — if one can use such a grandiose word for reading what I please and occasionally writing about it — at Trinity College. I suppose one could say I'm a sociologist."

"In what area? What do you read and write about?"

"Oh, you're the one for the questions, aren't you? You remind me of some of my more inquisitive students." She laughed her bright laugh again. "Well, I suppose I have a number of interests, as befits an eclectic, intellectual gourmand," she said, her eyes gleaming like the departing sun on the plane's wing. "Of late I've become interested in social ecology, how social systems evolve and their role in shaping human society and framework. Doesn't that sound terribly boring?"

"Not at all. What is it all about?"

"Are you sure you want to hear about this?"

"Absolutely!"

"Well, in the first stage of our social development, our environments determined everything: where we lived, what we ate and how we perceived the world and interacted. But, once we were able to conquer those geographical factors, we were able to reach the next stage where our societies emphasized time and tradition. Thanks to technology, we're now on a different plateau where we seem bent on digitally recreating all those things I mentioned — the environment, time, tradition — as we start living more and more in our heads through our computer screens. Previously, we tried to dominate our environment, but now we just ignore it — like everyone on this plane. We've gone one step further in eliminating our connection with nature. We've literally put ourselves above our environment. Oh — but listen to me. I'm going on and on like some boring old...university lecturer! Ha ha ha ha."

Jason was fascinated. Recently, the pendulum of his life had swung over so far to the emotional from the intellectual that he relished this kind of theorizing. "So are you suggesting it'll get worse?"

"Have you read that wonderful story by E.M. Forster, called *The Machine Stops*?"

"No, I haven't."

"Well, read it if you can. Forster was amazingly prescient — he essentially foresees the Internet. To simplify the story, Forster's Machine evolves until it becomes society's central controlling force. People lie sedentary in chairs, looking up at the screen and talking to the Machine. There's no physical contact and all the senses are devalued. No touching. No love or sex or any of that delicious stuff which makes us people, for better or worse. Surely that's the ultimate tragedy.

"I read somewhere that touch can increase premature babies' weight, and heal the immune system, and reduce heart disease—" She stopped. Something had grabbed her attention.

She leaned towards Jason and spoke in a conspiratorial whisper. "Remember when I was saying what a shame it would be if we became so isolationist and removed from other people that love and sex and warmth disappeared?"

"Yes," Jason whispered, feeling like part of some secret society and wondering where she was headed.

"Well, if that happened, then we'd miss out on things like that." The professor pointed up the aisle with her chin.

"Like what?"

"Like that." She repeated the gesture. Jason craned but still could see nothing.

"What is it? I can't see," he whispered.

"There, the toilet. Look at the door. Watch the door and you'll soon see what I mean."

Jason watched and waited. "What is it?"

"Be patient, young man," was all she said.

Perhaps five minutes passed. Then the door opened and a woman in her early twenties stepped out.

"There," said Jason's seat companion.

"What? I still don't get it."

"Just a moment longer." The older woman leaned back in her seat, apparently very satisfied.

After another minute or so he received his reward. The very same toilet door opened but this time it was the face of a young man that appeared. He poked his head out, looked quickly around and then hurried back toward the rear of the aircraft. The professor was shaking with glee.

"The Mile High Club has just welcomed its two newest members." Jason and the professor laughed, so hard, in fact, they woke up several other passengers.

"But, oh dear, we've just shared a wonderful

moment and I haven't even properly introduced myself. I'm Fiona Morton." She held out her hand.

"Jason Chiron. From Hot Springs Island, British Columbia." Her students must adore her, Jason thought.

"And what do you do on the attractive-sounding Hot Springs Island, Mr. Jason Chiron?" That twinkle again.

"Well, I've just moved back there. From Vancouver. I'm a web developer, a designer."

"Ahhhh," was all Professor Morton said. Jason felt compelled to fill the pause.

"But I'll be traveling to Bath," he said. Professor Morton remained silent, letting Jason choose how to proceed.

"To...well...to look for my mother. My birth mother. I've just found out I was adopted and I'm going to see if I can find her." He felt a fool the moment the words were out. Once or twice on the bus in his Vancouver commuting days he'd been on the receiving end of some poor soul blurting their life story to him, a complete stranger.

"Listen, I'm sorry. I must sound ridiculous and—"

"No, not at all. And I think I should tell *you* something. A mutual confession, if you will. I'm adopted as well," said Professor Morton. "My sister, the one who just died, well, she was adopted, too."

"Excuse me for asking, but you said the two of you weren't close. Could the fact that you were adopted have anything to do with it?" Jason was thinking about how he might have brothers and sisters and what might become of them after they discovered each other.

"Who can tell," she replied, the jovial expression leaving her face, for the first time. "It could be the reason, I suppose, or one of them. But it also may not be. I know estranged natural brothers and sisters as well. I suspect we all do."

"True," Jason said.

"But, listen, is there anything I can help with on my side of the Atlantic? I'd be glad to."

"Well, this might not be exactly what you meant, but please tell me about your birth parents. Did you ever search for them? Or find them?"

"No, Jason. My parents were killed in a fire and I was taken in by a foster family, friends of my parents, actually. It was all arranged through the church. I was not quite five, and I don't remember much about my real parents or really much about anything at that time, I'm sorry to say. I was the only child. Of my natural parents, I mean." She paused.

"But, when I was talking about helping you, I meant on the practical side — are you sure there isn't something I can do or find out for you?" Professor Morton asked.

Jason considered her offer. "Thank you. That's very kind. There's nothing that I can think of, off-hand, but here's my number in London. I'm staying with a friend." Jason wrote Dianna's number on a page from his day planner. "I'm not sure how long I'll be there. I'm planning on heading west, to Bath. I think that's where my mother lives." Those four words struck him as startling and unreal. His mother used to be dead but now she's alive. *Where my mother lives.*

• • •

They bid farewell in the plane's crowded aisle. As her tweed back moved off in the direction of the transit area, Jason headed towards immigration and wondered if he'd ever see her again. How many people does one meet during a lifetime and how many are remembered?

Jason sailed through immigration before collecting his guitar, his backpack and another suitcase. Customs went equally smoothly. Even better, he found Dianna waiting when he emerged. That Dianna and Tina were identical twins had always given Jason a start. To have left this face on one side of the world and then arrive to a perfect replica on the other was surreal.

On the Paddington Heathrow Express into central London, Jason filled Dianna in on Hot Springs life. They talked about Tina and their parents, and finally about Jason's discovery of Elizabeth. In sidebars he told her about Golly, about Al, about Human Designs and quitting — even Kevin and Phillip, people Dianna knew of but had never met. Dee Dee he mentioned only casually, almost as an aside, and Kiriko not at all. Kiriko could wait. As he thought of her, he remembered her envelope in his inside pocket, which he patted. Stored away in the plane's overhead compartment, he couldn't easily access it on the plane. He'd read it later, alone.

On their way to Camden Town and Dianna's flat, Jason felt a continued sense of disbelief — he was actually in England, starting the search for his mother.

"How long have you been here now?" Jason asked.

"God," Dianna said. "It's been almost seven years. Art school and now two years as an account exec. It's amazing how quickly it goes." She'd picked up a slight British accent

"And you're happy here?"

She didn't answer immediately.

"Sure…" she said. "I mean England's great. London's great. You know what Samuel Johnson said, right? When a person's tired of London, they're tired of life. Anyway, you're welcome to stay as long as you like."

"Thanks, but I want to try and get to Bath as soon as I can."

Although her basement flat was in a long line of row houses, the living room's large picture window brightened the room and gave it an undeserved sense of spaciousness. A small vestibule opened onto the dining room to the right and the living room to the left, where Jason would sleep. Dianna's bedroom at the back completed the layout.

Jason was dying for a shower but the tiny bathroom contained only a bath. His years at the hotel's hot springs made him dislike traditional Western baths. The idea of soaking in your own dirty water seemed entirely counterproductive; he washed first, and then ran the water painfully hot and slid in.

Ahhh, the warmth, the enveloping luxury...the fatigue of his long journey dissipated. As usual, the heat also quickened his pulse and made his heart pound against his chest. Naturally, he thought of Hot Springs and all the baths he'd taken. For most people, bathing is solitary. By contrast, Jason's life had been measured by those he'd bathed with.

Jason's head suddenly banged against the tub, waking him. He toweled off brusquely, unsure of how long he'd been soaking. Outside the bathroom, the smell of garlic and tomato sauce wafted through the hall.

"What brought you to England, Dianna — I mean, you could have studied at Emily Carr or wherever you wanted." Jason popped a piece of garlic bread into his mouth.

"Besides the obvious lure of living abroad and all that, what it really came down to was getting away from home. I mean, sure, I wanted to get off the island and away from small town life, but the real reason was my parents."

"What was going on?"

"It's hardly unique. I was tired of them — of anyone, really — telling me what and what not to do and trying to run my life. I hated their conservatism and the constant worrying about money. They don't know how to be happy. They probably can't even spell the word. C'mon Jason, *you* know what they're like. All they care about is what other people think. How'd you like to grow up with that all the time? I mean, look at you. Dada and Mary were so totally cool. I must have wished I'd had your parents a hundred times." The words barely out of her mouth, Dianna realized what she'd said. "Oh...I'm sorry, Jason. I didn't think...I'm acting like Tina." Tina had always been the more incautious of the two.

"Don't worry about it," Jason said. "I haven't gotten used to this adoption thing yet, either."

He noticed Dianna's hair was the same length and style as Tina's. When first dating Tina, Jason had read several stories about the closeness of identical twins, even when they were separated.

The phone rang and Dianna picked up. Five seconds into the call, her expression changed and she turned away from Jason. Dianna hurried to the bedroom and shut her door. With the stereo on, Jason could hear nothing. He guessed it was a guy. On her return, Dianna chose not to acknowledge the call and Jason directed the conversation towards the safety of old times and his plans for the next few days.

Despite his fatigue, Jason had trouble sleeping. Light from the streetlamps slithered in under the living-room curtains. Tires scrunched on pavement accompanied by the occasional footsteps of passersby. A dog barked at an emergency vehicle in the distance.

Suddenly, it came to him. Kiriko's unread note was still in his pocket. Clicking on the lamp, he retrieved it. The envelope was thicker than a normal letter or card. There was a reason. Inside he found a letter and four smaller envelopes, a bit like a Russian doll. The main note was written on thick paper the color of clotted cream, in a beautiful hand, as might be expected from an artist of her caliber.

Dear Jason,

Since the day of our drive, when you told me your secret, I had many things I wanted to say. Also, on that day when we sat in the waiting room of the hospital with your father. Then, too, I had many things I wanted to say. But I couldn't say anything then, either.

Now that you are gone, I can say one thing. That, even if you must go against your loving father, the decision to embark on your search is just and good and true. You must find your own truth and embrace it for there is no other but one's own. I can understand that more than you can know.

In this letter, I give you four more letters. Whenever you want to remember the people on Hot Springs Island who care for you, please open one. I hope it will make you remember and I hope it will make you happy.

Kiriko

• • •

Jason woke to the sound of water running in the bathroom; aspiring to be Guest of the Year, he was up and had the sofa bed stored before Dianna emerged. Soon after, the phone rang and Dianna again took it in the bedroom. It wasn't even 7:30.

After she left for work, Jason set out on a quick tour of the neighborhood. Walking helped him think and he'd write everything down when he returned.

The whole day was his and he had plenty of time to refine his strategy for finding Elizabeth.

He went halfway up the Parkway. He traversed Camden High Street and next De Lancey. He strolled through Regent's Park with the white classical residences of Cumberland Terrace in the background. Next were the Camden Locks and the market — already bustling by 10 a.m.

Sipping from a cup of steaming tea in a local café, Jason reread Kiriko's note. Outside the window, people walked by him on their way to work and school. A thought arose: I'm one of them. I'm actually English. Not Canadian. These are my bloodlines. On first learning of his adoption, Jason considered the ramifications of his newfound heritage in terms of immediate family — never once did he expand it to include nationality or culture. It was head-spinning stuff.

. . .

Dianna recommended the double-decker bus rather than the tube as cheaper and more entertaining; views from the top were terrific, she said. Jason, laptop safe inside his padded backpack, was heading for Trafalgar Square where he intended to get online in a wireless zone he'd researched before leaving.

Something else had happened prior to Jason's departure. Al had hit the jackpot. "I found them, Jason. They were in the basement — the records go right back. They were in a bunch of boxes behind some old furniture. I had to do a lot of dragging and digging, but I found them." She laughed, almost dizzy with satisfaction.

"You're *amazing*!" Jason said. "The absolute *best*!" He grabbed her.

"Stop it, you," she said, pushing him away. Trying to suppress a smile, Al removed a slip of paper from her apron pocket. "I left the actual register in your room so you can look at it in private. But here's the relevant information. I'm afraid there's not that much.

"Her name was Elizabeth Barnett and she listed her address as Bath, England. That's all. No street number or anything — no phone number either. Here's the date she arrived, about five months before you were born." She pressed the paper into his hand.

He stared at Elizabeth's handwriting. Like the puzzles they'd done as a family in the lounge on long winter nights, the pieces were starting to form a coherent picture. He had her full name, her photo, her town. He now had something substantial to work with.

He found the guest register under a pile of laundry on his bed. Al reveled in this cloak and dagger stuff. As suggested, there wasn't much to go on. Elizabeth Barnett's entry consisted solely of her name, a date, and a place written neatly in fountain pen. Jason considered getting it analyzed. He also considered next steps: more detailed Net searching, of course, and possibly private detectives.

Settled inside the cybercafé, Jason copied his search string looking for recent additions to Elizabeth

Barnetts in Bath, England. His first stab brought a manageable 170 results. Using Boolean logic and trial and error, he reduced the number to 49. He'd be able to check them all.

Among his finds was a woman of the same name who'd ridden round England on a horse. Another was a young woman on a dating site. Some were too young, some too old. One candidate he ruled out because she spelled her name Elisabeth, which sent him scurrying back to the register to check. But, no, it was as he thought. One Elizabeth Barnett was a teacher who'd just retired. Another was a professor of nursing. There was a biochemist and a librarian. He had leads. As he made notes and added flags to names and dates, he pictured the reunion meeting in which he'd become whole again. He stopped writing and sat up. That was it. When Dada had severed their biological connection, some part of him had been amputated. A hunk had been whacked from his core.

By the time Jason emerged, evening had almost arrived. He walked through Trafalgar Square, staring up at Nelson's column and sat for a few moments next to Lutyen's lions and fountains. Having only eaten some cookies and muffins washed down by numerous cups of coffee, Jason was famished. With Dianna busy, he'd been planning to eat dinner out anyway. Luckily, he met some American travelers wandering like himself and they linked up for an Indian dinner. Jason enjoyed the meal and the company. Forgetting himself and his mission even for a few hours refreshed him.

Back in Camden Town, Jason let himself in with Dianna's extra key. The flat was quiet. Shoes in the entrance and closed bedroom door meant that Dianna had beaten him home and was already in bed. As quietly as possible, Jason brushed his teeth and retired. Rare for him, Jason was wrapped by the warm blanket of sleep remarkably quickly.

The next day brought more research mixed with sightseeing. Jason started calling names on the list but he got nowhere at first. Although he felt intrusive and awkward during his first few calls, by the time he'd definitely eliminated ten names, Jason was already starting to feel more comfortable with the respectful but dogged approach that seemed most effective in getting people to talk. He wrote postcards to Kiriko and Tina (separately) and Dada and Al (together).

Pleased with his day's accomplishments, he rewarded himself with a trip to the British Museum on Great Russell Street across from a college of the University of London.

While gawking at an example of Egyptian funerary archaeology in one of the Roxie Walker Galleries, Jason was slightly startled when a tall, spectacled man with dark hair and a beard spoke to him.

"There's an amazing amount to look at, isn't there?" His accent was English and educated. Physically, he was very thin with broad shoulders. At first, something about the man's appearance unsettled him. Unable to figure out why, he shrugged it off.

"I know what you mean," Jason said. "In some ways it's almost too much."

"I've been coming here every lunchtime for fifteen years and I still feel that way," said the man.

"You must know every nook and cranny by now."

"I suppose so. Although I've never really thought of it in those terms. You see, I'm very interested — some might even say, fascinated — by antiquity and history. Everything in the world that's come before us. Through all of this," he swept his hands around, expansively, "we have an unbroken link to the past. It's like a vast, encyclopedic, three-dimensional diary of the human experience. This is what we thought, this is how we acted, this is what we believed." The tall man continually looked round as he talked. His absorption with antiquity was compelling. The power of the past seemed suddenly more present and apparent.

"This particular limestone example," he said, "was probably placed in or near the family shrine as a way of ensuring fertility and a safe birth." The carving stood some twenty centimeters tall and ten wide. Particularly touching was the protective arm of the mother around her child. Face tranquil, the mother looked at peace knowing her child was lying safe beside her.

They were bent over another Egyptian object when the man suddenly straightened. "Wait a moment...Didn't you say your name was Jason?"

"That's right."

"Well, perhaps you might be interested...several items in the museum, three or four if I'm not mistaken, deal with the myth of Jason and the Odyssey. Is that whom you're named after?"

Truth told, Jason knew nothing of his name's origins. His adoption threw the whole thing into question. How had he actually received his name? Had Elizabeth chosen it? Or what of the opposite — perhaps Elizabeth had named him differently and he wasn't Jason at all. These were revelations. At every turn his past grew more convoluted. Even something as fundamental as his name was up for grabs.

"Yes, yes. I'd like that very much. Thank you."

The first Jason-related item they examined was a marble relief of a physician and patient that bore no connection whatsoever to Homer's character. The next was a pen and wash drawing by Pietro da Cortona of the Homeric Jason with his mother, Medea, as they attempted to remove the Golden Fleece from the branches of a tree without waking the sleeping dragon below. Several dodgy background characters were performing inexplicable actions including playing the violin — hardly a clever move in the vicinity of a sleeping dragon. The real Jason laughed at how anguished and, well, unathletic, his highly stylized namesake looked. But before Jason could comment, his erudite guide looked at his watch.

"I'm sorry. I must be going. My lunch hour's over."

"But—" Jason said, looking for words of thanks.

"Yes?"

"Well, thank you," he said. "What a wonderful introduction to the past, mythology, and any number of other topics. I can't tell you how much I appreciate your time."

"Not at all." He appeared pleased at the compliment; a shy man warmed by kind words.

Before the moment became awkward, Peter raised a hand and walked off. That's when it struck Jason. Something had thrown him off when they'd first met but now he knew — he was a taller, thinner, bearded version of himself. "That could be me ten years from now," he thought. Again, he wondered about siblings and other long-lost relatives.

His look-alike's departure made Jason feel very alone. Although his first few days in London had been busy and interesting, he knew he'd have enjoyed everything more with a companion. With their shared connections to Tina and home, Jason had expected an instant friend in Dianna. He vowed to work harder at rekindling that friendship.

On Jason's return Dianna's bedroom door was closed again but he could hear her on the phone. Murmurs wafted forth but no distinguishable words. As Jason drifted off after rereading Kiriko's note, he thought he heard sounds from Dianna's room that sounded less like words and more like crying.

At breakfast Dianna seemed chipper enough, and they discussed Jason's agenda for the day: more phone calls and another tourist spot. Although Dianna informed Jason how to get inexpensive theater tickets, she declined to join him in the West End. She seemed stressed and distracted. Perhaps he was imposing. He had yet to set a departure date for Bath. He'd been hoping to firm his plans and narrow his leads while at Dianna's, but now he was beginning to doubt his welcome. Best to leave sooner rather than later.

Once more, Jason divided his time between Dianna's and the cybercafé. After eliminating fifteen more possibilities and finding five new leads, he headed home early. He'd try and snag Dianna for dinner in Camden Town. Despite good intentions, Jason learned his plan was flawed only seconds after entering the flat.

An empty bottle of wine, two glasses, and some half-finished snacks announced the presence of another visitor. The stereo was playing and the volume was up — but not nearly loud enough. Patently audible from the back bedroom were the unmistakable sounds of a man and woman making love. He departed as quietly as he could. Once more, loneliness nipped at his heels. So, a solo dinner in Camden Town. He hated eating alone and hoped this wouldn't become his English lot.

By the time he returned to the flat after a post-dinner stroll and two pints at the lively pub on the corner, Dianna's partner had left. Traces of Ghost Lover had been wiped clean, and Dianna was in the bath. When she emerged from the bathroom and said hello, Jason tried reading her expression. Did she have that glow, that aura? All she looked was tired.

She made herbal tea and they recounted their respective days. That's when she remembered.

"Oh Jason! There was a message for you. On the machine."

"From Canada?" Jason's heart went "thud." Not Dada, please. Or bad news about Angel.

"No, no. Someone from Ireland. Here. I'll play it for you."

A beep and then: "Good afternoon. My name is Fiona Morton calling from Dublin. I'm trying to reach Mr. Jason Chiron from Canada. Jason, I have a lead about Bath that I think you might find intriguing." She gave her number, repeated it and asked Jason to call back.

He was glad and intrigued. It was too late to phone tonight, of course. He'd try first thing tomorrow.

"You can call from here, Jason. Long distance rates are nothing these days, ridiculously cheap from home but a fortune from a public phone."

"Thanks."

"I hope you don't mind that I listened to the message but I couldn't help it…and… So, what do you think it's about? An interesting lead, she said. Do you think it's about your mother — your birth mother?"

"I wish I knew. She's someone I met on the plane. A professor in Dublin. An amazing person, I might add. She's adopted, herself."

"I hope it's good news."

"So do I. I don't think she's the type who'd have called unless it was important."

Dianna scrunched her eyes at him, "Are you okay? I haven't seen much of you, I'm afraid, and I know you must be going through a lot. A new country, the whole adoption thing. But I want you to know that you don't have to make yourself scarce, you know."

"Don't worry about it," Jason said. "I've been getting a lot done and enjoying London." He began his story about the British Museum but, not long in, he noticed Dianna seemed distracted. He changed the subject.

"What about tomorrow night? Are you free for dinner? I'd like to take you out and show my appreciation."

"Oh, that's not necessary," she said, her hair and eyes identical to Tina's. "But, no, I'm sorry. I've got a company thing, a dinner, on. That's the PR world, I'm afraid."

"Of course, no problem," Jason said — but didn't really mean it.

Not long after, they said good night.

Jason spent a long time getting comfortable. Like most sofa beds, the mattress was about as comfortable as a stack of manila envelopes. The frame rubbed and poked Jason's boniest parts and the whole apparatus seemed an elaborate, but cleverly successful, sleep-deprivation experiment.

He thought about Professor Morton's message and reference to an "interesting lead." Had she actually discovered something about Elizabeth? Finally, his racing mind slowed down enough for sleep to catch up.

• • •

Jason and Dianna shared their morning ritual: coffee, toast, fruit and conversation.

After Dianna's departure for Bloomsbury, Jason had some time before he could phone Fiona in

Dublin. He tried writing in his journal but couldn't concentrate. He checked his notes and leads, and then left for a newspaper and a walk in Regent's Park.

He called exactly at 9:30. "Professor Morton… It's good to talk to you. This is Jason Chiron calling from London."

"Jason! How nice to hear your voice. How's your trip been so far?"

"Very good, thank you. Excellent, in fact. But I still haven't made it to Bath. Which is partially why I'm calling. Thank you for the message."

"Oh, not at all. I'm sorry I missed you yesterday."

"I was a little surprised to hear from you. I was wondering — does this have anything to do with my mother?"

"No, I'm sorry, no, not directly. And, yes, of course you must have been wondering all night what I was calling about. I apologize for sounding so mysterious. I have a job introduction for you. Not that I'm sure you even want one, mind you. But I was talking to some colleagues here in Dublin and the friend of an acquaintance of mine is moving to Bath to take over a small publishing house there. He's looking for a web designer or developer or something. Anyway, they need someone who's familiar with the States and the technology and I thought of you."

"That's very kind of you," Jason said.

"Well, of course I wasn't sure if you were even interested in working in Bath or not but it just seemed too apropos not to tell you about."

"Yes," he kept his voice from sounding disappointed, "it sounds amazing." The thought of working in Bath or anywhere on this trip hadn't occurred to him.

"The chap who's going over to run it is named, wait a moment, Seamus Healey, and my friend suggested you give him a call since he's the one who'll be doing any hiring."

"Seamus Healey? Like the Nobel Prize winner? The poet?"

She laughed. "No, no, that's Seamus Heaney. Seamus is quite a popular Irish name — the Irish form of James."

"Oh, I see," said Jason. "Well, I'll call him for sure."

"Have you got an e-mail address where I can reach you? I could send the details there. Mr. Healey's phone number and all the rest."

"Yes, of course," said Jason and gave it to her.

She repeated his address, promised to send the details right away, heartily wished him good luck, and then rang off. What an incredible person.

The more he thought about it, the more the possibility intrigued him. He hooked up his laptop using Dianna's Internet connection in her bedroom. Her dresser was a mass of tubes and jars. Clothes were literally bursting from the closet and framed photographs covered one wall.

Many were from Hot Springs. There was even one of Jason taken on their final day of high school when everyone traveled to Cape Sansum to celebrate. It was early summer and the late-afternoon light accentuated the twins' smiles. Even looking at a photo he could see the siblings shared something from which he was excluded. A blood link, a genetic pairing deeper than love or sex or anything within human control. Again he wrestled with the idea that somewhere he too might have brother or sister.

He spent a half-hour wading through the spam and messages. Then he wrote to Tina, Al (with a word to Dada), Phillip, and Cristine. Angel was okay and in Alberta with Cristine's sister and Tina was getting a new dog; Al wrote that things at the hotel were running smoothly. He also wrote a note to Kiriko, although he wasn't sure she'd reply.

As hoped, Professor Morton's e-mail wasn't long in arriving. Jason sent a sincere thank you and then a note to Seamus Healey.

He logged off and planned his call. What tone should he take? Did he really want to work in Bath? How long was he planning to stay? For the moment, money was the only factor limiting his time in England — Dada aside, that is. And Kiriko…Jason was certain this Seamus would ask how long he'd be staying; he'd best have an acceptable response ready.

The call came sooner than expected; the voice was male and Irish.

"Jason! Good — what luck! Seamus Healy here. I'm calling from Dublin. I just got your e-mail."

"Great. Thank you for calling so quickly, Mr. Healey."

"Not at all, not at all. And cut the 'Mr.' crap. The

name's Seamus. Listen, how much do you know about the job?"

"Not very much. Only the little Professor Morton told me."

"Well, let me brief you then. I've been hired to head up a small publisher in Bath. Destination Press, it's called. I've been up a couple of times already and I'll be moving there full-time shortly. The place — the Press, I mean — is a bloody mess, still in the dark ages, and needs some major shaping up. I intend to totally revamp their so-called systems and drag them kicking and screaming into the digital age, not to mention establishing some kind of presence in North America — and I need some young, energetic blood to do it. I've checked out the links you sent me, the sites you designed and developed, and I was impressed. Bloody good work. That's if you actually did them, of course." A huge laugh erupted. He reminded Jason of a bear.

"So," Seamus continued, "are you in or are you out?"

"What? That's it? Do you mean you're offering me a job on the phone? I should tell you that, as a Canadian, I'm not sure about working here. Proper visas and…"

"Who gives a shite about crap like that? If you're good, we'll work it out and if you're not there's no need and no one's the wiser."

"But what about an interview?"

"What do you call this?" replied Seamus in a tone of voice that Jason could only describe as aggressively humorous.

"I guess—"

Seamus laughed. "They don't mean shite, laddie. Working together is the only way to find out if we can work together, believe me. *I* am the voice of experience." Jason thought about Human Designs where he'd been through a three-week process including tests and three rounds of interviews and endless consultations with HR androids.

"So when can you be there?"

"Ah...well, I'll have to find accommodation."

"I'll take care of that, at least temporarily until we see if we're going to love or hate each other." Seamus did his big bear laugh again.

"So, let me ask you again: are you in or out?"

One beat. Two beats, then: "I'm in." He couldn't for the life of him say exactly why.

"Splendid! I'll whip you off an e-mail about where to go and all that malarkey and I'll expect to see you up there at the start of next week."

Jason wanted to ask more, but he was sure this charming Irish steamroller named Seamus Healey wasn't interested.

The rest of the day sped by. All in all, Jason was pleased. He was getting closer to Elizabeth; he'd landed a job in a foreign country — and all this in just a few short days. And what did he have to lose? If things didn't work out, he could walk away — Seamus had made that clear.

He got on the phone and crossed out a few more leads. Gone was the traveler on her horse, and the woman from the dating site. By four o'clock, his ear was sore and he wanted some fresh air. Remembering the Americans he'd dined with near Trafalgar Square, he called their hotel and found them in. They arranged to meet at a pub and, hours later, Jason was tipsy and heading home on the bus.

Dianna's flat was unlocked. Pocketing his key, he stumbled in, hoping she was up. He wanted to tell her his big news. She was up all right. In fact, she was standing inside the vestibule like she'd been waiting there for him to get home — which, he would momentarily learn, was exactly the case.

"Jason, I need your help." She was biting her bottom lip and her voice was a whisper. She looked distraught.

"What is it? What's wrong?"

"I'll explain it all later..." she looked down, trying to gain control. "But, right now, in my bedroom, there's a man. I want him to leave but he won't go."

"A man? Is this someone you know?"

"Yes."

"Can't we call the police?"

"No. Listen, Jason, this is awkward." She paused. "He's my boss. Can you just try and get him to go home?" Her voice trembled.

Jason looked at Dianna. Her face was mottled. Her voice was raspy and hesitant.

"I'll try," said Jason without a clue how to go about it. Then his eyes got steely. "Did he hurt you?"

"No, no. Oh god. Where do I start...please, can't you get him to leave?"

As he moved towards the half-closed bedroom door he took a deep breath.

When he slid open the door, a man looked up from the bed. "Who in blazes are you?"

"My name's Jason. I'm a friend of Dianna's. She told me that she wants you to go." Damn! I should have said I was her brother.

"Well, why don't you just go and tell Di that I don't want to go, that I won't go, and that I have no intention of leaving whatsoever. In fact, I think you're the one who should fuckin' well leave."

"What's your name?" Jason tried another tack.

"None of your fuckin' business," the man slurred. Jason seriously questioned Dianna's taste in men; scrawny with a rather scraggly reddish beard, this guy had more hair sprouting from his torso than his head.

He closed the door and turned to Dianna.

"What's his name?"

"You'll laugh."

"No I won't. What is it?"

"Harry."

"Harry?"

"Yes, like the prince." Actually, it did seem funny. "Doesn't seem much of a prince to me," Jason said.

"That's not helping," Dianna said.

"Sorry," said Jason. Then, "He seems somewhat aggressive."

"He's been drinking."

"I could tell." Trying to think laterally, Jason recalled how Cassidy had spirited L'il Abner out of the Hot Springs Island Hotel. Although Cassidy's method wasn't an option, it helped. Jason whispered a question: "Is he married?"

"Why?"

"Come on. Is he married?"

"Do I have to tell you?" she asked.

"I guess you just did."

"All right. Yes."

"Good," Jason said.

"And is he the top guy at your company or does he have a boss too?"

"He's in charge of my section. There's a CEO, a CFO, and a chairman above him. The board of directors, too, of course."

"Excellent," said Jason. He asked another related question.

"I do," replied Dianna, "but...what? Why?"

"Just get it," Jason said. She went to the cupboard and handed it over.

"Turn on all the lights. As many as you can."

"Harry! Oh Harry!" called Jason in a sing-songy voice, as annoying as he could make it. Harry looked up. "Wha the fuck...?"

"Surprise, you're on candid camera." Jason pointed Dianna's Handycam directly at him. The recording light glowed purposefully, accusingly, red.

Harry stood up. "Gimme that!" He staggered towards the retreating Jason who continued filming.

"Yes, ladies and gentlemen, welcome to the home of Dianna Love, Harry's mistress *and* employee, where it's late on a Friday night and good old Harry here refuses to go home despite polite requests to the contrary." By now, Jason had backed into the living room and Harry was halfway down the hall in lurching pursuit.

"Di! Why don't you open the front door?"

"Yes, Harry, I'm sure both your wife and your CEO will enjoy this footage. Which do you think will cause the bigger stink, Harry? The sexual harassment charges or the adultery?"

Harry reached the door; it was increasingly evident the game was up. He was shirtless, in bare feet, and inebriated; there was no way he was going to catch Jason — and even if he did, they were about the same size. Harry withered.

"Listen. I'm sorry, mate. Just had a bit too much to drink, you know. You know what that's like. ...Be a good lad and hand over that tape now, will you?" Jason just kept filming.

"One bloke to another. Di and I are fine, just a little squabble is all. You're a man of the world. You understand these things."

"Dianna, get his clothes and shoes and throw them out here," Jason said. Harry managed to catch most of the garments but his shirt fluttered to the ground.

"Now," said Jason. "I'm going to stay just far enough away from you to make sure you don't do anything stupid. ...And then you're going to get dressed and get the hell out of here as fast as you can. Is that clear, Harry?"

"Yes. Fine. Whatever."

"Oh...and Harry? Don't forget to apologize to Dianna while you're at it."

"C'mon..."

"Apologize." Jason's voice was harsh.

Reluctantly, Harry turned to Dianna standing just inside the door. At the same time, lights came on in the flat upstairs. Jason saw shadowy faces through the drapes.

"I'm sorry, Di. Got a bit carried away, is all. It's just that...well, I don't want to lose you. Sent me off my head a little bit. We'll work things out."

"We're through, Harry. Just get out. Go. Leave."

Harry dressed and then, finally, climbed the stairs. As he was about to move off down the street, he turned to Jason and yelled, "Fuck you and that slut of a friend of yours, as well!"

"Ah, quite the English gentleman, aren't you, Harry?" Jason flung back. "Hope you enjoy this on the BBC."

As Jason descended the stairs, drama done, the light in the flat above clicked off.

Dianna shot into Jason's arms, sobbing and laughing. When the embrace ended, Dianna looked at him with tear-rimmed eyes — Tina's eyes.

"Jason, that was brilliant! *You* were brilliant! How did you think of the camera?"

"None of that's important," he said. "But you've got some decisions to make. Like what to do about your job. And your boss."

"I need a drink," Dianna said. She was a little wobbly, too. She poured one for Jason as well and they collapsed on the couch. "Well, the first thing I'm doing is telling him to give me some time off," she continued. "God, do they owe me. I don't ever want to see that little prick's face again."

"Did I hear him call you Di?" Jason asked and Dianna burst into laughter so infectious he couldn't resist joining her.

"Yes," she gasped, "he likes to call me 'Princess.'" Their laughter doubled.

"Sorry for asking," Jason said when the laughter settled, "but what did you ever see in that jerk? Married…your boss…a total asshole to boot…and named Harry…"

"I'm beginning to wonder myself," Dianna said. "But," she said, after a moment's contemplation, "if it's okay with you, I'd prefer not to talk about this anymore. I've had enough of Harry for one night. I'm sure you have too."

"Listen, I have to tell you something. I'm leaving for Bath on Sunday," Jason said. He explained Professor Morton's call and the job offer.

"That's great, Jason," Dianna said. "But I'm sorry you're leaving so soon. I was hoping you'd stay longer." Finally, the warmth between them had begun.

An hour later in bed Jason reached over to the shelf next to his sofa bed and found Kiriko's letters. He'd originally planned to open one a week, to ration her thoughtful notes like water on a desert island. He felt the thick weave of the envelope. He held it up to the light then brought it near before extracting one of the smaller unopened letters. None were marked. As Jason examined the smaller envelope, the larger one slipped through his fingers and fell to the floor. Jason switched on the small halogen shelf-light to search. The light cast a bright but narrow beam onto the creamy whiteness of the envelope, which Jason found between the shelf and the sofa bed.

Jason pulled out a letter. He imagined Kiriko writing it at her desk or perhaps even at her easel.

> *Dear Jason,*
> I remember an old poem. I can't remember the writer, except that he lived almost a thousand years ago. I tried to translate it best as I can, but please forgive me if I make a mistake. From my heart, I wish you much
> success on your search. Then you can come home again to those who wait for you.
>
> As thick clouds
> are torn apart by the winds,
> the sudden cry at dawn
> of the first wild geese
> winging their way
> over the mountains.
> *Kiriko*

Jason reread the poem and letter and then again. He wanted to repay Kiriko but didn't know how. Then he got an idea. Digging into his backpack, he found his old Cambridge notebook and wrote this song.

Make You Strong

Do you measure distance by an inch or by
   a mile
Or is the scale a frown against a smile?
Do you measure distance by a kilo or a meter
Or is the scale a moment or a while?

Do you measure distance by the cost it takes
      to get there
Or is distance just a castle in the air?
Do you measure distance by the time that you
      are gone now
And does it make you weak or make you
strong?

CHORUS
Make you strong, make you strong
Does distance make you weak or make you
strong?

Do you measure distance by the ones you
      leave behind you
Or by those you seek so far away?
Do you measure distance by your lips against
   a cheek now
Or by words and poems and things that we
      can say?

Do you measure distance by the cost it takes
      to get there
Or is distance just a castle in the air?

Do you measure distance by the time that you
   are gone now
And does it make you weak or make you
   strong?

CHORUS
Make you strong, make you strong
Does distance make you weak or make you
   strong?

Chapter 11 iNovel Link
The Chapter 11 Hot Springs iNovel Link is another
musical one. Please go to **www.HotSpringsNovel.com/
chapter11/** if you want to hear Jason's latest song about
longing and distance.

Chapter 12

"I hope you'll enjoy your stay."

The train left Sunday just before 7 p.m. and arrived an hour and a half later in Bath Spa — its official name. The train was sleek and modern, and the multihued cars reminded Jason of the rainbow sprinkles on his childhood ice cream cones. He enjoyed the trip but was aware he was once again hurtling into the unknown.

Dianna's travel guide described Bath as "one of England's most beautiful cities." He wondered why a fiction publisher would operate in this smallish, tourism-centered city in Avon instead of London.

Despite the almost certain distractions associated with a new place and job, he couldn't stop thinking about Elizabeth. Bath was her home — or so he hoped. And maybe his ancestral territory, his roots. Had the hot springs connection decided Elizabeth in her choice of refuge?

Seamus had e-mailed Jason the name of his lodging house, a place ten minutes from the city center. Jason grabbed a cab outside the station and soon found himself at Flaherty House. Mrs. Flaherty herself met him at the door.

"Ah, you must be Mr. Jason. I've heard so much about you from Mr. Seamus," she said. Her grin displayed a hole where a tooth — or perhaps two — should have been.

"You must be tired from your trip," she said, hefting his heaviest bag and brushing him aside with a wiry strength when he protested. "Ah, and I see you're a musician as well."

"Well, I play around."

"Jolly good, jolly good," she smiled. "I mess about myself — on the piano, that is." She gave a chuckle. "I love the old piano songs and the show tunes, you know." A stair creaked loudly as they headed upstairs.

"So do you know Mr. Healey — Mr. Seamus — very well?" asked Jason.

"I do, I do. But then, so does everyone." She laughed and gave Jason a wink.

"I've put you in the Robin," she said as she clunked up the stairs. "All of our rooms are named after birds, you see. Mr. Seamus is in Owl."

"Ah, he's a wise old owl then, is he?" Mrs. Flaherty looked back at him in genuine surprise.

"Why that's exactly right. Now aren't you the smart one to figure that out — just like Mr. Seamus said."

"Is he in now? Mr. Seamus?" Jason asked.

"Oh no. He's stepped out for dinner. And he's usually a wee bit late in the evenings, if you know what I mean…"

The Robin Suite had a sitting room, bedroom, and WC. The bathroom was by far the most spacious of the three rooms. A large and intricately carved mirror hung over the washbasin and reminded Jason of a song he'd written called "The Mirror."

The other rooms were decorated in a style that Jason thought of as "high nun." Doilies covered every available surface and a crucifix loomed large over the bed. An overstuffed armchair, holy pictures on the wall, and brightly flowered wallpaper dominated the sitting room. This is what traveling's all about, he thought.

"There you go now, dear. I hope you'll enjoy your stay. Mr. Seamus said it wasn't decided exactly how long you'd be here but I'm sure you'll let me know when it all comes a bit clearer." Before Jason could even think about the appropriateness of a tip, she was gone.

After perfunctorily unpacking, Jason took out his guitar and played "The Mirror."

> I looked into the mirror
> I looked into the glass
> And there I saw my future
> And there I saw my past
>
> Oh, oh, what do you know?
> Oh, oh, the mirror says it so

• • •

BAM! BAM! BAM! Jason jolted up. What city was he was in?

"Jason! Jason! It's Seamus. Wake up! Get up and let me in, lad. We're going out!"

He struggled to the door and flicked on the atrocious

overhead light. His watch read just after midnight. Seamus stormed in.

"C'mon, lad. Get dressed. We're going to a party." Seamus threw clothes at him, then entered the cavernous washroom and, door open, began urinating so loudly that it echoed into the other room.

Then Seamus grabbed his arm and marched him out into the cold, crisp, night air. After a brisk ten-minute walk, they'd reached what Jason thought must be central Bath before ducking into a narrow side street that Seamus called "one of the passages."

Seamus led him down some stairs and suddenly they were in a different world. The smoke-filled bar was awash with people and ear-splitting music. A spinning mirror ball — a mirror ball! — shot sparkles of colored lights from tiny spots overhead onto the walls and clubbers.

Even Seamus had to shout to be heard. "This is a private club. Run by a friend named Archie. What'll you drink?" He handed Jason a beer and pounded back straight whiskey. With one arm around him like they'd been friends for millennia, he crashed his glass against Jason's, spilling some of the stout. *"Go maire sibh bhur saol nua!"*

"What does that mean?" Jason asked.

"May you enjoy your new life."

"I sure hope so," Jason said. But Seamus was off, talking and shouting and gesturing to one person, then another and another. After twice trying to strike up a conversation and failing because of the noise, Jason was starting to get pissed. An hour passed. Is this what he woke me up for? It seemed an unimaginable way to welcome a new employee to the company. Why would he invite me out if he didn't plan to talk to me? With Jason wondering if he could find his way home, Seamus returned.

"C'mon, let's go," he said and grabbed Jason's arm again. Soon they were up the stairs and out. They'd left as quickly as they'd come. "You were feeling deserted, weren't you," Seamus said out in the fresh air. "Wondering why I'd even bothered to bring you here if all I was going to do was talk to other people and leave you all alone."

"Well, yes. It's late—"

"But you stuck it out, laddie. You're a good sport and I like that." He then sang in a low, deep and surprisingly melodic voice all the way back to Flaherty House.

. . .

BAM! BAM! BAM! At least it was light this time. Seamus came in and tried to haul him down to breakfast.

"I need a shower, Seamus," Jason protested.

"Details, details, details," Seamus laughed, speeding down the stairs.

Meals were buffet-style in the doily-intense dining room with Mrs. Flaherty and a young helper presiding. By the time Jason arrived, Seamus was already heaping his plate with bacon, sausages, fried tomatoes, and scrambled eggs. Jason used this opportunity for a really good look at his new boss.

He wasn't very tall, but what he lacked in height he made up in girth. Yet he wasn't fat, just solid; shaped like a whiskey barrel formed from aged oak, and just as hard. His arms and shoulders were particularly powerful and he owned a thick helmet of dark hair cut in a modified bowl style with streaks of gray and a voluminous, mouth-hiding, mustache.

Seamus's eyes were his most electrifying feature: a piercing almost maniacal blue set deep below thick black eyebrows. When the man looked at you, you were totally and completely looked at. The only person with a stare approaching it was Layla. But where hers held wonder and innocence, Seamus's carried something ancient and disturbing.

Seamus refilled his plate several times and never missed the chance to joke with Mrs. Flaherty or her helper — always from a distance of two inches or less. Once he went into the kitchen, and gales of laughter cascaded out from there as well. It seemed his *modus operandi* was to invade your personal space like a friendly army.

Then it was off to work. Shirt and tie weren't necessary, Seamus said. "Wear something warm instead."

"Don't worry, I'm Canadian."

A cold rain poured down, heralding winter. Seamus had found them bicycles and intended to ride to work. Fifteen minutes later they arrived at the office, soaked to the skin. Seamus didn't mind in the least. "Told you to wear something warm," he winked.

They locked the bikes in a rack on the edge of the lawn behind the car park. Jason guessed the slightly ramshackle building in front of him was once a large private home. A brass plate next to the door proclaimed that this was, indeed, Destination Press.

DP, as everybody called it, was a mess. Floorboards creaked. Paint flaked from the ceiling. If ever a place needed an infusion of money, energy and ideas, this was it. Jason hurried behind Seamus on his whirlwind tour. His overriding impression was of stacks and heaps and piles of paper. Why would a London publishing conglomerate buy this place?

DP was organized into divisions. One published local travel guides, another was something called *Farming News*, and a third was a vanity publisher. Its largest division, however — and champion money loser — was Destination Fiction.

"They got it cheap, that's why," said Seamus, answering Jason's unspoken question. "That, plus the Group CEO is from around here and wanted a place to employ his family. I'm not kidding. But it'll happen over my dead body."

"So here's the buzz, lad," Seamus said. "You'll be stationed here but I want you to set up a system, a network, and then get cracking on a website. First, for the whole company, and then individual ones for each division."

"There's no network or website?"

Seamus rolled his eyes. "Look around. We don't even have bloody computers." Seamus wasn't strictly accurate, but the number of terminals in relation to desks was minimal. "So, from now on, you're also in charge of IT."

"*What?*"

"Good on you, Jason," said Seamus. "Now, get on with it, will you? I've got ten million other things to do."

"But wait! Seamus! Where do I buy stuff? Who do I report to? How do I pay for it all? And...and...I don't even have a contract."

Seamus whirled again, pirouetting a perfect 180 degrees and arriving mere centimeters from Jason's nose. "Okay, first thing. You find out where to go, and I'll pay for everything. About how things work — or don't work — try to figure out things yourself or just do them how you think they should be done. I'm interested in change around here so the more you want to shake things up, the better. If you need advice then talk to Maddie McDonald. She's one of the editors in DF — that's Destination Fiction — and just about the only one around here with any brains, even if she did go to Oxford. As for your contract, you'll have to trust me, lad. Do you or don't you? If we're going to work together, that's the bottom line right there and we may as well have it out right now. Do you trust me or not?"

There was only one answer. "Of course I do."

Seamus's intense, almost frightening, gaze was instantly infused with warm Irish charm. He clapped Jason on the shoulder like he was beating a mattress during a spring cleaning. "Great. Now off you go."

The rest of the morning was spent meeting people and finding out what he could do about this sleepy collection of underperforming lists and underenthusiastic personnel. Generally speaking, the staff were friendly, if guarded. Maddie was a passionate, bright light in the otherwise grim Destination tunnel. Huge brown eyes and an infectious smile and laugh matched her can-do attitude, her Oxford First and her pragmatic intelligence. She hadn't been at Destination long and Seamus was right to see in her a ready ally for change.

• • •

The first week sped by. During the day Jason worked non-stop, and every evening he forced himself awake, working equally hard with his cell phone or his e-mail, sometimes even going door-to-door trying to track Elizabeth. He had yet to unearth any solid clues, but his list was shrinking. Every night he collapsed on his bed at Flaherty's with a sense of accomplish-ment.

Jason was asleep at 11 p.m. when his phone woke him. The only person he could imagine calling at this hour was Seamus.

"Hello."

"Jason, it's Al."

"Al! What is it?" Jason's first thoughts were pan-icked. Al wouldn't call at this hour unless the news was bad — possibly, horrible.

"Jason, I don't want you to worry, but I thought you'd want to know that Dada had one of his attacks last night, just after midnight — you know, the short-ness of breath, the racing heart."

"Is he okay?"

"He's fine. Same as all the other ones. Once he got to the hospital his symptoms disappeared."

"Where is he now?"

"Resting."

"Can I talk to him?"

"Jason, he didn't want me to tell you."

"Why not?"

"He doesn't want to worry you."

Jason thought for a moment.

"I know what you're thinking, Jason, but in my opinion there's no way you should come back. It was just another anxiety attack. They all are."

"Elizabeth didn't call by any chance, did she?" Perhaps his inquiries in Bath had struck home and prompted Elizabeth to phone.

"I thought about that, too. There was nothing in the phone log. I don't think so."

"Okay."

"But whatever you do, stay put, Jason. Remember why you're there. I'll look after things here. And try not to worry."

"That's like asking Dada to give up his checked shirts."

"Good, I'm glad you've kept your sense of humor."

"Keep in touch, Al. And thanks."

Jason reached for another of Kiriko's letters within a letter.

> *Dear Jason,*
> This poem is also very old. How many thoughts are there over a thousand years?

How many lives, how many loves pass over that time? I hope you have success on your search. When you read this, please know that we are thinking of you.

In a village by the mountain
When autumn has ended
Is a place
Where the meaning of sadness
Is in the power of the winter wind
Kiriko

•　ა　•

Seamus was infecting the DP staff with energy and enthusiasm. He was also busy finding other jobs for those who didn't meld with his culture or plans — it was his preferred form of downsizing. "Take care of your people, Jason, good or bad. Take care to get the bad ones good jobs and take care to keep the good ones. Do that and you'll never go wrong."

One Thursday night around eight o'clock Jason looked up from his desk. He was starved. He hadn't eaten lunch and his stomach was making sounds akin to Mrs. Flaherty's cackle.

"Hey, Maddie? You want to go and get some grub?" Having watched how Seamus worked for weeks now, darting in and out of people's offices, invariably knowing everything about everyone, Jason was taking a leaf from the Mad Irishman's book.

"Sure," said Maddie. "The pizza joint or — dare I say it — the pub?"

Jason laughed. "The pub, huh? You saying you want to call it a night?"

"I am. The kids don't have school tomorrow and David's taken them to spend the night at his parents."

"Then the pub it is."

They found a reasonably quiet table near the back of the Duke. They ordered salad, Cornish pasties and Guinness.

"Jason," said Maddie, "tell me how you got here. I don't mean Seamus and all that, but why you came to England in the first place."

Jason wondered if he'd fielded one too many personal calls.

"Well, the truth is…I did come here for a particular reason," Jason said, and paused.

"So what's the big dark secret, then?" Maddie asked, with a smile. "A skeleton in the closet? A ghost from the past?" Her eyebrows rose in mock horror.

"Actually…yes. On all counts. Or a boogie woman, to be more precise."

Maddie slapped herself on the forehead. "I'm sorry Jason. How insensitive of me."

"No. It's okay. It's my mother." Once again he told his story. At first Maddie said nothing. Then, with an expression indicating she'd taken Jason's revelations very seriously, she went for more drinks.

"I thought you might need another one," she said. "I think we both might."

"Thanks."

"So, no real clues?" Maddie asked.

"None to speak of."

"Oh Jason, what you must be going through. ...I can't imagine how difficult it's been. I can understand why it must be hard to tell other people. But at least now you've told somebody, haven't you? I mean besides the people back home. And getting it out in the open is the first step." She paused, searching his face. "You do, don't you? Feel a little better telling someone?"

"I do feel better," he paused for effect, "or maybe it's just the drinks. ...But now I've spilled the beans, it's your turn. What are *your* big dark secrets?"

Maddie's usually bright eyes dimmed and it was Jason who'd caught foot in mouth disease. "Sorry."

"What a pair!" They could only laugh.

"I didn't know putting your foot in it was so infectious," Jason said. "A regular epidemic." Then he grew serious. "But you don't have to tell me if you don't want to."

"No, you were honest and straightforward with me," Maddie said. "I should be the same with you." She waited a second. "Actually, although I try and seem all together and give the appearance that everything's hunky dory at home, it's not. Not by any means. And I'm not sure what to do about it. If it weren't for Carolyn and Connor, I'd probably have left long ago. In fact, I'm sure I would."

Jason thought for a moment. "What happened? How did it reach this stage?"

"Well, this is hard for me to talk about. A year ago I found out that...that my husband, David, is either, well, he's either gay or bisexual. And that he's had affairs. He swears it's been years since the last one, but regardless of whether I believe him or not, he has put me at a terrible risk."

Jason felt her betrayal and disappointment in every word. "It's not that I'm homophobic, because I'm not. It just seems rather essential in a marriage to know your partner's sexual orientation beforehand, wouldn't you agree? And the dishonesty — I mean, he's lied to me about it since the time we first met. He told me that he'd been lying to himself, too. You know, upright uptight parents. Conservative social circle and all that. Not wanting anyone to know.

"Anyway, that's why he's off with the kids. We've been spending some time apart to see how it feels when we're not together, to see if it will heal or...I don't know, to see if living separately is what we want. What *I* want. The long and the short of it is that it's a mess. It's a mess, Jason, a total unmitigated mess."

"Oh, Maddie—"

"No, don't. You don't have to say anything, Jason. I've been over it in my head a thousand times, and I don't know whether to feel ashamed or defeated or enraged."

Neither said anything for a good ten seconds. When Maddie continued, her tone was a shade brighter and her face visibly less bitter.

"But that's enough of that. And you know what? I was right. Talking about it *does* help. We're not usually very good at this, you know, the British. We tend to keep things all carbonated and pressurized."

"Canadians aren't much better," Jason said.

"You may not believe this, but you're the first person I've told. The very first. So please, anyway, please keep this absolutely to yourself. You will, won't you?" Her eyes questioned him. "And you should feel very flattered, I might add. It's a bit like losing your virginity, this confessional business." She tried to sound jocular.

"Thank you for trusting me, Maddie. Mum's the word."

"Well, you told me your secret, after all. Would've been less than fair if I'd held mine back now, wouldn't it? I suspect it's been eating away at me since the day I found out."

They continued talking and drinking until the barman called time.

"See you tomorrow," said Jason. They were standing outside. Jason had one hand in his pocket and the other on his bike. He was searching for something brilliant to say to keep the evening going.

"Thank you, Jason. I needed this. I needed it a lot."

"I did too," he replied.

She gave him a peck on the cheek and walked off in the opposite direction, the sounds of her boots echoing on the deserted street. She was wearing a bright orange beret that he could see for a long time under the halo of the streetlamps. Then she faded into the distance of the long curving road in the mist of the late autumn night.

• • •

At dusk on a Sunday afternoon Jason was alone at his spanking new workstation in the freshly painted Destination Press office, putting finishing touches on the Destination Travel Guides website. He was hoping to go live sometime next week.

Jeff Wiggins (who reminded Jason of an English Kevin) and raven-haired Sally Navrof had been in earlier with a few others; that, in itself, was symbolic of the tide changes happening at DP. According to Jeff, nobody worked on weekends before Seamus. Even so, by five o'clock, Jason had the office to himself. He was alone when this e-mail from Tina arrived.

Jason,
How are you? Sorry for not replying sooner to your last e-mail. I'm glad you're doing well, it seems. Keep at it with the search and it sounds like you're making some progress. Persistence!

I'm fine. Ginger — my new dog — has finally gotten used to things and it's great having a dog again. It'd been too long! Speaking of dogs, I was down at the hotel the other day and saw Golly and she's still hanging in there. Her foot seems much better :) Al told me she talked to you about Dada's latest episode. He's fine now — I have to agree with her diagnosis, however. You know what I mean. But I thought you would want to know how he is.

I haven't written cause I've been really busy. Lots of big news and changes here. First, I found a new place!!! Finally out from under my parents' thumb. You might know it, it's the Reids' old place, out on Donovan Road, that cabin with glimpses of the water through the Arbutuses (sp?). I move in on Sunday.

Also, another piece of big news. I got a job!!! Yes!!! There's a new vet in town from Edmonton and he's expanding and he hired me!!! I'm working 3 days a week to start and I'm ecstatic!!! But I'm afraid what this means is that I'll have to put off visiting you and Dianna in England, like we talked about. How about your plans? How much longer do you think you'll stay in Bath? In England? In Europe?

I saw Kiriko and Cassidy the other day at Salty's. They're fine and Cassidy promised to write to you soon so expect an e-mail. Anyway, that's about all the news I've got. Say hi to sis if you talk to her. Have you seen her since you went to Bath? And tell me how the search goes. Good luck.

Lots of love from all of us,
Tina

Maddie walked in and Jason minimized his e-mail window.

"Hey pardner," Maddie said. "Whacha doing?"

Jason's accent was by now a standing office joke; everyone teased him with pseudo-cowboy talk.

"It's the DT site," he said. "I'm almost done."

Maddie sat down behind him and spun Jason's swivel chair around so they were face-to-face. At first he wondered if something serious was afoot. The glow on Maddie's face suggested otherwise.

"Listen, Jason. I've been thinking. And doing some research. And I've decided, if it's okay with you, I'd like to help you."

"What do you mean? Help me with what?"

"Finding your mother. I'd like to help you look. The last few days, since you told me what was going on and why you were here, I've been doing some digging on the Net and at the library and I called a few people. I'd like to become what they call 'an adoption search angel.'"

"A what?"

"A search angel. An adoption search angel." She pulled her chair closer. Her excitement made Jason think of a sailboat's rigging trilling in the wind.

"They're people who help adoptees and birth parents find each other. Some of them are adopted themselves and the others are just good Samaritans. Anyway, I'd like to do that for you. I'd like to help you find your mother. If you want me to, that is."

Jason suddenly found himself with a lump in his throat. Maybe now he'd get somewhere. Her local knowledge would be a huge asset.

"I realized I've been wallowing in my own self-pity for too long. I needed perspective and you helped give me that. And I want to give some of it back — if that doesn't sound too ridiculously pompous and self-important. Besides," she finished, "this may be my only chance in my entire life — including the hereafter — to become an angel.

"And listen," said Maddie. "If you've got the time, I've got another surprise."

"What is it?"

"If you want, we can go to the spa." She looked at her watch. "It shut a few minutes ago, but David said, if we wanted to, we could go. Even if he's left already, I've got a key. You've been wanting to go for ages, so how about it?" Maddie's husband worked at one of the new spas primed to revitalize Bath as a true hot springs resort.

"Sure. Let's do it."

The car park of the New Bath Wellness Center was around back. Maddie tried the rear entrance but it was locked, so she used her key. A light glowed at the end of a long hallway. "That's the reception area."

David was tall and slim with a trim brown beard. He was Seamus-lite. "David," said Maddie. "This is Jason. From work."

"Jason, I've heard so much about you," said David. Jason wondered what he'd heard. How had Maddie described him?

"Thanks for the use of the spa. It'll remind me of home. It's very kind of you."

"Not at all. And since I hear you're quite the hot springs aficionado," David said, "I'm afraid to have to tell you that what we've got here isn't authentic thermal water. It's just heated city water and we add mineral supplements to replicate the hot springs experience."

"Well, I just grew up around them. I suppose it kind of gets into your blood," Jason said.

"Lucky you. My father's a co-owner, you see," David eyed the neatly stacked shelves. "It's nice but I wouldn't exactly describe it as a passion."

"Quite," said Maddie as if implying that passion and David were unacquainted. "It's why we moved to Bath from Oxfordshire," added Maddie. "David's father wanted someone he could trust to run the place." Jason heard her sarcasm.

"Funny that both our fathers run hot spring facilities," Jason pointed out.

David changed the subject: "I hear you're looking for your mother. Is the search progressing? Any luck so far?" David cast a look at his wife.

"Nothing to report so far, I'm afraid."

"David, I've just told Jason that I'm going to help him search."

"Very kind of you, Mad, I'm sure," David said. Although superficially pleasant, David's tone carried implications.

"You going to join us?" Maddie asked her husband.

"No. I've got about five minutes more here and then, as you'll remember, I'm picking Connor and Carolyn up at my mother's. You remember how to set the alarm, don't you Maddie?" Condescending.

"I think I can manage." Sarcastic.

David handed Jason some disposable swim trunks and directed him to the changing room. After a shower, Jason examined the bathing area. The hot springs section of the spa was narrow, with a small swimming pool and three hot tublike enclosures, all of different temperatures. Massage rooms, hair, nail, and facial salons and a workout center were accessed through a separate locker room door. The decorative motif was pseudo-Roman. He couldn't help comparing the sterile sports club–feel of the spa with the natural setting of his beloved Hot Springs Island. But Jason was here to relax and enjoy himself.

The steam rose, the jet streams bubbled, and the water performed its usual magic. His sinews transformed from stone into something more pliable, more human. Eyes closed, he could have been back on Russell Point, the sea lapping at the shore, with Golly and Dada and Al and everyone close by.

When Jason opened his eyes, Maddie was already immersed and sitting across from him — her arrival masked by the spa jets. Her sudden arrival in the bath was a déjà vu of the night he met Kiriko.

Kiriko. Despite the lovely notes she'd left, she hadn't answered any of his e-mails. And had Tina been trying to let him down gently by hinting in her last letter that Kiriko and Cassidy were more than just friends? He remembered the way Cassidy placed his hand on Kiriko's hip.

"Maddie?"

"Uh huh," she answered. Now her eyes were shut.

"I've got a rather…I don't know…unusual question."

Her eyes opened. "Go ahead."

"Well, I hope this doesn't sound strange, but doesn't David mind you being here alone with me like this?"

"Frankly, I couldn't care less what he thinks."

"Oh."

Maddie gave him a look he couldn't translate.

"The thing you have to remember, Jason, is that I'm the injured party. David has nothing to be suspicious about and never has. And, even if he did, considering what he's done in the past…

"You know, Jason, all I think about these days is whether to end my marriage or not. On the one hand, I keep thinking that, deep down, he's a good person, a confused one, mind you, but a good one. He's an excellent father, and the kids love him and need him. But in terms of being a husband, I'm entitled to think about my needs in all this, sexual as well as emotional. It's been months since we've slept together and I hardly imagine that's going to improve over time."

Jason responded with respectful silence. Then he closed his eyes. The sound of the spa's motor and the bubble jets, a low-key constant rumble, soothed him. As was his habit, Jason reached up and started massaging his neck, working out the kinks of the day. But then, without warning, Jason felt Maddie's hands replacing his. "I once took an acupressure course," she said.

Maddie's strong fingers kneaded his neck muscles.

She found the tender spots and gauged perfectly the amount of force to apply. The pressure was always long enough but never too long. She was wonderfully skilled and it felt terrific. After working both sides of Jason's neck, Maddie's hands moved to his shoulder muscles. How long had it been since a woman had touched him? A new stream of bubbles from the spa's jet machine shot onto Jason's leg as Maddie shifted position. He missed such intimacy. The moment and the water were rushing over him. His eyes remained shut. Her hands kept moving. He sighed without knowing he'd done so.

Suddenly, Maddie stopped.

"Did you hear something?" she asked. Jason opened his eyes. The bubbles kept churning the surface. Maddie turned towards him. There it was again.

"Yes, someone's there." Maddie pulled herself out and headed towards the locker room. Then a door swung open and Carolyn and Connor rushed loudly in for a dip and splash.

Chapter 12 iNovel Links

Please go to **www.HotSpringsNovel.com/chapter12/** to see two iNovel links for Chapter 12. The first is a series of websites (with brief explanations about them) related to the city of Bath. The second is another musical one, a recording of the song "The Mirror."

Chapter 13

"Cold is nothing. Warm is everything."

"Okay, everybody, gather round, gather round." This was Seamus, a month later. One of his innovations was holding more meetings but of shorter duration — this he achieved by conducting them chairless, even in meeting rooms.

"Two things. First, I bid everyone here to cast your eyes to the windows and see the golden light emanating from them. And by golden light, I'm not referring to the rays of old sol. Instead, I refer to our very own solar flare...Maria Kresse." The blonde and bespectacled Maria was startled to hear her name. "The reason I ask you to take notice of this super nova in our midst is because there — there — standing before you is the person responsible for our brand-new filing system and it's just totally bloody terrific. You did a fabulous job, Maria, a thoroughly bang-up piece of work that is miles — *miles* — better than any system I've personally ever seen. First-rate work!"

On cue, Andrea, Seamus's PA, handed him a bottle of champagne, which he delivered complete with a huge grin to the red-faced but thrilled Maria. As he planted a loud kiss on her cheek, everyone cheered and stamped their feet. Imagine applause and public commendation for a filing system! This was Seamus's genius — or at least one aspect of it. He knew the strengths and weaknesses of everyone at Destination Press and how to get the best from each of them. Some, like Maria, he praised publicly. Some he praised privately. But the praise was always sincere, if flamboyant. He gently scolded those in need of a surrogate father and trod lightly with the more sensitive types.

But most of all, Seamus cared. He cared about excellence and he cared about people. Through the grapevine, Jason knew the custodian's wife had been diagnosed with breast cancer and that Seamus had arranged for a specialist — a friend of his — to come especially from Bristol to look at her. "Treat people warmly, Jason," Seamus told him one drunken night. "Because without warmth we freeze up inside and die a sad, lonely, and ice-cold shriveled-up death with our willies falling off from frostbite. Remember, lad. Cold is nothing. Warm is everything." Then he winked. "Especially to frigid Canadians."

Seamus moved to his only other agenda item.

"Now — to the second thing. Thanks to your amazing hard work and dedication, this is a changed place, as I think we can all agree. It's a place with changed attitudes, a changed work ethic and a new corporate culture. And I'm damn proud of you for doing it. Not many people have the courage to move forward and embrace change as you all have. I mean that. I sincerely do."

Seamus always had something extra up his sleeve; this time it was thunderous applause, his hands smacking together like two great slices of ham. "This applause is for you," he shouted over his own din. "For each and every one of you."

Finally, he stopped clapping. "I've asked a lot of you all, I know I have," he said. He looked around with a sly grin and impishly angled head, playing to nuanced perfection the role of hard taskmaster converted into humble servant. "But you've performed exceptionally — and with just the bare minimum of grumbling and abject whinging." There was widespread laughter. "So, in honor of the changes we've made, to symbolize the strides we've taken, we must now move into the next phase of our rebirth. We're changing our name."

There were gasps. Destination Press had been around since 1949 and they were stunned that more than fifty years of tradition could be tossed so blithely.

"Andrea," Seamus said, nodding again. Andrea appeared from Seamus's office pushing his portable whiteboard — now covered by a rich blue velvet cloth.

"It gives me great honor to present you with your new home. Your new name. Your new logo. Your new identity." He whisked away the cloth and presented a new sign in gleaming gold letters: "Destiny Press."

"There it is. Your fate is mine and mine is yours and Destiny Press is a symbol of the symbiotic relationship we all share." He inserted a long pause and then abruptly ended the meeting.

"Thank you everyone! That'll do it! Meeting adjourned!" Seamus twirled at his usual top speed, amazing really for someone of his bulk, and disappeared into his office. A minute later, however, he poked his head out again and called to Jason.

On Seamus's gesture, he sat down while his boss paced the room.

"Listen, Jason, I've been thinking. I'm looking for something for Destiny Press and I want you to help me find it. Something big. We've changed our name and now we've got to actually do something. We have to show the world that we've changed in fundamental ways. That we're something to be reckoned with. I want something big. Something huge! Something that's *The Next Big Thing*!"

"Have you got anything in mind?"

Seamus's high-beam eyes careened around the corner of Jason's face to stare him down.

"What do I have in mind? What do I have in mind?" Seamus threw his hands in the air and rose up to his full height, appalled. "Do I have to do *everything* round here?" He whirled again and sat down on the edge of the table. Papers flew but he didn't notice.

He spoke quietly. "The reason I hire brilliant people is to give me brilliant ideas. I mean that. Go away and use that fertile mind of yours to conjure up something inspiring, something grand, something that has never ever *ever* been done before." He got off the table and came close, gripping Jason's shoulder so hard it hurt. In a voice as compelling as any Jason had ever heard, Seamus said to him: "Because if anyone can do it — it's you."

"Andrea!" Seamus called, and then was gone, quick as a jump cut in an action film.

• • •

BAM! BAM! BAM! Damn, damn, damn. Jason groaned, rolled over, and checked his watch. Sure enough. Midnight.

"Jason! Open up lad! We're going out." A reprise of that first awful night.

"There's something I want you to see. I think you'll like it."

"What is it?"

"You'll find out soon enough. And bring your guitar."

"Bring my guitar?" Seamus had already fled. Before long their cab was headed god knows where with Jason half-asleep and Seamus smelling of drink.

They reached their destination soon enough. Seamus paid, had an impassioned five-minute confab with the driver about horse racing, and then strode up the path to a rather tired looking house that Jason guessed was somewhere on Bath's northeast boundary. BAM! BAM! BAM! Seamus pounded and they entered.

The kitchen was crammed, music was playing, and people were everywhere. But the music wasn't recorded. It was live. The living room was filled with musicians dominated by a troupe of acoustic guitar players, singers, an electric bass player, and a single squeezebox pounding away on U2's "Sunday, Bloody Sunday."

"What do you think, laddie? It's the Music Club, UK version!" Seamus shouted.

Seamus introduced him to the host, a rather scruffy character in black leather pants, black leather vest, and a black silky shirt with one tail hanging out.

"Isn't he the greatest, our Seamus..." he slurred. "Isn't this just the greatest bloody idea? This drop-in jam session thing. This is the third time we've done it and everyone likes it so much we're going to hold it every week. At a different house every time. It'll be like a revolving party, you know. Wild man, the stuff he comes up with..."

Jason arrived home after three. Like smell, music catalyzes the memory and gives dimension to the past. The Music Club. Hot Springs Island. Dada and his family. Jason reached for Kiriko's third letter, still wondering why she didn't answer his e-mails. He opened it.

Dear Jason,
More than anything, I hope you have success on your search. When you read this, please know that we are thinking of you.

This poem is about water and memory. I thought it would remind you of your beautiful Hot Springs Island.

This poet's name was Yamabe no Akahito. He lived long ago.

As the mist rises
Above the still pools of water
Memories do not pass
With the speed of a river

Kiriko

• • •

"I've got a good feeling about this one, Jason," said Maddie. She had taken on the role of search angel with gusto and intelligence. Jason was deeply impressed and equally grateful. Her search skills dwarfed his own, and he was astounded not only at her breadth of abilities, but also by her determination. In the first week she'd learned how the adoption process worked and ways to hunt for b-parents, as they were called within the community.

Her optimism concerned their latest initiative. They'd cropped, enlarged and enhanced Jason's photograph of Elizabeth and used it on a new website, posters for the local community and classifieds. Jason imagined how she would react. Nonchalantly leafing through news of bazaars and church lunches when, a turned page, and she would be kidnapped, transported back to a distant country, a distant time. Keeping this in mind, they had worded the ad carefully. A question of outstanding inheritance needed resolving — true, of course, but not in the usual sense.

Jason thought about how much time he and Maddie spent together. And, of course, there was that evening in the spa, how her hands had felt on his neck and shoulders. Neither of them had mentioned that night since.

"But there's something bothering me," Jason said. "I'm feeling guilty that this search is taking up so much of your time. It's time you could be spending with Connor and Carolyn."

"The kids are with David and my mother. That's part of the plan, whether you're involved or not. Okay? If I ever want out, I'll just tell you. I'm hardly one to beat around the bush."

They went over Maddie's chart, listing all possible search options. They'd registered on several adoption sites, and trolled reunion registries at all of the major Internet adoption sites in both the UK and Canada, but they'd drawn blanks there too. Scouring libraries, phonebooks, court and public records hadn't worked either, particularly since they believed they were laboring under one huge disadvantage: Jason hadn't officially been adopted. His birth certificate declared Mary Chiron as his natural mother. Jason and Maddie believed Elizabeth impersonated Mum for the birth by using all her personal information so that Jason wouldn't show up on the records as adopted. If such was the case, there was no official trail. Jason wrote to Dada's brother's family to see what they knew, but they were either ignorant of the facts or unwilling to talk. "It was a long time ago," was all the return e-mail said. Also, there was no guarantee — in fact, it seemed highly unlikely — that Elizabeth Barnett was her actual name. Through Al, Jason had e-mailed Dada for more information. He'd asked if she had another name, and if Elizabeth had used Mum's name and information for his birth. Dada hadn't replied.

Jason contacted passport and immigration officials about entry records into Canada by Elizabeth but, once again, he'd come up empty-handed. Their search was suffering from too many years and too few unverified facts. They'd also checked out umpteen genealogy and ancestry sites, but this incredibly time-intensive task was another proverbial haystack in which Elizabeth was lost.

His true motives in coming to Bath became common knowledge as a result of his higher-profile search. Jason had overestimated the negative reactions and underestimated the positive: support was immediate and unstinting. His colleagues were universally kind. "Now you've got a search angel team," Maddie joked, "Jason's Angels." Even Mrs. Flaherty had learned of Jason's quest and sent out feelers into the considerable network she'd created during her thirty years in Bath. Jason sat with Seamus one afternoon while his employer made dozens of calls on his behalf. But even Seamus had been stumped.

All the unsuccessful leads and dead ends had led Maddie and Jason to wonder if they should enlist a professional. Neither the Bath phonebook nor Net search listed any local specialists, but there were a number in London and one in Bristol.

"Well, if we're going to hire someone, doesn't it make sense to use the local person? The one in Bristol?" said Jason.

"What about cost? How big a factor is that?"

"It's worth whatever I've got," he said sounding as noble as he could. In truth, Jason's finances were limited. In any event, they postponed making a decision. Feelers were out all over; they should give them time to work.

• • •

When Jason arrived at work the next day, he had an e-mail from Kevin (listing definitions of "loyal" and "loyalty" from several dictionaries) and one from Tina.

Tina's note was long and the tone, if not exactly forlorn, reminded Jason of the feeling articulated in Kiriko's second poem, when we know autumn is moving into winter and there's nothing we can do. She had started seeing someone, the new vet who'd recently hired her. Yes, she realized he was older — again — and her boss, but he was kind and caring and…she liked him. Jason was happy for her. But he also felt the same tinges of regret that Tina implied but left unstated in her note: that she was sorry it wasn't Jason, that it was a shame they'd been unable to regain the magic of their youth. He kept the tone of his reply light, cautioning that vets "could be animals, and I'm not even going to bring up the bestiality issue." He wished her luck and happiness.

• • •

"Hello, my name's Jason Chiron. I'm calling for Ms. Elizabeth Barnett, please."

"Speaking," The voice was guarded.

"I'm sorry to bother you, but let me begin by assuring you I'm not calling to sell you anything."

"Yes? How may I help you, then?" The woman's voice remained wary, or perhaps it was just curious.

"I'm looking for a woman named Elizabeth Barnett who stayed in a place called Hot Springs Island, British Columbia, in Canada for six or seven months almost thirty years ago. It's a question about inheritance...I found your name on the Internet and I was wondering if you might be that person or know anything about her."

"Oh, you're the same one, then, who put that ad in the paper, aren't you?"

"Yes, that's me."

"I must say, when I saw that ad I did think it was an extraordinary coincidence that you would be in Bath looking for a person with my name. But, it isn't such an unusual name, I suppose, so..."

"So I've been finding."

"Well, I'm sorry to have to tell you, Mr. Chiron, that I've never been to British Columbia, although I did once visit a cousin in Toronto — and a very lovely city it is. I must also tell you that the photograph most certainly wasn't of me, either — although I wish it was, seeing how attractive she is and now with an inheritance and all. Also, I'm quite a bit older than this other Elizabeth Barnett you're looking for."

From her voice, Jason knew this might be the case.

"So you're calling up all the Elizabeth Barnetts you can find, is that it?"

"Yes, that's right. You don't know any others, do you?" He kept his tone jovial.

The woman laughed. "Not that I can think of." Then: "I hope you don't think me rude, but what's your relation to this Elizabeth Barnett?"

"I'm a relative."

"I thought usually solicitors conducted these kinds of inheritance searches," said the woman.

"Well, I wouldn't know how other people go about it."

"Would you be her nephew then, or perhaps her son?"

Jason hesitated for a moment. "I'm her son and, anyway, thank you for your time, Ms. Barnett. I'm very sorry to disturb you."

"Not at all. I wish you all the luck in the world on your search. And keep trying, you never know what may turn up."

"Thank you," Jason said and rung off. On the other end, however, this older Elizabeth, a retired teacher who was most definitely not Jason's mother, sat down to think. After a few minutes, she rummaged through some old boxes for a yearbook and flipped through it until she settled on a small black and white photo. She searched for her telephone directory in a polished walnut credenza, and then looked up the number. After a moment's hesitation, she made a telephone call to a suburb north of London.

Chapter 13 iNovel Link
The Chapter 13 iNovel Link is a web-oriented link. By going to **www.HotSpringsNovel.com/chapter13/** you will be able to see the homepage designed by Jason for Destiny Press, including the company's new logo.

Chapter 14

"You have to understand that. Right now.
Right away. Don't you see?"

Although Jason continued his private mission, he was committed to making the new Destiny Press a success. His usual Saturday routine was to travel to the office early by bike, check his e-mail, surf the Net and then attempt to scratch from his lengthy To Do list as many items as possible.

One morning Jason emerged from Mrs. Flaherty's. He examined the sky to gauge the weather, then unlocked his bicycle and pedaled off towards the office. Jason often took varying routes to work. He liked looking around and growing familiar with the different neighborhoods as he cruised up one street and pedaled down another. When he rode, he tried to think of The Next Big Thing, that brilliant mind-blowing idea Seamus had demanded of him all those weeks ago. He had yet to deliver.

A white car was parked halfway down the block on the opposite side of the street from Mrs. Flaherty's. Until Jason's appearance the engine had been running, at which point, a woman in the driver's seat turned it off. She watched intently as the young man threw on his backpack, checked the sky again, inserted his ear-phones and rode into the distance.

The key has got to be innovation, he thought. He

had to conceive of something innovative enough to generate publicity as opposed to advertising. To get tongues wagging. Word of mouth sells. The concept had to build enough steam to reach critical mass and drive it past the tipping point into full-blown success. It had to be mainstream yet at the same time appeal intellectually. The challenge was daunting.

He barely registered that the same white car was now traveling slowly half a block behind him on a long and bumpy, well-treed road.

Half a mile from the office, Jason stopped for a traffic light. Glancing over his shoulder, he saw the same white car still a half-block behind. The road ahead was clear, but still the car just dawdled along.

Just as the traffic light changed to green, the white car pulled into a driveway, thus explaining why it was traveling so slowly. He didn't give it a second thought. The moment Jason disappeared, the white car and its solitary driver headed for the motorway.

Sometimes, like now, she bitterly regretted her vow to never make her presence known, to never intrude. Other times, the guilt of what she'd done paralyzed her with such intensity she questioned who and what she was. She had lived with this for thirty years. She'd waited for time to dull the scar to acceptable pink from angry red. She recalled her conversation with Elizabeth Barnett, her former teacher whose name she'd borrowed and who'd led her to this spot. She saw herself in the rear-view mirror. The light, almost honey, hue of her brown eyes had changed little as she'd aged, but now, along the edges, wrinkles and cracks had appeared. She imagined they were the tributaries of some great river breaking away from the mother flow, finding their own way to the sea.

• • •

Of the publisher's four divisions, Destiny Fiction plainly had the most potential for growth and success, and it attracted Jason in ways the other offshoots didn't. Rumor had it that Seamus was planning to flog both *Farming News* and the self-publishing division if he could, and possibly even expand Destiny Travel.

To build the DF website, Jason needed to familiarize himself with the list and authors. After spending time with the editors and books, faithfully bringing home a new volume or manuscript every night, he'd come away favorably impressed. He'd underestimated the quality of the fiction they'd published in the past and planned for the future. Seamus said that the dismal financial picture of the firm wasn't attributable to the product itself but to mismanaged resources, ridiculous personnel decisions, and — most importantly — pathetic marketing and distribution described by Seamus as "diseased and dysenteric — classic D&D." Editorially, the company was sound, if a tad conservative, but Maddie was helping DF create a niche as *the* place for young writers. "We innovate or die," she succinctly put it in one of Seamus's infamous stand-up meetings.

Jason's desk was stacked with books, newly printed flyers, author bios, catalogues and point-of-purchase materials. He kept shifting his gaze back and forth between his screen and the pile and wondering what in god's name he could do that would meet Seamus's criteria for something inspiring, something unique, something grand.

Jason never worked without his iPod, a tool he believed as essential to his craft as his laptop or degree. He even planned to deduct it as a tax expense. His preferred musical genre when coding was fusion — the lyrics distracted him and the driving beat urged him to completion. Baroque was great for more sedate, artistic tasks — the influence of Mum and The Pit, he suspected. A recent discovery was the eclectic Russell Rose, one of DF's authors and a budding Renaissance man. In fact, Jason was listening to Russell's music while examining sample *Absolution* covers circulated by the design staff for feedback. Russell's new book, *Absolution*, was to lead the spring list and the cover choice was important. To get a better sense of *Absolution*'s essence, he picked up a galley and started reading.

That's when it hit him — BAM! BAM! BAM! — the intellectual equivalent of Seamus pounding the door in the middle of the night. He looked again at the cover on his screen, then down at the passage he was reading, then at his iPod. Jason was reading a passage where the protagonist, waking from a prolonged coma, finds his loved ones dead — when the music shifted in sublime unison from one minor key to another, a transition of mood that matched perfectly, exquisitely, the tone of the book. There it is, Jason thought. *There it is.* It seemed so obvious, so bloody obvious. A literary-musical fusion. Just as music adds power to film, Russell could link his compositions to certain book passages or chapters. Readers could don their headphones or switch on their stereos as they read these chapters. They'd become part of the process. They could even rearrange the music sections. Destiny Press could include the CD with the book. They could sell it separately. They'd have two versions. Why, they couldn't even podcast it…."Damn!" Here was a chance to revamp the whole DF list.

So…what to call it? Enhanced novel, bonus features novel…or what about making up a new word like Google and Yahoo had done — a Movel, say, or Mook. Looking over at his iPod again, it twigged: how about M-Novel?

What if it's already been done? With urgency verging on panic, he typed in all the search variations he could think of. He learned that someone had published a CD of songs found in the novels of James Joyce. There was a large community of hypertext novels, e-novels and stage musicals based on famous works of fiction. But no mainstream publisher had produced a novel with soundtrack. This couldn't wait. He had to tell Seamus now.

To Mrs. Flaherty's extreme disappointment, Seamus had departed the guesthouse's Owl Suite ("I'll make it up to you, luv, just you wait") for new digs. He had found an extraordinary place to live: a converted wooden narrow boat docked at the far end of Sydney Wharf. Jason rang ahead to tell Seamus he was coming and the Irishman greeted him dockside. A wood stove glowed warmly inside the lovingly constructed craft's living room. Predictably, a bottle stood ready as well. Books (mainly DF titles) dominated the room and Seamus shifted some volumes onto a sideboard to clear space to sit.

After preliminary small talk and the requisite toast ("May you live to be a hundred years, with one extra year to repent"), Jason made his pitch

"So here's what I think, Seamus. I've read lots of the novels on our backlist and, you know what, they're good. They've very good. But I've never heard of them. There's so much fiction out there these days, the question becomes how to separate our titles from the rest of the crowd. How do you make them stand out and generate buzz? It seems to me that with the best-sellers, either your author is already a huge name, they win a big award or the book is about some huge news topic — something everybody wants to read. But there's something else, another way: innovation garners interest.

"But you have to be careful. People like new ideas but not radical ones. And that's what this idea is." He paused. "I think we should call it the M-Novel."

Jason described his idea and made a case that DF would gain a reputation for innovation that would attract new literary talent. "And we can redo our backlist as M-Novels!"

Seamus neither dominated the conversation nor interrupted with his customary astute questions. Even more uncharacteristically, he lowered his glass, balled his hands into fists and placed them against his cheeks, elbows on knees, head down — a classic thinker's pose. Jason took fifteen minutes. The room's only sounds were the ticking of the antique walnut clock above the bookcase and the gentle lap of the canal's water against *Hera*'s thick dark hull.

Then he leapt to his feet, hurtled like a ball from a cannon, and grabbed Jason under his arms, lifting him to his feet. The space between their faces was so minimal that drops of whiskey were visible clinging to Seamus's salt and pepper moustache. His voice had the texture of a hammer banging nails into wood.

"Good on you, Jason!" Seamus said enthusiastically, "Good on you. I like the idea. I like the idea a lot." Seamus's mind was traveling a million miles an hour. "I like the balance between innovation and practicality. I like that you've thought about this from a commercial perspective while never forgetting that the book itself has to be good. The M-Novel idea can generate the first wave of buyers and then we let Russell do the rest. And you've thought about all our key stakeholders and come up with the backbone of a great plan. But what I like most, Jason — what I like most — is that you came through for me. I asked you to come up with something new and different and innovative — not an easy task in an occasionally moribund industry — and you did."

And then Seamus gave Jason such a crushing hug that Jason feared broken ribs. When he released Jason, Seamus began pacing about so furiously he literally rocked the boat.

Seamus's thumb and forefinger continually pinched his moustache as he rattled off words and ideas at a dizzying rate. "But but but…although this is fantastic — fan-fucking-tastic — we also have to be careful. There are bastards out there, Jason, bastards around every corner. Believe me, I know this business and the competition and they're all bloody snakes in the grass and you can't trust a single one of them. It's a solid idea — but it's also one that's eminently pinchable. Whoever's quickest off the mark, they're the ones who'll gain the recognition and the publicity and that has to be us. It has to be. We've got to keep this quieter than a priest with a prostitute, is that understood? Not a single solitary word!"

They spent the rest of the night talking about implementation. When Jason left (slightly sozzled, his usual state after a Seamus session), he felt as puffed and powerful as the Egyptian pharaohs he'd seen in the British Museum. Seamus's final words, "Well done, my lad," rang long and loud in Jason's head. He felt like one of Tom Wolfe's masters of the universe, riding home on bike tires made light with glory.

• • •

The phone rang in the Robin Suite. Jason answered.

"An outside caller for you, Mr. Jason," said Mrs. Flaherty. And then in a whisper: "I think it's about your mother. He said something about that ad in the paper. I'll put you through quick as a wink."

"Jason Chiron speaking."

"You the chap that put in that ad with the photo, the one in the paper? Asking for information about a Miss Elizabeth Barnett?" The voice was male and probably middle-aged. Maybe West Country with a touch of something else — Jason was unable to tell. The man spoke slowly and deliberately, wanting Jason to understand every word.

"Yes. That's me. Could I have your name please?"

"I think we might leave that till later," the man drawled.

"What do you mean?"

"Well, are you interested in finding this lady or are you not?"

"Yes, of course I am."

"Well, then it should be worth something to you, no?"

"What exactly do you want?"

"You know what I'm saying. Information's usually worth something, wouldn't you agree? It's valuable, is what I'm saying."

"Where could we meet?" Jason asked.

The man named a teashop in the center of town. They agreed to meet in an hour. "You'll know me by a copy of the newspaper on the table," said the man.

"I'll be there." Jason phoned Maddie but couldn't reach her. He decided to walk instead of taking his bike and he could already feel the cold. The temperature hovered barely above freezing. He pulled the dark woolen scarf tighter around his neck and wondered what was in store.

The man was in place as promised. A half-finished cup of tea was on the table along with a well-worn plaid cap and the newspaper. Jason thought about shaking hands but the man's expression stopped him.

With a nod he indicated that Jason should sit down. His beard was red mottled with gray and his skin was pallid but splotched, matching his grog-blossom nose.

The man leaned forward. "I've got the information you want."

"And what would that be, exactly?" Jason remained calm. How could a man like this have anything to do with his mother?

"I have an envelope in my pocket with an address innit. You slide fifty quid inside this newspaper here and I'll hand over the envelope. That's how it works." He looked like a bulldog — a bearded, alcohol-dependent and fifty-year-old bulldog.

"And this address...are you saying it's the address of Elizabeth Barnett, the person in the picture?"

"I'm saying that this address will help you find her."

"How did you get it? And how do I know you're telling the truth."

"You don't. It's totally up to you, mate. Take it or leave it." He leaned back in his chair. Jason sensed it wouldn't take much for Bulldog to leave.

"I don't have fifty pounds. I never carry that much cash."

The eyes grew narrow. "How much you got, then?"

Jason took out his wallet and counted. "Just over thirty."

The man thought for a second. "All right then. Put it in the paper."

Jason slid in the cash as directed. The man removed a soiled-looking envelope from an inner pocket. It was sealed but bore no name or writing. The second the money was inside the folded newspaper, the man slapped cap on head and hurried out of the restaurant. Hands shaking, Jason tore open the envelope and removed a piece of paper. Scribbled in pencil was an address: St. Stephen's Hospital, Watley Road, Salisbury, Wiltshire.

A hospital of all things. ...What did this mean? That she worked there or was a patient? Could she be a doctor or a nurse? Jason had to learn more. Throwing coins on the table, Jason dashed into the street, his breath visible in the cold and momentarily reminding him of steam rising from a hot spring. He scanned the street twice, three times; Bulldog had vanished.

That night Jason dreamed of Kiriko standing on the outer rim of the beachside hot springs.

. . .

Maddie came by Flaherty House the next day after dropping the kids at a birthday party. Mrs. Flaherty flashed a traffic warden's disapproving look at Maddie climbing the stairs to the Robin Suite and Maddie smiled sweetly in return.

Before long they were huddled in front of the two-bar electric fire.

"Listen," said Jason. "I popped down to the office this morning and checked out this St. Stephen's place on the Net."

"And?"

"It's an acute mental health-care facility run by the National Health Service."

"So it's a psychiatric hospital?"

"Yes." They both went silent. "So do we go?"

"We could phone first," said Jason. "It'd be much quicker."

"Yes, of course. But don't you want to go and see it for yourself? I would if it were me. Isn't the suspense killing you?"

"I'm half-afraid of what we'll find. I have to tell you, there's more of a sense of dread than anything else. I mean, a mental hospital..."

"I understand," said Maddie.

"How far is it?" Jason asked.

"Maybe fifty miles, give or take. On the A36, I think. We could easily get there and back in a day."

He loved that Maddie said "we."

"But what if we found something? Could we stay over if need be?"

"I don't know. I haven't thought about it. I suppose so. I'd have to talk it over with David. Make sure he's okay with the kids."

"Or you could just leave me there and come back by yourself. In fact, you don't even need to come at all if you don't want to."

"I'm your search angel. We're in this together."

"Hey — isn't Salisbury close to Stonehenge?"

"Indeed."

"I was thinking...if nothing pans out maybe we could do a quick detour, after. I'd love to see Stonehenge. We could play it by ear."

"Listen," Maddie said, "how does this sound? You call the hospital and make an appointment for, say, I don't know, Tuesday. Give them the general picture. We'll supply the details when we get there."

"Sounds good."

"So we drive down early Tuesday to visit the hospital, and we could stop at Stonehenge, either on the way there or the way back, depending on the appointment. That'll also tell us if we need to stay over. I'll talk to David."

"Sounds like a plan." Jason continued thinking. "But, you know what, I'm going to book a room anyway. I haven't seen anything of England outside London and Bath so I'll stay there for a night, regardless. Plus, I wouldn't mind taking a couple of days off. I've got so many back days owing, it's ridiculous. But — it's not a problem you taking Tuesday off?"

"Actually, I'd love to. David and I had a terrific row last night." She was glum.

"What about?"

"You know, it's getting to the point where it's not just the affairs or the lies anymore. It's just him; who he is. The real question is, can I continue living with this man without becoming someone I hate or driving me stark raving mad or...oh, don't get me started.

But, listen," Maddie said. "I have to dash." She stood up quickly. "I'll see you at work tomorrow, Jason," and she kissed him gently on the cheek.

● ● ●

He called St. Stephen's Sunday and Monday and was finally able to arrange to meet Dr. Roger Nutall, for noon on Wednesday. He also booked two rooms in Salisbury, in case Maddie stayed, and rented a vehicle.

Maddie cleared her trip with David and Jason informed Seamus he was taking time off to travel and follow some leads in his search for Elizabeth.

"No longer than two days, though," cautioned Seamus. "The Project is entering a crucial phase. I need you here."

"For sure. I'll be back on Friday at the very latest. Probably earlier."

Jason was looking forward to a road trip with Maddie, but he couldn't stop imagining Elizabeth with some horrible affliction.

He picked Maddie up at 8 a.m. The day was cold. The forecast suggested snow was possible, the first of the year. When they stopped for warm scones and tea at a roadside café, Maddie began telling Jason about Stonehenge and other sites on the Salisbury Plain. Halfway to their destination it started snowing. The rich flakes were shaped "like thin slices of ice cream," Maddie said. Her mood grew lighter the more it snowed and the farther they traveled from Bath. By the time they reached Stonehenge, the snow was falling steadily. The road remained clear but the open fields around the prehistoric site looked like acres of recently milled paper or a vast bridal train.

They parked the car and headed towards the site — history on the horizon. Huge snowflakes kept catching on Maddie's long eyelashes, and this made them laugh. She was wearing a black tam, a thick muffler and a dark coat; when the snow lit upon her, Jason thought of day and night, brightness and dark.

"Look at them," she said. Whether due to snow or just luck, they were alone. "When I was a child, you could walk right up to the stones. None of these restraining ropes were here. You could get so close."

"These larger ones on the outside are called Sarsens, if I remember correctly. The inner ones are bluestones, and, if you chip away the surface, they *are* really quite blue underneath. But the amazing thing is, they're probably from Wales, transported all this way."

"From Wales?"

"Yes. Three or four hundred kilometers away. Carried by rafts, mainly, on rivers."

"Wasn't this place some kind of early observatory?"

"They think so but no one's really sure. The Heel Stone," she said pointing, "that's the key. If you align it with the center of the ruins, it predicts the position of sunrise on the summer solstice."

Jason and Maddie stopped talking to let the past settle around them. This was the most ancient man-made structure Jason would ever likely see. It forced him to think of the continuity of human civilization and how, although we only live one generation at a time, we build on the present like stairs rising from the past. This place had an undeniable power — just like hot springs, humanity and nature fused here.

They stood before the ancient bluestones and the Sarsens. They also stood very close to one another, trying to stay warm but also wanting to share in these miraculous moments. The snow continued unabated. You could almost hear the sound of the flakes falling onto the monoliths.

Jason wore no hat. His thick hair was turning white. Maddie removed her glove and gently brushed the top of his head. Then she said, "I bet you taste like snow."

• • •

Driving to Watley Road on the outskirts of Salisbury, Jason felt like the swirling snowstorm had found its way inside him. He felt guilty but released. As they neared St. Stephen's, he knew he had to put aside the events at Stonehenge. The immediacy of what lay before them demanded unwavering attention.

The facility looked well cared for. Ivy on the exterior walls even suggested a certain pastoral quality. Maddie guessed it was a manor house in an earlier incarnation. Once inside, that universal hospital odor brought memories of Angel and her baby.

An inquiry at reception led them to Dr. Nutall's office. Jason's pulse raced and he felt flushed. The doctor was momentarily out. They sat on two maroon leather chairs facing a large desk covered with neatly piled file folders. It was the room of a busy but organized professional.

The door opened. Roger Nutall was a large, rather handsome man with a deep voice and firm hand-shake. His face and smile were kind and he moved with a former athlete's grace. A photo of his wife and four children stood beside the stack of folders. Although Jason had no psychologists or psychiatrists as friends or even acquaintances, he tended to picture them as off-kilter or eccentric — neither label applied to this man.

Loath to waste time, he told the story of discovering Elizabeth, his arrival in England and Bath, and the purpose of his visit. Dr. Nutall listened and examined Elizabeth's photo with equal care. Jason described his meeting with Bulldog and laid the soiled envelope and piece of paper on the desk.

"And that's all you have?" asked the doctor.

"Yes. Nothing more. I have no idea if she ever worked here, or was a patient, or what. Nothing."

"And what about a time period? Nothing there either?"

"No."

"I'll get someone to check." He copied the details from the paper onto a yellow pad then studied the newspaper again. "If you don't mind, I'll take this and have the photo circulated. If anyone knows her or recognizes the face, then we'll see what we can do. I'll also call some of my counterparts at other institutions.

And of course I'll check our records. I can't promise anything beyond that, I'm afraid."

"That's actually a lot. Thank you," said Jason. "We appreciate you seeing us like this. My number's on the ad."

"I'll do what I can," said the doctor. "But, as I said, I wouldn't get your hopes up. In any event, if we find out anything, I'll call."

On the outside steps, Jason and Maddie heard screaming. A woman's piercing shriek escaped from somewhere within the large building. Jason stopped. Silence.

Maddie spoke: "Let's look on the bright side. We're not any worse off and we can discount that she is a patient right now."

"At least under that name," Jason replied. "That's the thing. We need to know her real name."

"Well, maybe the photo will do the trick. All we can do is wait and see."

"Yeah, I know. But I thought we were on to something."

"Look on the bright side," Maddie said. "Think how much time we have together."

They lunched in Salisbury and then strolled through the town, finally arriving at the cathedral, one of the country's most famous. "The spire's the tallest in England," said Maddie. Although not as old as Stonehenge, it was one of the most beautiful structures Jason had ever seen and more than seven hundred years old.

By the time they returned to the main entrance

from the Close, the Bishop's Walk and the Palace, it was after five. Maddie wanted to hear Evensong, which began at 5:30 p.m.

In red and white robes, choirboys filed into a side chapel and began to sing. The ethereal sound was chilling. Goose bumps formed on Jason's wrists and neck. He imagined peasant farmers from seven centuries ago attending such a service. Sitting beneath overwhelming, soaring vaulted ceilings while listening to heavenly voices echoing and reverberating, they must certainly have felt the presence of God. No wonder religion exercised the grip it did. Even Jason, critical of organized religion and the ills it brought, couldn't help be moved by the voices and harmony and the pure quality of the acoustics and the place and the moment.

He wondered if Elizabeth had ever been here. Perhaps she'd sat in this very pew and heard the exact same hymns. And if she'd been here, what went through her mind at the time? Could she have been induced by the place and mood to reflect upon her life and the decisions she'd made? Had she sat here and regretted giving up her child, wondering about what he'd become and how things might have been different?

When it was over, they walked back to the car park, still reliving their moments in the great cathedral.

"It's quite rare to see it white like this, I suspect," Maddie said. "As if it were somehow more pure than usual. Virginal almost."

"Yeah," Jason said. "A virginal phallic symbol. Good one."

Maddie decided to stay the night in Salisbury. They checked into separate rooms to clean up and make phone calls.

They agreed to meet in Jason's room for a night-cap. Maddie wanted to freshen up first. While she was gone, Jason opened a bottle of wine they'd picked up earlier while strolling through the snowy town. Maddie took some time to arrive. Each hallway sound seemed unusually loud. Jason could feel his shirt brush against his skin. He looked in the mirror and removed an imaginary something.

Jason heard footsteps. He went to the door. On Maddie's soft knock, he opened the door and she was inside. They moved deeper into the dusk of the room, and he poured the wine. They clinked glasses and drank the dark red wine that he'd opened earlier to breathe. They were both breathless.

Maddie wore a long skirt of some silky material that looked impossibly smooth. She had a crisp white blouse with two buttons undone revealing a lacy peach-colored camisole and tantalizing skin.

Although the bedside light was on, it was the flame of the gas fireplace that lit the room. They sat in twin armchairs near the fire and finished the first glass of wine. When their hands touched as they put down their glasses, they twined and untwined hands and fingers.

Jason looked directly into Maddie's brown eyes. "Maddie."

"Yes." She returned his look.

"I don't know how you're feeling, although I think I do. But I just wanted to tell you that being with you today...I can't tell you what you and your help have meant to me these past few weeks, these months. You've truly been my angel."

"And you me," she replied, her voice husky. "You don't know what it's been like for me since I found out about David. I felt devalued and unattractive. It's meant so much to me to feel alive again. You've been...my rock, really. Remember the heel stone at Stonehenge? How it aligns with the center of everything, how it predicts where the sun will rise. Well, that's what you've been to me." Maddie reached up and stroked the skin on Jason's cheek. In response, Jason took her hand and began kissing it. Then, his lips found hers, or perhaps hers found his. It didn't matter. All seemed inevitable now. Jason could feel his heart pumping strongly in his chest. Their kisses grew longer and longer. Both knew the bed was only feet away. Breathless, Jason broke away for a moment.

"Maddie, I have to ask you something. I feel obliged to."

"Ask me what?"

"That you're sure. Are you absolutely sure this is what you want?"

"Just stop talking, you goof," she rewarded him with a kiss of such probing sensuousness that it could leave no doubt whatsoever.

"Maddie..."

"Oh Jason," she sighed and upon them was the moment when words became superfluous. The wineglasses were set aside. She moved onto his lap and their lips intertwined then came apart. Accompanied by short gasps and breaths and wordless encouragements, their hands became extensions of their desires. He could feel her weight against his firmness and every time she moved she brushed against it, sending him to another level of expectation.

They were on the bed now kissing necks, eyes, faces, and hands. Though they both longed to tear their clothes from themselves and each other and deliver the gratification they both knew awaited them, they were equally aware that prolonging each moment heightened their senses, their touch, the experience.

The kisses were a continuation of those this morning, as if the hours between hadn't existed. Now, though, their kisses were not confined to face or head or neck. Now it was hands and arms and fingers, anywhere and everywhere. Jason helped Maddie remove her blouse; her shoulders and back became new territory to explore. She felt Jason's length through his corduroy trousers and he shook with pleasure and anticipation. How long since he'd felt this — this power, this intimacy.

She understood the power of temptation and lingered often. She slowly undid Jason's shirt, button by button. Every minute they drank deeper of each other. Soon her skirt was undone and off, draped on the armchair like a flag no longer needed. Maddie wore white sheer stockings with lace tops that stayed up without assistance. She was braless under her camisole and Jason had already dampened her nipples through the peach silk with his mouth and slid his hand around and under and over so that he now knew, instead of imagined, the texture of her breasts, the firmness of her nipples, the circumference of her aureoles.

They continued their kisses; each piece of clothing finding the chair or floor was the curtain rising on another act. Each minute deepened and strengthened what was to follow.

Maddie was breathless. "Now. I want you now. I can't wait any longer. I want you inside me." Jason was completely unclothed now and only Maddie's stockings remained. They had already tasted each other, separate, then together, and then separate again. He now knew what her grip on him felt like, her hand touching him and moving him. She had made him shudder and him her.

"Hold it," he said, almost unimaginably, momentarily breaking the spell. "Wait. Protection."

"No, I'm safe," she whispered, "I'm on the pill." Maddie didn't want to wait. She wouldn't wait. She reached for him and guided him into her, both of their backs arching as he found her. She sighed so loudly Jason thought she might be crying.

"Are you all right?" He feared hurting her.

She said "yes, yes" over and over and she called his name repeatedly until it became part of their rhythm, her voice and his voice and the sighs and the moans one aspect of this rhythm, this motion, this physical and deeper wanting. He remained atop her and then he was behind and then beside her. Then she demanded him below her, underneath her, so she could set the rhythm and see his face and rest her hands on his chest while finding the sweetest contact and losing herself in the slide and the friction and the pulses that came like waves. Although he wanted to go longer, and tried stopping to regain his breath and his control, she wouldn't let him, her rhythm insisting that he continue, her body demanding that he release now, release deep into her. She'd already been there twice, she whispered, and now she wanted him to find his, which he did, shaking and shuddering like a sailboat suddenly catching the wind. His breath was heaving and beads of sweat dotted them both.

"Oh Jason," she sighed and hugged him close. He responded. Before long, their kisses refreshed their briefly spend ardor and they made love again. This time it was more leisurely, more poignant. They lay entwined and exhausted until Maddie rose to use the bathroom.

When she returned sometime later, she asked him if he wanted something to eat.

"I'm plenty satiated," he joked but she didn't laugh.

"What about a drink?" she asked.

"No, love. I'm fine. Come and join me." She stood a few feet from the bed.

"I'm hungry," she said, "I've got some snacks in my room. I'm going to get them."

"What?" Jason asked. "Now?"

"Yes." She started dressing. Jason raised himself on an elbow, surprised. He'd been expecting pillow talk and soft caresses. Not the munchies.

"Is something wrong?"

"You're not hungry?" she asked again.

"Maddie...what is it? Are you okay?"

"I'm fine," she said, but didn't sound fine. Before he knew it, she'd slipped from the room.

Until he heard the key he was afraid she wasn't coming back. She peeled an orange and arranged nuts and biscuits on a napkin. Poured some juice into the glasses that she'd emptied of wine and then washed. With her completely dressed, Jason felt awkward naked. He slipped on his T-shirt and underpants.

"Here," she said, and handed him an orange slice. She wouldn't meet his eyes.

"Maddie...what is it? What's wrong? Has something happened? Did I do something wrong?"

She said nothing. Just nibbled on her food, eyes down.

"I wasn't that bad, was I?" Jason tried to kid.

"You were wonderful. That's part of the problem. In fact, I've never experienced anything like that in my whole life." But the timber of her voice belied her words. He'd never seen her like this before. He reached out and touched her forearm as she was putting some nuts in her mouth. She stood up.

"Jason. I have to go. I have to go home and make things right," she said suddenly.

"What? What are you talking about?"

"I'm sorry, but I have to go home. I have to go home and make things right."

"Home? I don't understand."

Jason could see the tension in her throat, her larynx moving up and down.

"Jason. This is wrong. I didn't feel like this at all when we were making love. But now I know. It's all wrong."

"Maddie. It's nothing, it's...I don't know...it's probably just a letdown after making love or something." He was babbling. This was totally unexpected. "I asked if you were sure and you said—"

"I just have to go home and make it right. You have to understand that. Right now. Right away." She started gathering her things.

"You mean you're really leaving?" He was dumbfounded.

"Yes. I'm leaving. I feel so guilty...oh my god, what have I done..." She was close to tears.

"Guilty? But after what you told me about David, this hardly seems—"

"Don't you understand? It's not David. That's not who I feel guilty about. It's my children. My babies. It's them I'm betraying. I can't put everything at risk like this. I can't put *them* at risk like this. Not my babies. I've made a huge mistake, Jason. I have to go *now*."

"But what does this mean for us...and, how are you going to get back?" His thoughts smashed together like random atoms.

"Please let me have the car, Jason. You're not in a hurry. You can take the train tomorrow or later or whenever."

"What about the snow?"

"I don't care—"

"I'll come with you."

"No."

"But Maddie…"

From his window he watched her leave the car park and drive into the night. The snow had stopped. The sledgehammer slamming into his heart told him that it was over. He felt like a cage had been placed around him and he couldn't escape no matter what action he took or no matter what course he steered.

Chapter 14 iNovel Link

This iNovel Link is a dramatized reading of the section when Jason and Maddie arrive at Stonehenge. The passage begins on page 210, with the words: "Halfway to their destination it started snowing." Please go to **www.HotSpringsNovel.com/chapter14/** to listen.

Chapter 15

*"Then and only then can we perhaps
move on with our lives."*

Jason e-mailed Maddie repeatedly. He was desperate for another chance. He even tried phoning her at home when he knew David was out but, unsurprisingly, all he got was her machine. Two days had passed since his return from Salisbury. Maddie had called in sick every day since. Jason wondered if she'd told David or how she'd handled things at home. Regret consumed him.

He slumped at his desk, staring into his screen. Was this some kind of karma? A repayment for giving up on Kiriko? Did Kevin's intimations of smoke and fire resulting from betrayal have more merit than he thought? Or perhaps these were Dada's dire warnings being served. What had he said — that the inevitable result was some messy reality.

Jason's cell phone buzzed.

"Jason Chiron."

"Jason. This is Roger Nutall from St. Stephen's."

"Dr. Nutall...thank you for calling. How are you?"

"I'm fine, thank you. I did some checking to see if I could find anything about your mother, Elizabeth Barnett."

"Yes?"

"I'm sorry to say that I've only got bad news and

bad news. Or, better put, I've got no news and bad news."

"What do you mean?"

"First of all. I found no trace of an Elizabeth Barnett as either patient or employee anywhere in the mental health system."

"Oh, I see."

"As for the bad news, it's related to that chap you referred to as...let me see...the Bulldog."

"Yes?"

"To be direct, I think you've been a victim of fraud. Two of my counterparts at other facilities have met with people like yourself who'd been directed to them by a person matching the description of this Bulldog character. We think he finds missing person ads, meets the interested party, takes their money and then sends them to a suitably far and complex place like ours. An easy getaway. There's no shortage of people trying to take advantage of the innocent, believe me." The doctor seemed to speak from experience. "Might I suggest that you consider consulting the police?"

"I see," said Jason. Though unhelpful, one possibility was now eliminated. It should hardly have come as surprising.

"I'm sorry to be the bearer of bad news."

"Thank you for going to so much trouble. It was very kind of you."

"Good luck, Jason. I hope you find her."

So, another hope punctured — not that he'd held much of one after the visit to St. Stephen's. But any possibility was better than none. He was absolutely nowhere in his search and, combined with the disaster of the Maddie affair...Jason slumped back again. What would have happened with Maddie if he'd done things differently? Taken things slower. Despite what had happened, he wanted her back. He wanted her friendship back.

Seamus called him into his office.

"What's wrong, laddie? You've been moping round the last few days like a drunk at closing time. Out with it."

"I thought I was onto a big lead in Salisbury but it fizzled like all the rest. I'm no further ahead than when I arrived."

"Even with Maddie's help?"

Jason looked up quickly. Seamus fixed him with squinty eyes. Did he know something? Had he drawn conclusions from his and Maddie's overlapping days off?

"Yes. Even with Maddie's help."

"Well, then. You'd best hire that pro you've been talking about. Go for the one in Bristol if you ask me. And do it now. Cause I can't have you fucking about. We're too close to releasing *Absolution*—. Do you know how important this is? Have you any idea?"

"I do."

"Well then, don't let me down, lad. And don't let your colleagues — or yourself — down either. There's too much riding on this."

"I understand."

"Well, get cracking then. And, listen, give me the name of this people-search pro and your files and I'll call him for you. While you," he said, finger stabbing the air in Jason's direction, "get back to work." Seamus held Jason at arm's length and gave him a penetrating look, "I know what you're going through. I'm 100 percent behind you."

The talk helped. Jason left Seamus's office newly motivated and resolved. He'd lose himself in work. If he'd learned one thing from Mum's death, it was the banal truism about time healing wounds. Things do move on. Life does return to normal. You come out of the troughs to see land ahead and eventually sun on the horizon.

• • •

Finally, late on Sunday night, Jason received an e-mail from Maddie to his private account.

> *Dear Jason,*
> I'm sorry. I'm sorry about what went on and how I've behaved. I'm sorry about everything. I'm coming to work tomorrow and I need you to pretend that nothing ever happened, to act like you barely know me. Please don't talk to me about anything besides work and, even then, try and keep it to a minimum. I know you're hurting but I am too. I'm feeling fragile beyond words. I can't offer anything beyond my sorrow.

I'm sure you were surprised at what happened. But even more than surprise, my overriding emotion is one of shame at my actions and my willingness to put my children at risk purely for my own selfish reasons. I hope that you, of all people, understand this. That the welfare of my children, all children, must be paramount always and unconditionally. I failed to realize that for one foolish moment, and now I don't know how to reconcile my reprehensible actions with the person I thought I once was. I have condemned David for something I willingly did myself. It is not easy understanding how one can be a hypocrite when there is nothing I despise more.

I'm counting on you. Then and only then can we perhaps move on with our lives. I don't know what else to say.

M.

● ● ●

Early on Monday, Jason received a call from the search professional in Bristol contacted by Seamus. An hour later, John S. Morgan was well briefed. He promised to do what he could as soon as possible. With Maddie almost certainly out of the picture, Mr. Morgan — a jolly-sounding character — seemed his last and best chance.

Her timing ironic, Maddie arrived in the office during Morgan's call. She looked pale and drawn. Another nail found its way into Jason's heart. Once or twice he saw her reflection in the window. But Maddie didn't turn towards him, not even when she passed him.

Destiny Press had never been busier. With only a week till the Christmas break, everyone was desperately trying to ready *Absolution* for its launch. Flyers and posters were arranged and the office hummed with purpose. Seamus brought staff from other divisions to help, and arranged a mystery-mailing package, called a teaser, to be sent to key reviewers and journalists hoping to pique their interest in the M-Novel concept. Jason was feeling equal amounts of pride and trepidation. The *Absolution* site was scheduled to go live in February and Jason was working closely with author/composer Russell Rose clearing up this and ironing out that. With Russell's blessing, Jason had even recorded and contributed a song to *Absolution*, called "Song for New York." With Andrea, Seamus was planning a publicity tour in North America.

When the office bustle suddenly fell quiet Jason realized just how close Christmas was. Weeks ago Maddie had invited him to spend it with her family. Now, his Christmas would be spent with Dianna in London.

Given the short December days, it was still dark when Jason reached Destiny on his last day of work. He was expecting to be alone — it was the 24th, after all — but the door was unlocked. Maddie was at her desk, transferring papers and files to her soft leather briefcase.

"Maddie."

She looked up.

"Jason." She'd managed to avoid being alone with him since Salisbury. "What are you doing here today?"

"Seamus asked me to work on his computer."

"You didn't come in just so you could catch me, did you?"

"Is that what you think of me? A stalker?"

"No, no...of course not." Maddie resumed collecting things. "Seamus called. After the holidays, I'm going to spend some time with Russell here and then bring him to the States with me. Seamus thinks the whole thing, the Music-Novel concept, is going to be big." This should have meant celebration: hugging and dancing.

"Oh. I see. That's great," said Jason.

"I'm working at home today," she said. "I needed some files and...I should really get going. I'm taking the kids to David's parents..."

Maddie moved towards the door, cutting Jason a wide berth.

"Jason. I hope you understand that it's over. Maybe David could do it, but I can't. This whole episode forced me to look very hard at myself, and I'm less than enamored with what I see."

And then she walked down the stairs, out into the still-dark morning.

• • •

The train took Jason past the green and brown countryside still dotted with snow. Inside, the car was overheated and he felt overinsulated. The wheels hummed on the tracks and the carriage creaked and groaned.

Jason carried only his backpack and a padded briefcase for his laptop. As cars and towns flashed by, he reached into the case. He'd been saving Kiriko's fourth letter. The reflections in the train window reminded him of her. And the dreamlike state he felt, this sense of drifting, of floating above the tracks, awakened the need to reconnect. He'd read her previous poems over and over. Especially since Maddie. They evoked Kiriko's spirit through and through. Her depths. Her thoughtfulness.

Jason sorted through his bag and found the envelope. But, instead of the fourth letter, he found only the original letter and the three notes he'd already read. He searched his bag again, and then went through his backpack. It was gone. He turned back to the glass and tried to find some essence of her in the unfurling ribbon of scenery.

The day was overcast and London emerged painted with a charcoal palette. Wreaths and cheery shop lights evoked Christmas as he walked from the tube station to Dianna's flat. Though he looked forward to seeing her, his mind, even now, was occupied with the search specialists he'd read about in London. Maybe this short trip could bring him closer to what he truly wanted.

. . .

The Christmas Eve party was hosted by one of Dianna's clients, a coiffed and tailored heiress who'd grown even wealthier selling her own brand of perfume. The house boasted butter-colored pillars, a granite entranceway, glittering chandeliers and even a monstrous curved staircase.

Liveried waiters passed silver trays of tall crystal champagne goblets. A string quartet played in one corner of the vast entrance hall.

Jason and Dianna snagged some champagne and toured the house. As they moved into what Dianna called the drawing-room, Jason asked who all the people were.

"Anyone and everyone," Dianna said. "She's on hubby number three, an aging has-been rocker. I bet half the people here are his friends looking for some good free grub."

It seemed that Dianna knew most of the other half of the crowd and a goodly portion of the ex-rocker's friends as well. As she chatted and air-kissed and was accosted by Jasmine-this and Bertrand-that, Jason made his way to the sumptuous buffet supplemented by the roving tuxedoed waiters carrying plates of pâté on pumpernickel and seatrout on salted biscuits too divine to be called crackers. The table glinted with heavy silverware and brilliantly polished plates. There was lobster, prawns, veal, savory lamb chops, something Jason thought was pheasant, smoked salmon and a hundred varieties of cheeses.

Dianna and Jason ate, drank, talked, mingled and gawked their way through the evening. He felt like a cultural voyeur spying on the glitterati. He had no stake in any of these people beyond Dianna and he was simultaneously attracted and repulsed by the conspicuous wealth and the need by so many, apparently, to see and be seen. It was dazzlingly shallow, and made him miss Hot Springs Island in ways he could never have anticipated.

Late in the evening, Jason left the overheated indoors for some air. "You can find me hiding in the manger," he told Dianna. In reply, Dianna kissed him on the cheek.

Even in the chilly courtyard, Jason had to inch around the crowds. The majority smoked cigarettes but some puffed on expensive oversized Montecristos. Jason detected the sweet smell of marijuana as well.

Suddenly, a camera flash was stuck directly in Jason's face and set off.

Jason could literally see stars but not the person who'd blinded him.

"So it is you, then, is it?"

It was Harry.

"I'm surprised you recognized me, actually, considering how drunk you were that night."

"I think you'd had a few yourself," Harry said. As much as Harry sought a little verbal payback, Jason was having none of it.

"If you'll excuse me..." Jason said, more than willing to leave Harry behind.

Harry blocked his way. Not aggressively, but it was obvious he wasn't finished. "So, have you done it with her? Is that what that whole night was about? Can't blame you, really, for being jealous — she's a lovely bit of tail, I have to admit. And next time — give her one for me, eh?"

Before Jason could respond, Dianna grabbed him 'round the waist, rosy-cheeked with sparkling eyes.

"I've got to tell you, I've got to tell you!" Dianna said excitedly to Jason. Then she saw Harry. Her body language not so much changed as melted. "Oh, it's you."

"I was just leaving," Harry said. "And don't forget what I told you, sport." He bled into the crowd.

"Oh, I'm sorry," Dianna said. "I knew he might be here. I was hoping he wouldn't but—"

"I'm sorry you had to see him."

"Was he beastly?"

"Nothing a good video screening wouldn't cure."

Dianna laughed. "Listen, do you want to go?" she asked.

"How about you?"

"I just have to say my goodbyes."

"Go for it."

• • •

The streets were busy well past midnight. Both Jason and Dianna were tipsy as they wove their way down the stairs into the flat. She hung on Jason's arm and chatted about Christmas on Hot Springs Island and how London was so different.

She made them rum hot toddies and continued her theme.

"Jason, did you ever see that film made by Ken Morrow?"

"Which one?" Ken was a high-school classmate. After graduation, he'd gone on to make documentaries.

"The one he made at uni. It was called *Christmas Spirit*, I think, and it was all quite depressing, really. How suicide rates soar at this time of year, how illness spikes, how many more people die, how lonely people get while everybody round them seems so full of good cheer."

"I've always thought the darkness and cold have something to do with it, too," Jason said. "The winter blues. After all, we've just passed the shortest day…"

"And the longest night," Dianna added. "And cities, I think cities bring people down, too. I understand Ken's film more now than when I first saw it. I feel a little bit of that, to be honest — the loneliness, I mean. I never did on Hot Springs, but here…Sorry, Jason, I don't mean to get maudlin on you. But anyway, that's the end of that. Let's change the subject. What did Harry say to you at the party?"

"Nothing worth mentioning. He's just a nasty man with a nasty little personality. I still don't get how you could have ever ended up with him."

"Well…new boss attracted to reasonably attractive account executive acts solicitous and — don't laugh please — charming. Reasonably attractive account exec feeling lonely and vulnerable and wondering what the hell she's doing with her life is glad of the attention and a warm body. Was it a mistake? Obviously. But, given where I was at that time, hardly surprising. Do you want something more to drink? How about a brandy?" Jason shook his head. Dianna filled a glass and downed most of it in one go.

"I mean, absolutely, he was the wrong guy. The problem's finding the right one."

"You must meet loads of people on the job. Look how many people you knew at the party tonight."

"Yeah, but did you look at them? As for the office, the good ones are married or involved or they're gay or they're crass."

"So who's the right one, the right type, for you?" Jason asked.

"Oh, I don't know," Dianna sighed. "I wish I did. Someone funny, intelligent, caring, some sensitive artist type, I suppose. I don't care that much about looks."

"As we could tell with Harry," Jason said. Dianna laughed in spite of herself.

"See! Someone who can make me laugh. That's what I need. London's a massive cold city, you know. And after you've been here awhile...not every day's fun." She finished off the glass. "I just want to say that I had a great time tonight, despite Harry." Dianna started laughing.

"What's so funny?"

"Harry and the videotape. It was so brilliant. *You were so brilliant*. God, that video..." she giggled. "I thought I was going to have to call the cops. I was so glad you were here."

"Ah, shucks," said Jason.

"Anyway," Dianna said, "I've drunk way too much and I'd better go to bed before I fall down on top of you." They hugged good night.

"Thanks for a great day," Jason said.

Jason lay on the spiky sofa bed in the dark. Somewhere between sleep and wakefulness, he heard something. Dianna was sitting close to him on the side of his thin mattress. She reached for his left hand, the one closer to her. She was wearing a diaphanous nightie, which he knew he could see through if he looked hard enough. He could almost feel her soft skin radiating warmth as if her cells had minds of their own and were inching irrevocably towards him. Pieces of mercury seeking each other. "You know, Jason. I was thinking about what we were talking about. About the kind of guy I want and need. Well, I realized something. What I need — who I need — is someone like you."

Her hand moved up his forearm. She looked at him. He was well aware they'd both been drinking and that they were both vulnerable. Cognizant that every single thing about the situation was wrong, he also knew that some other part of him, the realm of his body, wanted this. He was teetering, standing on the thinnest of edges, balancing, with the prospect of falling, falling, falling. The silence was overwhelming. Something had to happen to replace this static seam in time with motion and action.

He lay back on the bed to try and have a little distance — room to make sense of what was happening. His right arm dangled off the edge and grazed something. Immediately he identified the texture and knew what it was: Kiriko's final letter.

"Dianna, I don't think this is...going to work."

"I know. It would be...it would be too hard, way way too hard in so many ways. It would complicate things between you and Tina and, more importantly, it would change things between Tina and me. I couldn't do that to Tina. Or to me."

Jason recognized how close they'd come. Another minute and they might have been entwined. They'd danced on the rim of the volcano but survived.

She sighed. "I don't know," she said. "I'm sorry." Her kiss on the cheek was sisterly and belied the sheer nothingness of her nightgown. Her retreating footfalls meant that this moment would never return.

The sealed envelope was now streaked with dirt on the outside but its contents remained as pure as its brethren. Like the others, it contained a brief message and a poem.

Dear Jason,
When you read a letter like this, your thoughts fly across oceans and over the highest mountains and come to us. Time means nothing. Distance is only a state in the country of your thoughts. So it is with searching. You can find things even when you are not looking, though perhaps they are not the things you thought to look for at all. But you will still have found them. This poem is very old but it, too, has

crossed time and place and language. You and
I can cross those things, too. I wish you success on your search.

In the paths of my dreams
I walk to you without resting
but all of these dreams
are less than one moment
of seeing you
in the waking world
      Kiriko

Chapter 15 iNovel Link
By going to **www.HotSpringsNovel.com/chapter15/**
you can see Kiriko's fourth poem to Jason, including her
Japanese calligraphy.

Chapter 16

"People exist so they can be found."

After the New Year's break, with the help of Maddie and other DF staff, Russell Rose went on a major UK-wide campaign to try to enlist book chains, literary critics and even music-store owners to the M-Novel cause. Then, in late January, the whole team, including Seamus, would travel to the States and do the same thing all over. From all accounts, *Absolution*'s prospects in the US were optimistic. The early reviews admired "the sexy innovation showed by the plucky little publishing house."

Although impossible to tell if *Absolution*'s early success would continue, one thing appeared certain: Seamus enjoyed the limelight like "a porker in excrement," as one office wag described it. Every day it seemed reports filtered into the office that Seamus was fast becoming America' latest media darling and that he and Russell Rose were the new tag team of celebrity literati. Nothing topped the videotape sent over from the States, though — Seamus on a late-night talk show. People gathered in the meeting room to watch.

"So, Seamus," asked the host. "How did you come up with the idea in the first place?"

"Well, do you want me to be modest or truthful?" Seamus laughed, and winked at the audience. The camera loved him.

"Whichever you prefer."

"Well, as you've probably heard, we Irish like to say that if you kiss the Blarney Stone you're then blessed with the gift of eloquence — the gift of the gab."

"So I've heard."

"Well, when I went up to see it for the first time, I found out that most people — and I was one of them — are unaware that the Stone is actually set high up on a battlement of Blarney Castle and it's actually quite a long climb. Well, after the trek to the top — I was so tired that, without noticing what I was doing, I leaned against the wall. And, there I was, completely oblivious, but leaning my rear end right up against the Blarney Stone! Can you *imagine*?"

"So what happened next?"

"Well, there were unforeseen consequences."

"Unforeseen consequences?"

"Well, truth be told, ever since I've had brilliant ideas coming out my arse!" The audience roared.

• • •

Despite doggedly tracking down every hard-won lead, Jason was no closer to finding Elizabeth than he'd been months ago on Hot Springs Island. John S. Morgan, the man charged with flushing out Elizabeth, had made negligible progress too and, making things worse, he didn't come cheap. Unanticipated extras overran the first invoice and, besides the resource drain, Jason feared he might be getting bilked. Morgan remained upbeat, however.

"People exist so they can be found," he said. "It may take a while but sooner or later almost everyone gets tracked down, trust me."

With Jason's help, Destiny's new head of publicity and promotion set up an Intranet site for the now considerable press and media coverage of *Absolution* and DP. The site had references to dozens of interviews and articles from magazines and newspapers as well as reviews from both professional critics and readers from online bookshops. By now, Maddie's name had started appearing in some of the American media as the editor of *Absolution*, but Jason had received little credit for his contribution.

Normally, money didn't overly concern Jason. But with the increasing costs associated with the Elizabeth search cash was diminishing and he found himself wondering how much Seamus and Destiny were making from the M-Novel idea. With his money running out and *Absolution*'s stock rising, Jason contemplated approaching a lawyer to see if a small slice of the pie might rightfully be his. But he held back. In a part of his mind, he hoped there'd been some huge misunderstanding — that before long Seamus would inform him and everyone else that this was just phase one of the publicity campaign and that in phase two, Jason would get the credit he deserved. Of course, he considered calling Seamus and asking him. His hesitation, however, wasn't just ethical; in debates with Seamus, Jason always lost.

● ● ●

Despite a daunting workload, Jason left early one Friday to visit John S. Morgan in Bristol. After Bath, Bristol seemed large and modern. Morgan's office was in a nondescript four-storey building of steel and brown glass. The man himself was a roly-poly caricature with florid hair and face, and an equally bright red, badly knotted tie. His clothes were too tight and he boasted a trio of fresh shaving cuts. He was as loud in person as he was on the phone.

"Jason! Sit down sit down sit down." After preliminaries including biscuits and tea, they talked business.

"Where are we on this? What progress have you made?"

"Well, we've eliminated all sorts of possibilities and red herrings. Yes, indeed. But, at the same time, we still have a number of difficulties to overcome, the number one item being her name, as I've mentioned before. I'm convinced, Jason, that Elizabeth Barnett was a pseudonym. To be honest, I've even got doubts about Elizabeth as her first name. Normally we have more to go on but in your case, I'm afraid we don't have much foundation. The overseas nature of your birth confounds things further, as does the fact that your other mother, Mary, appears on all your birth records. I can say this, however: Elizabeth Barnett, or whatever her name is, is certainly skilled at covering her tracks." He gave his jolly laugh.

Jason agreed. He and Maddie had banged their heads against the name issue time and again. Finding her true identity was fundamental. Morgan then anticipated Jason's questions about cost.

"Now, I'm sure you're thinking this is costing you a pretty penny for not very much, so let me tell you what I'm doing. I have two private investigators working on your case, one in this area and one in London. The local chap found out that you're not the only one who's been had by this Bulldoggy fellow," Morgan checked his notes, "as your Dr. Nutall said. And I've hired a database firm to check insurance records and the like for any Elizabeth Barnetts within a certain age range, as well as the phone number your mother used to call your adopted father."

"And, any luck?"

"In fact, yes."

Jason moved to the edge of his seat.

"But, I'm afraid it's not helpful. She called from a public phone. In central London. Using an international phonecard."

"So it wasn't even Bath."

"No. I'm afraid not. So, I hope you can see how all this costs money. Hiring people. Having searches done. As I think you can see, Jason, I'm hardly getting rich doing this," Morgan said.

"I understand," said Jason. "Now, I'd like to ask you something else."

"Of course."

"It has to do with intellectual copyright."

"Hardly my field. Most of my cases concern paternity and family matters, as one might expect."

"I see. But just let me ask you this. Have you read or heard anything about this new M-Novel we've published? It's called *Absolution* by Russell Rose."

"Yes, of course."

"Well, the M-Novel was my idea."

"Very clever of you. Congratulations."

"Except I've been wondering if the idea's been, well, misappropriated, if that's the word."

"Misappropriated? Do you mean stolen? By whom? What do you mean?"

"By my boss. The man who originally called you on my behalf."

"But you both work for the same firm. ...In fact, he's the managing director, isn't he? How could he steal it?"

"He's taking all the credit."

"Did you do the work on company time?"

"I did."

"And is Mr. Healey profiting financially from this? I mean personally. Himself, not the company."

"Not that I know of."

"And did you do anything to protect yourself in case he is?"

"Um...well, no again."

"If he's not making any private money, and you did the work on company time...I'm sorry, I don't see there'd be much of a case. Not that I'm an expert, of course. As I was saying."

Jason realized how foolish he sounded. He stood up.

"Thank you for your time, Mr. Morgan. I'm not sure how much longer I can keep the search going, but I'll let you know."

Morgan stood up as well. Jason noticed a missing shirt button revealing a taut, white, belly that made Jason think, perversely, of Moby Dick.

• • •

It was fifteen minutes before eight on a weekday morning and Jason had already been at the office a half-hour. He was alone with his music cranked; he didn't notice his cell phone ringing. The persistent caller reached him finally on her fifth attempt.

"Jason, thank God I've reached you." It was Tina. "Jason," she said, her voice both sober and sobering, "I've got some bad news."

His mind went blank while details pulsed through: quitting his job, finding a plane, packing, money, telephone calls, and...

"It's Dada, isn't it?" Before Tina could utter a word, Jason knew. And it wasn't just another anxiety attack. This time it was real. This was retribution for him trying to find a new parent when the only parents he'd ever loved were on Hot Springs Island.

"No, Jason. It's not Dada. It's Al. She had a stroke a couple of hours ago and she's in a coma. It's touch and go right now. The doctors don't know if she's going to make it. I've been trying to call you but couldn't get through. You've got to get home, Jason. Dada needs you. Al needs you. Everybody needs you."

Chapter 16 iNovel Links
There are two Chapter 16 iNovel Links, one literary and one musical – although they're related. *Absolution* is the first M-Novel released by Destiny Press and written by

Russell Rose, which means that *Absolution* has both a literary and musical component of its own. By going to **www.HotSpringsNovel.com/chapter16/** you will be able to read an excerpt from *Absolution* as well as hear a related song (composed by Jason) called "Song for New York."

PART III

HOT SPRINGS ISLAND, BRITISH COLUMBIA, CANADA

Chapter 17

"I thought you'd want to know."

Jason had left Hot Springs Island in the autumn and now it was February. Spring was not far off.

He wished Professor Morton was next to him again. She was calm and wise. Wisdom seemed in particularly short supply. He'd ask her what do about his search for Elizabeth. He'd ask about debilitating strokes and how to cope if Al remained alive but diminished. He'd also ask her about love and remembrance. And death.

He'd failed. He'd come away empty-handed. He told John S. Morgan to continue hunting till the money ran out, but he didn't hold much hope, especially without a search angel. Even the triumph of the M-Novel was qualified. The quest to find a mother to replace one forever gone was based on the idea of renewal. Now Al, dear surrogate-mom Al, hung near death.

He was on his cell phone all the way to the plane, most of the time with Ellery. Al had been rushed to Lady Peace Hospital, but they would transfer her to the Royal Vancouver the moment her condition stabilized. She remained in a coma but her vital signs had stabilized. Jason was to phone the second he landed in Vancouver, which was momentarily. He called from inside the terminal. It shook him to know that Al wouldn't answer. That she might never again.

"Nothing's changed," Ellery informed him. "She's

still at Lady Peace. Dada's down there now and they're still not sure when they can move her. You can try calling your dad on his cell but it might be off — you know, hospital regulations. Dada said just to get home as soon as possible."

Jason had no luck reaching either Dada or Tina. He left a message telling them he'd be there soon and then rushed to catch a seaplane. He was in Troy less than two hours after arriving from England. Jason found Al wired and tubed. It was impossible to connect the vigorous, full-of-life Al to this figure lying in white sheets, connected to machines. When he exited into the hall, exhausted, he found Tina.

"Didn't you see Dada? He's in the waiting room. He called the hotel and Ellery told him you were coming."

He shook his head.

"How is she?"

"No real change. They might move her tomorrow morning if her vitals hold."

"Jason." It was Dada. He was further diminished, even older. Al's stroke had hit him hard. Jason tried to impart his love, his guilt, and his regret that he'd felt the need to focus on Elizabeth in his life instead of these people who loved him like no other. If he hadn't gone off seeking a phantom, he would've been here. He'd let them down badly.

"I'm glad you're home, son," was all Dada could manage. His voice trembled. Tina wiped her eyes with the back of her hand.

The head nurse confirmed that unless major

changes occurred in the night, Al would be airlifted to Vancouver late tomorrow morning. "In the meantime," said the nurse, "I think you'd all better get some sleep."

The gathered crowd resembled that of Angel's tragedy. Well meaning as everyone was, Jason found the small talk and solicitousness difficult. He wanted answers while people could only ask questions.

Cassidy's blond head towered over everyone. Kiriko wasn't far behind. Cassidy rocked and told Jason to bear up, that everything would be fine, that the family would grow stronger. Jason had no idea if Cassidy knew why he'd gone to England but it didn't matter.

Jason's attention could now be turned to Kiriko. She approached him. They embraced. He took in her fragrance and immediately recalled their journey together across the tidal plains, through the tunnel under the river and into the city. He remembered her letters. He saw her as she stood in the airport waving goodbye.

Even after the long moment ended, Kiriko continued holding both of Jason's hands as she tried to soothe him, not with words but with everything else she possessed. She was elemental and totally lacking in artifice. With both Al and now Kiriko, hope had never seemed more important.

● ● ●

Everyone was exhausted, even Golly. Tina drove the Chirons home. Dada and Jason agreed to meet in the hot springs right away. Midnight was too far away.

The hot springs confirmed his second homecoming. His prolonged absence made every moment exponentially powerful. Mum had been the first to make him aware of the connection. They'd been sitting in the oceanside bath and Mum pointed out how the surrounding ocean joined them to Asia. They talked about the tides and then about the hot springs water, one of her favorite topics, and how it reconnected us to the depths of the earth. As they readied to leave, it started raining. Even now, Jason remembered the smell of that rain, a different kind of water.

Dada arrived. He showered and then lay in the bath with his eyes closed.

"I'm glad you're home, Jason."

"I am too, Dada."

The steam rose. A dead leaf caught by the wind blew into the bath.

"It was my fault, Jason."

"What do you mean?"

"Al's stroke. It was all my fault."

"What are you talking about? That's impossible."

"We were arguing."

"What about?"

The moon disappeared behind a cloud.

"Al was castigating me, saying I never called you. She said that you wouldn't come back until I told you how much we needed you. She pointed out the irony of the situation, that my worry about losing you to Elizabeth was a self-fulfilling prophecy. She was very upset with me. I told her that what you were doing was your choice, and it was beyond my ken except to bear what responsibility was mine."

"What did she say to that?"

"That if I hadn't kept this secret so long, then none of this would have happened. She had a headache and didn't want to talk about it anymore, but I wouldn't let it go. I called her interfering and an outsider. How impossibly, unforgivably, cruel was that? She was trying to bring us closer together."

The stars struggled to shine through the cloud cover. A deer passed by, heard but unseen in the woods.

"How can I live with myself, Jason?"

"She'll get better, Dada. Just you watch. Al's tough. You know she is. Then you can say you're sorry to her yourself."

"I pray that I can, my boy. I just pray that I can."

Jason waited for Dada to default to Shakespeare. This time nothing came.

• • •

Al was stable enough for transport to Vancouver the next morning. Only one family member could ride the medi-vac plane to Vancouver and Jason volunteered. The hotel had to keep running and, without Al, Dada had to step up. Jason called Phillip Hung and got an anonymous voicemail instead of Irene's usual message. Jason reached him on his cell.

"Phillip Hung."

"Phillip — Jason here."

"Jason! Where are you? Are you back?"

"Yeah, I'm on Hot Springs."

"For how long?"

"I don't know. Al's had a stroke and they're airlifting her to Vancouver. I need a place to stay."

"Al's had a stroke? Omigod, that's terrible…is she going to be okay?"

"We don't know. She's still in a coma but she's going into the Royal Vancouver. I don't know how long she's going to be there. I was hoping you could put me up."

"Jason."

"What is it?"

"I should have e-mailed you or something, I know, but…"

"What is it?"

"Irene and I split up."

"*What*? You and Irene?"

"I know."

"When did this happen?"

"Just after you left. It's been coming for a while, though."

"I'm sorry, man. I don't know what to say."

"So, I don't have my old place anymore. Irene's got it. I'm in a new place, it's small, I've just moved in and I've got a roommate so I…"

"Don't worry about it. I'll find something else. I'm sorry, Phillip."

"Listen , it doesn't matter. Al's much more important. I hope she gets better soon. I'll come and visit. If you want me to, that is."

"Thanks. Of course. I'll call you later when I know more about what's happening."

"Sure. Good luck with everything, Jason. Call me if you need anything."

He could always get a hotel. Jason scrolled through his addresses and stopped at Dee Dee's. He should call her and leave a message. Dee Dee and Al were close. Which made him think of Kevin.

When Kevin visited Hot Springs, Al had taken him under her wing. He had preened at the attention. In fact, he'd never been better behaved. The poor boy just needs some love, Al said. Maybe this was an opportunity to mend fences. He'd call him from Vancouver and if it happened, great. If not, so be it.

• • •

Normally Jason loved flying. But not today.

The turbulence started as they approached the Strait of Georgia. The light plane dipped and then lifted. Then it rose and dropped again in a move so stomach-wrenching that the restraining straps on Al's stretcher snapped as taut as guitar strings.

"We'll be there soon," said the nurse. She gripped the armrest so hard you could see her veins.

Beginning their descent on the Vancouver side of the strait, they hit their worst pocket yet. The plane must have dropped fifty feet in a single second. At that moment — whether through the force of the jolt or by pure coincidence — Al raised her head.

"Where am I?"

"Al! Al! Are you okay?"

"Don't try to talk too much, dear," said the nurse. "You take it easy now."

"Where am I? Am I inside…a plane?" Although Al's speech was weak and slurred, she was intelligible.

Jason reached for her hand through the blankets. "Al…"

"Now, dear," said the nurse. "Do you know your name? Can you tell me your name?"

"My name is Alexandra Koval." Jason and the nurse exchanged hopeful looks.

"And where do you live?"

"On Hot Springs Island. Where am I?"

"You've been quite ill, dear," said the nurse. "We're taking you to the hospital."

"I'm a bit tired. I just want to sleep," said Al and drifted off. Thankfully, the turbulence abated. The pilot lowered the landing gear and they prepared to land.

• • •

Al woke twice on the way to the hospital and once more after admission. "The prognosis is very good. We'll have to run some more tests over the next couple of days but she can stay out of the ICU, and physio can help her get back many, perhaps all, of her motor functions. Most of the effects seem to be on her left side, but we'll know more in a couple of days." The doc's smile was warm. "It's generally good news. Very good news."

Jason slept in a lounge on Al's floor. Tomorrow one of the rooms for out-of-towners like Jason was opening up.

Because of restricted visiting hours, Jason had much of the next day to himself. Exhausted from his restless night, he decided walking would be good. Sunshine helped jet lag. He headed towards and then across the Cambie Street Bridge. The domed stadium and Science World reminded him of Human Designs. He decided to walk by.

They spotted each other at the same moment. Kevin ran across the street towards Jason, oblivious to swerving cars and bellowing horns.

"Jason," Kevin gasped, though he hadn't run very far. "I got your message. Bad news but good news, man. I'm sorry Al had the stroke but I'm glad she's getting better. She's a nice lady. But you — what the hell are you doing down here? Come to spy on the gang-that-couldn't-code-straight?"

"I was just getting some exercise. Where you off to?"

"To get a Coke or lunch or something."

"Can I join you?"

"Sure, man, sure." Soon they were at one of their old haunts.

After the tale of Al's miraculous awakening, Kevin brought Jason up to speed with the office.

"The biggest news is, Walter's gone," said Kevin.

"Walter? That's amazing — a lot of people will be glad to see the back of him," said Jason.

"Yeah, the board of directors axed him. *Coup d'é-tat.*"

"When did this happen?"

"A coupla weeks ago."

"Kevin. Can I ask you something?"

"Sure." Kevin made sucking sounds with his straw.

"What was it with all those e-mails?"

Kevin's eyes flickered up towards Jason.

"Don't you know?"

"No, I don't."

"Have you talked to Dee Dee?" asked Kevin.

"Not yet. Not in months. I called and left a message about Al, though. A little while ago."

"And did you call Phillip?"

"Yes."

Kevin's manner changed. Both arms flattened on the tabletop and he leaned forward so his face, almost Seamuslike, was close to Jason's.

"He told you?" asked Kevin.

"Yes," said Jason.

"And you're totally okay?"

"Well, I never imagined he and Irene would break up—"

"Oh fuck..." Kevin said, throwing his hands in the air before running his dirty fingers through equally squalid hair. "That's what you think, I meant?"

"Yeah. What's the big deal?"

"You total stupid asshole ignoramus. ...Man, you are the dumbest thing on two legs. You couldn't take a hint if it came right up and kicked you in the balls."

"What're you talking about?"

"Jason, Jason, Jason," said Kevin. Imagine it. Here was Kevin — Kevin! of all people — talking down to him.

"It's Phillip and Dee Dee. Got it? That's what I was talking about. Why do you think Phillip and Irene broke up? I had your back, man, and you didn't even come close to getting it." And then Kevin laughed — a long, dark laugh.

"Why didn't you just tell me?"

"Wasn't my place, man."

"But it was okay to send me crazy e-mails?"

"I wanted you to find out but I didn't want to tell you," said Kevin. This twisted logic made perfect sense to him. You had to remain loyal to your buddies but you couldn't interfere. To Kevin, this was honor.

They finished their lunch.

"I'll maybe come by tonight to see Al. Like I said, she's a nice lady."

"Sure. I guess...thanks."

"No sweat, man. See you." He walked off, flicking his headphones from neck to ears in one well-practiced motion.

• • •

Jason felt compelled to make his next destination the building where Phillip worked. Looking up at the reflective windows glass, he thought about the activity and people inside, about Cynthia and Tom and Taylor and the charity run and how much money they'd raised. And Phillip, of course. And what friendship meant. No one came out. Fifteen minutes later he was on a bus to the hospital.

Armed with a bag of goodies, Jason arrived at Al's room only to find someone already there sitting and talking. Dee Dee was holding her hand, and from the looks of things, Al had improved even since last night.

Jason hadn't a clue what to say to her.

Al spotted him first, and Dee Dee's eyes naturally followed. He walked into the room to forestall any awkwardness.

"Al, I'm sorry I wasn't here when you woke up. How are you feeling?" He reached for her other hand.

"Better. Much better. A little weak, though. And I can't move my left arm very well. But otherwise all right, all things considered..." She sighed.

"Hello, Dee Dee."

She smiled. "Thanks for calling me."

"I thought you'd want to know."

"I did. Thank you."

"Where's Phillip?"

"He's in the car." She looked down. "So I guess you've heard..."

"Uh huh."

"Jason, is there a coffeeshop or somewhere we could go to talk?"

He was tempted to say why bother. But not in front of Al.

"Al, do you mind if we go for a cup of coffee?" Jason asked.

"Not at all, dear. I'll just rest my eyes for a while," she said.

Dee Dee and Jason left the room. They talked about Al until they were seated with hot drinks.

"So, when did it start?" Jason asked.

"You mean Phillip and I?"

"Of course I mean Phillip and you. What else would I mean?"

"Jason...can't we discuss this rationally?"

"I'm perfectly rational. I'm just feeling as if I've been stabbed in the back...although in this case you need a double-handled knife."

"I can understand how you feel—"

"Dee Dee, with all due respect, you don't have a clue how I feel. So, when did it start?"

"That depends on what you mean. If you mean, when did I first become attracted to Phillip, well, I've always liked him. You know that."

"That's not what I mean."

"Not till you and I had broken up. Of course not. I'm not that kind of person."

"Oh right. But you are the sort of person who starts dating her boyfriend's best friend and then conveniently forgets to inform him. Minor detail, I suppose."

"Ex-boyfriend, Jason, ex-boyfriend. Initiated by you, I might add. By Mr. Commitment-phobia."

"So who went after whom?"

"Nobody went after anybody. It just happened. Can't you understand that? I originally e-mailed Phillip because I hoped he could help me with you. Help me understand why you were leaving. And he wrote back. He was very understanding and sensitive. And then we started chatting and...but Jason, when you told me you wanted to go back to Hot Springs by yourself, can you imagine how I felt? And what about you? I know that Tina's back on the island, Jason. What about her? How do you think *that* made me feel?"

"There's nothing between Tina and I. And how do you think Irene feels, while we're at it?"

"Jason…"

"Okay, okay. Listen. This is pointless. Phillip doesn't have to hide in the car anymore. He — both of you — should have had enough guts to at least let me know. Don't you think I was at least owed that?"

Dee Dee looked down. "Yes, of course you were. I'm sorry. We were planning on telling you…but after you went to England, well…we just kept putting it off."

"You sound like Dada."

"What do you mean?"

"Nothing," Jason said. "So how serious is it?"

"I don't know. But Phillip is much more stable and serious than you'll ever be, Jason. You know that. And I think that's something I need."

"Yeah, just ask Irene how serious and stable he is."

"Jason!" She was close to tears.

"Sorry. Sorry. Cheap shot. That was the last one. Phillip told me that he's got a roommate."

"Yes."

"And that roommate. It's you, isn't it?"

"Yes. He had nowhere else to go, really, after he moved out."

Jason thought of a million snappy rejoinders. But there was no point. He stood up.

"Listen. Thanks for coming by. I mean it."

"I came for Al. But thank you for calling me. That was sweet of you."

"Tell Phillip to phone me. We'll go for a beer or something. And tell him to stop hiding in his Beemer and face me like a man." He said this with a smile.

"I will, Jason."

Salvaging the last of his dignity, Jason executed a Seamus maneuver and spun toward the door. Dee Dee sat at the white Formica table as Jason walked past the long line of semitranslucent cafeteria windows.

Chapter 17 iNovel Link
The Chapter 17 iNovel Link is visual. Go to
www.HotSpringsNovel.com/chapter17/ where
you'll find two sketches. The first one is a view from Al's
ambulance plane over the Georgia Strait and the second
one is of Kevin and Jason talking in the restaurant.

Chapter 18

"Nothing would please me more."

Al returned to Hot Springs Island less than a week later. She began physio in Troy and although her speech was slightly affected and her left side still drooped, she was progressing. Jason and Dada moved her into the hotel and her fighting spirit resurfaced. Jason was hopeful.

Dada, too, was recovering from the malaise that had gripped him since Al's stroke. Visitors inquiring about Al's condition were a tonic — people never failed to energize him.

Cassidy was a frequent visitor. But he rarely came alone. Kiriko usually accompanied him and together they made a striking if unmatched pair. Despite her quietness — particularly beside the hyperactive Cassidy — it was Kiriko's presence that dominated the room for Jason.

She possessed this most astonishing composure. It wasn't just the economy of her movements. It was also their fluency. Jason had noticed it even that first time in the bath. You were unable to detect exactly when an action started or stopped.

Whether such grace was her culture's or hers alone, Jason couldn't tell. What he did know, however, was that in her presence he felt a sense of peace that he rarely encountered elsewhere except in nature, when sailing, or in the hot springs. He had never felt this calm emanating from other people. In this, she resembled her art. Her paintings invariably expressed nature draped in the same repose.

Jason asked a number of people if Cassidy and Kiriko were a couple. No one could supply a definitive answer. Their non-verbal behavior seemed too aloof to be romantic — but since his experiences with Dianna and Maddie and Seamus and now Phillip and Dee Dee, he had begun doubting his instincts.

Today Cassidy hadn't come just to tell stories.

"Dada, Al. What do you think? I was hoping to have a Welcome Back Party to show how much we love and support you. You know, the Music Club plus all of your friends. Make it the best party ever because you're the best lady ever. What do you think?" Kiriko smiled. Jason was reminded of a more beautiful version of the *Mona Lisa*. He'd forgotten he'd already used this comparison to describe Elizabeth's smile.

"I'd love it, Cassidy. Thank you. Nothing would please me more. I might not be dancing very much, though."

Jason sensed her excitement. "You don't worry about that dancing, Al. I'll swirl you around in that wheelchair like you're the belle in the fancy ball scene in *Gone with the Wind*!" Al's all-time favorite movie. Cassidy's energy sparked a flame that leapt from person to person.

"Al," said Dada "Don't you think you might be rushing things a bit?"

"It doesn't have to be right away now, does it? We

can ask the doctor. And if I have another stroke, then I can't think of a better way to go, can you? Dancing, with music and all my friends around me?"

"Al! Don't even *suggest* something like that," said a theatrically cross Jason.

"Oh Jason," Al sighed. "All this worrying...you're beginning to act like me!" Everyone laughed. But, truth told, since the stroke, Al seemed reborn. She was far more accepting and worried less. When he mentioned it, Dada replied with a quote from *Much Ado*:

> For it so falls out
> That what we have we prize not to the worth
> Whiles we enjoy it, but being lack'd and lost,
> Why, then we rack the value, then we find
> The virtue that possession would not show us
> Whiles it was ours.

• • •

As families do when confronted by crisis, the Chirons and friends put their heads down and plowed ahead. Shorthanded as they were, Jason worked from before sunup to well past dark. England seemed distant, like a dream.

The American and Canadian media were full of *Absolution* and this new literary development from the small town of Bath. Seamus was being hailed as a visionary and the giant North American publishers were all scrambling to produce Next Big Things of their own. Seamus had been right. Whoever got off the mark first had an advantage. Destiny Press was becoming a household name.

One morning an envelope arrived. Enclosed was a substantial cheque and a long handwritten letter praising Jason's work and character, as well as expressing deep concern over Al and the regret that Jason had been forced to leave. Seamus hoped Jason would return to Bath and Destiny Press because "that's where your Destiny lies."

The letter upset Jason's equilibrium, bringing back thoughts of England that meant Elizabeth. He found himself re-reading it. "You're a person of insight and intelligence," wrote Seamus in his large bold hand. "Your grasp and understanding of technology and the future are rare, I hope you know that." And then: "You're a warm lad who I think of as my own. If I had a son, I'd want him to be just like you — or, better yet, to be you." He wanted to believe every word.

Rejoining the flow of island life, Jason reconnected with friends. He called Cristine.

"Layla! Jason's here!" shouted Cristine. "Layla!" There was no response. Cristine muttered under her breath.

"What is it?"

"Computer games," she sighed. "Biggest mistake I ever made. It's gotten so bad I almost wish she was addicted to TV. Wait a second." Cristine went to get Layla, who came back scampering ahead of her mother.

"Hi Jason!" said Layla brightly. He tried to ask her about school and tell her about Golly but she was distracted. Only when he asked about her game did they connect.

"I've got two kinds. One's on my computer. And the one I'm playing with right now, it's called a Tamagotchi. Have you ever seen one? I can show it to you! It's from Japan. I call him Dino — he's like a cyberbaby — and I've got to take care of him and play with him and feed him and love him and stuff and if I don't, then, well, like…and I want to get another one cause I think he's getting lonely. Oh! I've got to go and feed him now," she said this in a great rush of breath and then ran from the room.

"You see what I mean?" said Cristine. "I got it for her after Angel. …I thought it would give her something to take care of, to nurture, you know."

"I understand. I've seen her with Golly."

"And now I've created a monster. I can't take it away from her. I've tried and it's not worth it." She pursed her lips.

"How's Angel?"

"She's doing okay. She's still in Alberta. She doesn't want to talk to me much. She talks to Layla more. But it looks like she's getting on all right with my sister, so there you go. She's talking about going back to school. She's thinking about going into web stuff. If you wouldn't mind, maybe you could talk to her about it sometime."

"Sure. Of course."

"God, Jason, I never thought motherhood could take so much out of you for so long. I just wish I had somebody to share it with, you know." Jason nodded.

"Being a single parent is the loneliest job in the world. And that's besides wanting a partner, you know. Do you know how long it's been since I had a boyfriend?"

"We all care about you, Cristine."

"It's different. But why's it all so hard? Raise some kids and find someone to love you. Is it too much to ask? There's nothing simple. But, listen...how about you? How are you doing?"

"Actually, Cristine, for a second there, I thought you might've been talking about me."

• • •

The official Welcome Back Al Party was scheduled for eight o'clock but people were already arriving an hour early. Cassidy and Cristine (but not Layla — she was playing with her Tamagotchi babies at a friend's) had been decorating since early afternoon and the party mood was infectious. A stage had been built and a dance floor cleared and everyone agreed tonight was a grade up from the usual Friday nights. Cassidy had slipped on a tuxedo jacket over his jeans; with his long ponytailed blond hair trailing from under his top hat, he looked positively dashing.

Kiriko and Cassidy arrived separately, Kiriko dazzling in a shortish dark skirt and a sparkly gold and black top.

Although not complete, Al's recovery was faster than even the most optimistic prognosis. Dada attributed it to the party. Tonight was gala. Tina and her new boyfriend, Adam, were already there, and Kevin was ferrying in from Vancouver. Phillip and Dee Dee had other plans.

By nine the band was belting out a medley that had everyone dancing and rocking. Kevin had arrived and although "this isn't exactly my bag, music-wise," he'd stuffed his skinny frame with food and found an electro/heavy-metal musical soulmate in Ellery.

The guest of honor looked happiest of all. Al had a mammoth overstuffed armchair that Cristine covered in gold lamé, complete with a professional-looking sign that read: "Queen for the Day." Like royalty, she received her stream of visitors — makeup applied by Cristine adding to her regal air.

If Al was Queen, then Golly was Princess or at least Lady in Waiting. Cristine had also gold-laméed Golly's bed and placed it beside Al's chair. Golly received a pat from each visitor and the old Lab was as much in her element as her human counterpart.

This was to be a night of visitors,

The first surprise crept in unsure of himself and wary. Where had Jason seen that face before? A Music Clubber? Someone from town? His shoes were caked with mud despite the dry weather. "Can I help you?"

"Jason?" he said. "Jason, right? It's me."

"Uh huh," said Jason. Who the hell was 'me'?

"I'm Frankie. You know, Al's son. We talked on the phone before."

"Frankie!" There was reason for surprise: Frankie was a consistent no-show. Not on birthdays, not during

Al's illness or recovery, not even during her coma. Dada spent hours chasing him from old number to old number. After finally tracking him down, even then he couldn't convince Frankie to come despite the severity of his mother's condition. No money or time, he said.

"How did you find out about the party?"

"Your dad called me."

So, Dada had worked his magic. From Jason's perspective, hulking Frankie was just one more disappointing man in Al's long line of them. He looked like John S. Morgan more than his mother; he even mumbled and avoided eye contact like him. But Al's night would be made.

"Your dad said I could stay free of charge."

"Sure. Right. Well, your mum's over there. Why don't you say hi to her?"

"What about my stuff?"

"I'll put it behind the front desk."

Frankie suspiciously watched Jason store his bag. Then he shuffled over to the Queen. When she saw him, she literally sprung from her chair. Even from a distance Jason could see her clinging like a person in a capsized boat. Frankie just looked embarrassed and awkward.

Al and Frankie's relationship had fallen apart because of Frankie's drug problems and his refusal to seek help. She played the ultimatum card, and to her endless regret, Frankie called her bluff and dropped out of her life. Except when he needed money, of course.

Jason got Frankie a beer. It disappeared in two practiced gulps. The next couple didn't last much longer. By the fourth, though not totally relaxed, he held his mother's hand as he crouched next to her.

Dada had waited until he could talk to Frankie away from Al.

"Hello, Frankie. I'm Joseph Chiron. We talked on the phone. I'm glad you could—"

"So you got a room for me, like you said?"

"Yes. Of course. It's upstairs," said Dada.

"I'm kinda tired from the trip, you know." Jason watched their introduction and then approached.

"Of course," Dada said. The trip from Calgary had taken less than three hours. "When are you leaving?"

"Tomorrow."

"*Tomorrow*?" This was Jason. "Does your mother know?"

"Nah. I'm just gonna leave before she gets up."

"What? Why wouldn't you tell her?" Jason asked.

"She'll just make a big scene. I can't stand that stuff," Frankie mumbled.

Jason could see Al smiling; her three men, together at last.

"And when," Frankie asked, "can I get the rest of my money?"

"I'll get it for you, Frankie. Just wait here," said Dada. Frankie took another hit of beer.

Jason followed Dada into the office.

"Money? Dada, what was that all about?"

"Make your worst guess and you'd be right. He said he couldn't come because he didn't have the money. So I said I'd pay."

"His plane?"

"Plane fare plus expenses. Pocket money, he called it. He said if I didn't give him three hundred dollars on top of airfare he couldn't come. Even to see his sick mother — who'll probably leave him every cent she has."

"Oh man..."

"He's part of the reason, Jason."

"Reason? Reason for what?"

"The reason for the stroke. I said some terrible things, Jason. I invited Frankie to try and make amends."

"What do you mean?"

"I told you about our argument. How Al blamed me for driving you away."

"Yes."

"Well, I struck back. I said that if *she* was such an expert on raising children then why hadn't she done a better job with Frankie. That at least you'd stayed out of prison. That at least you called. And that at least you loved me. And look at him. I'm so ashamed of myself."

Jason placed a hand on his father's bony shoulder. "Give me the money, Dada. I'll pay Frankie."

"I didn't know what else to do."

"It's all right, Dada. You made Al happy. It's all good."

Jason stuffed the money into his pocket and opened the door. Standing at the front desk, a big folding suit bag and bulging briefcase on the floor next to him, was none other than Seamus Healey.

"Seamus! What are you doing here?"

"Laddie!" he called out. Before Jason knew it, Seamus had him in his bear hug grip again.

• • •

"What are you doing here?" He could barely speak.

"Great to see you, laddie! It's a surprise. I had to come back to the States on business and had something in Seattle. And now, wonderfully, I've got some time off. I knew you weren't too far away in beautiful British Columbia, so here I am. And look at this! I've come right in the middle of Music Club night, haven't I?"

"Sort of."

"I'm one lucky sod, I tell you. One lucky sod. So are you going to introduce me around or what? And get me a drink. And a room. Christ, this is absolutely fantastic!" Seamus lunged at Jason for another mighty hug.

His energy was irresistible. Jason called over friends and music clubbers, but Seamus literally needed no introduction. He flattered Dada about his wonderful son and circumspectly said nothing about Jason's English sojourn or his search for Elizabeth. Seamus told Al how often and affectionately Jason spoke of her. Only on seeing Kiriko did Seamus pause. "Who is she, mate? She's a vision."

"She's someone very special to me," Jason said. Seamus obviously was no longer listening.

Someone called Jason into the kitchen. Al was still

sitting in her chair but clearly searching for the absent Frankie. Tina stood with a group of women singing Neil Young's "Heart of Gold" while Adam hovered nearby watching her.

Seamus wasted no time in applying the charm to Kiriko. Or trying to. He got nowhere. Every time he tried closing the gap, Kiriko subtly escaped. He stepped forward. She moved away. It was a kinesthetic chess match and Kiriko was winning. Then Cassidy arrived.

An instant rivalry was born without them exchanging a word. A clash seemed predestined. All they needed was an excuse. As the two eyed each other and cloaked their mutual aggression with politeness, Kiriko slipped away. Seamus broke eye contact with Cassidy first and sought out Jason.

"I'm buggered. Absolutely knackered. I've been on the move all day and tomorrow's my first day off since god knows when. Where's my room?"

"There's a problem, Seamus. We're fully booked."

"Then where am I staying?"

"You can spend tonight in my room. It's got two beds."

"Lead the way."

Seamus tossed down his bags and began undressing. Jason knew if he was to broach the issue of the M-Novel idea, it was now or never. Seamus's remarks about Kiriko added impetus to his words.

"Seamus."

"Yes, lad..." He looked up and saw Jason's demeanor. "What's the serious face for? Oh, oh, this looks like a heavy one. Fire away then." Seamus plunked himself onto the bed.

"You know, Seamus, I don't know what to make of you."

"What's that?"

"You're so convincing; people always believe you no matter what you say. I know I did."

"What are you talking about?" Seamus asked, genuinely puzzled.

"When I first met you, you gave me this long speech about dedication to your people and dedication to your principles."

"I don't have a clue where you're going with this," Seamus said.

"I'm talking about the best idea I've had in my whole life. I trusted you with it but then you took it and used it like you were the one who thought it up in the first place."

"Jason. Listen to me. Is that what this is about?"

"Of course it is."

"You think I stole your M-Novel idea?"

"I do."

"Well, there's gratitude for you," said Seamus. "And after all I've done for you. Think back now, Jason. I gave you a home in England — in Bath, no less. I challenged you and taught you and I found Morgan for you and even tried to find your mother for you myself. I kept looking, even after you left, because I want to help you. And my letter, and the check I didn't have to send.

"Can you deny I was your mentor and that you

learned more from me about publishing and business in a few months than you've learned the rest of your life? Can you? And if I hadn't said to you, go on, think of something, find the big idea, would you have? And Jason, what would you have done with it? Who would you have talked to? You don't know how the media works. It's what you do with ideas that makes them huge. And I made this happen, Jason. Can you deny that?"

"That letter meant a lot to me. So did your help with my mother. But that doesn't mean I'm wrong about the other thing. They're not mutually exclusive, you know. It's just like the music night."

"What are you on about now?"

"At Len's or whatever his name was. When you took me to see what you called the British version of Music Club. You got that idea from me. I gave you the idea for the Music Club and everyone was going around saying what a genius you were."

"Jason, listen to yourself. Listen to how small and petty you sound. For every moment in life, every hour, every day, you have the choice between making something happen or sitting there like the rest of the goddamn lazy world. So, you've got all these great ideas, do you? Then do something about them. And, tell me, just so I know, was it you who invented the Music Club idea in the first place? I didn't notice you putting forward anyone else's name." He was right.

"Jason, Jason, Jason…" Seamus stood up and wrapped one beefy arm around him. "What is it you want? Tell me what you want and I'll try and make it happen."

Jason had nothing to say. Words seemed so pointless when, on the fundamental issues, Seamus had hit the mark. At the same time, he knew Seamus thought the world revolved around him. The problem was, much of the time it did.

"What I want, Seamus, is something you can't give me."

"And what's that?"

"To know what's right."

Seamus let go and looked into Jason's eyes the final time that night. "Ah, don't worry about it, laddie. All you have to do is understand one simple thing and one thing only. In life there are no absolutes. Only relatives. Now, give me a hug and get out of here. I need some sleep."

• • •

The breakfast table on Saturday morning was an unusual gathering: Dada, Jason, Seamus, Al and Frankie were joined by Cristine and Layla and, moments later, Cassidy and Kiriko, who'd come to help clean up. Al clung to the arm of the visibly uncomfortable Frankie, who'd made it clear he was leaving later that day. She was making the best of what little time remained. The old Al wouldn't have remained as positive.

Seating arrangements turned into a chess match between Cassidy and Seamus. They vied to sit next to Kiriko, and Jason cringed, feeling her discomfort. Despite this, breakfast was fun. Cristine asked Seamus about Destiny Press and that got them talking about technology. Seamus told them the inventor of the World Wide Web had just been knighted by the queen.

"That's a good one, isn't it?" Jason laughed. "A dated elitist award being bestowed on the inventor of a revolutionary technology that's the ultimate tool of democracy and egalitarianism. What irony."

After breakfast, everyone got down to work. The hotel was soon spotless. As the island residents readied to leave, Cassidy cornered Jason.

"Got a second?" Cassidy asked.

"Sure." Cassidy took Jason's arm and led him outside.

"Who's this guy, Seamus?"

"My old boss in England."

"Yeah, I know that. But what's he doing here? And tell me about him. Is he married, got a girlfriend, what?"

"No. He's a widower."

"What happened?"

"It's a long story."

"Tell me anyway," Jason sensed him looking for an edge.

"Why do you want to know, Cassidy?"

"It's just the way he's been hanging around Kiriko. Hovering around, trying to get close to her. I don't like it. I think he's doing it just to get to me. I wanted to find out if you knew anything."

"What's the story with you two? Are you involved romantically?"

"No, no. We're just friends. Nothing more." This wasn't overly informative, however. Cassidy always described his girlfriends as "just friends."

"But, you know what," Cassidy continued. "I don't trust the guy. How about you? Do you trust him? I need to know."

That was the question, wasn't it? He remembered that first day in the office when they'd been discussing his contract and Seamus had asked the exact same question.

Seamus opened the door and joined them with such impeccable timing it was as if he'd been reading their lips through the window.

"What're you lads talking about?" The silence was uncomfortable. Cassidy glared. Jason made his face blank.

"Nothing, Seamus, nothing," Jason said.

"Well, if I could get a word with you when you're done..." he said, and then left them alone.

. . .

When the guests were gone, Seamus went looking for Jason.

"You ready to go?" asked the Irishman.

"What do you mean? Go where?"

"You're going to show me around."

"Didn't you hear? At breakfast? I'm taking Frankie to the ferry."

"We'll go in my rental car. We can drop him off and then we're free."

"Let me check with Dada."

"No, you're fine. I talked to Dada already. He doesn't mind at all. While you and the others were dusting and tidying, Dada showed me your accounting system and I pointed out some cash-flow tips. It should make a big difference. I think he's pleased."

Despite Seamus's attempts to draw him out on the way, Frankie said little. Who knew what the trip had meant to him — besides a cash infusion, that is. Al begged him to visit again but it was hard to interpret his grunted responses as promises. He didn't want Al to see him off. "We've already said our goodbyes, Ma," he said. At least he'd called her Ma. They left Frankie at the waiting room without so much as a handshake.

He took Seamus on his usual sightseeing tour: a drive around the island punctuated by trips up Mt. Sansum and the other two hot springs. They stopped at Valdes Beach to skip stones across the flat water and ended their jaunt in downtown Troy.

"That's Kiriko's gallery, isn't it?" said Seamus. "Dada told me about it. C'mon, let's go." Jason's efforts to redirect Seamus went unheeded.

Seamus was immediately smitten by Kiriko's work. "I'll tell you right out," he said to the salesclerk. "I love Kiriko's work and I'm going to buy some. I just haven't decided which ones. I'd like Kiriko to explain them to me in great detail first. The more I know, the more I'll be interested. She'll help me decide." The gallery called Kiriko about a very interested prospective buyer and she promised to be there soon.

Kiriko's English was skilled but measured. Her vocabulary was wide but she took time relating her thoughts — not that the enthralled Seamus minded. The two paintings he was most interested in were both done since Kiriko's arrival on Hot Springs. Both were of the sea. The first one, titled *Pier*, depicted a dock stretching in a diagonal across the bottom of the painting, with glittering ocean and mountains behind. The lines of the wave crests were gold reflecting a sun barely visible behind distant hills.

"When I painted this," Kiriko said, "I was trying to show the blessings we receive from the sun, the ocean and the mountains. That blessing is not just physical. It is spiritual as well. We look at them...in awe, and we receive from them feelings of wonder. In these things we recognize the power of life and nature. As I was painting, I realized that nature is our teacher and that I was having a dialogue, a conversation, with my teacher."

The second painting was called *Mt. Baker & Waves*. Again, the ocean seemed to leap off the wall with Mt. Baker (which she called "Baker-san") a bit player in the background.

"I have always wanted to paint the ripples of the ocean," Kiriko said. "I had to wait a long time for calm weather and smooth seas. The waves are one part of the ocean and the ripples are one part of the waves. They are connected. Both of these parts change constantly. Their colors are also changing and there are so many that it's almost...what's the word...infinite. I wanted to show the motion of the sea that never stops combined with the stillness and the calm of Baker-san. The mountain is never-ending and the ocean is never-ending too but they are both so different. I hope you can understand."

"I do," said Seamus. "I understand very well. That was a beautiful explanation, Kiriko, and they're beautiful paintings. I'll take both of them." The clerk clapped her hands in delight. Kiriko bowed slightly, smiled her smile and said, simply, "Thank you very much."

While Seamus's credit card was being processed, he turned to Kiriko again.

"Now Kiriko...we must celebrate with dinner tonight. And I won't take no for an answer."

"I'm sorry. It's impossible."

"Seamus—" said Jason.

"What about tomorrow night?" asked Seamus.

"I'm sorry."

"Seamus." Seamus returned Jason's look and at least stopped talking.

"Thank you very much for buying my paintings." She extended her hand. Seamus held it as long as he could before she pulled free. Then she left.

Seamus turned to Jason. "Christ...can you beat that?" He was incredulous. "I buy two of her paintings — thousands of dollars — and she won't even have dinner with me." He thought for a moment. "It's Cassidy, isn't it? That's got to be it."

"Seamus..."

"Well, are they?"

"I don't know. I honestly don't know."

• • •

They'd just returned to the hotel when the front-desk phone rang.

"Hot Springs Island Hotel, Jason speaking."

"Jason!" She sounded surprised. "It's Cristine."

"Hey, how come you're using the hotel line?"

"Well, actually, I was hoping to speak to some-body else."

"Really? Who?"

"Not that it's any of your business, but...Seamus."

"Seamus? Why? Tell me to go to hell if I'm being too nosey."

"Go to hell. You're being too nosey." They laughed. "I thought he was charming and I was won-dering how long he was going to be around. I thought we could get together for a drink or something. I *know* he likes to drink," Cristine said with a laugh.

"You're calling to ask him out?"

"Anything wrong with that? I talked to Cassidy this morning and he told me that Seamus was asking about me."

So that's how it was. Cristine was a red herring to get Seamus off the Kiriko trail? What should he say to Cristine? "Jason? Are you there? What is it? There's something you're not telling me, isn't there?"

"No, it's just—"

"What?"

Talk about no-win situations.

"Okay, here's the thing. I think Seamus might be interested in someone else."

"You mean he's dating another woman?"

"No. Just that he's interested."

"And has he actually gone out with her?"

"No."

"And has he said anything about me to you?"

Actually he had. In the car after dropping Frankie off.

"Yes, actually."

"Well, out with it! Come on! What did he say?"

"He said he thought you were really nice. And funny. And talented. He saw some of your stuff at the Troy Gallery."

"Well, that sounds pretty good."

Jason settled his position. Cristine could decide for herself. He remembered how lonely she'd sounded the other day. How long it'd been since she'd dated. Even if they went out, it seemed unlikely Seamus could break her heart in only a few days.

"Do you want me to get him for you?"

She hesitated a bit. "Sure."

"Wait a second. I have an idea. Why don't we all go out in a group? If it works, you give me some kind of signal and I'll skedaddle. What do you think?"

"That's perfect!"

"Seamus was saying he wanted to hit the hot springs. We could all have a dip and take it from there."

• • •

Cristine couldn't find a sitter at short notice so Layla joined the party. They decided on the beachside hot springs, Cristine dragging Layla from the office where she'd been playing on Jason's computer. Normally she loved cavorting in the hot springs, especially on the beach with Golly.

The tides were perfect and there was a good chance of stars. Another advantage of this beachside bath was that the brave-hearted could swim in the ocean to cool off. Layla particularly enjoyed such dips. She was an accomplished swimmer for her age and liked to demonstrate her skills.

Seamus, Cristine, Jason and Layla soaked and laughed and splashed. Despite the little moment between mother and daughter earlier, Layla was animated and excited. They'd been in and out of the bath for around an hour when Cristine starting looking around. "Where's Layla?" she asked.

They couldn't see her, either. The pool wasn't that big.

"Layla!" They called individually and in unison. No answer. Only a minute ago Layla had been swimming next to them.

"Layla! Layla!" Jason and Seamus scrambled up the pool's rim for a better view. They saw nothing but ocean.

"Is her towel here?" asked Jason.

Cristine checked. "It's over on the beach where she left it. She wouldn't have gone to the house without it, would she? I don't think she'd have left without telling me."

Their cries increased in volume and frequency.

"Could she have gone off for a pee?" asked Seamus.

"I don't think so. I think she'd have just gone in the ocean."

Seamus leapt off the rocks and started splashing around in the cold ocean calling Layla's name. The water was around ten degrees and a shock to the system. She could easily have gone in over her depth or been overcome with cold or fallen or...Seamus continued calling and thrashing his arms about in the waist-deep water.

"Layla! Layla!"

"I'll turn on the floodlights," said Jason. "I'm going for help." His voice was grim. The wind had picked up in the last few minutes and now whistled ominously through the trees. Waves slapped onto the rocks and the shoreline.

Jason scrambled to the gate as fast as he could.

"Surprise! Surprise! Here I am! Here I am!" Layla stood triumphant behind some rocks twenty meters down the beach. "Fooled you fooled you fooled you!" she shouted in glee. Relief flooded over them like a wave breaching the pool's wall. Then came anger.

"What do you think you're doing?" Cristine shouted. "Why would you do something like that? Don't you know how awful that was? How scared everybody was? What were you thinking, Layla, what in heaven's name were you thinking?"

"I *told* you I didn't want to have a stupid bath." Layla spat out. "If you'd let me stay in the office none of this would have happened. It's all *your* fault!"

Cristine visibly tried to contain her anger.

"You know what it is? It's that bloody computer again," Cristine stormed to Jason as she gathered their things. "The thing's a curse."

• • •

It was Sunday and they were going sailing. The trip had been suggested by Dada some weeks back during a Cassidy-and-Kiriko visit to see Al. Dada was exaggerating some boating adventure when he asked Kiriko if she'd ever sailed.

"It's one of my dreams," she said.

"We're in the dream-come-true business," Dada said. They'd set a date. Dada also invited Seamus and Cassidy. "What better place for them to make up?" he asked. "'This music crept by me upon the water, / Allaying both their fury, and my passion, / With its sweet air.'"

Jason invited Cristine, too. "I can't," she said. "Layla's grounded. It's a mother-and-daughter prison camp right now. I'm thinking about putting up barbed wire around the house. Or better yet — around the computer."

At the last moment Dada pulled out for work reasons. Jason would skipper the trip, with Cassidy, Seamus and Kiriko as crew and passengers.

Jason and Seamus arrived first and began prepping the boat. Kiriko and Cassidy arrived a half-hour later. "Look," said Kiriko. "This dock reminds me of my painting. The one titled *Pier*. Do you remember it?" Jason did. It was leaning against the wall in Seamus's room next to *Mt. Baker & Waves*. Jason went in to look at them every day.

"So you're still here," Cassidy said to Seamus.

"Excellent observation, Cassidy, excellent observation," Seamus said in a jovial-enough tone.

The day was overcast and blustery, with a wind of fifteen knots gusting to twenty from the north. As Dada predicted, it was cold, but everyone was warmly dressed, including Seamus, who'd been forced to purchase winter clothes for his North American adventure. He nosed *Argo* out of the slip and into the long finger of Troy Harbor. She was a thirty-five-foot C&C Mark II with a bright blue hull. After clearing the rocky islets dotting the harbor entrance, they headed into the wind. On Jason's direction, Cassidy hauled up the mainsail, which was reefed to make the ride more comfortable. Cassidy had done some sailing as a teenager, but Seamus, a newcomer, was quite happy to sit in the cockpit close to Kiriko.

As they moved from Pilot's Passage into Swayburn Channel, they were running with the wind directly behind them and making more than six knots. It was a chilly day so Jason went down into the cabin to turn on the propane heater and get Kiriko a blanket. Cassidy was at the helm.

Jason was lighting the temperamental device when he felt the boat shift and then heard and felt a loud "THANG" and a frightening jolt. The sails flapped chaotically. They must have accidentally jibed, the wind catching the mainsail from behind and sending the heavy metal boom flying across the cockpit. He rushed up the companionway.

"Everyone okay?" he asked. They nodded. "What happened?" He tacked to get the headsail under control. Seamus was white-faced and motionless. Jason had never seen him so quiet.

"Accidental jibe," confirmed Cassidy. "Sorry. I should have been more alert." Kiriko's face too was ashen.

Seamus spoke. "You could've fucking killed me."

"Why don't you watch your language? I said I was sorry," Cassidy said.

"What happened exactly?" Jason asked again.

Seamus answered. "I was standing up, pointing. I thought I'd seen a dolphin...something, over there. I was leaning over on the left side, when suddenly the boom swung around and came right over top of me. I just managed to duck. It missed me by inches. I could have had my head cut off or smashed open or been knocked into the water or...Christ knows." Seamus glowered at Cassidy. Although Cassidy appeared calm, his eyes were flashing too.

"I said I was sorry, man. It was an accident."

"You didn't warn me or anything," accused Seamus.

"Yes, I did."

"A little fucking late, it seemed to me." Seamus's face was regaining its color.

"Why don't I take the wheel?" suggested Jason.

Not long after, sailing conditions changed and the wind was literally taken from their sails. Jason reluctantly decided to cut the trip short. Cassidy and

Seamus barely exchanged two words all the way home. Kiriko was equally silent. They pulled into the wharf and secured the boat. Seamus went ahead to wait by the car. As Jason said goodbye to Cassidy and Kiriko, Cassidy looked him in the eyes and said: "It was an accident, brother. I'm telling you. It was an accident."

"Of course it was," said Jason. Kiriko looked at the ground.

After dinner, he slipped into the office and phoned Kiriko.

"I'm so sorry about this afternoon," he said. "I wanted to say something when you were leaving but—"

"I understand," she said. "Please, there's no need to say you're sorry. Thank you for inviting me and taking me out on your boat. And thank your father, too. The sea was beautiful."

"That's why I called you. I want to make it up to you. What if we go again tomorrow. I want to show you what sailing's really all about, how peaceful and wonderful it can be. I don't want that to be your last experience out on the ocean in *Argo*. I want you to enjoy yourself."

Kiriko hesitated. Jason wished he knew why, but he pressed his case.

"I haven't been able to talk to you alone since I got back from England. There are things I want to tell you."

"What time?" Kiriko asked.

• • •

Kiriko was dressed smartly and carried a backpack. Inside was a Thermos and lunch she'd packed for them along with her sketchbook and pencils. The sky was clear, the sun shone and the wind blew a perfect fifteen knots. As they passed the Sailing Club with Second Brother Island to port, the wind picked up in earnest and *Argo* responded, springing forward like a big horse given its head. The boat heeled to starboard and the sound of the water rushing by the hull made Jason realize how much he loved being out in a good boat on the gunmetal ocean with a good breeze and the Gulf Islands scenery as backdrop. Another sailboat appeared on the horizon, its white sails contrasting with the green-forested hills behind it. Misty gray clouds hung to port. Buoys and crab traps bobbed on the surface. A seal's head popped briefly up reminding him of Golly.

Kiriko sat on the starboard side of the cockpit and looked out at the sea. Her eyes sparkled with lightness and rapture. Jason looked up at the new headsail. Its shape was perfect and its color a mass of white against the blue sky. The sheets leading back to the cockpit were snug and the telltales on the mainsail streamed out behind in unison.

"Where do you want to go?" He called. The only other sounds were of the wind and the water.

"Let the wind take us," Kiriko replied.

"Sounds great," Jason said, and meant it.

The sun dazzled off the constantly shifting water

like infinite diamonds. The wind carried a faint trace of brine. Again and again they filled their lungs with the purified air.

They carried the headland past Buckles Provincial Park and pointed towards Portland Island. *Argo* was holding a steady six knots and trailed a good wake. If they held to their current course they'd sight Russell Point soon.

Despite the fine weather, there were few other boats. Jason taught Kiriko to release the main sheets when they tacked and she tailed for him as he worked the winch. In only two or three tries they were tacking effortlessly.

They were making excellent time. They passed between Portland and Piers and continued heading southeast.

"Look!" said Kiriko. "It's Mt. Baker. It's exactly like my painting. See how silver the water is. This is just how I imagined it!" He had never seen her so excited. "Thank you, Jason, oh thank you. You don't know how happy this makes me. When I painted *Mt. Baker & Waves*, it was from a photograph I took from the ferry. This is so different. Now I feel part of the ocean. This is how I saw it in my mind. It's like a dream. Another dream." She removed her sketchbook and pencils from her pack. Her hands flying across the broad white pages, she did half a dozen renditions of Baker and the water and the surrounding islands. They were beautiful and Jason was amazed how so few lines could convey so much. Seeing her work up close thrilled him.

As midday approached, the wind started fading like it had yesterday. The water was flattening and the day grew warmer. By now, Hot Springs Island and Russell Point were far behind them. Jason locked the steering wheel. "How about some lunch?" he suggested.

They drank hot green tea, tendrils of steam rising from the cups and disappearing in the sunny cockpit. When Kiriko called the boat "dear *Argo*," he wanted to kiss her.

"Do you realize this is the first time we've been alone since I got back from England?" Jason asked.

"Yes," Kiriko said. "I'm so glad you're home."

"I wanted to say thank you for your letters."

"You already did."

"That was just a quick one. I wanted to tell you how much they meant to me. And the idea of the letters within the letter — what a wonderful surprise. It was like finding money in your pocket or...suddenly coming across a mysterious woman in a hot springs."

Kiriko smiled.

"And the poems were so beautiful and layered. They said so much in so few words. I'm sorry I couldn't read the Japanese but the calligraphy was wonderful."

"I wanted to remind you of home."

"Actually, they made me think of two things in particular," Jason said.

Kiriko tilted her head in lieu of asking.

"They made me think of Japan."

"I see."

"And," said Jason, "naturally, they made me think of you. Especially the last poem I opened."

"Which one was that?"

"The one about 'seeing you in the waking world.' Do you remember that night in the hot springs, when you asked me to sing 'Stars Tonight'?"

"Of course," said Kiriko. "You didn't want to, but then you did it, anyway. Thank you."

"Well now it's my turn. I'd like you to recite that poem? Do you remember it?"

She closed her eyes for a moment and then began the poem in Japanese. Forced to focus on the sounds and the rhythms and Kiriko's intonation, it seemed more music than poetry. Then she recited it again in English: "'In the paths of my dreams / I walk to you without resting / but all of these dreams / are less than one moment / of seeing you / In the waking world.'"

"You remember it in both languages."

"It's one of my favorite poems."

"Why?" asked Jason.

"There are many reasons," Kiriko said.

"This one had a different tone from the others. The others all evoked the seasons or images from nature."

Kiriko paused. "Yes. It is a love poem," she said softly. Then she changed the subject. "I'm very sorry that I haven't asked you about your search," Kiriko said, "and if you found your mother."

"No, I didn't. But I think I found a lot of other

things while I was there. Actually, many of the things I found I didn't even know I was looking for," he said.

"What things? What do you mean?"

"Not things, actually, but people. I found out I cared much more about certain people than I'd ever realized. It made me understand how much I care about Dada and Al. And, Kiriko, I found out how much I care about you, as well. After reading that poem over and over, I came to a conclusion. And the conclusion that I reached is that you care about me, too. I need you to tell me, Kiriko. You have to tell me how you feel."

In answer, Kiriko placed her right hand over Jason's larger one. With these delicate fingers she transferred thoughts and beauty onto paper, preserved them like ancient life captured in a piece of translucent amber. Through these gifted hands, she conveyed meaning. Jason didn't move. He wanted her hand to remain exactly where it was.

"Jason…these things you ask of me, they are very difficult. It's so…impossible."

"What's impossible? What do you mean?"

"I can't explain. I can't say anymore," Kiriko said. "Why do you ask me about things I can't explain?"

A gust of wind from the north caught the rigging and heeled the boat dramatically. He leapt to the helm and tried to restore equilibrium. The suddenly strong afternoon winds made the ride home a wild one. As always with the ocean, conditions changed instantly.

Only when the docking lines were taut and cinched was Jason able to reflect on what she had said. That Kiriko cared for him, Jason was certain. Of everything else, he was unsure.

• • •

The hotel hadn't been this quiet in some time. After dining last night with Cristine, *sans* Jason, Seamus was now in Vancouver for interviews.

Taking advantage of the calm, Dada asked Jason to meet him in the bath that night, although an hour earlier than usual. "Getting too old for the witching hour," he said. The request pleased Jason. Since his return from England, their old ritual had for the most part fallen by the wayside.

At eleven o'clock father and son reunited in the mineral-rich waters with faithful old Golly lying in her usual place on the worn green bathmat.

"I wanted to talk to you," Dada said. They watched a bird fly overhead. "I was listening to the radio today," Dada continued, "and there was a story on about a girl who'd been adopted."

Never before had Dada mentioned adoption of his own accord.

"It was a documentary thing. The girl's name was Jenna. She'd known she was adopted from a pretty young age and, in her family, it wasn't a big thing. But still it wasn't simple. When she saw her birth mother, she realized how alike they looked. It was like seeing herself in the future. When she said that to her mother, whose name was Sylvia, Sylvia said that seeing Jenna was the opposite; it was seeing herself when she was young. So there they were. Two people crossing boundaries.

"Then they talked about this writer from California who'd written a book called *The Primal Wound*. Her thesis is that all adopted children suffer deeply and profoundly because they're separated from their mothers at birth. She said that, even just after birth, babies already know their mother's voice and smell and when they're separated they never feel the same again or as safe.

"Jenna said that she didn't know if she'd suffered from this primal wound or not. But what she did know was that meeting her mother was one of the most important events of her life. Until then she hadn't felt real or free, she said. Before she'd always felt like there was some kind of bond or tether holding her back and now it isn't there anymore. It's gone."

Jason asked his question softly. "So what happened with her adopted parents?"

"They were still her parents and she still loved them the same, if not more. She was grateful to them in a new way. She said, genetics counts for something, but if you think about it, we're all related somehow or other anyway. It just depends how far back you want to go."

"What about her birth mother?"

"They exchange Christmas cards, but that's about it."

Dada stopped speaking and there was silence for a while.

"Dada?"

"Yes, son."

"Why are you telling me this?"

There was a pause. "You'll think I'm a pretty sorry excuse for father when you hear."

"No I won't."

"Until I heard this, I'd never really understood what you were going through. I know you tried to tell me. I mean, we haven't really talked about what it was like for you in England, searching for your mother, because I didn't want to know. I was afraid of what you'd find out. This whole time I was thinking about it solely from my perspective and, I guess, trying to somehow protect your mother— if that doesn't sound too crazy.

"But then, when I heard this girl speaking, I don't know. Something clicked or cracked."

Jason didn't know what to say.

"There was one other thing. I saw in the office today that you'd opened an invoice from your lawyer in England, that Morgan fellow. It was lying on the desk and I looked at it. I saw how much it was costing you. That it was still that important to you."

"Thank you, Dada. You don't know how much this means to me."

"Don't thank me yet."

"What're you talking about? What do you mean?"

"I've held back on you Jason. Again. You asked me and I didn't tell you the truth."

"What're you talking about? I don't understand."

"Elizabeth Barnett. That's not her real name. I

know her real name. You asked me and I avoided the question...whatever. It's the same as a lie."

"Then what is it? What's her real name?"

"Elizabeth Robertson."

"Elizabeth Robertson?"

"Yes."

Although he didn't want to, Jason couldn't stop himself from asking, "Why didn't you tell me? Do you know what I've been through and...?" Words failed him.

"I was afraid of losing you, Jason. I was afraid of losing you and I didn't want to share you. You're our son. Mum's and mine. But now I know. Now I know that unless you find her, this'll never be done with. So I'll help you any way I can from now on. I promise you. Jason, please forgive me."

"Dada..."

"Do you forgive me, Jason?"

"Of course I do," said Jason.

"Jason. You're all I have. You and Al. Really. The two of you are all I have left."

Jason had to break the tension. He didn't want to see Dada remorseful and sad. "And don't forget Golly. She's one of us too."

• • •

"So, Jason," said Tina in Penny's Pastries, Hot Springs Island's most famous bakery and coffeeshop, "I'd like to have you over for dinner on Friday for your birthday. You can invite what's his name — your old boss — if you want."

"Seamus," said Jason,

"He's been here quite a while," said Tina.

"Yeah, longer than expected. I guess he likes it here. He's done some work in Vancouver and Seattle and Portland, day trips and a couple of overnighters. But, sure, that'd be nice. Thanks for the invite. Who else is coming?"

"Just Adam. And it's my pleasure. You only turn thirty once."

As expected, Seamus was keen to attend and wanted Cristine invited as well.

Jason suspected that Tina's invite was the front for a surprise party. He'd seen the furtive phone calls and whispered conversations between Al and Dada. Whenever he'd show up they stopped talking and attempt nonchalance. This would be his first and the surprise party idea appealed to him even if he'd figured it out in advance.

It was Friday. At breakfast, Dada, Al and Ellery and a new helper brought out a little cake and sang "Happy Birthday." Dada gave him a cool tuner that you attached to your guitar stock with a spring and Al a sailing book. The new girl planted kisses on both his cheeks.

Jason was born at seven in the evening. They pulled into Tina's driveway in Seamus's rented SUV at exactly that time. Cristine's green VW and Adam's white van emblazoned with "Hot Springs Veterinary Clinic" were parked in front. They'd hidden the other vehicles well. Ringing the bell, Jason prepared himself for the big SURPRISE!

Adam opened the door. "Happy Birthday, Jason," he said. "Tina and Cris are in the kitchen. Come on in." There was no leaping. No shouting. In other words, no surprise party. He did get some lovely hugs and more presents but that was it. Dinner was fun. Seamus and Adam clicked intellectually and they bantered most of the night.

While Tina readied coffee and dessert Jason cornered Cristine on the back porch as she grabbed a smoke.

"So how're things going?" he asked.

"Good. Great."

"With Seamus, I mean…"

"Mr. Bird Dog's at it again," Cristine laughed.

"Okay, okay, don't tell me. But I think I know. If things were going badly you'd be complaining faster than Dada quoting Shakespeare."

Cristine grinned. "Yeah, I suspect you're right. Actually, Jason, it's fine. But at the same time, he's leaving next week, you know. These days, my motto's 'one day at a time.'"

"You can say that again."

"But, Jason, I wanted to ask you one thing about him."

"What's that?"

"Has he got a temper?"

"Well, he's Irish if that means anything. But seriously, why? Have you had a fight or something?"

"No, no. That's not it. I've seen glimmers of it, and after Abner, I want to be careful."

"He's feisty, but he's no Abner, that's for sure."

When the dinner party ended, Seamus and Jason headed home on the North-South Road. Although a more than pleasant evening, Jason had been counting on the surprise party. Thirty was a milestone. He realized now why he wanted the party so much. It was a way of transforming his feelings of rejection into something more positive. Before, birthdays had been celebrations. Now he associated this day with Elizabeth and searching and unanswered questions.

As they approached the hotel turnoff, Seamus threw a pile of CDs Jason's way. "Choose one," he said. The sudden toss caught Jason off guard. The discs spilled all over the floor.

"Whoa, Seamus, what was that?"

"Sorry, mate, sorry," said Seamus. Busy collecting the discs from under the seat, Jason missed Seamus's grin.

"SURPRISE!" They were all there. Jason's family and friends. Dada, Al, Kiriko, Cassidy, Ellery, Kevin, the Music Club — even Dee Dee and Phillip. Seconds later in walked Tina and Adam and Cristine. About the only person missing was Layla. "No way," said Cristine. "I'm not taking any chances *this* time."

The plan was done flawlessly. The feint at Tina's. Even Seamus's toss of the CDs to prevent him seeing familiar cars. No need to fake his shocked expression this time. Hug after hug after hug. It was glorious.

Phillip Hung entered Jason's line of sight. He was obviously nervous and just as obviously wanting to talk. "Jason...I don't know what to say. Except that I'm sorry."

"Well — Hung!" said Jason.

"Very funny," said Phillip, completing the ritual. They'd be okay.

"I...well, I think Dee Dee told you what happened. I know it's unforgivable but..."

"You know what Phillip? You're probably just what she needs. Stable. Employed. I was also going to say loyal but—"

"Bastard," Phillip grinned.

"How's Irene taking it?"

"Ouch. You can probably guess. And it's not just Irene. It's her whole family. Mine, too. I'm getting it from all sides."

"Serves you right."

"Okay, okay. Enough with the guilt tripping, will you? That's all I've been getting for months." While Phillip talked, Dee Dee watched keenly "But, you know, Phillip. It took balls coming here," said Jason.

"It was Dee Dee's idea. She talked it over with Al and your dad."

"That's what I meant, it took balls." Jason winked.

"Actually, Jason, when I said it was Dee Dee's idea, I didn't just mean coming here. The surprise party was her idea, too. She arranged it with your dad and Al."

"What?"

"Yeah. She knew you'd always wanted one. A big one. Your place and her place in Vancouver were too small so she thought this would be a good chance."

"You're kidding?"

"I'm not."

Jason turned to her. "Dee Dee…"

How it is possible, Jason wondered, to be standing with your ex-girlfriend and friend, now a couple, and feel like this? Their arms found each other.

"Good luck, you two," Jason said. "Good luck." Then he moved to the bar. Why rehash when you can celebrate? He felt like another drink.

Before he could reach the liquor, however, Jason felt a tap on his shoulder. It was Ellery.

"Jason, over there," Ellery said, and pointed to the door of The Pit. It swung open and there were Dada and Al, together carrying the biggest birthday cake he'd ever seen. Thirty candles lit up their smiling faces and the room burst into song — and thanks to the Music Club, their version of "Happy Birthday" was even somewhat harmonious. Jason cut the cake, Dada popped the champagne, and everyone surrounded the birthday boy to offer congratulations and best wishes a second time. Some people gave him small presents, and he was kissed and hugged too many times to count. But the final one was best.

"*O tanjobi, omedeto gozaimasu*, Jason" — Happy birthday — and Kiriko kissed him. "I have a present for you, too," she said. "But I don't have it with me. Would you mind coming with me?"

Kiriko took him by the hand and led him toward the front door. When they reached the front hallway, she turned to the wall. "There," she said.

Her paintings, *Pier* and *Mt. Baker & Waves*, the same two he stared at every day in Seamus's room.

"I don't understand."

"They're for you," she said.

"How?"

"I asked Seamus to return them. I told him why and he agreed."

"But...but they're so valuable," spluttered, Jason. "They're worth thousands of dollars — I can't accept them, Kiriko."

"I want you to always remember our day together sailing. To always remember me. Please accept them. They are all I have to give you."

• • •

Before Jason could say another word, Dada bolted from the office. Urgency gripped his voice.

"Jason! Jason! Come here. Quick!"

"What is it?"

He grabbed Jason by the sleeve and half-pulled him towards the office.

"It's Elizabeth, Jason. It's Elizabeth."

"What is? What're you talking about?"

"It's you're— It's Elizabeth Robertson. She's on the phone."

"What?" Jason couldn't believe this news.

"It's true, Jason. Elizabeth's on the phone," said Dada. "She calls around your birthday. I told you that. She's on the phone now."

"What did you say?"

"That you were here. That you'd gone to England to find her. And that you're here now and want to talk to her. I freed her from her vow, Jason. I want to do everything I can to help. Talk to her, Jason. Talk to her."

He was immobile. Usually, we only recognize our lives' pivotal moments after they've gone, Jason realized. But not this one. All his time and efforts in England had been for this moment.

"C'mon, son. Hurry up. She's waiting."

The receiver lay atop a pile of papers. His arm felt ponderously heavy, like moving through liquid. He took a breath and then spoke: "Hello."

She didn't answer.

"Hello," he repeated more urgently. But still she didn't answer. Whether in panic, whether unable to break her vow despite Dada's release, Elizabeth had hung up. Instead of his mother's voice all Jason heard was a dial tone.

Chapter 18 iNovel Links
Chapter 18 has two iNovel links. Please go to
www.HotSpringsNovel.com/chapter18/ and you'll
find the following:

- a painting link: paintings by Kiriko of *Mt. Baker & Waves* and *Pier*; and
- a photo link: several photos of the sailboat *Argo*.

Chapter 19

"Heaven with hell's central heating."

Jason had been expecting words. Instead, all he could hear was the sound of an empty humming wire, the faint clicks of a switching system and some circuits. The receiver weighed in his hand but he couldn't put it down. Maybe she'd come back on.

Then he had an idea. He punched the callback number, but international numbers weren't connected to the system. Then he wrote down the time so he could later check the phone bill. He would get her number and, now that he knew her real name, he would call John S. Morgan and then…He stepped back. What was he doing? He felt like an idiot. She didn't want to speak to him. Otherwise, why would she have hung up? He remembered Dee Dee's words about the pathetic nature of unrequited affection.

But why had she called? What if she'd been disconnected? A soft tap on the door. Dada came in.

"Jason? Are you finished? What happened?"

"I'm waiting for her to call back."

"Why?"

"What did she say to you when you told her you were going to get me?"

"Nothing. Why?"

"When I picked up the phone, there was nobody there."

"What?"

"Either we were disconnected or she hung up. Maybe she couldn't deal with it. With me. I don't know."

"I'll wait here with you. If you want me to, that is."

"Sure."

A minute passed. Then another. Then several more. Dada laid a hand on Jason's back as sounds of the birthday celebration drifted through the door.

* * *

To come so tantalizingly close to Elizabeth without talking to her left Jason in a fog of disappointment. He got a phone number for Elizabeth from his long distance supplier and passed it on to John S. Morgan along with Elizabeth's real last name, but it felt rather useless. When he'd tried the number he got nothing, not even an answering machine. For all he knew, it could have been a public phone.

Another change was more concretely imminent. Seamus was leaving. Two more days in Hot Springs and he was off on business to Toronto, Montreal and New York. Then back to England. Of late, Seamus had taken to disappearing during the day. Where and for what cause Jason didn't know.

Jason hadn't talked to Kiriko since his birthday party. In fact, when he'd emerged from the office she'd already left and he'd been unable to reach her since. He needed to talk to her about the paintings.

With a quick word to Ellery, he jumped into his car and drove to Kiriko's place. She wasn't home. She wasn't at the gallery either.

Cristine didn't know where she was; neither did Dada or Al. He went to see Tina.

"Hey Jason! What's up?" They went for coffee.

"I wanted to ask you about Kiriko."

"Ask me what?"

"I haven't been able to reach her since the party."

"Actually, I haven't seen her since then, either. What about her other friends?"

"I've tried everyone I can think of," said Jason.

"What's going on, Jason? Is something wrong?" Tina asked.

"I can't figure it out," he said.

Tina's cell phone rang. She was needed at the office.

"We should talk later, Jason," Tina said. She was concerned. "Call me — I mean it."

That night, Cassidy called Jason. He was looking for Kiriko, too.

"So you don't know where she is?" asked Cassidy.

"I haven't seen her since the party."

"Me either. She's not with your old boss, then?" Cassidy wouldn't even call Seamus by name.

"No," said Jason. "But, if you find her, call me right away. I'm starting to worry."

● ● ●

The night before Seamus's departure, Dada and Jason sat in the hot springs at day's end. As far as Jason knew, Kiriko had ceased her midnight visits. On misty nights he remembered the way she'd surprised him, how she'd walked up the steps and then left.

"Dada, you still haven't heard from Kiriko, have you?" asked Jason at one point over the sound of the bubbling water. Despite even more attempts, Jason remained unable to reach her. *Pier* and *Mt. Baker & Waves* hung in the hall as a reminder of her absence.

"No. And, frankly, it's starting to worry me. What's that line in *As You Like It*... 'Beauty provoketh thieves sooner than gold...'"

Jason heard something outside the bath. He stopped breathing. His heart started thumping.

"Hello? Anybody there?" called Jason.

"I know it's closed to regular guests but I've this mighty chill that needs taking from my bones," said Seamus.

Jason unlocked the door.

He plunged right into the bath without showering. Normally, Dada set guests straight quickly, but Seamus could do no wrong.

"Ahhhh," Seamus released a long sigh. "Heaven on earth. You know, Da, you've got a great thing going here. Heaven with hell's central heating." Dada thought this observation wonderful.

"Seamus, we haven't seen much of you the last few days," Dada said. "Where've you been and what've you been up to?"

"'The gaudy, blabbing, and remorseful day / Is crept into the bosom of the sea,'" replied Seamus.

"Wait! Wait! Good one, Seamus...*Henry VI*, no? Part II, Act III?"

"You're impossible to trump. Good on ya, Da."

"What do you mean? Where've you been?" asked Jason.

"I've been exploring the island, in particular the other hot springs. The New Spring and also the one at Etna. Not a patch on yours, mind you, but still worthwhile. You've got me hooked, you know."

Dada chortled in delight.

"The hot springs — is that what you meant by 'the bosom of the sea'?" asked Jason.

"Well-spotted laddie. But no, actually, truth be told, I've been taking sailing lessons. Kayaking as well."

"Sailing lessons? Why — you should have told me," sputtered Dada. "Or Jason. One of us, anyway. We would have been happy to take you out anytime. *Argo*'s just sitting unused most of the time." Dada sounded almost offended.

"I've been trouble enough as it is," said Seamus.

"Don't be silly, my boy," countered Dada instantly.

"There's another line, isn't there, Da, from King Henry? — 'Unbidden guests / Are often welcomest when they are gone...'"

• • •

Finally, the mercurial Seamus Healey departed. Dada and Al were teary at the departure of their loud but remarkable guest. As for Seamus, he was his usual hail-fellow-well-met self.

"Stay in touch, Jason," he'd said and then applied one of his bone-crushing hugs. He peeled away in his SUV, the sound of his laughter disappearing into the morning, along with the crunch of tires on the gravel.

Not long after, a car pulled up in the hotel driveway.

"Jason!" It was Officer Hardy of the Troy RCMP, Hot Springs Island's sole police force.

"Duncan? What are you doing here?" They'd been classmates.

"Hi Jason."

"Hey buddy — is this social or professional? There some kind of problem?"

Duncan came closer. "I really don't think so, but is there some place we can talk privately?"

"Sure...of course." Jason led Duncan into the office.

"I'd like to talk to one of your guests, Jason. The Irish fellow." Duncan consulted his notebook. "Seamus Healy."

"What? What's wrong?"

"Is he here?"

"No. You just missed him. Why? What's going on, Duncan?"

"Do you know where he is?"

"He was supposed to go to Toronto, Montreal and New York and then back to England."

"Do you know where he's staying?"

"I didn't ask. But I could probably find out."

"Would you do that, please?"

"Sure. But what is it?"

"Someone called and reported that Kiriko Shimizu is missing. Have you seen her?"

"No, I haven't. Who reported it?"

"Cassidy Maher. And, according to him, this Healy fellow might have some relevant information. He said they'd been seen together and that nobody's seen her since."

"You're kidding? But, listen, this has got to be some kind of misunderstanding. Is Cassidy suggesting that, what, that Seamus did something to her?"

"No, nothing like that. But, still, I'm obligated to find out what I can."

"Yeah, of course."

"Nine times out of ten people show up sooner rather than later. Usually some kind of romantic entanglement." Duncan paused. "There's one other thing. And this you have to keep to yourself."

"Sure," said Jason.

"When I checked out her apartment, the place was in a mess. And we also found some traces of blood in the kitchen — not much, mind you, but there was still blood."

• • •

Jason forced himself to ask the question. Were either Cassidy or Seamus capable of violence? His answer

363

was no. But, unlikely as it was, anyone who watched the news saw stranger things happening every day. Nothing could be completely discounted — hard as that might be to imagine.

After endlessly examining and reexamining scenarios, Jason reached a conclusion. Kiriko had returned to Japan. She must have. Something from her Japanese life had beckoned. Something or someone had called her home. During their conversation on *Argo* that day, Jason felt she was being constrained by some invisible shackles. The more he thought about, the more convinced Jason became that Kiriko had fled to Japan.

Jason had to decide. To go or not to go. Going seemed reckless, silly even. Illogical and impulsive. But where had well-thought-out planning got him?

And Kiriko might need him. For too long, he'd been hesitant. He wanted to prove himself to her. Even though Dada and Al needed him here. Even though Elizabeth was on the verge of being found. He told no one of his plans. His passport was in order, he confirmed his flight on the web and he e-mailed his only contact in Japan, Professor Kawamoto, his Japanese language teacher at UBC. She'd left Canada almost five years ago but still sent a yearly e-letter to her former students.

"Dada. Feel like having a bath?"

"At this hour? Why?"

"I've got something to tell you. I'm going to Japan."

Chapter 19 iNovel Links

In this chapter, Seamus joins Dada and Jason in the hot springs. Of course, hot springs are a major setting for this book, so this chapter's iNovel Links are about them. The first shows three paintings done by Kiriko (not mentioned in the book) of the beachside hot springs on Russell Point. The second lists some hot springs–related websites all over the world, particularly (though not exclusively) ones in Canada, the UK and Japan. Please go to **www.HotSpringsNovel.com/chapter19/** to see them.

PART IV

KUROKAWA ONSEN (HOT SPRINGS),
KYUSHU, JAPAN

Chapter 20

"It's our way of staying in touch with the past,
however symbolic."

A third continent beckoned. They cruised at thirty thousand feet over the invisible ocean — as if the physical world was below and forgotten and above it a sunlit heaven. Inside the silvery exterior of the wafer-thin fuselage, the cabin air passed through filters and exchangers and the whispering whoosh was a softer constant than the roar of the powerful jets on the shining wings. Although hurtling along at hundreds of kilometers an hour, the sensation was more of floating than of speeding, the air a cushion of nothingness instead of a barrier.

The flight was direct from Vancouver to Narita airport. Approximately ten hours later they began the final approach, a wide circle over the Boso Peninsula and Chiba Prefecture. From his window seat Jason could see ricefields divided up into Tetris-like blocks with narrow roads between them. Coming the opposite way, had Kiriko felt something akin to this, trepidation tinged with excitement?

Tired from the long flight, he sleepwalked through the line at immigration. The shuffling crowds were separated into Japanese and foreign passports. Jason stole glances at his line mates from China, Taiwan, Korea, the Philippines.

Narita had much in common with Heathrow and Vancouver and other international airports. Officials in uniforms and signs directed you to lines, phones, washrooms and customs. Everything appeared well scrubbed and ran with admirable efficiency. The Japanese travelers dressed tastefully; their clothes seemed of better quality and fit than those of their fellow voyageurs. Tour groups large and small gathered in circles and engaged in elaborate goodbyes. All were laden with bags of chocolates or cigarettes, gifts for those who'd stayed behind — token penitences.

Jason hoped his two years of UBC Japanese would help. From what he'd heard, English wasn't spoken much outside the big cities so he reviewed his old notebooks on the flight over. Eavesdropping, however, his confidence faded. Everyone spoke so quickly. He could barely make out words, let alone phrases. Thankfully, he'd heard back almost immediately from Professor Kawamoto; she was willing to help in Kyushu and said she'd love to see him.

The spring weather was warmer than what he'd left behind and more humid. An unpleasant stickiness crept up his back. Fatigue set in and he felt a throbbing in his forehead like he'd been clamped with a steel band.

You could reach central Tokyo by train, limousine bus or ridiculously expensive taxi. Jason chose the bus; it would take him directly to the hotel he'd found on the Net. The fare was so high he recalculated the exchange rate several times to make sure he'd got it right. Professor Kawamoto warned her classes that Japan was expensive. Only now did he fully understand the difference between theory and practice. Hopefully the countryside would be cheaper. His search for Kiriko would begin in earnest there.

The orange and white buses pulled into numbered stops with dizzying frequency. Drivers zoomed up to the curb, passengers and luggage were disgorged, and a new set loaded every two minutes. Twice, Jason attempted to board only to learn he was reserved on a bus leaving just minutes later. He attempted several surreal conversations in which his rudimentary Japanese was met with equally unintelligible English.

From what he gathered, the Narita area was about seventy kilometers from Tokyo's center. Even at this distance, it wasn't long before they left bamboo copses behind for a busy highway bordered on both sides by factories and huge buildings. Space was at a premium. Things were jammed into spots undreamed of by North American city planners, the occasional house plunked in the middle of a pipe-infested industrial area.

Before long the steady vibrations of the bus lulled Jason to sleep. He awoke to find them pulling into the New Takanawa Prince Hotel. Soon enough he was checked into a clean yet smallish room, but a glance at the room service and restaurant prices appalled him. He left the hotel and walked down the hill to the station area. He'd try and find something there.

Stretching his legs felt glorious, though the hum in his forehead remained, and, if anything, had increased in intensity. A quick shower hadn't helped. His body didn't feel like his own. He realized he knew nobody in a city of twenty million.

Darkness had come. This section of the city, at least, had grown more attractive by night. The gray hodgepodge of buildings was hidden behind a plethora of neon signs and lights; color had claimed the night shift.

The bullet train, called the *shinkansen*, left from Shinagawa Station and Jason thought he should reserve tickets for the next day's travel. The station was massive. Even with the many English signs he was soon lost. There were at least a dozen train lines and entrances and exits everywhere. Considering the hour, the volume of people astonished him. It was pure bustle. The otherworldly nature of the station combined with his fatigue and jet lag to make him feel like he was floating over his own body. It was as surreal as one of Dada's old paintings.

"Excuse me, do you need help?"

"Pardon?" Jason came back down to earth. He'd been standing, dazed, almost hypnotized by the motion, lights and sounds.

"Can I help you?" He was a well-dressed, middle-aged Japanese man carrying a wafer-thin briefcase. His look was sympathetic and helpful, that of someone picking up a stray cat or dog grazed by a passing car.

"I'm trying to buy a *shinkansen* ticket for tomorrow."

What kindness. The man not only led him to the ticket office, but facilitated the transaction as well.

"Thank you very much. That was incredibly kind of you," said Jason.

"You're welcome."

"Where did you learn your English?" It was lightly accented, passably fluent.

"I worked in New York City for several years. My company sent me there." Reaching into his pocket, the man produced a blue leather name-card wallet and from it a business card. "Here's my *meishi*. My name is Hiroshi Oshima."

"Thank you Mr. Oshima. *Domo arigato*. I don't know what I would have done without you. My name's Jason Chiron. Sorry, I don't have a card. And...can I ask you another question?"

"Please."

"Do you know somewhere good to eat around here? Not too expensive? I just arrived and I'm a bit hungry."

Hiroshi Oshima thought for a bit.

"Perhaps we could go for a drink and some food together?"

"Are you sure? That'd be great."

"There is *aka chochin* around here. It is a small local bar with food. Please come this way."

They passed the hill near Jason's hotel and then made half a dozen quick turns.

"There," Jason's guide pointed to a bright red paper lantern hanging from the eaves of a small establishment fronted by narrow sliding doors. Delicious smells wafted forth. "That is *aka chochin*, red lantern."

Before very long, Jason was drunk and Oshima-san his best friend in the whole world. They'd started on beer and moved to sake (*Nihonshu*, Oshima called it) and now the room was shifting perspective. Jason knew that Japan was prone to earthquakes but he hadn't expected one so soon — particularly inside his skull.

The bar was long and narrow and they sat at the counter. Oshima-san was a regular, it seemed, and his foreign guest was the center of attention. People kept pouring him drinks and they must have eaten fifteen different dishes. The cooks and servers were loud and garrulous — nothing like Jason's image of Japan as a staid, formal place. Here it was all slaps on the back and raucous laughter, like Oshima himself. Until reaching the bar, he'd been the picture of decorum. Now his hair was ruffled, his tie was loose, and he kept putting his arm around Jason like they were blood brothers or in-laws or something.

"This area, this area," said Oshima, his face as red as the lantern outside, "is very close to the famous Sengakuji Temple. Do you know Sengakuji Temple?" Oshima was slurring.

"No, what is it?"

"It is very famous. You must visit tomorrow. Because it is the place where the Chushingura *samurai* are buried. Do you know Chushingura?"

"No, I don't."

Oshima was very surprised. "What? You don't know?" At this point, Oshima informed his bar buddies of Jason's startling ignorance.

"It is one of the most famous stories in Japan.

Chushingura is sometimes called the story of the forty-seven *samurai*."

"Why is it so famous?"

"That is an excellent question." Oshima was sagging and his forehead was in danger of colliding with the countertop. "It is famous because it is the story of *giri* and *ninjo*. Do you know *giri* and *ninjo*?"

"No, I don't."

"Hmmm," said Oshima. "I will try and tell you the story. Once upon a time, there were 47 *samurai*. The master *samurai*, their lord, did something to another lord, so he was forced to do *seppuku* — you know *seppuku*, *hara kiri*, cutting your belly with a sword?" Oshima gestured. Jason nodded. "Well his *samurai* now had no master so they became *ronin*, which means they are like children with no parents. But these *samurai* decided that the death of their lord was unfair; it was unjust, so they had to get...revenge. Yes, revenge. For one and half years they planned the attack, which they finally did. And then, after, they did *seppuku* too. They were very brave and loyal and had much honor. That is the story. Now many people go to their graves to visit, to honor this loyalty and *ninjo*."

Jason had the drift, and the parallels made him shake his head. It was a tale of loyalty and commitment against all odds.

Finally time to go, they tumbled from the doors, propping each other up like human crutches.

"Can you find your hotel?" asked Oshima-san. "Because I must go the other way."

"I think so. It's not far. Thank you for a wonderful evening," Jason said. Oshima staggered off, his right hand held high approximating a farewell. Jason immediately got so lost he ended up catching a taxi only five blocks from his hotel.

• • •

The next stage of Jason's journey began.

He watched the megalopolis speed by for an hour until everything outside the bullet train's Plexiglas windows blurred into one long streak. Jason unfolded his newspaper. A story about the hot springs in Nagano Prefecture, somewhere up north, caught his eye. Although the area was renowned for its milky-white water, it seems they'd been artificially coloring it with bath salts.The natural hot springs source had dried up eight years ago. The government was closing the inns to investigate and they planned to check all 1,150 hot springs in Nagano. He tore out the story. Dada would be interested.

They'd already passed Shin Yokohama and Nagoya and whizzed by many other stations. Next stop was ancient Kyoto and then Shin Osaka. The PA announced regularly that Jason occupied a "Nozomi Super Express bound for Hakata with stops at Shin Kobe, Okayama, Hiroshima, and Kokura."

They were traveling at well over 240 kilometers per hour. Although Jason had been looking forward to these speeds, the reality was an anticlimax. Smooth and quiet, the ride resembled a plane more than a train. The only time you truly sensed you were traveling three times that of a speeding car was when another *shinkansen* passed going the other way. There was a deep almost violent shudder as the two trains met and the other train remained visible for only the briefest of moments before instantly disappearing in a blur and Doppler-effect.

• • •

Both during Japanese class and outside it, Jason and his fellow students had called Professor Kawamoto "Sensei." Jason had phoned her before leaving Tokyo and she'd offered to meet him at the main *shinkansen* exit in Hakata Station. "And don't forget to keep your ticket," she reminded him.

As the train slowed, Jason began to worry if he'd recognize her. Years had passed since they'd met. Back home, Jason had printed one of her old newsletters, and he skimmed it again now before reaching Hakata. The more he remembered, the better.

She was teaching both English and Japanese literature at a university and several junior colleges in the area. The rest of the letter, written in English, Japanese and simplified Japanese for beginners, was an essay on the theme of seasons in Japan. Her English writing was astonishingly good — she'd been educated at Columbia and somewhere in England.

Even before exiting, Jason saw her waving and realized he'd worried needlessly. She'd changed remarkably little. Perhaps a new wrinkle or two and her hair dyed brown (like the majority of women he'd seen in Japan so far) but that was all.

"Jason, how nice to see you — *ohisashiburi*," she said and bowed. They didn't hug or shake hands, but her smile was easy. That's when it came back to him — her remarkable voice. She had a naturally resonant timber and a melodic cadence. Several of her students had remarked on her speaking style, how precise yet soothing, both in English and Japanese. One girl had called her voice "crystalline."

She then said something in Japanese. When Jason couldn't catch it, she switched easily to English. "How was your trip?"

"The plane ride or the *shinkansen*?"

"In Japan, I mean. My car's parked this way." Jason's suitcase wheels clattered against the pebbled station floor. Like everyone else, Sensei walked briskly.

Her cream Toyota Camry matched her neat suit in color and style. Inside her exquisitely pristine vehicle, Jason perched on the edge of his seat like a parrot on a branch in a tropical breeze.

Kawamoto Sensei drove like she spoke, with a comfortable rhythm and deft efficiency.

Buildings dominated the immediate horizon. Once they reached an elevated highway, however, the ocean came into view. Sensei told him about the substantial port and northern Kyushu's industrial and shipbuilding history. When she finished, Jason asked what he thought was an innocuous question.

"How's Professor Kawamoto? Your husband, I mean." Sensei didn't answer for a second.

"I suppose you don't know, Jason."

"Pardon?"

"My husband passed away. More than two years ago."

"Oh...oh...I'm so sorry. I'm so sorry to hear that. Ah..., um, I didn't know...I'm sorry. I don't remember reading it in your newsletter." Jason was stunned — at his blunder and the enormity of the news.

"I wrote that there'd been a tragedy in my family and that I wouldn't be sending a letter the next year."

"Of course. I'm sorry. I remember. But I didn't know that the tragedy was—"

"Yes. He died of lung cancer. He'd been sick for a little while but when the doctors found out what it was, it was really too late. His illness is the main reason we returned to Japan."

"It must have been very hard on you."

"Death is never easy. It was also difficult when my mother passed away — a few years before we came to Canada. Now, the only ones left are my father and I. It may be a popular...what's the word — truism? — that health is the most important thing in life but it is true. Health and family. They are both immutable." She'd lost none of her remarkable vocabulary.

"If you like, we could visit his grave on the way home. It's not far. On the way."

"Of course. But I'm afraid I don't know the customs. Should I bring flowers or..."

She turned and smiled at him; it was the first time she'd looked at him in some time. "No, that's not necessary. But, thank you."

By this time they'd left the highway and were traveling a main thoroughfare lined with shops and restaurants. A modern area, all the establishments seem fronted with large parking lots, Japanese-style strip malls. Japan too had been seduced by the culture of the car. They turned right and passed a series of large beige buildings whose purpose Jason couldn't begin to imagine. Another right, and they were motoring beside a small river, the banks of which were lined with concrete blocks like a sluiceway.

Ten minutes later they were in a residential area, with houses interspersed by ricefields. Hazy hills on the horizon broke up the otherwise flat terrain. As Sensei pulled up and parked, sunset hit its climax, the sky turning the pink of rose-colored glasses.

A gully separated the road from the cemetery and Sensei and Jason had to cross a narrow arched bridge to enter.

Although the cemetery was recognizable as such, its features were distinct. Tall slats of wood covered with calligraphy stood behind meter-high stone obelisks. Surprising to his North American sensibilities was the lack of greenery. The square monuments resembled buildings in miniature and reminded him of Tokyo.

Cut flowers protruded from glass vases in front of most gravestones. Other offerings included cigarette packs and even jars and bottles of *sake*. Sensei brought a wooden bucket from her car trunk, which she filled with water to douse the graves of her mother and husband in a ritual cleansing. Then they put their hands together in the universal gesture of prayer and bowed in silence.

Jason watched her as she prayed, her eyes closed and her body motionless. How much she must miss her husband. For Jason, the experience of mourning before the unfamiliar graves of two people — one he'd barely known, the other not at all — underlined just how few talismans or links to his own past he possessed.

As they were leaving, a diminutive statue of Buddha wearing a small red bib caught Jason's eye.

"Sensei. Excuse me. I don't know if this is appropriate to ask or not, but could you tell me what that is?"

She followed his gaze. "Oh. Oh." She hesitated a moment. "That is a grave for an unborn child. The child's mother probably put it there."

"They don't have memorials like this in my country," Jason said. He knew several people who could've used one.

• • •

Sensei's home was a two-storey single-family dwelling in a relatively new neighborhood of smart clean houses with colorful tiled roofs. They pulled into a carport protected by a brown-tinted Plexiglas overhang. A tiny patch of lawn and gardens back and front defined the circumference of the house. Jason schlepped his stuff from the car into the entranceway. Once inside, they removed their shoes and replaced them with slippers.

Kawamoto Sensei lived with her father. Now in his

eighties, Dad was a tall, gaunt, spare man with bad false teeth but a ready smile. He spoke no English but Sensei effortlessly handled the introduction which included Dad's left-handed handshake while they were bowing — kind of mid-Pacific style, Jason mused. He liked the old guy immediately.

Jason stored his things in Sensei's office where he would sleep on a *futon*. Her father — Ji-chan, she called him — slept across the way in the Japanese room, the one with *tatami* mats. "Even new Western-style homes have them," Sensei said. "It's our way of staying in touch with the past, however symbolic." She served green tea while they talked.

"So tell me why you're here," Kawamoto Sensei asked. "In your e-mail you just said you wanted to explore Kurokawa Onsen."

"I'm sorry if it sounded mysterious," said Jason with a smile. Too many times since Dada's revelations about his adoption, Jason had faced a predicament about what to reveal and what to hold back. He was tired of half-truths. By the time he'd reached his arrival in Bath, Sensei stopped him.

"Wait," she said. She rose from the dining chair opposite Jason's and returned from the nearby kitchen with a bottle, some ice, mineral water and three glasses. "Do you drink whiskey?"

"I do."

"Let's have a drink then. This story sounds like too much for just green tea." They laughed. "About two fingers, water and ice for both me and Ji-chan, if you would? Pour whatever you like for yourself. I'll just fix a quick snack to go with it. In Japan, it's the custom to eat when drinking."

"I remember you saying that," Jason said and mixed the drinks. The first went to Ji-chan.

"*Dozo*," Jason said, moving to the TV room and offering the glass. The old man flashed his awkward grin and then went into a long monologue about something linguistically miles above Jason's head. He could only smile and nod in response like a bobble-head doll.

"He's just saying thank you and wondering if you drink much whiskey in your country," called Kawamoto Sensei from the kitchen.

She joined them and there was another long speech in Japanese, this time by the daughter.

"I didn't get a single word," Jason said. "Not exactly the most brilliant of your students."

She laughed. "Don't worry. We're speaking the local dialect. Even many Japanese people have difficulty."

"There's a lot to learn," Jason said.

"Yes, there is," said Sensei.

"About everything," Jason added.

"About everything," Sensei agreed. "Now, since we're talking about everything, I'd like to learn more about what happened and why you're here. Please continue. And please tuck in at the same time." They returned to the dining area. On the table lay a variety of *o-tsumami*, small dishes not quite a meal but more than snacks. There was broiled squid and Japanese pickles and vegetable sticks with *miso* mayonnaise.

Jason continued his story. He told her about his search for Elizabeth, his job at Destiny Press, Seamus, the M-Novel and on it went. They talked like this until it was time for bed.

Chapter 20 iNovel Link
The Chapter 20 iNovel Link is about maps. By going to
www.HotSpringsNovel.com/chapter/20/ you can find maps of key locations in Jason's Asian travels: Japan, Tokyo, Shinagawa, Kyushu, Fukuoka and Kurokawa.

Chapter 21

"I think it's a shifting landscape."

Despite his exhaustion, Jason couldn't sleep. His body had been ready hours ago but his mind nagged him like a telemarketer at dinnertime. He tried counting sheep. He tried regulated breathing. Nothing worked.

After finally closing them for what seemed only moments, Jason's eyes opened just after 4 a.m. The room was dark except for soft slivers of light eking in through the blinds in Sensei's small office. Beneath him lay a heavenly soft, double-layered blue futon. His head was braced by a small pillow filled with noisy rattley things that felt and sounded like dried insects. They crunched when you moved; Jason couldn't imagine what the inventor was thinking.

The traveling, the air and the alcohol had left Jason parched. Although the air in the Fukuoka region seemed substantially cleaner than Tokyo's, his nose had been clogged since his arrival and wasn't improving. He also had to pee — he'd never figured out how you can be thirsty yet still need to urinate. Considering his jet lag and general dazedness, he found the washroom easily. Inside the door were light green corduroy slippers with the word *Toilet* embroidered on the tops. They only covered about three-quarters of his size tens. He flushed the rather complex-looking toilet called a "washlet" and washed his hands in the clever device that first brought the water to a small sink over the tank and then recycled it. He could find nowhere to get a drink, however.

Jason padded into the dining/kitchen area in search of potable water. He could hear Ji-chan snoring across the way. The closed sliding paper doors, called *shoji*, provided minimal sound insulation and actually vibrated every time Ji-chan let one of his earbusters fly.

Jason managed to find a glass, fill it and then wash and rinse it in the darkened kitchen without making a sound. Until, that is, he attempted to place the glass in the dish rack — which he missed. The heavy glass dropped onto the stainless steel counter with a loud bang and rolled off the edge, plummeting to the floor with a sound equal in volume and violence to a Ji-chan snore.

Kawamoto Sensei awoke immediately; Jason could hear her overhead. She descended the stairs in pink slippers and white robe, a *yukata*, if he remembered correctly, decorated with porcelain blue Japanese parasols.

"Jason," she stage-whispered in the dark, "is that you?"

"It is. I'm sorry. I was just getting a glass of water."

"Are you all right?"

"Yes, I just dropped the glass. But don't worry, it's not broken."

Sensei found a small light on the stove's exhaust hood.

"I hope I didn't wake Ji-chan."

"That's impossible," she laughed. "He once slept through an earthquake so powerful it knocked over the television."

"I'm sorry I woke you."

"That's all right. I don't really sleep very well since my husband died. The nighttime is always the worst." She looked older without her makeup, and more vulnerable. She gathered some paper towels and stooped to wipe the wet spot. She suddenly stopped wiping and stared at Jason's feet.

"What is it?" Jason asked.

At first she said nothing — but her expression spelled horror.

"Jason...your feet..." He looked down. There they were, the green corduroy undersize slippers half on, half off his feet, the word *Toilet* glaring up at them. The only thing worse would have been walking on the *tatami* with them. He scurried off to the toilet barefoot. What a gaff — a major toilet blunder at an early stage.

Returning, Jason helped wipe down the entire kitchen floor. There was a hint of a smile on Sensei's face. After finishing, she washed her hands vigorously and filled the stainless-steel kettle.

"How are you feeling now?" Sensei asked. "Did you manage to sleep?"

"Not too bad, thank you."

"I'm going to make some English tea. Do you want some?"

"Won't it keep you awake?"

"I doubt I'll go back to sleep now, anyway," she

said. It was almost four-thirty. The sky through the kitchen's frosted window was already lightening.

"Sure. Why not?"

Soon enough, steaming cups of Earl Grey Breakfast Tea rested on placemats in front of them. They drank from dainty porcelain cups decorated with tiny pink flowers.

"You didn't finish telling me your story. About why you're really here," Sensei said.

"No, I didn't." By the time the sun was up, he had.

• • •

"That's quite a story. It's very surprising in many ways," Sensei said.

"It is, isn't it? I'm sure it sounds ridiculous, coming here, traveling all this way, based on not very much," said Jason.

Sensei was silent for a good fifteen seconds. "Why don't I go down there with you, to help you look for Kiriko-san? We could take Ji-chan and he could enjoy the *onsen* while we do the searching."

"That'd be fantastic! But don't you have to work?"

"It's the weekend."

"Of course. My clock's out of whack."

"The only thing is, on weekends it can be hard to find a room, especially now that it's cherry blossom season. I could either call in a few hours, or we could just go and try our luck."

"But are you sure you don't mind? It's asking a lot."

"You didn't ask. I offered. Besides, Kurokawa is a wonderful place and I can enjoy the *onsen*, too. We all can."

"Thank you so much. I don't know what to say... except, remember when I told you about the woman I worked with who tried to help me find my mother?"

"Yes."

"Well, she called herself my search angel. So now you're my Japanese search angel."

They planned the day and then Sensei went to pack for herself and Ji-chan while Jason dressed and folded his bedding. Before they left, Sensei knelt, bowing before a picture of her late husband adorning what Jason supposed was a small Buddhist shrine. Incense smoldered and he noticed a cup of green tea and a bowl of rice — both steaming — placed on the altar's ledge. He wondered about the frequency of this ritual and how often she visited his grave. This was devotion of a kind he'd never encountered; his remembrances honoring his mother seemed shallow and inadequate in comparison, and he vowed to emulate her.

Ji-chan was ready in the backseat even before Jason had loaded the car and Sensei closed the house. Through the doorway, Jason could hear the lingering sound of the bronze altar bell — Sensei's temporary farewell to her husband. Despite heavy traffic, they arrived in the Kurokawa area less than four hours after departure, including a stop to eat the scrumptious lunch she'd prepared. The final part of their drive took them down a winding, tree-lined road, not quite a highway but more substantial than a local road. The spring day smelled of promise, and after a quick nap in the car Jason felt rejuvenated.

Sensei found them a Japanese-style inn, the Ryokan Yamanokawa, several kilometers south of the main town in a place called Kurokawa Ichiban Shita.

"How much of a hurry are you in?" Sensei asked.

Jason wanted to balance his urgency with politeness. "One of my recent goals is to live in the moment," he said. Sensei suggested they check in first.

The entrance to the *ryokan* was down its own narrow, hilly road ornamented by knee-high, thatch-covered lanterns. The parking lot was back from the inn for aesthetic and noise purposes — all cleverly done. The heavily treed grounds already made Jason feel at peace. Birds chirped and branches rustled. The entrance area was all dark wood, glistening floors and impressively thick beams under a gray-tiled roof. A sign at the sliding front door was lit to welcome guests.

An elderly staff member in kimono guided them over several small bridges, through labyrinthine halls, past dark staircases and eventually to their room. Some rooms had large private bathing facilities while others catered to families with baths called *kazoku buro*. The general public could use two outdoor baths (*rotenburo*), one for women only and one mixed — not to mention several large indoor baths segregated by gender. In scale, style and ambiance this place far outdistanced the Hot Springs Island Hotel. For the first time, Jason understood the impetus behind some of Dada's ideas for the hot springs. Of course, Yamanokawa lacked the ocean on its doorstep. But the nearby river underlined the complex's harmony with nature. It was a masterpiece.

Their room was ten *tatami* mats in size with a small sitting area near the window. A low wooden table dominated the main room and was surrounded by four legless chairs topped by silky tasseled cushions. Tea was served and they were given instructions for dinner and breakfast. Sensei had booked them for two nights. They decided first to bathe and to see the old town later. It was already three and dinner was at six. Not much time to search for Kiriko. "The morning is a good time to start," suggested Sensei. The two men set off for the large outdoor bath while Sensei headed to the women's facilities. All were supplied with narrow white towels and Sensei outlined the procedures for Jason: before entering the bath, wash thoroughly using the buckets near the taps. The towels, she said, served two purposes: cleansing oneself and modesty. Jason immediately recalled Kiriko's dexterous use of a similar towel. At least one thing had fallen into place. He hoped it was a harbinger of some sort.

Ji-chan talked the whole way to the bath but Jason hadn't a clue what he said. It didn't seem to matter.

Yamanokawa's *rotenburo* was another minor masterpiece. You entered through an elaborate steel-roofed gate and immediately to your left was a place to wash and a stone fountain for drinking the gushing mineral water. Across was a thatched roof under which hot water poured into the pool through elevated bamboo pipes. To the left of this stone sat a statue depicting some kind of froglike animal. Artfully placed rocks ringed the bath, and trees bordered the entire enclosure, as did two high wooden fences fringed with bamboo. The water itself was even hotter than on Hot Springs Island, with a milky hue. It felt soft and silky to the touch. A single maple leaf floated on the water as if placed for effect.

The bath took on new visual aspects from whatever angle you chose. Jason imagined it in different seasons. In snow's pure monotone or with rainbow autumn throwing red and yellow highlights off the water, it would be sublime. Dada would love it.

They'd been immersed only a few minutes when a Japanese man about Jason's age entered the bath and bowed almost shyly towards them. After finishing his initial ablutions he entered the bath, his rectangular towel dangling before him with practiced skill. Ji-chan seemed less sensitive to such formalities. Perhaps this was an advantage of getting old — you cared less about form and disregarded meaningless social conventions.

"Hello," said the man in English, "do you mind if I ask your country?"

"No, not at all. I'm from Canada. From BC — the west coast."

"Oh, I see."

"How about you? Are you from around here?"

"Well, not exactly. I come from Kita Kyushu. Do you know that place?"

"I do. I came from close to there myself today."

"Do you work in Japan?" asked the young man.

"No, I'm just a tourist. I'm staying here with my friend. This is her father."

The man greeted Ji-chan and the two exchanged introductions. It was fascinating to watch the young man's manner change. His body language grew formal despite his nakedness.

"Excuse me," said Jason when they'd finished. "Do you mind if I ask you a question?"

"Please," said the young man.

"This statue...what is it for?"

"Oh, that is a *kappa*. Hmmm...how to describe it? Oh...it is very difficult."

"It's not a real animal, is it?"

"Most people say no. It is animal from legend. It lives near the water usually and likes...cucumbers and sumo wrestling. And you must be very polite to it."

Jason tried not to laugh.

"Yes, I know. It must sound very strange."

"Is it a fertility symbol?" Jason asked.

"I'm sorry, I don't understand. Please say again."

"Is it supposed to make you virile...wait...is it, you know, to make a man strong — with women?"

The young man sucked in his breath and bent his head to one side. He didn't know. Jason erroneously took this as confirmation of the *kappa*'s role.

"Where did you learn your English?"

"I study at a private language school."

"Really? Why's that?"

"But I must study harder and harder."

"Why must you study harder?" asked Jason, trying to speak slowly.

"Oh…because I will be going to Taiwan for working. I must use English there. We will dig out subway tunnel."

"Have you ever been there before?"

"No. I have never been abroad before. This is my first time."

"You must be very excited."

"Actually, I don't want to go, really."

"Can I ask why not?"

"Because I cannot take my family. I must go alone."

"Oh, I see. How long will you go for?"

"Maybe one and half years. Maybe two."

"That's a long time."

"Yes. And specially because my children. My boy is about two years and my wife will have one more baby soon. I probably won't see my new baby until much later."

Jason realized something. Death's not the only way to lose parents, or to lose a child. Once more, a chance encounter had given him insights: he was luckier than he thought and he didn't appreciate it anywhere near enough.

● ● ●

On returning to their room, Jason guessed at sleeping arrangements. There appeared only the one room for the three of them so he guessed it would be *futons* on the floor. He'd wait and see. The other reason he was interested was that the long hot bath had left him rubber-legged and ready for a nap. Ji-chan too.

With no bed or *futon* handy, Ji-chan pulled a *zabuton* cushion from one of the legless chairs and folded it under his head. Jason followed suit. Before Sensei had even returned, the two men, young and old, were sacked out on the hard but yielding *tatami*, both dressed in identical *yukata* embellished with the inn's logo.

Sensei let them sleep.

By the time Jason's lids flickered open, the quality of light had changed. Although not yet fully dark, evening approached. The room lights were off. Ji-chan remained still next to him while Jason did a lazy visual examination of the room. Sensei was in an armchair in the little alcove near the window; she looked like she was daydreaming. Jason eased his eyes completely shut so he could delay, even by a few moments, his arrival from the country of sleep. Perhaps a minute passed, then another. The room remained still.

Jason got up. Ji-chan rose soon after. Dinner would be served shortly but, before it arrived, Sensei extracted some lovely cold Kirin beer from the pint-sized fridge in the alcove and they toasted the day. The beer slid down gloriously. Pouring the next glass, the amber color reminded him of Kiriko's unusual eyes. He couldn't wait to get started tomorrow.

Dinner was served in their room — probably the most remarkable meal of Jason's life. Jason ticked off seventeen different dishes. They savored delicacies like *sashimi*, fish and vegetable *tempura*, crab, grilled shrimp with lemon, wild boar barbecued on individual pottery burners, and something he couldn't name — all washed down by more of the amber Kirin. Dessert was melon and green tea ice cream. The word "feast" failed to do the meal justice.

After digesting their majestic dinner, Sensei and Ji-chan wanted another bath. Jason decided to walk around for a while before taking his bath, and he set off alone to experience the night atmosphere of this magic place. He might never get the chance again. The omnipresent knee-level roofed lanterns were all lit — a reminder of a romanticized Edo-era. It might not reflect the reality of the past, but it played to people's idealized visions of history. The lights glowed like his general sense of well-being and he felt prepared for whatever the next few days might toss at him.

The light gravel of the pathways crunching under his sandals, he came across the small wooden bathhouse, which Ji-chan had probably already entered. His destination. Eager to catch up with the old man, he slid open the door and strode in — only to find himself three meters away from a half-disrobed Sensei who immediately grabbed a towel to cover herself. Her jaw dropped and eyes widened. Jason's did the same as he stuttered and gasped, backing up, searching for a suitable apology.

"Sorry! Sorry!" I thought...I thought this was the *men's*...I didn't know which...I...I..."

"Just go. Go. GO!" Sensei said.

He felt imbecilic as he skittered out of the women's door. Sensei — no prude — was shaking with laughter. "The look on his face…oh…" She laughed so hard her ribs actually started aching, and she enjoyed the rest of her bath tremendously.

Whipping into his side of the bathhouse, Jason thankfully found himself alone with Ji-chan. After an extremely thorough ritual cleansing, he dunked his head under water and stayed immersed in the hot liquid until the red of his face could be accounted for. Thinking that time heals all wounds — and renders most major embarrassments less so — he spent so long in the bath that his fingertips grew more wrinkled than Ji-chan's.

• • •

Sliding open the interior door to their room, Jason was surprised to see the table gone and three *futons* lying in a neat row across the width of *tatami* mats. Ji-chan already occupied the middle bedding and was leafing through a magazine.

Sensei removed her reading glasses.

"See, I got the right door this time," Jason said.

Sensei laughed. "You were gone a long time."

"Trying to wash away my embarrassment."

"If you stayed in the bath that long, you must be thirsty. Would you like a beer?"

"Yes, please. And, listen, I'm so sorry about—"

Sensei cut him off. "You can hang your towel over there," she said.

He was thankful to be offered a graceful out, and placed his damp towel on the silver rack alongside father and daughter's. Before long, Ji-chan was snoring while Sensei and Jason talked in the soft light of the hardwood alcove.

"Jason, do you mind if I ask you a question?"

"What kind of question?"

"Well…I hope it's not too private."

"This sounds serious." Jason's tone was light but he sensed the frivolity wouldn't last.

"You didn't say so earlier but, this girl, Kiriko-san…are you in love with her?"

Jason smiled and looked down. "There's something about her that draws me to her in a way I've never felt with anyone before. She intrigues me, she fascinates me, she gives me a sense of peace and calm. She's also deep and sensitive and a real thinker. Not to mention, extremely, wonderfully talented. I'm risking a lot by saying, yes, I do love her, but the truth is, that's why I came here. To find out if I really have what I think I have. And, for once, I'm willing to take my chances, with my head up, knowing what they are. I really am. I've never done this before. I always sort of fell into relationships without making an actual conscious decision that said, yes, this is the person I want to be with.

"Also, maybe because that's how I feel, I also feel more comfortable with whatever happens. Somehow I feel sure that whatever I do will be worth it. Even if I can just help her in some small way it'd be worth it. If she is here, like I think she is, then I'm guessing she probably left Hot Springs Island so suddenly because she was facing some kind of crisis. That's the only thing I could conclude. I want to find her, Sensei. I really want to find her and help her. So, if that's being in love, I guess I am."

Sensei grew thoughtful. "So before you were searching for your mother and now you're searching for Kiriko."

"I suppose you could put it that way."

"Either that, or they're two parts of the same search."

Before Jason could sift through the implications of Sensei's last statement, she asked another question.

"So tell me more about what you think love is," she said.

"If you don't mind, I'd like to hear your views, Sensei. I've been doing all the talking up to now. Please tell me what you think."

"Perhaps we could start by you not calling me Sensei. My first name is Yuko."

Jason laughed. "Well, I'll try, but I can't promise. Remember, this is a guy who can't find the right door."

"The reason I asked is because it's a question I've been thinking about a lot over the last few months," Sensei said. "This term I'm teaching a course on the Romantic and Victorian poets for the first time. It has forced me to think about what romance is, what love is. From the terminology down to the underlying meaning."

"And what do you think?"

"First of all," said Sensei, "I think it's a shifting landscape. Love and romance are like sand on the dunes. Some things that were considered highly romantic at one time or another are no longer so. The opposite is also true. Love and romance also differ from place to place, from culture to culture, and even by age. Definitions change. What Ji-chan and what I think, for example, are probably very very different. At least I suspect so — and probably hope so too…"

"It sounds like you identify with the Romantics," said Jason.

"That's interesting. I've never thought of that before."

"Is it true?"

"I don't know. It seems strange if it is, I suppose."

"Have you ever found true love like the poets write about?" asked Jason. It was a bold question.

"I'm not sure I know what 'true' is, anymore," Yuko said.

"There's still time."

"Do you think so?"

"Of course I do."

"I miss my husband very much. I feel there are gaps in so many places. I miss the companionship. I miss part of being a couple, a team, if you will. I miss the *situation*, if that makes sense. Now I am alone and I wonder if I will ever find it again."

"You've had it, once, with your husband. And you still do, although in a different way. I could sense your depth of feeling when we went to his grave in the house this morning, when you knelt before his photo. How you set out the green tea and the rice. I'd never seen anything like that before. Some people never have that — never. And even still you could find it again, although perhaps in a different way."

There was a brief silence between them. A bird hooted in the distance. Yuko spoke. "Thank you," she said. He hoped she'd found a new — even if minor — vein of optimism to carry her forward into some still unknown relationship. If anyone deserves it, thought Jason, it's her.

"Now I think the beer has done its job. Please forgive me but I must go to sleep."

"Don't let the bedbugs bite," said Jason with a smile. His mother had said these words every night as she flattened the white strip of bed sheet with her hand, then kissed him on both cheeks, and then his forehead, to send him into "dreamland," as called it.

Chapter 21 iNovel Links
There are two Chapter 21 iNovel Links. The first is a photo link, with a series of photos of the *ryokan* and Kurokawa Onsen. The second is an audio link, so that you can hear the sounds of the river and the hot springs' water from these same two locations. Please go to **www.HotSpringsNovel.com/chapter21/** to experience these links.

Chapter 22

*"So much has happened. I don't know
what to make of it."*

Before the sun had risen into the azure sky they were
bathed and dressed and heading for Kurokawa proper. After crossing the bridge they made a long lazy
curve into the crowded parking lot in front of the
Ryokan Kumiai — a tourist information center run
by the inn association. Behind this office was an outcrop where you could look down at the quaint resort
village filled with hot spring hotels, gift shops and
restaurants. It was a remarkable place, all hilly and
bushy and bent with narrow streets and all manner
of traditional architecture jumbled together with
more modern structures. The most charming hodgepodge Jason had even seen, and Kiriko's hometown.

They descended a narrow winding street so steep
that the concrete was pitted for traction. Shops lined
both sides of the descent selling boiled eggs cooked in
the sulfurous hot springs, slippers, cakes and sweets
and a hundred kinds of *sake*. Between the river
bisecting the town and the hot springs' water churning through pipes, the sound of running water followed them everywhere. Hotels and *ryokan* lined
both sides of the river like jumbled books on a tot-
tery shelf, many of them with beckoning entrances so
wide open and welcoming that they seemed part of
the outdoors.

"If you like," said Yuko, "we can buy a pass for many of the different hot springs and baths, just for the day."

"Would later be okay? I'd like to concentrate on finding Kiriko."

Yuko became Sensei. "Of course. That's why we came."

They only had two names to work with: Kiriko Shimizu and her late mother, Kiyo Shimizu. There'd been a return address in a letter from Kiriko's mother but Dada had lost it. Nor could he remember the inn's name. Hopefully, like Hot Springs Island, everybody knew everybody.

Sensei did the talking. After a dozen dead ends, however, Ji-chan was growing tired and they made new plans. Sensei would drive Ji-chan back to the hotel to rest while Jason would continue walking the town. She wrote him a note he could use to ask after Kiriko and they practiced some relevant Japanese phrases. Then she left.

"I'll return soon," she said with a smile, all competence and resolve.

Almost everyone said *konnichiwa* to Jason as he wandered first on one side of the river and then the other. When he was ready for a break, he sat on a bench in a shelter just over one of the bridges. He'd brought a notebook with him and as he watched the water tumble downstream, he started jotting down some lyrics. In only twenty minutes, he'd written a new song.

The Problem with Rivers

Our lives are like rivers, they flow north and south
We go to the source and we go to the mouth
We go to the heart and we go to the tributaries now
Our lives are like rivers, they flow east and west
Ambling and rambling on some distant quest
On the routes to the ocean and its tributaries now

CHORUS
The problem with rivers we can't see where they go
And where they come from, we just never know
They go round the bend — and they're gone now

I went down to the river to see how it flowed
Was it coursing its route, traveling fast or slow
To nourish the land or carry it away
Eroding the banks, sometimes filling the wells
Dipping and dancing and rising in swells
Rivers can be heaven or they can be hell — you just
    can't tell

CHORUS
The problem with rivers we can't see where they go
And where they come from, we just never know
They go round the bend — and they're gone now

Sometimes a drought and sometimes a flood
Sometimes it's so clear and sometimes it's mud
And sometimes it's a mirror so we can see ourselves
Our lives are like rivers, they flow every which way

And though our words fail us I've got something
    to say
Just listen to the rivers and its tributaries now

CHORUS
The problem with rivers we can't see where they go
And where they come from, we just never know
They go round the bend — and they're gone now

   • • •

They'd agreed to rendezvous at the bottom of the steep hill below the tourist information at three. Jason made sure he wasn't late. Yuko Sensei, however, was late. Jason started up the incline towards the parking area. Halfway up Yuko still hadn't arrived, so he ducked his head into the *sake* shop he'd seen earlier. The selection was amazing. He could easily have spent all day admiring the bottles and the beautiful elaborate labels. Japan's *sake* culture was far more developed than he'd realized. Before getting carried away, he had to check that Sensei hadn't arrived. He stepped out of the shop and there she was, not three yards away, half-running down the steeply inclined road.

They saw each other at exactly the same moment. "Jason!" she cried, her toe catching the front edge of one of the indented circles in the pavement. She hurtled forward out of control — a steep pitch, at running speed, over a brutally hard surface.

He leapt onto the road in a desperate bid to

catch her or at least to slow her. He snagged her with one arm then maneuvered the rest of his body in front of her before she hit the concrete. Her momentum carried both of them backwards, however, Jason fighting to stay steady and upright — one step, two steps — and then he stopped. Both were gasping with fright and exertion.

"Jason..." was all Sensei could gasp.

"That was close. Yuko, are you all right?" he asked.

Only now did they break the embrace. Other pedestrians had seen the stumble and continued watching the minor drama unfold.

"I don't know how to thank you," Yuko said. "You saved me."

"No I didn't, I almost caused it."

"I shouldn't have been hurrying. I was late and—" She was on the verge of tears.

"It's okay, it's okay," he said. "Everything's fine." She visibly forced herself to regain calm.

"Jason...do you mind? I think I'd like to go back to the *ryokan*."

"Of course. I understand totally. Let's go. But be careful where you walk!"

Yuko's wan smile showed appreciation for his humor attempt, but she wasn't quite there yet.

Back at the hotel they bathed and napped. For the most part, equilibrium was restored. Later, another stupendous dinner helped divert their minds, as did the *sake*. The *sake*, more commonly called *Nihonshu* (meaning liquor of Japan), arrived on a red lacquer tray in three porcelain containers, white with indigo designs. Three small cups completed the set. It was served hot and the taste blanketed his tongue. The spreading warmth filled his inner spaces like a long hot springs bath. Drinking heated alcohol was relatively novel for Jason. Besides making the alcohol work quicker, it added a burning sensuousness, a fiery flavor. The soft texture was highly pleasing but also contained a hidden sweet smoothness. Sensei described it as elegant.

They'd ordered more *Nihonshu* and by dinner's end all were a little tipsy, Ji-chan in particular. He was asleep even before the *futons* were arranged; they had to wake him to go to bed.

In a replay of the previous evening, Jason and his ex-teacher sat in the alcove and conversed. In the occasional silences they drank beer and listened to the night.

"Jason, I have to thank you," Yuko said at one point.

"What for?"

"For saving me. Twice."

"Twice? What do you mean?"

"The first one was today, on the slope, and the second time was last night. Because of our talk, for the first time in a long while I feel...if not happy about past events, then appreciative of what I had with my husband. I almost feel like I've reached a new stage of acceptance about my husband's death, and you helped me. There's this unspoken taboo in

Japan about voicing things that are too raw, a fear that once the door is open into the soul, it can never be closed, and that that picture is frightening."

Jason recalled his conversation with Kiriko about warmth and intimacy and human contact in Japan. How hot springs and baths were essential vehicles by which people touched and became physically closer. Sometimes, she said, you'll see a son or grandson, daughter or granddaughter, washing the back of their elder or massaging their shoulders or neck. "It's a...substitute for words," Kiriko had said "It's one of the few accepted ways to touch."

That night, both Yuko and Jason slept well and soundlessly, their dreams comforting and unconfused, their composure bolstered and unbattered. They awoke rested and ready to face another day.

• • •

Jason's eyes opened late to find himself alone and the *futon* of Yuko and Ji-chan folded neatly by the side of the room. He dressed, intending to join them in the bath, but he was too slow — as he piled his bedding, the door slid open and Yuko entered.

"Good morning," said Sensei. "You looked like you were having such a good sleep, we didn't want to wake you."

"Good morning. How about you?"

"I feel wonderful."

"Where's Ji-chan?"

"In the lobby. I hope this isn't a problem but..."

"What is it?"

"Well, I should have mentioned something, but on trips like this, Ji-chan tends to get impatient to arrive but once it's almost over, he gets just as impatient to get home. Remember how he was so eager to leave home that he sat in the car before we were ready? Well, it's like that, only in reverse. He even wants to skip breakfast."

"Sure. I understand."

"But it means that I won't have time to help you look for Kiriko more. I feel so bad that I helped you so little. We hardly looked at all."

"Don't mention it."

"I can drive you into Kurokawa proper."

"No, no. It's fine. You said there was a hotel bus, right?"

"Yes, it leaves at eleven o'clock."

"Then I'll take that one."

They sat on the room's elegant woven straw mats that cooled in the summer and retained warmth in winter. Their thoughts played over the past three days, alighting on certain moments or words like birds gathering on branches.

"If you come back to Fukuoka, you can stay with us."

"Thank you. I'd like that." But both of them knew this was unlikely.

"I'll help you with your bags."

"This must seem sudden. I should have told you."

"It's fine," said Jason. She offered to make arrangements for a different hotel and to help him in other ways, but Jason declined. It was time to regain his independence and resume his solitary journey.

When they passed through the front entrance, the staff bowed and called out in unison something Jason couldn't understand. Yuko's father was absent, however. Although she'd left him sitting in the lobby, they found him quietly ensconced in the car's back seat.

Once again, Jason loaded the vehicle.

"I want to thank you for everything," he said.

"Not at all. It is I who should thank you," Yuko said.

Although words had drawn them closer, now they seemed to serve a lesser function.

"I guess we should get going," said Yuko.

"Of course."

"Let me know if you find Kiriko-san," said Yuko.

"I will."

"I'd like to meet her."

Although both would have liked to hug, they observed the local proprieties and bowed. With a quick wave from her and Ji-chan, the creamy flash was gone — like a silk cord that had been severed. Jason wondered if it could be retied.

• • •

The bus for Kurokawa left shortly after checkout and Jason was bowed away by a bevy of maids and employees in a departure more fitting royalty.

His plan was simple. He'd go to the Ryokan Information Center and find someone who spoke

English. Then he'd find a reasonably priced inn with staff used to dealing with foreigners.

The clerk at the Info Center spoke English and Jason had the option of several inns accustomed to foreign guests. None were cheap, however, and Jason realized that his time here would be short unless he came up with a more economical plan. Thank god for Seamus's check.

Kurokawa was satisfyingly small; Jason didn't have to lug his bags far. The only way down the hill, though, was the same steep route where he'd shared that critical moment with Sensei a scant twenty-four hours ago.

Check-in wasn't until three so he left his bags to wander the town again. It was already becoming familiar. He'd kept Sensei's note and took up where they'd left off yesterday. Some people didn't know what to make of him while others displayed great kindness and concern. There were frequent consultations and discussions among the people behind the counters and, most of the time, Jason hadn't a clue what was going on. He was Alice in Blunderland occupying a world of unknown rules. Currents that he'd created but couldn't control were sweeping him along.

Jason lunched in a cutesy café that seemed an anomaly in this traditional *onsen* village. Jason chose it purely on the basis of an English menu posted outside. After ordering curried rice served with red Japanese pickles, he gulped down several glasses of refreshing ice water from the pitcher on the table.

Jason continued visiting shops and inns until check-in time. The possibility that Kiriko might already have been found in Canada wasn't lost on him, however. Hoping for news from home, he kept looking for an Internet café but found none. His hotel had no hookup for guests either.

Hot and sweaty from his search, Jason headed for the bath directly after registering. His new *ryokan* was downscale from the Yamanokawa and had no *rotenburo*. Making up for it, however, the men's bath looked newly renovated with wooden walls and a pleasing mixture of fitted stone and polished marble.

He scrubbed vigorously and doused his head and body with the hottest water he could stand. When he emerged from his first long soak his skin was as pink as a newborn's. In his room, dressed in his own clothes instead of the undersized *yukata*, Jason made immediately for the mini-fridge and drank a large bottle of beer. He was still sweating and had nothing to do until dinner. He would relax and gather his thoughts.

Meals were served in-room, and the knock on the door came sooner than he expected. Jason said, "*Dozo*," meaning "come in." The outer door opened and he heard the maid remove her footwear before entering. Then the inner door slid open.

"Kiriko!"

• • •

He should have readied something to say. Nothing came to him but he didn't care. Kiriko's presence made everything else secondary.

"Jason. I was so surprised. Somebody called us to

say that you were here, in Kurokawa, looking for me. Now you've found me. ...Or I've found you."

Joy, gratification, justification, relief. They hovered round Jason like the fireflies Kiriko once hunted on a summer night.

"Our house is outside Kurokawa," Kiriko said, filling the silence. "I wanted to see you, but I couldn't get away because...it took time for me to get here."

"I'm just glad you're fine and that you're here."

"You were asking about me in shops. One of the people told someone else and they called us. They said you were looking for me with a woman named Kawamoto Sensei."

"That was my Japanese teacher from UBC. I told you about her."

"And she came here to help you look for me, too?"

"Yes."

"You wanted to find me so badly?"

"Of course," Jason said.

"Your being here seems like a dream."

"Do you know what happened when you left? After you left?" Jason asked.

"I don't know anything."

"Some people thought you'd been hurt or injured. The way you suddenly disappeared. ...This may sound hard to believe but some people even said that someone might have hurt you, or at least tried to."

Kiriko's eyes widened. "I...don't know what to say."

"You never checked your e-mail."

"No," said Kiriko. "I didn't want to." Jason knew Kiriko's attitude to the cyberworld and technology.

"There was blood in your apartment," Jason said.

"People went into my apartment?" Kiriko looked at Jason uncomprehendingly.

"Yes."

"I only cut myself while I was packing." She held up her left hand to show her flesh-colored Band-Aid. "Didn't they notice that some of my clothes were gone, too? And my suitcase?"

"I don't know," said Jason. "All I know is that I'm happy to see you. You can't believe how happy I am."

"You care enough about me to come this far? Even though you don't know why I left?"

Jason didn't hesitate. "Yes. I came this far because I care that much about you."

Kiriko was kneeling on the *tatami* in the *seiza* position. She lowered her eyelids. She bowed her head. Jason had never seen so much emotion conveyed by such nuance.

"I was really worried," Jason said. "I had to find out that you were okay. Kiriko — can't you tell me why you left so suddenly without telling anyone?"

"There are many reasons."

"Can you tell me?"

"It would take a long time."

"You can take forever if you want. I've come all this way to hear your story. And if you don't want to tell me now, I'll wait until you're ready."

A dozen seconds passed before Kiriko spoke

again. Sensei had told him that silences were more frequent in Japan. That people were comfortable to let the quiet speak.

"You ask me such difficult questions that sometimes I can't answer or know what to say."

"I can wait," Jason said.

Kiriko opened her bag and removed a perfectly creased handkerchief. She placed it in on her lap. Then she started slowly moving it back and forth, back and forth, between her fingers.

"What if you found out that I came back for reasons that would make you think less of me?"

"It wouldn't matter," said Jason.

"What if you found out that I came back for reasons you could never forgive?"

"Kiriko, please just tell me. Tell me why you left the way you did."

"I couldn't tell you or anyone because...because of...my shame."

"Shame?"

"Yes, my shame. My greatest shame. *Haji.*" Kiriko then spoke in Japanese, hoping to explain herself more truly, hoping to use words closer to her past and her heart, hoping that Jason might understand something important in her context, for once, instead of his. But even in her own language she found walls.

"I'm sorry, Kiriko. I don't understand."

"I'm sorry, too. I don't know if I can explain and I don't know if you can understand. Shame has always been a larger part of my culture than yours. But I thought I was different. I didn't know that I could be moved this deeply by the shame of what I've done and the worry of what someone else may think of me and my actions."

"Kiriko..." Jason said.

"There are things about me that you don't know."

"You told me that before."

"Do you remember when we talked on your beautiful *Argo*?" Kiriko asked.

"I remember everything about that day."

"I wanted to tell you everything, then," Kiriko said.

"Why didn't you?"

"Because I was afraid."

Kiriko placed both hands on her knees and then, in one motion, her back a perfect line, she rose gracefully and walked to the window. This particular *ryokan* was built at an almost impossible angle into the side of a steep hill, and Jason's room had a spectacular view overlooking the river that divided the small *onsen* town in two. The front of the structure was supported on concrete stiltlike pillars while the rear half burrowed into the hillside. Kiriko slid aside the already half-opened screen in front of the window so she could look out over what was probably the defining landscape of her childhood.

"Please wait just a while longer, Jason. Then, I think, you can understand everything. No matter what."

"Kiriko. I'd like to let people back on Hot Springs know that you're safe."

"I suppose so."

"We have to tell them, Kiriko," said Jason. "At the very least, the police need to know."

Kiriko lowered her head, perhaps in resignation or perhaps because of the shame of which she spoke.

"I'll only tell my father. He can talk to the police and we'll keep everything quiet," Jason said. "We won't let anyone know who doesn't need to."

"You can come to our inn. You can telephone from there," Kiriko said.

"I'd like that."

Kiriko looked down at the rushing river that coursed under the town's many bridges and around the rocks and boulders that could divert the flow but never stop it. "Even the largest stones are worn away by the water," she said. Jason wondered if this was a line from another poem.

Jason felt a rumble. He couldn't tell from which direction. It sounded like a truck, perhaps, or some large piece of machinery being used on the road. The pitch sounded too low, however, for anything man-made. You could feel it more than hear it, like a giant subwoofer.

A big bang, a thump, came next. The room actually moved — like a giant in the basement had struck the ground floor with an uppercut or a blow with a sledgehammer. "*Jishin*," Kiriko said. "Earthquake." A massive shaking immediately followed the thump. Instantly, things in the room started rattling violently. The *shoji* shook so hard Jason was afraid they would fly from their grooves. As though in slow motion, the teapot lid lifted from its flanged resting place. The heavy wooden table in the center of the room bounced up and off the *tatami* mats. Kiriko hung on to the window ledge but the earthquake forced her to her knees.

He tried to rise and move to her but he couldn't. The shaking of the building was so intense that he actually could not get to his feet. He had to crawl. For an instant, panic welled and he had to force himself to stay calm. Recalling the slender yellow concrete columns on which the hotel rested, he thought for the first time, *we might die*. The building would pitch forward, out of the crumbling hillside, and tumble like so many random pieces of rock and cement down the steep banks of river and into the water itself. Clouds of dust and smoke. Only then did he make a connection between the placid, warming waters of the hot springs and the violent, molten core of the earth's underground volcanoes.

On his hands and knees, he reached Kiriko and flung himself on top of her.

The overhead light swung in great, shaking, pendulous arcs. After the initial up and down movement, the earthquake had mutated into side-by-side shaking and yawing. A crack opened in one of the earth-colored plaster walls, like a diagram of a blood vessel. Secondary cracks sprung outwards from the main fissure and little chunks of plaster fell to the floor.

And then, as suddenly as it started, the earthquake ceased. The building hadn't fallen. Jason wanted to get outside as quickly as possible. The overhead light still swung, although in smaller arcs now. Some kind of alarm blared several streets over. The dust was literally settling over them and the town itself.

Kiriko's breaths were labored, not only because of the earthquake's violence, but also because of Jason's weight.

"We should get out of here," Jason said only a moment before the first aftershock hit.

"Get your head down," Jason yelled, and that's when the overhead light finally broke loose from the ceiling and crashed down on them. Jason felt a sharp pain in his side. Still, the second quake banged and rattled on. The cruel irony of making it through the first quake only to perish in the second wasn't lost on him. In earthquakes, one's sense of time alters radically. It is not so much slow motion, more that each millisecond becomes packed with such intensity and sensation that we live the equivalent of a week in only the half-minute or so one takes.

But, like the first shock, the second one subsided without total calamity. Kiriko and Jason were alive. They were alive. They were fully alive.

Jason spoke her name and she responded. "Jason."

Jason lay on his right elbow. Spoonlike, Kiriko had been under him, her back to his chest, her arms protecting her head. Now she turned so that she was lying on the *tatami* mats between his arms. Their faces were only inches apart and out of love, out of hope, out of gratitude at being spared, Kiriko and Jason kissed for the first time. It was impossible to say how long they would have continued because it was cut short by one more — albeit much shorter — aftershock.

"We have to get out of here," Jason said. "Are you all right?" He untangled himself from the light cord and brushed the broken plastic and plaster bits from around them.

"Kiriko! There's blood on your dress."

She looked down. She was wearing a honey-colored button-down blouse and a beige skirt patterned with flowers. Jason was right. Blood spotted the front of her skirt near her hip.

"Are you hurt? Where?" Jason momentarily forgot his own pain. Kiriko examined herself and found nothing.

"It's you, Jason," she said. "It's you." She touched a rip in his shirt and felt the stickiness of blood. "The light must have cut you. The blood on me is from you." Throughout both earthquakes, Kiriko had continued holding the handkerchief she'd been clutching earlier. She moved it to the gash on Jason's side and kept it there as best she could while they scrambled down the steep stairs and out of the building.

• • •

Jason's cut was less serious than feared. They cleaned up using a tap outside Jason's *ryokan* while, all over the little town, people milled around the narrow streets comparing notes and assessing the aftermath. There was no time to find out more; Kiriko wanted to return home as quickly as possible.

They drove to the inn in a spotless old white Nissan Silvia, a towel behind Jason's back to catch the blood. Traces of light still filtered through the thick tree canopy over the twisting road but darkness was pending. At least no fallen trees barred their way. Before long they pulled into a parking area in front of a traditional wooden house. Cherry trees surrounded the space. Kiriko's delicate features were briefly framed by the blossoms as she climbed from the car.

"That's the inn, over there," in the gathering darkness it was difficult to tell much except its shape. Kiriko and Jason entered the house through a dark *genkan* and stepped up and into a hallway.

"*Oto-san*!" Kiriko immediately called to see if her father was present. "*Tadaima*!" — I'm home. She called again but there was no answer. Then they heard another door slide open. It was Kiriko's aunt.

There was much bowing and smiling. Auntie expressed great concern over Jason's injury and she scurried away, returning with disinfectant and a bandage. With that out of the way, Kiriko translated the many thanks expressed for the care shown to her niece in Canada. Her aunt said she must tell her husband and Kiriko's father, then she and Kiriko had a long talk in Japanese and Jason was directed to follow the two women upstairs.

The stairs were of dark wood, steeper and narrower than Jason was accustomed to. He could only imagine trying to climb them during the earthquake. Reaching the second floor, the three of them stepped into a narrow hallway floored with the same dark wood. Kiriko and her aunt whispered for a moment, deciding something, then Auntie slid open one of the doors. After more whispering, the aunt turned and silently passed behind Jason.

"Jason, look," Kiriko said softly. He moved to the door.

In the middle of the *tatami* room was a sleeping child of perhaps three or four. A wet cloth lay atop the child's forehead making it difficult to determine its gender. They remained silent and kneeling just inside the door, watching the easy breathing of the child. After perhaps half a minute, Kiriko slid the door close and motioned Jason to follow her downstairs. Before she could say anything about what they'd seen upstairs, her father and uncle arrived and began immediately falling to their knees, bowing and expressing sentiments similar to those expressed by her aunt a few minutes ago. As the family discussed the earthquake, beer and snacks were quickly set out on the low table in the house's main *tatami* room.

Jason used this flurry of activity to look at Kiriko's father. Of diminutive stature, Mr. Shimizu's face was even more deeply tanned than Al's and was topped with dark hair even though he was probably in his sixties. His manner bespoke good cheer and his clothes had a certain dandyism. The most remarkable thing about him was his eyes — they were of the same clear amber as Kiriko's.

Jason was poured beer again and again and offered snack after snack. He was also kept busy answering translated questions about the earthquake, his family, and all manner of things when, suddenly, the large clock on the wall above the TV chimed and everyone except Jason rose.

"It's time to lay out the *futon*," Kiriko explained. Kiriko moved to help but was directed by her father to remain with Jason. The doors slid shut and Kiriko and Jason were alone again.

She took a sip of hot tea and placed the mug on a coaster.

"You must be wondering about the little girl." Ah, a girl.

"Yes."

"Her name is Aiko. She's my daughter. You may have guessed already, but she's my secret. Aiko is my secret."

"I don't understand."

"She's the reason I had to come back so quickly. She was very sick."

"Is she all right now? What was wrong with her?"

"When I knew you were here, when I knew that I was going to tell you, I looked up the word in the dictionary." She pulled a piece of paper from her pocket. "Meningitis," she said, pronouncing the word hesitantly.

"That's very serious."

"Yes. But the doctors say she'll be fine. I'm very thankful and grateful."

"I'm glad."

Kiriko smiled, although it was less an expression of joy than of tiredness and relief.

"But I still don't understand," said Jason.

"I'd like to explain everything," Kiriko said, "but it's a long and difficult story for me."

"Would it help if we took a walk?" asked Jason.

"We can't leave Aiko," Kiriko said quickly.

"Of course. I'm sorry."

"We can go when my aunt comes back. She won't mind. Can you wait?"

"Of course," Jason said.

"How's your cut?" Kiriko asked. She moved closer to him.

"It's fine," Jason said. "How about you?"

"I'm just a little stiff," said Kiriko, as she rolled her shoulders and then stretched her neck first one way and then another.

"Here," Jason said, and moved behind her. He laid his hands lightly on her long neck, and began to knead the muscles within.

Gradually, she began to relax. Her skin was smooth, almost flawless.

"Do you know about the origins of *shiatsu* — acupressure?" Kiriko asked.

"Sshh, don't talk," Jason said.

"It arose from injury. When you...bump into something, you always touch and rub the spot you've bumped. That's how it began."

His fingers continued searching for Kiriko's *tsubo*, her meridian points. He closed his eyes, too. The world was centered on the tiny spaces between his fingertips and Kiriko's skin. He felt a change in

Kiriko's breathing, if tiny spasms were causing her to move.

"Kiriko? What is it?"

At first she didn't answer. "Kiriko? What is it? Did I hurt you?"

Finally, she spoke. "No, no. It's not that."

"Then what is it?"

He let his hands rest on her shoulders. They were united by the fundamental universality of touch, and both felt in their bodies the profound intimacy of true connection.

"What is it, Kiriko?" Jason repeated. "Why are you crying?"

"I'm crying, Jason, because I'm happy. Because I'm happy."

Chapter 22 iNovel Link
The Chapter 22 iNovel Link is another musical one.
This time it's "The Problem with Rivers," a song
written on the piano by Jason. Please go to
www.HotSpringsNovel.com/chapter 22/ to listen.

Chapter 23

"The only thing we can do is try."

When Kiriko's father, aunt and uncle returned, Jason asked if he could call the Hot Springs Island Hotel, collect.

"It'll be very early there," Kiriko said. "Maybe three or four in the morning. Perhaps you should wait."

Kiriko translated and a long discussion took place. It would be better to call later. Why didn't they go for a walk and bath, and Jason could call when they returned? Also, Mr. Shimizu would phone and explain to the owner of Jason's *ryokan* that he was staying with them and that they'd come by in the morning to collect his gear and settle the bill. Jason was given a *yukata* and a towel. Aiko would be looked after. Jason and Kiriko set off into the night.

The house's wooden door slid shut behind them. They both wore wooden sandals and *yukata* and Jason had difficulty walking because of the tightness of the robe and the too-small clogs. The sound of wood against tarmac echoed in the air and Jason noticed the difference in night sounds from those on Hot Springs Island.

As he explained at great length — and made even longer by the need for interpretation — Kiriko's father was proud of his inn and the outdoor bath he'd created. His hand-built *rotenburo* (separated by gender) backed onto a small stream behind the inn and were reached by a small flagstone walkway from the back entrance. Instead of following the signs (which Jason had learned to read at Yamanokawa Ryokan) to the inn's outdoor bath, Kiriko took Jason's hand and said, "This way," as she led him in the opposite direction.

The flagstones soon transformed into concrete and then, another twenty meters uphill, into a dirt pathway.

"Where are we going?" Jason asked.

"You'll see," said Kiriko, and they continued walking. The foliage darkened their route as they traveled uphill and Kiriko extracted a small torch from the sleeve of her cotton *yukata*. They curved up and around and, by then, they'd been walking for more than five minutes since leaving the back door of the inn. Once or twice they had to step over a fallen branch and Jason's fingers brushed moss when he stumbled slightly and used his hand for balance. The path made two more bends and then dipped, whereas before it had only risen.

"Where are we going?" Jason asked again.

"We're almost there," Kiriko said.

She was right. Thirty steps later, they rounded a curve and Kiriko switched off her light. They'd arrived. Jason's eyes took some moments to adjust to the return of darkness. When they did, he saw before him a rustic but very private outdoor bath set into the ground. The interior was lined with cypress boards while the top was surrounded with rocks reminiscent of the beachside springs on Hot Springs

Island. Water fed the bath via a raised bamboo piping system and the soothing sound of the falling water Jason knew well. There were no lights, no changing room, no shower. A few wooden basins and two benches sat beside the bath.

Kiriko took Jason's hand again as they stood side by side. Although he didn't really understand the need for quiet, she whispered when she spoke.

"This is my secret place," she said. "It's a special bath used only by our family. When I was a child, whenever I wanted to be alone or to escape from something, this is where I would come."

"Does your father—"

This time it was Kiriko who said, "Shh."

Without another word, Kiriko moved to the bench and placed her towel upon it after brushing it clean. Her back to Jason, she pinned up her hair and undid her *yukata*, which she folded neatly and placed on the bench. She stepped out of her undergarments which she then tucked into the folds of her *yukata*. Her movements were calm and unhurried.

She went to the side of the bath and washed with her long towel and the wooden basins. Then, her back still facing him, she paused on the rocks lining the bath. Jason had an overwhelming sense of déjà vu.

Only after she stepped down and into the bath did Jason follow her, first at the bench and then beside it. He cleansed himself as Kiriko had done and joined her in the bath.

He heard, rather than felt, the first spatterings of rain. Drops bounced off the leaves and branches of the surrounding trees and, as they grew more abundant, he could see the raindrops colliding with the surface of the steaming bathwater. He remembered bathing in the rain as a child.

It was intensely private. He was overjoyed that she would allow him into her refuge.

She sat so close to him in the cramped confines of the *hinokiburo* (cypress bath) he could touch her simply by lifting his arm. Their towels were draped on a rock next to the bath. Her legs were positioned gracefully to one side and her hands rested modestly in her lap.

In this magical place in the falling rain, the whisper of her words carried a power far greater than any shout or scream.

"Now I can finally tell you my story," Kiriko said. She collected herself for a moment, seeking the English words that she hoped would make Jason understand what to her, for so long, had been beyond understanding. Jason waited, his hair growing wet from the rain.

Her story was of a young girl in a big city alone. Takayuki was her first boyfriend. They met in art school and then, unplanned, three years into their romance she became pregnant. Marriage followed but the child, Kiriko said, changed everything. "It changed me," she said. "It changed him," she said, "it changed both of us and everything that we were."

"And then he left me," Kiriko said, "for another

woman. I felt very young and alone and abandoned. My parents had been against the relationship and the marriage from the beginning. They told me to endure. They were upset that I had gone against their will in the first place and they were, at first, unforgiving. I had no choice. Not only for me, but for Aiko. It was difficult to accept that my first love could love some-one else. I thought it was because of the child and how it had changed us, but, then I learned it wasn't Aiko he wanted to say goodbye to, it was me."

"What do you mean?"

"He remarried, and wanted to take Aiko with him. He said he couldn't give her up. That they could raise Aiko better than I because they were husband and wife and I was alone. They told me they would have other children so Aiko could have brothers and sisters. They had more money than I and they had support of their family. And, then, with all this, two things happened. My mother died and I got sick and I couldn't take care of myself, let alone Aiko. I didn't know what to do. I was torn. I was sick in the deep-est part of me. I had to choose the most difficult thing in the world. I had to choose to give up my daughter, to give her the chance at happiness that I couldn't give her. I broke down. I got sicker and sicker and I was in a hospital and I saw doctors…"

Jason looked up into what parts of the sky could be seen through the gaps in the trees. The rain had abated, although not completely. He was hoping the clouds had cleared enough so that perhaps, as he lis-tened, he might catch a glimpse of even one star for the briefest of moments. As he did, a single raindrop fell onto his forehead, an unerring piece of marksmanship from so high. He felt the minute splash and the splattering of the water that told him that even this one tiny drop could subdivide.

"After I got a little better, I knew I couldn't stay here any more. There were too many memories and too much pain. I thought if I could go far enough away to a foreign country, things would be better. My mother had always told me about meeting your father so I thought about Canada, your place, the place that was an island with an *onsen*, that's where I could go.

"Then I learned that Kana — my husband's new wife — was going to have a baby of her own. Aiko would have a new brother or sister. Not long after that, I came to Hot Springs Island. I liked my new life there. I thought it was a chance to start over in a place where no one knew me. Your father was very kind to me. Everyone was. And then Aiko became sick. The new baby was about to be born and they worried about Kana's health and the baby coming. They had trouble taking care of Aiko and they asked my family to help, to care for her until she was better and the baby was born. My father called me. I knew I had to come back. I had to come back. Like you flew back for Al."

"And Al is fine now just as Aiko is fine, too," said Jason.

"So is the baby," said Kiriko. "Now Aiko has a brother."

"So this is your secret," Jason said.

"I thought about telling you many times, Jason. But when I heard your story about your parents and your mother in England, it reminded me so much of Aiko that I cried. That's why I cried. I felt sad and ashamed."

"Why didn't you tell me?"

"How could I? How could I tell you all these things after what I knew about you? How could you ever want to be with someone like me who did what I did? I thought...you would hate me."

"Why? I could never hate you."

"Because I did the same thing as Elizabeth. I abandoned my child. I heard how you talked when we were in the car. I understood your pain. How could you trust me? I thought you wouldn't want a person like me who already has children, especially one who could do the same thing that was done to you."

"But you did it all for Aiko. You did what you thought was best for her." Jason understood he was not only empathizing with Kiriko; he was gaining an understanding of Elizabeth's actions, as well — and for the first time.

Kiriko said nothing.

"This is why you thought things between us were impossible?"

"Yes."

"Nothing has changed for me, Kiriko. My being here means that it wasn't impossible, that it isn't impossible. Now we can start again."

"Now we can start again," Kiriko repeated.

• • •

It was midnight by the time they returned. Kiriko's father was still up and suggested that Jason call Canada. They went through an operator and the connection took time. Although this was Dada's normal waking time, his voice was sleepy.

"Jason, is that you?"

"Yes, it is. How are you?"

"Is everything okay?" asked Dada.

"I've talked to her, Dada. Everything's fine."

"Then you got the e-mail Al sent for me."

"No, I haven't checked my e-mail for a few days. What do you mean?"

"Oh my god, Jason, then you don't know? When you said you talked to her, who did you mean?"

"Kiriko, of course. Dada, what's going on?"

"So Kiriko's all right?" Dada asked. Jason looked over at her.

"She's fine, Dada. But—"

"They found her, Jason. *He* found her. Morgan, that English fellow, your search agent...he found her. He found Elizabeth. And I asked her to meet you and she's agreed. To talk to you, to meet you, whatever you want. She wants to see you, son. She called here again and I talked to her at length. She's sorry she hung up the other day, she was crying and she just couldn't deal with it at the time. She was unprepared, overly emotional. She wants to start over with you and she's waiting for your call. She even said she could come to Canada."

For the second time in a few short hours, Jason was too stunned to talk.

"So now I've found them both," Jason said.

"I guess you have," said Dada.

"But, listen, Dada, Kiriko's here and she's okay. Tell the police she's okay — but don't tell anyone where she is. She doesn't want anyone to know where she is. It's very important. Here, I'll put her on."

Kiriko took the phone. She told him Jason would explain why she left. She didn't want to. She couldn't. She returned the phone to Jason.

"I'll tell you everything later, Dada."

"Jason, are you okay?"

"I'm just...I don't know. I'm reeling. So much has happened. I don't know what to make of it."

"Are you going to call her?"

"Yes. Yes, I will. Of course I will. Have you got the number?"

"It's in the office...can you wait a second, I'll go get it," said Dada.

This time, the miracles of technology were on Jason's side. On the other side of the world Jason could hear his father leave his bed and place the receiver on the oak table where he always kept his book and glasses. Jason could picture everything: Dada slipping on his cracked brown leather slippers and checked dressing gown. Footfalls on the dark wooden floor as he went to the bedroom door and opened it. Despite the time difference and the breadth of the Pacific, they were part of the same experience.

Dada came back and picked up the receiver. Jason wrote down the number, double-checking it. He promised to call with all of his plans when he knew more. When he knew himself.

• • •

The time for Aiko's return to her father and new mother had arrived. She was a bright and curious child and her bubbly spirits and bright brown eyes had won over even the hard-core stubbornness of Kiriko's father. They were sorry to see the child go.

Kiriko's ex-husband now lived in Fukuoka. By arrangement, they would meet more or less halfway at the Mt. Aso Visitors' Center at five that evening. Although Kiriko tried to maintain a brave face as they left the inn, Jason knew she was wracked with guilt and misgivings. She felt she was abandoning Aiko a second time.

The drive was scenic. Aiko's face was plastered to the window the entire time. On their way to the rendezvous via long uphill climbs beside vistas and ridges rendered treeless by centuries of volcanic activity, Aiko asked questions that Jason struggled to understand. Once or twice, she used English words Jason had taught her, and he praised her unreservedly.

In the distance, not far from their final destination, they could see a plume of smoke rising from the giant crater.

They'd left purposely early. Kiriko wanted as much time as possible with Aiko so they stopped at every sightseeing spot they encountered. They could see eighteen kilometers across to the other side of the canyonlike caldera, the largest of its kind in the world. The sky was a magnificent cobalt blue. Up and up they went, closer and closer to their destination, closer and closer to losing Aiko again.

Except for Aiko's happy chatter, they didn't speak. He'd been here two weeks now and was accepted into the Shimizu clan with an ease he couldn't have imagined. He was making some progress with his Japanese and the Shimizu Inn had played host to Kawamoto Sensei and her father last weekend, a visit that signified for Jason just how many pieces of his life were now converging where before they'd been fragmenting. Kiriko and Sensei liked each other immediately. Jason felt a sense of pride escorting Ji-chan across the road to a special dinner in the Shimizu home.

Things were good back on Hot Springs Island, too. Dada and Al and Golly were healthy and the hubbub around Kiriko's disappearance had died down. Cristine and Layla and their new dog — a present from Tina and Adam, which successfully usurped Layla's affections — were visiting Angel in Alberta. Jason had even uncovered his name linked with Russell Rose's and the M-Novel — Seamus's doing.

They pulled into the parking lot of the Visitors' Center at 4.30 p.m. for an ice cream. Aiko took his hand as they entered the food area, holding Kiriko's on the other side. People smiled at them. To the world they looked like a young family out for a day of sightseeing, a young family without a care in the world.

The sun was transforming into a pink disk in preparation for its downward slide behind the distant ridges to the other side of the world. In a half-hour it would be gone, heralded by some final traces of lingering color.

The three of them sat at a long white table and looked at the spectacle outside the large plate-glass windows. Aiko stood to get a better view. Jason and Kiriko held hands. He'd never seen her this sad.

Five o'clock arrived but Kiriko's ex-husband didn't. Each passing minute increased the tension. Finally at 5:30, with Aiko restless, Kiriko telephoned from a public booth.

"There's been a problem," she said, on returning. "The baby's sick and they had to go back. They called my father. We'll have to arrange another time."

Jason spoke. "Kiriko, I've been thinking the whole way up here and now this. Doesn't this strike you as...as, I don't know, too coincidental?"

"What do you mean?"

"What if we try and get Aiko back?"

"Aiko back? We?" Kiriko couldn't believe Jason's words. "Jason, what are you saying?"

"We could talk to them. That they didn't come today, it could mean something. Maybe the new baby's too much. We could talk to them. We could ask them."

"I don't know what to say."

"We could try it. We could bring Aiko to Hot Springs Island and see if she likes it there. Or I could stay here awhile longer and see how that goes."

"But what about Dada and Al?"

"They'd love Aiko, I know they would. It's been far too long since that place had a child around."

"Jason, do you mean it? Do you mean what you're saying?" Her eyes were already lighting to a smile.

And for once, he knew. "Let's do everything we can."

• • •

The white car and its passengers flew down the mountain like a falling star briefly visible in the night sky. Kiriko opened her window a sliver. She turned on the radio. She smiled. In the back seat, Aiko fell asleep to the sound of the music and the vehicle's motion.

The caldera of the volcano was to Jason's left. In the waning light he couldn't see into its depths but knew it was there. Pinpoints of light, probably houses, were now visible on the far side of vast crater where in the daylight there'd been gray.

He returned to the day and moment he'd found Kiriko — or, more accurately, the day she'd found him. The earthquake, Kiriko's revelations about Aiko and her marriage and illness, the trip to her secret hot springs, the call to Dada — all these momentous events would stay with him forever. None, however, did he replay more frequently or in greater detail than his phone call to Elizabeth that same night he'd phoned Dada. It had become part of him. Every sound, every word, every moment.

It was morning in England when he'd called. He remembered looking at the number scrawled on the piece of paper like it was code to a vault. And the exact sound and feel of the old-fashioned dial on his finger, the way it spun back around to zero after he let it go. And then, from thousands of miles away, a gray telephone rang in a white house on a nice street. A woman picked it up and answered.

"Hello," the woman said.

"Hello, is this Elizabeth Robertson?" Jason asked.

"Yes, it is. Who is this?"

"This is Jason," he said. "This is your son."

Chapter 23 iNovel Link
You may have noticed that each chapter begins with an epigraph that is a quote from a *Hot Springs* character. Please go to **www.HotSpringsNovel.com/chapter23/** and you will find that the Chapter 23 iNovel Link is unique because it is the only exclusively poetry link. If and when you go to this link, you'll see that all the epigram quotes have been collected and shaped into a poem (with some minor changes and additions).

The End

WITH THANKS

Some say that novel writing is a lonely business. At one's desk on late nights and in early mornings, the steaming coffee cup and convoluted thoughts are often your only companions. While that is true, I've also been blessed with stupendous support, advice and help from a dazzling array of gifted, caring people. I hope you all know what you've meant, and mean, to me. My gratitude is like that coffee cup — very warm and close to overflowing. First, I thank beyond words Kim McArthur, Canada's most dynamic publisher and person extraordinaire. Thank you for believing in me. The same goes for Ann Ledden, without whom *Hot Springs* would never have become what it is. I also send my appreciation to Janet, Jim, Taryn, Thea and all the fantastic team at McArthur and Company. To my wonderful and talented editor Leah Fairbank: you made *Hot Springs* and me better — coincidences happen for a reason. I am deeply grateful for the intelligent and energetic assistance of Sam Hiyate and his associates, and thanks are also extended to the personable and painstaking Pamela Erlichman. I must also not forget to thank in advance the hard-working publishers' reps and the wonderful people who run and staff those glorious churches of the mind and my favorite haunt — bookshops.

Closer to home, Alan Bryce has long provided me with wisdom and unyielding support, and Warren Arbuckle gets special mention for his creative mind and insights. Andy Eastham and Julia Caranci were thoughtful readers, as was political historian Mark Ledbetter. I also received help and encouragement from Steve Barnes (on the music), marvelous Maryum Bowman, Mark Colby, Annie Horsburgh, the talented Solveigh, Bob and Kelly, John Ledden, the Roses, Robert Zacharias, Cliff McNeil-Smith, the Tanners, Lynne Jordon, Sharon McLeay, the top dogs at YellowDawg.com, as well as from Marilyn Herbert and all the cool people at Book Club in a Box. Special thanks go to my family, of course: mother Rosemary (who inculcated a love of words at an early age), late father Stan, sister Janina and brother Tony. Thank you, Ken, for being a loving son. And Kimiko has been an unwavering pillar of support from day one — your amazing talent and warmth of heart astonish me daily.